Hidden Secrets

A Green Dory Inn Mystery: Book 2

Janet Sketchley
janetsketchley.ca

Hidden Secrets, A Green Dory Inn Mystery, Book 2

ISBN 978-0-9951970-9-1 (epub)
ISBN 978-1-989581-00-1 (mobi)
ISBN 978-0-9951970-8-4 (print)

The characters and situations in this book are works of fiction and are not intended to represent any individuals, living or dead. The opinions expressed by the characters are not necessarily those of the author, nor is the grammar they use always correct. The Green Dory Inn, Captain Jack's Pub, and most other places mentioned in this novel are purely fictional and in no way intended to represent real locations. Where real locations are mentioned, they are used fictitiously for the purposes of the story. Considerable liberty has been taken with the geography around the inn.

Scripture reference: In Chapter 29, a character paraphrases Revelation 3:20 KJV. In the closing author's note, the quote is restated in the New King James Version (NKJV).

Edited by Brilliant Cut Editing.

Cover by E.A.H. Creative.
Interior dory image: iStock.com/Gunay Aliyeva.
Author photo by Amanda Walker Photography.

Published in Canada by Janet Sketchley.

FICTION/CHRISTIAN/SUSPENSE

Janet Sketchley

Books by Janet Sketchley

The Redemption's Edge Series:

Heaven's Prey
Secrets and Lies
Without Proof

The Green Dory Inn Mysteries:

Unknown Enemy
Hidden Secrets
Bitter Truth
Book 4 (TBA)

Daily Devotions:

A Year of Tenacity: 365 Daily Devotions

Tenacity at Christmas: 31 Daily Devotions for December

Readers Journals:

Reads to Remember: A book-lover's journal to track your next 100 reads
(Available in two cover options, print only)

Note to Readers

Lunenburg, Nova Scotia, is a real town—a UNESCO World Heritage site. The Green Dory Inn, Captain Jack's Pub, and most other places mentioned in this novel are purely fictional and in no way intended to represent real locations. The Ovens Park and Fisheries Museum are real places mentioned in the story.

I have taken considerable liberty with the geography of the inn, as I'll explain at the end of the book. Please don't peek there now, or you'll find spoilers.

Also, for my non-Canadian readers, please note I'm using Canadian spellings in this book. You'll see words like colour, neighbour, licence, and travelling, and they're not typos. You'll also see some hyphenated words like mid-fifties and mid-size. That said, and despite the many eyes that have checked the manuscript, I can't guarantee perfection. But I've done my best!

Meet the Key Characters

Anna Young: owner of the inn, recently widowed, 56

Bobby Hawke: Roy's grandson, visiting for the summer, 28

Captain Hiram Hiltz: built the inn, died 40 years ago at 81

Ciara Williams: childhood classmate of Landon, 24

Corey Seymour: local teen who does Anna's mowing, 14

David Hiltz: Captain Hiltz's grandson, missing for over 40 years, presumed dead as a teen

Dylan Tremblay: local police constable, 29

Elva Knapp: Anna's neighbour, difficult personality, 57

Glenna & Ivan McNutt: guests at the inn, 45 & 49

Gord Lohnes: Anna's friend, 59

Hart Brown: Meaghan's boyfriend, involved in previous trouble at the inn, 25

Jaclyn Carstens: Anna's neighbour, owns a local pub, 30s-40s

Landon Smith: Anna's friend, grateful for her love and support, 24

Maria Hiltz: previous owner of the inn, daughter-in-law of Captain Hiltz, 84

Meaghan Lohnes: Anna's housekeeper, Gord's daughter, 22

Nigel Foley: eccentric local man who roams the woods, 58

Quinn Dyer: teen grandson of Tricia and Blaine, living with them, involved in previous trouble at the inn, 15

Roy Hawke: Anna's neighbour, 77

Tricia & Blaine Dyer: Anna's neighbours, mid-50s

Chapter 1

Tuesday

THE AIR IN the university hallway hung thick with dust and summer heat. Dead, even though light glowed through windows in a few office doors.

Landon moistened her lips and drew a deep breath. The polished brass nameplate with its precise black letters reflected her anxiety back at her. Magnified, like a distorting mirror in a creepy carnival. She tried again to calm her thumping heart. Professor Tallin wouldn't have agreed to this meeting if there'd been no hope.

She rapped on the frosted glass pane. Assertive, but not demanding. Tallin should approve.

"Come."

At the brisk command, she eased open the door, the handle slick beneath her sweaty palm, and stepped inside to beg for her future.

The woman behind the plain wooden desk could have doubled as a department store mannequin, with her expressionless face and long white arms. Close-cropped dark hair, ice-blue silk blouse. Except a store display would complete the outfit with a coordinating necklace or wispy scarf. She focused on her laptop screen, eyes tracking side to side. Eventually, she snapped the laptop shut and pinned Landon with a cool stare. "Yes?"

Landon pressed her palms into the smooth cotton of her capri pants and refused to touch the back of her neck. No nervous tics, no sign of weakness. Tallin only respected strength.

"Professor, I wanted to discuss my mark for the last course."

One pencil-thin eyebrow arched. "I did warn you, Ms. Smith."

"With respect, your email said if I wasn't back in class the following Monday, I couldn't expect to pass." To which Landon sent an apologetic reply explaining she couldn't leave her friend Anna in the middle of a crisis. But the crisis had resolved. She'd met the deadline.

She maintained eye contact and kept her tone neutral. "I was present that Monday and missed no more time. While I was away, I submitted my assignments on time and kept up with the readings."

"Your final exam was weak. And there's the matter of class participation. Which is hard to do when one is not present."

"I understand, but given that I accomplished everything else on the syllabus, could you consider my participation while I was here and evaluate based on that?"

The slow shake of Tallin's head radiated disappointment. "You're almost twenty-five, older than the majority of the students, and you definitely have more life experience." Dry and sharp, her tone offered no trace of compassion. "My colleagues may have coddled you, but I expect better."

Landon's mouth shot open. She sucked in a mouthful of air, speeding through a silent count to ten. "I'm not asking to be coddled. I'm asking for a fair chance."

"You wasted your chance when you abandoned your studies to play nursemaid. Or detective."

"Those were extenuating circumstances. My friend is like a mother to me. She needed support, and no one else could be there for her."

The professor's lean cheeks puckered inward as if she'd taken a mouthful of especially sour wine. A sideways pinch of her lips enhanced the impression. Her gaze drilled Landon. "If you were assigned a case and you only showed up half the time, would you be considered an effective social worker?"

"That's different."

"It's not. Nothing must interfere with your work when someone else is depending on you."

"Someone else *was* depending on me. We thought her life was in danger."

Tallin flicked an imaginary speck of dust from her desk lamp. "Emotionalism and allowing your personal life to interfere are two weaknesses you must overcome if you ever hope to achieve your degree."

Landon's fingers tightened toward fists. She forced them straight and prayed for calm. "So there's nothing you will do about my mark."

"No."

"And because you were 'delayed' in processing the marks, my other course options are full."

Narrow lips formed a crimson line. "Unfortunately."

The tremors in her core made her strain for every breath. Her lungs ached. "I will be filing a formal complaint."

Professor Tallin placed her palms against the edge of her desk. In a slow, fluid motion, she pushed her chair back and stood, leaning forward. "Is that an attempt to intimidate me?"

Landon lifted her chin. "I wouldn't waste my time."

Eyes narrowed, Tallin mirrored Landon's motion. "You won't graduate without my courses."

"Then I'll repeat the first one in September." And miss her fall work-term opportunity because of this woman's petty power struggles.

Grinding her teeth to block a torrent of angry words, Landon spun on her heel and yanked open the door. She ducked into a connecting hallway and then out a side door before venting a low, primal growl.

In her back pocket, her phone buzzed. She waved it off like an errant wasp.

The phone vibrated again. If these were parting-shot emails from Professor Tallin, they'd be more ammunition for her complaint.

If enough students spoke up, maybe the university could insist on sensitivity training or something. Good thing Tallin wasn't still carrying a caseload, for the clients' sakes.

Landon unlocked her phone to two new texts. From her friend Anna, not Tallin. A little of the tension faded from the back of her neck.

You're on my mind... everything okay?

Are you free to chat?

A longing like homesickness swelled, and she tapped the phone's call icon. It wasn't about the location. Nova Scotia hadn't been home for years. But nothing said "home" like Anna's heart.

Anna answered. "Hey, how are things?"

The welcome in her voice softened Landon's mood. "I'll manage. Just remind me God has this, okay? He's working it all out?"

"He has good plans for you, and nothing is too hard for Him. Now, what's wrong?"

Phone to her ear, she walked down the concrete steps and escaped onto the sidewalk as she told Anna the basics. "It's bad enough I always struggle with the assignments, but what chance do I have against such a vindictive, mean-spirited person?"

"It's because you stayed to help me, isn't it?"

Landon kicked at a pebble on the sidewalk. "She had it in for me anyway. Because I'm not 'strong' and hard like she is."

A delivery truck rumbled past. The murky scent of its exhaust soured her stomach. A memory flashed from her visit with Anna—sparkling blue water, circling seagulls' high-pitched cries, and bracing clean air that tasted salty-good. Not like poison.

She walked faster. She had to get to the park, see at least a bit of nature. A tree, a squirrel. Something to refresh her spirit. For all the positives of the city, buildings and sidewalks never spoke peace.

"You, my friend, have a strength your professor can't see." A cool balm, Anna's voice carried assurance. "Don't let her diminish that. But what will you do for the rest of the summer?"

One more block, and she'd reach the tiny park, an alcove in the urban crush.

"Try to find a job, I guess. And you know she won't accept the same papers again when I redo her class."

A youth sauntered toward her, profanity stamped on his tee shirt and angry beats audible through his bulky over-ear headphones. He sneered as they met.

Right now her emotions agreed, but faith gave her a different choice. She countered his attitude with a deliberate smile and a silent prayer they'd both find peace.

Anna spoke again. "What would you think about coming here for the summer?"

Instinct made Landon's heart flip, but going back would be okay now. She'd faced that fear and won, even enjoyed her last visit. "I can't afford the flight, and you need your rooms for paying guests."

July was peak tourist season, and Anna's country inn only had four rooms to fill.

"Bookings are a little slow, and I wouldn't mind keeping it that way this year. I'm still not feeling like I should."

They'd thought all Anna needed was to catch up on her sleep once the prowler stress ended. Landon pressed the phone tighter against her ear. "What's wrong?"

"I don't know, but my energy hasn't come back. I'm achy, cranky, and still doubting myself, even now that the trouble's stopped."

Ahead, paving stones left the sidewalk for the pocket-sized park. Landon's pace slowed, and a bit of tranquility soothed her spirit despite Anna's news. "Have you seen a doctor?"

She sank onto a shaded bench, thin wooden slats pressing against her thighs, and let her eyes absorb the varying shades of green.

Anna wanted her to move back to Lunenburg. That was no secret. But Anna wouldn't stoop to emotional manipulation. This was real.

"I have an appointment next Monday. I just thought... if you're free anyway, some time together could be good for both of us."

On the street, a heavy engine ground gears. A horn blared, and someone shouted. Landon's ears were tired of tuning out endless traffic noise. Rural Atlantic Canada's appeal grew by the minute.

What did she have to stay for?

Nothing, until September.

She slouched lower on the bench. Anna's neighbour had paid for her last flight because he'd been so concerned about Anna. Landon couldn't ask for another handout.

"Landon? Are you still there?"

"Sorry, just thinking about it."

"If you want to come, I have reward points for your flights. But no pressure. You've met my friends, and you know I'm in good hands."

A siren wailed nearby. Landon cringed.

The city was alive and had so much to offer. She was happy here.

But not today.

It wouldn't be running away as long as she came back in the fall. It would be a summer break. Lots of people took them.

She sat up straight on the bench, pebbles crunching under her thin-soled sandals. "Anna, I'd love to see you. Thank you."

Chapter 2

Friday

When Landon exited security at Halifax's Stanfield Airport on Friday, Anna's broad smile was a beacon among the waiting strangers. Swallowing unexpected emotion, she raced into Anna's arms.

Home. Acceptance. The warm stability that Anna wore like a fragrance. Yet Landon's initial, misty-eyed read of her friend's face caught strain lines that should have faded since June. And a pallor only partly due to the wide white headband holding back her brown, chin-length bob. Amid the chatter of reunions and weary travellers, Landon squeezed her tighter and held the hug longer than usual as if she could love Anna back to health.

Anna had been her mother's friend first. The two were around the same age, now their mid-fifties. But her mom couldn't handle what happened to Landon—or her dad's death because of it—and Landon lost both her parents. When she needed them most.

Thank God for Anna, stepping in and showing all the love she could, including the love of Jesus. Anna's faith and prayers fostered Landon's ability to stand whole today. Scarred, but whole.

And now able to return to the town she'd been taken from, if not to feel at home, at least to find her way as an adult and lay her childhood memories to rest.

A buzzer blared, and the luggage carousel rumbled to life. Anna flinched more than Landon did.

Landon studied the tight jaw, the now-pinched lips. "You okay?"

"Just a bit of a headache. I'll get a coffee before we hit the road."

Pain might account for the brackets around Anna's mouth. But her brown eyes seemed faded, like something dimmed the light inside. Landon's mission for the next six weeks would be to restore the shine.

Watching uniform dark suitcases circulate, she stopped feeling self-conscious about the garishly flowered one she'd bought at the thrift store. At least she'd recognize it.

Beside her, a guy in a suit did a swift lunge-and-grab to wrestle a bulky case off the moving track.

A bright mass of pink and green slid toward them, and Landon pulled it free. She checked the tag to be safe, but there couldn't be a second one. Retro only went so far.

Anna snickered. "At least you won't lose it."

"Unless the airline decides it's too ugly to live."

"But then they have to buy you all new things. Win-win."

Fifteen minutes later, coffee in hand and likely cooling fast, Anna tracked down her car. "I was hurrying to get inside in case you landed early. I should have paid more attention."

Landon dropped her suitcase, and her arm muscles practically cried in relief. Wheels would have been a huge plus. She hoisted the case and her carry-on into the back seat of the bronze Honda and climbed into the front. "Thanks for coming to get me."

"It gives us an hour and a half of uninterrupted catch-up time before we get home and I put you to work." Anna navigated the concrete maze into the sunlight. "Just let me figure out which lane I need. They've changed it again."

Landon leaned her head back and closed her eyes, basking in the quiet praise music streaming from the car speakers. After the stress with her professor and the scramble to leave the city for the rest of the summer, relaxing felt good. She'd tried on the plane, with limited success.

Here on the ground, she could unwind.

The engine revs increased, and Anna exhaled. "That wasn't so bad. We'll be home in time to rest a bit before seeing everyone."

"I feel like I'm crashing a party." She'd wanted to come tomorrow, but Anna had several guests booked for the inn. Her housekeeper, Meaghan, could've checked them in, but welcoming people was what Anna did best.

Anna's welcoming heart was behind tonight too. The new neighbours had finally moved in, and she'd invited them and a few friends for a potluck.

She merged onto the highway. "You've met most of them." Her fingertips tapped the steering wheel. "I told Quinn he could come with his grandparents. If he behaves."

"How likely is that?"

"He's better than he was. And I couldn't very well exclude him."

Landon first encountered Quinn when he picked a fight with the boy who'd been mowing Anna's lawn. Fourteen or fifteen years old, the two had been friends until Corey decided to straighten out his life. Quinn's anger may have been what pushed him into the pranks to scare Anna away from the inn—the crisis that brought Landon here a month ago. Meaghan's boyfriend was the instigator, but Quinn had done his share.

Worst of all, Quinn had tried to implicate Corey, and the other boy had run away.

This time of year, Corey could sleep outside, but what would he do for food and clean clothing? Going back to his troublemaking friends might seem like his only answer unless he hitchhiked into Halifax and fell into bigger trouble.

He was small for his age and pretty for a boy. Bigger trouble could be very bad, indeed.

Landon rubbed the back of her neck. "No word on Corey?"

"None. My heart's breaking for him. And his father doesn't care."

Anna's emotions sounded as raw as they'd been when Hart and Quinn were finally caught. By now, she should be healing.

Seeing a doctor was a good idea.

They sped past trees and exits and a stretch of urban sprawl. Beyond the city, the highway dropped to two lanes with an occasional third for passing.

So many shades of green and sparkling glints of water. Each view expanded Landon's soul.

Anna took the Lunenburg exit, then bypassed the town for a narrow route that hugged the winding rocky coastline. Choppy ocean waves played in the sunshine to the left, and widely spaced two-storey homes slid past on the right, built well back from the passing cars.

The road kept to a few metres above sea level until Anna reached the final curve before the inn. Then the elevation increased, with a metal guardrail fencing the gravel shoulder from the rock face's vertical plunge to the waves below.

Ahead, the inn's sign beckoned—a green dory on an oval of cream-painted wood, framed with thick nautical rope.

Bright yellow pansies and orange marigolds overflowed the signature green rowboat on the front lawn, welcoming visitors with waves of exuberant colour. Typical of the region's older homes, the grey inn's twin dormer windows framed an extended "Lunenburg bump" dormer above a sunshine-yellow front door.

Landon drew another deep breath of salt-fresh air, glad they'd cut the air conditioning and opened the car windows when they dropped from highway speed. "I've missed this. Quinn's doing a good job on the grass."

"And he's usually polite about it. He knows it's temporary until Corey gets back, but this is a chance for some restitution."

"Restitution would be cleaning up the mess he made in the barn."

"I don't trust him in there alone." In the small lot at the end of a long driveway, Anna parked facing the windowless grey building. "If they were searching for something when they broke in, they didn't find it."

"But you said it's only junk."

"Nigel still insists there could be something important."

Nigel also believed in aliens and roamed the woods with a metal detector. "Have you let him look?"

"I think he's been spending his free time hunting for Corey."

"Does he have a job?" The man popped up at such odd hours, she'd assumed all he had was free time.

"He stocks shelves at the grocery store. Loves it because they let him bring home the dented cans."

Now Anna's voice held its customary soft acceptance. Nigel, Landon, Corey, even Quinn... never a misfit who didn't fit in Anna's heart.

Stepping across the threshold from the back deck brought an unexpected mist to Landon's eyes. Guests used the front door. Family and friends came in this way, from the rear.

An airy hallway ran through to the front entrance, ivory-hued walls catching daylight from the windows in the doors. On this end, it accessed Anna's private rooms and the kitchen, the inn's heart.

A warm, spicy aroma teased her. "Mmm, spaghetti?"

"Meat sauce for lasagna. Let's get you settled, first." Anna's heels tapped along the aged-honey hardwood floor to the front of the inn. "Same room as before."

The butterfly-themed room, so clearly decorated for Landon. Since she'd broken the fear of coming back, she could accept the room as a haven to visit, not an attempt to tie her here. She tugged her suitcase up the stairs.

"There are no guests tonight, so enjoy your space." Anna left her carry-on at the door. "Come down when you're ready, but there's no rush. Meaghan will be here soon to help."

Alone in her room, Landon spun in a slow circle amid the soft peach and green tones. She stopped at the butterfly prints, one a monarch with wings spread in full stained-glass orange-and-black glory, the other a Canadian tiger swallowtail, soft yellow with black stripes.

The front rooms with their ocean-facing dormer windows bore nautical themes, but the two at the back reflected the forest behind the inn. Here, the ceiling sloped toward the windows, creating a cozy intimacy.

Landon peered outside. There'd be no prowlers to watch for now. This time of day, she wouldn't even see a deer munching Anna's flower garden. She half expected to glimpse Nigel roaming the woods, but nothing moved. Even Anna's black and white cat would have gone to ground somewhere in the shade.

A deep yawn brought water to her eyes. Time to get away from the bed's lure, or she'd still be here when people started arriving.

She splashed cool water on her face and traded her crumpled travel clothes for a lemon-yellow sleeveless top and colour-swirled skirt. A quick redo of the blond ponytail low on her neck, and she shut the door firmly behind her.

The curved wooden banister slid silk-smooth beneath her trailing fingertips as she skipped down the stairs. She followed the savoury fragrance along the short hallway to the rear of the inn just as Meaghan stepped through the back door.

"Oh." The flame-haired housekeeper's blue eyes rounded, deepening the grey smudges underneath. "Landon. Welcome back."

Faint hollows in her cheeks hadn't been there in June. Finding out your loser boyfriend had been terrorizing your employer had to be hard. From what her father said, Hart had cost the girl her last job too.

Anna emerged from the sitting room on the right, her wide smile encompassing them both. "Many hands make light work. I'll put the lasagna together, and you two can tackle setup. We'll mingle on the deck and then come inside to eat."

Even with a square farmhouse-style table and four ample white-and-pine hoop back chairs, Anna's kitchen had plenty of room for the three of them to work without tripping over one another. White cabinets and brushed stainless-steel appliances lent a professional feel suitable for an inn, with a pale pink tint on the walls reflecting the homey rose and grey flagstone pattern from the vinyl floor.

The sparrow figurine Landon had given Anna last month sat on the window ledge beside a small aloe vera plant in a purple pot.

As Meaghan dropped her purse onto one of the chairs, Anna wrestled a large glass pan from a bottom drawer. When she uncovered the slow cooker on the counter and stirred the sauce, tomato-spiced comfort filled the room.

"Do we need fresh flowers for the tables?" Landon retrieved a pair of scissors from the oak knife block.

"Yes, please."

When she returned with a cluster of blue and white pansies from the rear garden, Meaghan had the four yellow-clothed tables laid with cutlery and glasses. "We'll fill these with water before dinner, and there'll be other glasses on the counter if anyone wants something else."

Landon collected empty porcelain vases from each table and divided the flowers. "I should have done this at the sink."

"One second." Meaghan fetched a plastic pitcher from the kitchen. "Anna said your second summer class didn't work out. I'm sorry." Wistfulness softened her voice.

"It's disappointing." Landon positioned the newly filled vases.

"I wanted to go to university. Although I really liked working in a gift shop in town. And Anna's great, of course."

Hart made so much trouble about her working. Maybe he also kept her back from more education. Her father, Gord, claimed the man wanted her at home to wait on him.

Landon pressed her lips shut. Meaghan didn't need her opinion. "What did you want to study?"

A shriek from Anna froze them in place, eyes locked. As one, they bolted for the kitchen.

Chapter 3

The back door slammed. Landon raced ahead of Meaghan through the empty kitchen and out onto the deck.

On the grass, Anna stood with Nigel Foley, arms wrapped around a third, smaller person in tee shirt and jeans.

Corey?

Lightning zinged in Landon's chest. "Thank God." The words released the weight of all the horrible things she'd feared.

She ran down the steps.

Nigel blinked at her and touched the brim of his camouflage cap. He stood taller than ever, shoulders proud. Up close, his grey eyes snapped with pleasure. "Smart boy. He knew where to go."

Corey squirmed in Anna's embrace. She released him but kept a grip on his arm.

Clearly, he'd had a food source. His face and hands were clean, and the musk of body odour was nowhere near the three-week level.

Landon reached out a hand. He wouldn't accept a hug from her, but she needed to touch him. To bridge the hurt of their last exchange. "Nigel told you you're not a suspect?"

The boy peered at her through overlong bangs, ignoring her outstretched fingers. “I said I didn’t do it.”

“I’m sorry I doubted you.” She’d wanted to believe him.

Anna steered him up the stairs to the inn. “We’ll get you some food, and Nigel can tell us how he found you.”

Nigel’s bark sounded like a cross between a cough and a laugh. “He ate well.”

Corey cut him a sideways glance, tan-shirted shoulders hunching toward his ears.

Bypassing the deck furniture, Anna seated them in the kitchen with Corey farthest from the door. It’d be a wonder if she let the boy go home.

Soon Meaghan plunked a thick sandwich in front of him, with a couple of chocolate chip cookies on the edge of the plate.

“Thank you.” Anna beamed at her. “Sit with us and hear the story.”

Meaghan’s heavy red braid bounced side to side against her shoulders. “I can listen while I finish the lasagna. We’re short on time.”

Corey’s breath hissed. He may have eaten well, but not Anna’s-cooking well.

“We’ll save you a piece.” Anna squeezed his hand. “You’ll be wanting to see your dad and sleep in your own bed.”

The boy’s expression hardened. He bit into the sandwich.

After bringing Corey a tall glass of milk, Meaghan offered Nigel his container of dried tea leaves.

He peered inside, waved it beneath his nose, and nodded. “Yes, please.”

While she worked at the counter, he adjusted the brim of his hat and blinked at Anna. “Found him in my bunker. Natural peanut butter has a short shelf life. I went to replace it, and there he was, living like a king.”

Nigel had a bunker. To hide from the aliens?

Corey ducked his head, fingers gouging into his sandwich. “I’m sorry I ate your food.” The words came out low and mumbled.

“That’s what it’s there for, boy. You were smart to get in. And to cover your tracks.”

Thin elbows tucked into Corey’s sides, and he seemed to shrink in on himself. “Nobody calls me smart.”

“Probably never let them see it.” Nigel tapped a crooked index finger against the side of his camouflage cap. “Besides, there’s book-smart and there’s life-smart.”

Meaghan brought a small white teapot for Nigel and a larger pot for Anna and Landon, then handed out sunflower-spangled mugs.

Landon caught her eye before she turned back to assembling the lasagna. “Thank you.”

Half the sandwich was gone. Anna fidgeted with her empty cup. “Corey, we need to let your father know you’re back. And the police, so they can cancel the missing person alert.”

“I guess.” He slid down in his chair. “So Quinn set me up. Are he and the other guy in jail?”

Something clattered against the counter. Meaghan stood statue-stiff, her back to the group.

“No.” Anna spoke gently. “The trial date is coming up. Meaghan’s boyfriend, Hart, is the other person, and she didn’t know any more than you knew about Quinn. Hart’s barred from the inn grounds as the accused leader. I asked for an exemption for Quinn so he could do the lawn until you came back. He’s admitted what he did in the barn and planting your hoodie there—”

Corey jutted his chin at Landon, his eyes hard.

“—and he’s willing to work as restitution.” Anna flattened a palm on the glossy pine tabletop, tapping her fingertips one by one. “When you’re ready, the mowing job is yours again. And I’d like to hire you to work with Quinn on cleaning up the mess in the barn. With you as the boss.”

A smirk thinned the boy's lips. "I'm good with that."

"But now I need to report that you're found."

Anna left the room with the cordless land-line phone, and Landon studied Corey as he ate. His hair, scruffy before he went missing, hung in his eyes. His shuttered expression gave no hint of the fear he must have carried that the police wouldn't believe his innocence. That this would be the crime that sent him to juvenile detention.

Still, he'd been snug in Nigel's bunker all this time while Anna fretted over his safety. "Why didn't you check your texts? Anna tried to tell you it was safe to come back."

He tilted his head back and squinted at her, upper lip curling. "Phones can be tracked."

In case she'd missed the body language, his tone radiated "too stupid to live." Warmth swept from her torso to the top of her head, and she clenched her teeth. With all he'd been through, this was a time to show grace.

Grace, but not a victim response. She held steady eye contact. "We've been praying for you. I'm really glad you're okay."

"Yeah." He drained the rest of his glass. "Why are you still here?"

"I'm back. For the summer." She kept her tone matter-of-fact. "I failed my course."

His face softened. For maybe a second. "Too bad. Hiding out meant I missed all my exams. I failed the year, except they're not allowed to fail us. Not that it matters."

"Of course it matters."

He bit a cookie in half. "Why? It's not like I'm going to university or anything. Teachers don't care. Neither does Dad."

Folding her arms on the pine tabletop, she leaned forward. "Will you let your future be decided by whether people care about it? Even the people who should care?" She pictured her professor. "Show them they're wrong."

"I agree." Anna slid back into her seat and offered him the phone. "Want to let your father know you're back?"

"He'll find out when he sees me."

Her posture slumped. "Will there be trouble because you ran away?"

The boy hiked a narrow shoulder. "Saved him grocery money."

The corners of Anna's lips pinched. "Well, there's no trouble with the police, but they do want to talk to you and ensure you're okay. Let me drive you to the station."

"Or I could go home."

"Would your father want them showing up there?"

He rolled his eyes. "All right. Let's get it over with."

Standing, she untied her apron and straightened her coral blouse. "The lasagna should go in the oven in twenty minutes, and I was going to make a salad. Will you girls cover that?"

"Of course."

"Nigel, we're having a potluck to meet the new neighbours. You're welcome to stay."

"Thank you, but no. Crowds." He mashed his camouflage hat more firmly on his head like a protective helmet and stood. "Mother will want to hear the news."

"Everyone will be glad to know Corey's safe."

The warm relief in Anna's voice revealed her loving heart, but the defensive tilt of Corey's head said something else.

With a rueful nod, Landon tried to show she understood. Spiteful tongues would be glad, too, for different reasons. To the ones who called him a delinquent and a lost cause, his running away offered proof. He didn't have to listen, but part of him would.

Nigel left with a half-bow and a series of nods, and Anna shepherded Corey out behind him. "Your bicycle's still here. I'll get it from the shed and load it in the trunk."

Meaghan cocked an eyebrow at Landon and tipped her head toward the forest behind the inn, Nigel's preferred means of access. "He has a bunker."

Her deadpan tone didn't hide her opinion of this rough-hewn, scarecrow man. Still, she treated him kindly. Not that Anna would permit any less.

"I'm glad Corey had a safe place to go."

"Yeah, but I bet it was creepy. You get into something sealed off and underground like that, you'd feel buried alive." Loose tendrils of curly red hair jiggled around her face with the force of her shudder.

Cold prickled the back of Landon's neck. "I don't do enclosed spaces."

She plunked cherry tomatoes and mushrooms into a metal colander and emptied a package of prewashed greens into the etched-glass salad bowl Meaghan had retrieved from a high cupboard shelf. "Anna said people were coming for five thirty. She won't want to leave Corey at the station alone, but she'll want to be here for her guests."

"You may not have noticed yet, but she's still stressing out. If they're not done when she needs to be back here, she'll be a mess." Meaghan pulled a pair of long-handled serving spoons from a drawer and crisscrossed them beside the bowl. "I'll phone Dad to go over. He's coming tonight anyway, and he's pretty good at calming her."

Landon twisted to rest a hip against the counter. "Has she needed a lot of calming?"

"I think she's getting worse." Meaghan's voice shook. "This shouldn't be happening."

~~~

Five past five, and no word from Anna. Landon gave the kitchen countertop an unnecessary wipe. "Have you met the new neighbours?"
~~~

"No, and I'm not sure who's coming. Anna could invite anyone at the last minute." Meaghan snorted. "She might come back with a cop who just went off duty."

"Dylan was here enough in June. He'd fit right in."

Meaghan's phone buzzed, and she swiped the screen. "They're done. Dad's driving Corey home, and Anna's on her way."

"Great." The lasagna was keeping warm in the oven, the salad chilling. They were as ready as they could be. "I'll fill the water glasses."

The other girl's rigid posture, her claw-hold on the edge of the counter, made Landon leave the pitcher.

"You should know Dad's been spending a lot of time with Anna. They're getting close."

"Okay." Gord's health issues and apparent loneliness made him a natural for Anna's friendship. *Close* couldn't mean romantically close. Not with Anna still grieving for Murdoch, less than a year since his accident. For Gord's sake, Landon hoped he understood Anna's nurturing nature. Why the relationship would trouble Meaghan was something else to wonder about.

She carried the water into the breakfast room—tonight, the potluck room. Flower watercolours on the walls and blooms on the square tables reflected Anna's hospitable nature. Lighthouse salt and pepper shakers at each table tied this nook to the inn's seafaring theme.

A dark-blue pickup truck rumbled past the side window toward the parking area. Anna's elderly neighbour Roy and his twenty-something grandson, Bobby.

Landon carried the empty pitcher back to the kitchen. She'd refilled it before Roy rapped at the door.

With a cheerful hello, Meaghan lifted the towel-covered basket from the seat of his walker. "This smells great. Oh, it's still warm."

"Bobby's brown bread. Better than store-bought."

Roy's incredibly wide jaw always reminded Landon of a satisfied cat. Sea-blue eyes in a weathered face presented a rough exterior that had intimidated her until she'd glimpsed the compassion beneath the crust. He raised a gnarled hand from the walker frame. "Well, look who came back. Could an old guy have a hug?"

Landon opened her arms. "This old guy can."

His bristly hair tickled her cheek. Roy smelled of summer sunshine and salt breeze as if he'd spent the day outside. With the ocean view across from these homes, maybe he had.

If Anna hadn't told her, she'd have never guessed he was in his late seventies. White hair, as thick as his grandson's, crowded his head, and his eyes flashed a mischievous twinkle. He radiated a brisk energy, even with a broken leg in a full cast.

Roy spun his walker and lowered himself onto the seat. "This thing has its advantages." His leg stuck out in front of him, the cast a kaleidoscope of scrawls and sketches.

Bobby carried in a slow cooker. "Hi, ladies."

He made eye contact with Landon. Brief, but deliberate enough that it still cost him. Whoever she reminded him of had left a mark.

When his gaze slid to Meaghan, his smile unfroze. "I'll plug this in on the counter, okay?"

Meaghan pointed to a free outlet. "Baked beans?"

Through the cover, Landon caught a hint of tangy-sweet scent.

"Special request from Gramp." He plugged in the cooker and leaned back on his palms against the counter.

Today a cartoon sailboat stamped his shirt. The casual clothes, flip-flops, and sandy hair splayed across his head like straw made it hard to remember this was a brainy guy who wrote books. Even the glasses didn't help because he'd gone for gunmetal rectangular frames instead of geeky plastic ones.

He caught her watching and flushed. "Where's Anna?"

"She's on her way." Meaghan peered out the window. "Actually, that may be her now."

It wasn't, but Anna's car came right behind.

Anna ushered the new arrivals into the kitchen. Tricia and Blaine lived a few houses away. Around Anna's age, mid-fifties, both wore the stooped, careworn posture of a much older couple.

Their grandson, Quinn, trailed them with a swagger that claimed more space than he needed. A young teen trying to appear older. As if there were any of his peers here to impress.

Still, he'd been making amends to Anna with the mowing, and he'd accepted her invitation to join them. If he could agree to work with Corey, they might heal the rift. That would help both boys.

Tricia deposited a potato salad on the table, and Blaine added a plate of squares.

A tap on the door announced a tall, frizzy-haired blond woman carrying a heavy-duty cardboard box. "Meatballs and rice. The liquor box is just for transportation. I know this is a dry establishment." Her blue eyes lit with her smile.

"Meaghan, Landon, meet Jaclyn. She's Roy's other-side neighbour. The one who was travelling last time you were here, Landon." Anna helped her unpack a pair of white casserole dishes. "Jaclyn owns one of the pubs in town."

Hard to imagine such a friendly, outgoing face commanding respect in a bar. Although the woman's height and colouring, with the straight blond eyebrows, projected a Viking warrior vibe.

Anna slid the box under the table and shooed everyone outside. "Let's enjoy the gorgeous day. And I have news."

Roy emerged last, and Anna clapped her hands like a child with ice cream to share. "Corey's back."

Excited voices peppered her with questions, and Anna, laughing, tried to answer them all at once. Too bad Corey couldn't hear the genuine pleasure in their voices.

Slouched against the wooden deck rail, Quinn stuffed his hands in the pockets of his baggy jeans and glared at his feet.

Two more cars arrived. The three newcomers clustered for a moment with the cautious posture and gestures of fresh introductions, then strolled toward the deck.

The couple climbed the stairs first, he lugging folding chairs under one arm and she holding a covered dish. In their early thirties, they'd be a few years older than Bobby and six or seven older than Landon.

Anna beckoned them into the group. "Everyone, meet Connor and Kelly, our new neighbours."

"Hey." Connor, thin-faced with a clipped beard, propped the chairs against the railing.

Black hair flowing loose to her waist, Kelly wore a garnet-coloured sleeveless blouse that accented her light brown skin. She flicked a smile toward Connor and then shared it around the group.

Meaghan held out her hands for the casserole. "I'm Meaghan. I'll take this inside for you."

As Connor and Kelly moved away from the top of the stairs, Landon glimpsed the woman behind them. A roaring sound filled her ears.

Anna's voice came through, distorted. "And this is Ciara. She's not new to town, but she's only been back a few months."

Ciara had grown into a petite but curvy woman. With her pointy little nose, round cheeks, and bright eyes, she resembled a cheerful rodent. Not as dangerous as she'd been in junior high, but still like she'd give a painful bite.

Smiling, she scanned the group. Until her gaze hit Landon's and she froze, eyes wide. The foil-covered platter lurched in her grip.

The next second her smile steadied. She stepped forward and offered Anna the platter. "Thank you for inviting me."

The roar receded to a rushing as if a river had sprung up beneath the deck. Water under the bridge. Landon's mind grabbed the cliché. She'd fled a store to avoid meeting Ciara in June, but since then she'd fought to forgive the past. Today, she chose to stand.

Chapter 4

As Anna introduced everyone to the newcomers, Landon smiled in time to her name.

"And I'm Gord." Meaghan's father spoke from the stairs, raising a white cardboard bakery box in salute.

His arms still looked too thin for his golf shirt, but his skin had better colour than when Landon last saw him. Heart trouble had pushed him into early retirement. Rest and treatment, and moving home to be near his daughter, appeared to be helping.

Anna repeated Connor's, Kelly's, and Ciara's names for Gord. "I think that's all of us. Elva declined."

"What did you expect?" Eyeing the new neighbours, Gord shrugged. "You'd have to meet Elva to know what she's like. But don't believe everything she says. She's been troubled since she was a kid."

As if that meant it was okay to dismiss her with such a tone.

Landon caught the pinch-eyed glare Quinn directed at him. If Gord's tires were flat later, she'd be sorely tempted to forget what she'd just seen.

She took the platter from Anna. "I'll take this inside."

Meaghan opened the door as Landon reached it. As she glanced past Landon, her expression blanked.

Too many people? Or had Meaghan been another of Ciara's targets in school? Anna said Gord moved away before having a family, but Meaghan had come back to live with her grandparents. Her being in a younger grade wouldn't have stopped Ciara.

How had Anna connected with Ciara, anyway? The girl had no reason to meet the neighbours. Landon choked. Anna didn't know their history. She must have invited her in hopes she and Landon could be friends.

Gord had followed her inside, and he slid his box onto the table. "How was your flight?"

"Fine, thanks. How are you?"

He thumped a palm on his chest. "Making progress. Must be the clean, sea air." Close up, the lines around his mouth didn't cut as deep as they had in June.

When they rejoined the group, Ciara sidled up to Landon. "So Corey's not the only runaway to come home. Where did you go, anyway?"

Cold slicked her skin. She hadn't run away. Although she'd wanted to.

Landon squared her shoulders and straightened her spine. Confidence and poise. Measured breathing. No hint of weakness.

The full truth would slap the smirk off Ciara's face, but not here. Not now. And never arm the enemy.

Even a forgiven enemy, because the other girl's attitude might not have changed.

Where had she gone? "Ontario." Via Moncton and what her abductor had called on-the-job training.

Hot pink lips thinned in a brittle smile. "I'm glad the rumours weren't true."

Rumours? There should have been a missing persons alert, nothing more. Even when she was found, she'd been underage so they'd withheld her name.

Landon kept her expression bland. As much as she wanted to know what Ciara heard before it blindsided her somewhere else, this was not the place to ask. Too many other ears.

The other girl eyed her up and down. "It ended well, whatever happened. New life. Probably a great career and a fantastic boyfriend."

The envy in Ciara's voice proved what Landon's counsellors had said. She'd come a long way toward wholeness. Even if it didn't feel that way on the inside.

She tried for a friendly tone. "I'm studying social work."

One perfectly sculpted eyebrow arched. "Didn't see that coming." Ciara sniffed. "But I didn't see myself back in this town working in a gift shop, either. Hey, I thought I saw you last month, but Anna didn't mention you'd be here tonight."

"I arrived this afternoon. But I did make a quick visit in June. Did Anna tell you she had some vandalism?"

"She didn't go into details." Ciara's fingertips rolled the hem of her shape-hugging pink tank top. "How long are you here? Maybe we could hang out. Put junior high behind us."

Was that an apology? Landon drew a slow breath. "It's not a place too many people care to revisit. If you want to do coffee or something, I'll be here for a while."

From the middle of the deck, Anna called out, "Let's move inside to eat while the food's hot."

Plates filled with a little of everything, guests clustered around the four yellow-draped tables. Clinking cutlery and the occasional scrape of a knife punctuated the quiet chatter.

Sitting with Roy and Quinn, Landon watched the old man try to pull the teen into a conversation. She prayed Quinn might find a mentor here, like Corey had with Anna's late husband, Murdoch.

"... that was the first and last time I tried cutting through that field. Never knew a bull could move so fast." Roy popped another meatball in his mouth.

A faint snicker broke Quinn's silence.

Landon leaned her elbows on the table and waited for Roy to finish chewing. "Bobby hinted there's a story behind breaking your leg. Want to share?"

Roy scratched the side of his head with a gnarled finger. "That boy has no respect." But his sea-blue eyes sparkled, and genuine warmth filled his voice.

At the next table, Jaclyn twisted in her chair. "I'll tell it if you won't. Connor and Kelly have a right to know what sort of foolhardy folks live around here, and we could all use a laugh."

Roy huffed. "You weren't there for it all, and only the squirrel was laughing."

Jaclyn stretched out an open palm. "Then have at it."

He tipped his head back and a little to the side. "Sometime the first of May, I was out back doing yard work when I spotted something dangling from the opening of one of the birdhouses. So I fetched the ladder, braced it *carefully* against the tree trunk—"

He narrowed his eyes at Jaclyn as if to underscore the care. "When I started climbing, this rusty banshee dove at me, chattering like mad. Dug its claws—all four sets—into my scalp. Well, it hurt. And it was a surprise attack. I started flailing at the critter."

He windmilled his arms, narrowly missing Landon's water glass. "The ladder wobbled, and down I went."

Jaclyn's blond brows shaped a straight bar. "And there you'd have been for quite some time if I hadn't needed to borrow your truck. Old men shouldn't be climbing ladders unattended."

"And young women should understand the fight for independence."

"Independence would have taken me to town to rent a truck instead of borrowing yours. Which would have left you on the ground for the squirrel army to return in force."

Roy threw back his head and laughed. "You win. And in the squirrel's defence, her babies were in that birdhouse. She didn't know what this two-legged predator might do."

Quinn's fingertips made a tiny drumroll on the table's edge. "Squirrel, one—Roy, no score."

The old man grinned. "Maybe not no score. It brought my grandson for the summer to babysit me."

"Hey, I visited before." Bobby's protest carried a laugh. "Next time, you don't need to be so extreme. Just ask."

"Suppose that'd avoid the cast." Roy shifted his leg. "I can't wait to ditch this thing and get into physio. And drive again, before young hotshot here takes his sports car back to Ontario."

Landon drained the last of her water. Anna's neighbour Elva had complained about Bobby's driving despite his obedience to the traffic rules, just because he was from away. Connor and Kelly might have a few hurdles there too.

At the table with Bobby and Meaghan, Ciara leaned forward. "Sports car? Are you the white Corvette?"

"Well, not personally, you understand, but my name's on the registration."

Ciara's bright lips pinched for a second before she produced a fake smile. Bobby, one—Ciara, no score. Not bad.

When they all migrated to the deck, Landon welcomed the soft July breeze skimming her cheeks. She clenched her jaw against a yawn. Falling asleep in the middle of Anna's party would be a bad idea.

Quinn sat alone on the steps, shoulders hunched like a shield to block the friendly chatter behind his back.

Water glass in hand, she edged through the chairs and perched beside him on the wooden step.

He ignored her.

She waited, watching the gentle wind playing in the tall pines, the voices behind her rising and falling in gentle waves.

Finally, he muttered, "What?"

"There's more dessert inside if you'd like some. That cake Gord brought is amazing."

"Too many chatty people between here and the door."

"Good thing you're tough, then." When he didn't move, she nudged his arm. "Corey could still use a friend. I think you could too."

He spat in the grass beside the steps. "He should've thought of that before he cut us off. Who needs him?"

Something moved among the trees, off to the right toward the new neighbours' house and Quinn's grandparents' place beyond. The same direction Quinn used to come sneaking to pull his pranks on Anna.

A raccoon maybe, or Anna's cat, Timkin.

"Did he cut you off, or did the group cut him off when he said he was through breaking the law?"

Quinn shifted his elbows on his denim-clad knees.

An orange marmalade cat emerged from the forest with a careful, weaving stroll. On a human, the gait would be arrogant or drunk. Or both.

Beside her, Quinn stiffened.

The cat came nearer, its dancer's nonchalance at odds with the matted fur and emaciated frame. The flagpole tail kinked at the top, and one ear dipped like it was signalling a left turn.

"Poor thing."

Quinn huffed. "He's been around the past week or so, but he'll run if you try to get close. My grandparents always chase him away. Nobody wants something like that hanging around."

Landon watched the animal, her senses tuned to the boy beside her. Bitterness marked his tone at the end. Not contempt for a mangy stray... more like resentment of the situation. Of being unwanted?

But his grandparents sacrificed for him to the point of ruining their health. He must know they loved him.

She leaned forward, echoing his posture. If he thought they only kept him out of obligation, it would be the same thing.

The cat paced across the backyard and through the pansies and other transplants in the flower bed. There was something lonely in that exaggerated strut. Or maybe she was just projecting what she heard from Quinn.

"Anna might let me feed him. If he can get along with Timkin, he'll be welcome."

Quinn unfolded himself from the steps. With a fair imitation of the cat's stroll, he retraced the animal's route into the forest toward home.

She expelled a harsh breath and pressed her lips tight. After his last fight with Corey, Anna had said he wasn't welcome on the property if he couldn't behave.

He probably thought Landon had just thrown it back at him.

Fine social worker she'd make if she couldn't handle a simple conversation with a teenager. She unclenched her hands and spread them on her skirt, letting the cotton fabric cool her heated palms. The vibrant colours cleared her mind.

Maybe this wasn't the right career path for her. She had to be open to that. But negative, accusing thoughts were not the voice of the God who loved her.

She stood and smoothed down her skirt. There'd be all summer to build a connection with Quinn and consider her future. Tonight, she'd focus on the here and now.

One of the dishes at supper had been saltier than she was used to, and her mouth felt like sand. She headed for the kitchen for more water.

On her way back outside, something creaked in Anna's sitting room.

The door stood ajar. Anna slouched at the desk, staring at the computer monitor, her expression hollow. She hitched the chair closer, and it creaked.

Landon slipped inside and closed the door. "Anna? Is something wrong?"

Anna gave a little cry and jerked around in her chair. Eyes wide, her hands flapped helplessly against the armrests. "I don't know what to do."

"Tell me." Landon squatted beside the chair and clasped her hand.

Anna's fingers fluttered like a bird's heartbeat. Her gaze bounced between the computer and Landon. Her first attempt at words came out in a croak.

Landon picked up the glass she'd set on the desk's edge. "Here. I drank out of it, but it should be okay."

After a swift gulp of water, Anna cleared her throat, then took another sip. "I came in to take a phone call. One of my reservations for tomorrow cancelled—because of negative reviews."

"What?"

"That's what I said. She told me which site she'd found them on and said the four- and five-star reviews sounded great, but these were newer. She didn't want to take a chance. And she'd booked two rooms."

Outside, laughter erupted.

Landon flashed Anna a wry smile. "One of Roy's stories? Or Jaclyn's?"

Anna's lips twitched. "Could be either one. I should be out there, but—" She waved a trembling hand at the monitor. "I've had more cancellations than usual lately. This lady was the first to give a reason. I should have waited until everyone left."

"You said 'these' reviews. So it's more than one."

Anna's broad, open features puckered like a frightened child's. "A lot. And on different sites. No wonder people are cancelling. This could ruin the inn."

Landon's thighs burned from holding the squat. She pushed to her feet and kneaded the muscles. "Let me see."

Instead, Anna shut off the monitor and pressed the back of her hand into her forehead. "I need to get back outside, and there's no point in us both being upset. Would you go through them with me later?"

"Of course." Another hour wouldn't hurt. Landon hugged her. "We'll figure this out."

They rejoined the others, but the discovery had erased any progress Anna had made after last month's stress. Her hands lay in her lap instead of gesturing while she talked. When she listened, her facial muscles sagged.

Soon Tricia and Blaine said they needed to go home and check on Quinn. Guests began folding chairs and gathering their dishes, thanking Anna and saying goodnight.

Last to leave, Gord lingered on the deck. He took Anna's hand. "Is everything okay?"

"I'll be fine. It's been a long day."

Landon collected a stray glass from beside a chair and headed inside. Not that privacy would help Gord pry anything from Anna.

She left the glass in the sink and started emptying the dishwasher.

For a person who'd do anything for anyone, Anna wouldn't let her friends know her own needs. Maybe she felt she'd used up too much of their care after Murdoch's accident, or maybe last month's prowler had given her a bit of a persecution complex.

Either way, at least she'd admitted finding these reviews and agreed that Landon could go through them with her.

Not that either of them would know what to do.

Anna popped her head in from the hallway. "I won't lock up yet. Timkin may wander home before we go to bed."

Landon rattled a handful of knives into the cutlery drawer. "I know it's still light out, but do you think you could sleep if we saved those reviews for morning?"

When Anna's face clouded, Landon held her gaze. "We need to be fresh to figure out what to do. And getting upset tonight will just make it harder to sleep."

Anna's shoulders slumped forward, her coral blouse drooping as if someone had laid an iron bar across her back. "I'll have to contact the different sites and ask for help. They're not likely checking messages on a Friday night."

"But will you be able to sleep, or will you worry?"

A brief flash of the old Anna showed in her smile. She rested her hand on a chair back. "You and I both know the secret to not worrying."

Landon reached into the dishwasher for the plates, face angled away from Anna to hide her relief. Throwing out the *worry* word had triggered Anna's faith response. They'd pray together, and then Anna would sleep.

Her part would be to hold back her own desire to check out these awful reviews and get some rest herself.

Plates clattered in her hands. One or two poor reviews were to be expected. You couldn't please everyone. But a bunch? And bad enough to scare other guests into cancelling?

There had to be something they could do.

Chapter 5

Saturday

THE HARD THING about crossing a time zone coming east was how Landon's body thought it was only six when her alarm went off at seven on Saturday. She launched out of bed before she could fall back to sleep.

Last night Anna hadn't told Meaghan about the reviews or the cancellation. She'd wanted to figure out damage control first, and Meaghan would arrive midmorning.

Gritty-eyed and headachy, Landon yawned her way downstairs, following the scent of coffee to the kitchen.

Anna popped bagels into the toaster. "Breakfast first, with a quick prayer for wisdom—and against a spirit of discouragement." The pouches beneath her eyes had darkened overnight.

Ten minutes later, Landon carried one of the hoop back kitchen chairs into the sitting room and angled it beside Anna's desk. She slid onto the contoured pine seat and propped a foot on the front rung. "Are these all from one person?"

"Different names and on multiple sites." Anna jabbed the power button. "I shouldn't have looked. No wonder everyone left when we went back out. I ruined the evening."

"You did not. They probably thought you were tired. Especially if they knew you'd driven to Halifax to get me. It was a nice time, though, and a great way to help Connor and Kelly get to know their neighbours."

The browser opened to the travel site Anna had been viewing last. Complaints about the food, bad water pressure, rudeness—Anna, rude? Rooms not living up to the photos on her website. Bedbugs.

Five one-star reviews, all from different usernames, and all within the last three weeks. None included their home province or country for Anna to know if they'd been actual guests.

Landon fought the urge to argue with these faceless people. "Do you think any of these are legitimate?"

Anna's fingertips worried a corner of the mouse pad. "Not the bugs. Beyond that, nobody said anything to me. Our guest book comments are all positive. And none of these reviews show up on the hotel booking sites. With those, you have to have actually stayed at the property."

"Which proves these are false. Can you copy and paste them into a document, and we'll compare with the other sites? We need to see the whole picture."

They ended up with a list of eight reviews, most repeated across various sites and social media.

Landon eased the felt pads of her chair legs sideways on the hardwood floor to give Anna more elbow room. "Click over to your site and show me the room photos?"

Whoever had taken the shots knew about angles and lighting. The bedrooms, breakfast area, and common room promised a comfortable, pleasant stay. There was even a picture of Anna's black and white cat, Timkin, guarding the inn's bright yellow front door.

"These are great. So's everything else. If the reviews are fake, what can we do?"

The tip of Anna's pen scratched a jagged row of question marks on the corner of her memo pad. "Bobby used to do computer work. He's helped me before, but I hate to bother him."

"Why not contact the sites and ask for help?"

"Good idea." She clicked back to the first review site and brought up a contact form. Her fingers hesitated over the keyboard. "It's more than just how to handle these reviews."

She swivelled to face Landon, soft brown hair falling forward along her jawline. Grey strands caught the light. "It's the timing. I thought the trouble was over, and now there's more. It can't still be Hart and Quinn. Surely they wouldn't be foolish enough to try anything else."

Dread clouded her eyes. "Who else has it in for me?"

Who, indeed? The steady hum of the computer, unmoved by human angst, seemed to mock their lack of answers.

Anna swallowed convulsively. "The inn was Murdoch's dream. I can't let him down."

The Murdoch Landon remembered would have been far more troubled by his wife's anguish. She took Anna's limp hand in hers and squeezed. "What's the first thing he'd do?"

"Contact those sites?"

The doubt in her voice, so tentative... so unlike Anna. Landon gave a brisk nod and filled her tone with confidence. "It's a start."

Ignoring the inner whisper that she was no use, she kept her chair by the desk while Anna worked. At least her presence proved Anna wasn't alone.

Anna had sent her last message when the back door opened.

"In here." Anna sounded almost like her usual, positive self. She minimized the browser screen and touched the back of Landon's hand. "I don't want her to worry about losing hours."

Meaghan stuck her head around the corner. "That was fun, last night. Did you get some rest after everyone left?"

"A bit." Anna stood, brushing the wrinkles from her tan capris, and tucked a lock of hair behind her ear. "Thank you both for pitching in yesterday afternoon while I took Corey into town."

Landon hooked a finger in the handle of her empty coffee mug and followed them into the kitchen. Meaghan was already tugging the blue plastic basket of cleaning supplies from the cupboard. "Where do you want me to start?"

"Just do the Schooner room. The other people cancelled."

"Not again." The basket wobbled, and a white-handled duster hit the floor. She scooped it up and turned troubled blue eyes on Anna. "If this keeps up, what will you do?"

"Don't you worry. We'll ride this out."

Meaghan slung her basket over her arm and hurried into the hallway as if to escape more bad news.

Anna stared after her. "She already needs more time than I can give her. Especially when Hart's case goes to trial. I hope they don't send him to jail, but he'll at least have a fine."

Closing her eyes, she seemed to gather her strength. Her back straightened, and the strain lines lost a little ground around her mouth. She slipped the neck loop of her sailboat-patterned apron over her head. "We still have guests to prepare for. I think I'll welcome them with a cinnamon loaf."

Last month, Landon would have scurried to find her laptop and catch up on homework or readings. She'd lived under deadlines for so long, she didn't know how to fill her time now. No classes, no counselling sessions, no friends here other than Anna.

The summer stretched outward like the ocean from the shore. With heavy fog rolling in.

Anna's kitchen, brimming with sunlight and a fading hint of grilled bacon, offered safe haven. Landon poured herself a glass of water. "I'll stick around."

One loaf became two, "because the oven's heating anyway." As soon as Anna put them in to bake, she leaned against the counter and checked her smartphone. "One of the travel sites replied."

Tight-lipped, she pushed her hair back from her forehead. "They say there's nothing they can do. Bad reviews happen, and I have no way to prove these aren't legitimate. One or two they'd let me contest, but not this many."

"But they're the same on multiple sites."

"Apparently that happens too. I can respond politely and acknowledge their concern, but I'm not to argue with the reviewers." Red stained her cheeks, matching the poppies splashed across her shirt. "I feel like if I treat them as legitimate, I'd be validating them. But I can't just leave it."

She tapped at her phone. "I need to talk to Bobby. Texting's safer in case he's writing, although I really do want to interrupt."

Landon flattened her palms on the table's satin-cool surface. "It has to be one person—these reviews are too close together for it to be more than one, unless you've had a steady stream of unsatisfied guests."

"I don't know what to think. It feels like an attack, but why?" The phone buzzed on the countertop, vibration skittering it sideways. Anna snatched it up. "Bobby?"

She explained the problem, then listened, scuffing one brown-sandalled foot against the other. "You're sure? That would be wonderful. Thanks."

Tucking the phone into the pocket of her capris, she released a breath. "He's coming over, and he told me one thing I can do now."

"What's that?"

"Well, I have no control over the review sites, but I do with my social media. I can write what he called a 'pinned post' for any account I can, apologizing for some recent negative reviews, which I believe to be false, and reassuring people the Green Dory Inn is the same welcoming place it's always been."

Landon pushed back her chair. "Go start now. I'll handle the baking dishes and let him in."

"Thanks." Anna untied her apron and hooked it in the pantry cupboard. She hurried out, hair bouncing in time to her hurried step.

The sink window overlooked the back of the inn property. Before Landon finished washing up, Bobby emerged from the tall trees to the left. The driveways around here were much longer than the two-car-length city ones, and the woods made a convenient shortcut. The sun gave him a short shadow as he crossed the parking lot into the inn's shade. At the stairs, the green blob on his white tee shirt resolved into a multiarmed alien with a gap-toothed grin.

Where did he find these things? She dried her hands and hurried to let him in. "Thanks for coming. Anna's pretty upset."

His gaze skirted hers. "It's probably not as personal as she thinks, but after last month, no wonder she's concerned."

He sidestepped into the sitting room. "Hey, Anna. Gramp says hi."

Landon followed, close enough to smell the coffee he must have been drinking. She'd stay out of his line of sight, but she wanted to hear this too.

Anna shot back from the keyboard like a student eager for assistance. "I wasn't sure how to word it. See what you think." Hopping to her feet, she waved him toward the black office chair. "You drive."

Flip-flops smacking the floor, he circled behind the couch to the desk and dropped into the seat. After a minute of studying the screen, he nodded. "Okay, this is a good start. We can play with it a bit before you post it."

Anna stood beside him, fingers twisting the wedding ring set she still wore.

Landon nudged her toward the kitchen chair she'd brought in earlier, then curled up sideways in one of the twin recliners. She pressed her cheek into the headrest's plush upholstery.

The desk chair creaked as Bobby swivelled to face Anna. "Did you bookmark the reviews?"

"They're already open in the browser. I wanted to see if there were any more."

"Were there?"

"No." The word came out guarded as if Anna thought it was only a matter of time.

As he read, Bobby bounced his fingertips on the edge of the mousepad. "These aren't your typical troll. If you hadn't said they were fake, I'd believe them."

He scrunched up his nose, hitching his glasses closer to his face. "The thing with reviews is you'll see one star and five stars for the same thing. Sometimes it's just a person's mood or expectations. Customers understand that, and they'll filter out the worst—and sometimes the best—to decide on their own."

"But..." Anna's voice quavered. She flattened her palms against her thighs. "They're lies. And guests are cancelling. This is someone attacking my business, and I have no way to stop them."

Naturally, the review sites couldn't take Anna's word for it. But what was she supposed to do—wait and hope new positive reviews buried these ones? What if the reviewer kept going?

Bobby's hands crawled through his sandy hair. "Writers see this too. Someone will run a campaign against them, get a bunch of people to trash their books, and for the most part, all they can do is move on and wait for the dirt to settle."

Landon wanted to protest, to fight for justice. Accuse him of not caring. Except Bobby wasn't the enemy and he clearly shared her frustration. "What about this post idea you suggested? Will it help at all?"

"It might, and we can point people to the sites Anna said aren't affected. The danger is it could encourage them to search out the bad reviews, which sound all too plausible. The upside is it may make legitimate, satisfied customers respond to those comments themselves."

"But the review site told Anna all she could do was leave a polite reply. Not to argue or deny anything."

Bobby's eyes narrowed slightly, and his mouth slid into what Landon thought of as his supervillain grin. She'd seen it before when he suggested digging a tiger pit to trap last month's prowler. "Anna shouldn't post anything defensive. But her customers can."

"Then we could make our own accounts and do that too." Except a false review was still a lie, even if she meant it for good. She ducked her chin and picked at a frayed spot on the hem of her denim shorts. "Never mind."

"I know it's tempting."

No judgment soured his tone. Instead, a hint of a dimple appeared in one stubbly cheek.

He tapped Anna's pen on the edge of the desk. "Travers would have some brilliant scheme to track this person and expose him as a fraud, but all I've got is to write that post and wait for the reviews to go stale."

Landon leaned forward on the recliner's padded armrest. "Who's Travers? Can we ask him?"

A faint grin stirred Anna's cheeks. "Travers is the hero in Bobby's books. If Bobby can't talk to him, we sure can't."

Bobby's eyebrows rose. "I didn't think you liked science fiction."

"You made me curious."

He opened his mouth, then seemed to reconsider. "Back to business. This could be someone with a grudge against you, but it could also be a random troublemaker who leaves bad reviews for a bunch of places."

"People do that?" In Landon's world, bullies held something personal against their targets, even though it wasn't justified. "Why pick on people they don't even know?"

"It makes them feel big to put someone else down. And who knows? Maybe he's thinking of another place and got the name wrong. Whatever the reason, you'll need to keep watch for anything else he leaves, but for now, let's work on what you want to say on your social media."

It might not fix anything, but having something simple to do and the reassurance of working with someone more experienced with words eased the tension in Anna's bearing. Her face had smoothed, and she'd stopped fidgeting with her rings.

That alone made Bobby's visit worthwhile. Other than one account Landon had to create to connect with her classmates for group projects, she stayed away from social media. It hadn't been a disadvantage until now.

As Anna and Bobby fine-tuned the message's wording, the oven timer beeped. Landon slid her feet to the floor. "I can get that."

"I'll go." Anna stood. "They may need more time."

Bobby kept focused on the computer, occasionally typing or moving the mouse.

A warm cinnamon scent wafted into the room. Landon inhaled deeply. "Thank you so much for helping Anna. Just having someone who understands makes a huge difference for her. It's out of my league."

Frowning at the screen, he shrugged without looking up. "Bad reviews, maybe, but social media's child's play for girls like you."

He tapped a few more keys.

Girls like you. The words spun in Landon's mind, gaining weight and bouncing from wall to wall.

She blinked. Swallowed. Stood and walked with as much dignity as she could from the room and out the back door.

Palms flat on the deck rail, she stared unfocused at the vertical stripes of tree trunks and the green splotches of foliage.

She'd heard those words before. "Girls like you" came from a place of judgment—or a place of power trying to dominate and steal her worth. In a way, Bobby's careless delivery cut deeper than the deliberately venomous tones from her past.

So much for thinking he was mellowing toward her.

She curled her fingers over the railing, squeezing until the wooden edge bit her flesh. This couldn't still be about the girl she reminded him of. No matter his past hurts, he had to see they were different people.

Roy knew her past. He might have told Bobby, expecting it to make him compassionate. She ground her teeth. If so, it hadn't worked.

For a nice guy who cared for his injured grandfather and took time to help Anna, he clearly had no heart left for someone with Landon's depth of wounds. Even if those wounds were healed.

She sighed. Or healing.

A red squirrel darted from the base of one pine trunk to another, then scooted up the rough bark to a branch and crouched there, chattering.

The rapid-fire sound echoed Landon's emotions at the unfairness of it all. She could put herself in Corey's place and understand his attitude toward her. She could ignore the verbal attack from Anna's neighbour last month because Elva had to be carrying her own pain. But this made no sense.

It just hurt. And somehow, she had to interact with Bobby without drawing further barbs—and without retaliating.

Pulling a deep breath of salt-and-pine air, she extended her hands, palms down. With a slow exhale, she imagined dropping the pain to the grass below the deck. She brushed her palms together for good measure.

Another burst of scolding from the squirrel drew her gaze back to the trees. The orange cat sauntered into view, crooked tail high, an elegant and slightly tipsy dancer.

Something in his gait prompted a name. Captain Jack.

It made her smile, and the residual ache ebbed. Eyeing the stray, she moved cautiously across the deck and down the steps. When her feet touched the slate path, he bolted.

"That one defeats even my attempts to approach him." Nigel Foley's voice came from the right.

Landon whirled. Nigel stood watchfully, metal detector slung over one shoulder.

She'd never met someone who could move so quietly in the woods. The first time he'd spoken out of nowhere, he'd been right behind her, and she'd panicked. This time he waited a safe distance away.

She tried to smile her appreciation. "He's so thin. I meant to ask Anna about leaving some food out for him, even though Timkin won't like another cat on his territory."

He nodded twice. "I expect he catches enough to sustain himself. No one knows where he came from."

"Quinn said most people chase him away. He sounded a bit sorry for him. I feel the same way."

"We outsiders share an understanding." He walked nearer, his battered tan work boots soundless in the grass.

Ordinary people could understand too. Anna did. Others... Landon glanced at the inn. Because he was helping Anna, it didn't matter if Bobby understood.

She smiled at Nigel. "I've named him Captain Jack."

He froze, grey eyes piercing. "Did he suggest that?"

His tone raised the hairs on her neck. "Quinn? No, it just came to me today."

Nigel blinked rapidly, then nodded. "Stranger things have happened."

Landon gripped the handrail at the bottom of the deck stairs. "I don't know what you mean."

"The secrets of Captain Jack. His spirit may have found a way to return. To guard them. Or to lead us to them."

Nigel had spoken before about a rumoured secret attached to the inn. Anna had told her about the man who built the house she and her husband had bought from the last surviving family member. "Wasn't Captain Hiltz named Hiram?"

Sharp grey eyes peered at her beneath bushy salt-and-pepper brows. "Everyone called him Captain Jack."

Now that she didn't have to decipher his words, her brain stopped flailing. "Did you come to see Anna?"

"Not today. Just patrolling."

Anna had enough on her mind anyway with the negative reviews and guests arriving. She was probably half afraid these people would cancel too.

The door opened, and Bobby emerged with a brick-shaped object wrapped in a tea towel. "Hey, Nigel." He made brief eye contact with Landon as she moved away from the stairs to let him pass. "Anna made me take one of her loaves. Gramp will send me over more often if he thinks he can get food."

He headed off through the woods.

Nigel slid a finger along the brim of his ever-present camouflage hat. "That one fits in well around here."

"He's been good to Roy and Anna." Even when it meant helping Landon by giving her drives last month. She'd do her best not to impose on him now that he'd made his opinion clear.

"Be careful of the captain." Nigel saluted and loped back into the forest.

The spot between Landon's shoulder blades prickled as if the ghost of the inn's long-dead builder stood watching her.

Chapter 6

STANDING IN THE grass behind the inn, Landon focused on her surroundings. The sultry air, spiced with sun-heated pine. A blue jay's strident call, and in the distance, the mournful cry of seagulls.

Reality. A reality that didn't include ghosts or messages from beyond the grave.

A bicycle darted around the side of the inn and stopped with a metallic wheeze that could have been a desperate plea to be oiled. Corey dismounted and wheeled his bike across the grass to the garden shed.

He leaned it there and came back. "Anna inside? I came to start the barn cleanup."

"You know she'll fuss over you being here when you just got home."

He jerked his head in a motion that flung his bangs out of his eyes. "Home's duller than Nigel's bunker." A grin slid across his face, and for a second, he lost the aloof vibe. "Some of his books are chill—survival tips and inventions. Then there's the weird alien ones you'd expect."

The mask snapped back in place, and he slouched up the steps to the inn.

Strolling after him, Landon reached the door just as Meaghan was coming out. Damp tendrils of red hair stuck to the girl's forehead from working upstairs in the heat, but the blue-grey shadows under her eyes had been there when she arrived.

Landon smiled encouragement. "Enjoy your Saturday."

"Thanks."

In the kitchen, Anna was talking to Corey. "If Quinn can come, I'll get you both started."

More energy vibrated in Anna's voice—from having Corey back or from what she and Bobby had done online? Either way, it was good. Anna deserved better than this stress.

Corey's thumbs danced across his phone. After a brief text exchange, he grunted. "He'll be here in a bit. Do you really expect him to get along with me?"

"I do. You were friends once." Anna planted her hands on her hips. "Leaving the activities you were into was the right choice. I don't think Quinn understood you were cutting those ties but not cutting him out. I think it triggered more abandonment for him. That's what he's responding to, not to you."

"It still burns."

"Of course. And he needs to learn how to behave. My prayer is that, by working together, you can rebuild on a different foundation."

He shrugged and edged toward the door. "Can I get started, and you can lay down the law to him when he gets here?"

Landon tagged along to the barn. She hadn't been inside since the day she'd found Corey's hoodie planted in the mess.

Anna unlocked the doors and propped one open before going inside and flicking the wall switch. The string of weak bulbs cast enough light to work with, but shadows lingered in the corners.

Dust motes clogged the summer-heated air, tasting of ancient hay and motor oil. Old machinery and heavy furniture crowded the walls, and a jumble of cardboard moving boxes littered the middle.

Many boxes still lay on their sides, household goods and clothing spilled on the wide-planked wooden floor. Some stood upright, refilled to either keep or toss. When Corey fled, Anna didn't have the heart to keep cleaning up the mess.

Quinn sauntered in, a red ball cap low on his forehead, as Anna was instructing Corey to get work gloves from the shed. A faded skull with chains snaking through its eyes leered on his tee shirt.

Anna's lips tightened briefly. "Thanks for coming on such short notice, Quinn. Remember, I've put Corey in charge because of his hoodie. It only seems fair. I expect you to work together and treat each other with respect."

The boys eyed one another like two fighters squaring off.

Anna must have taken Quinn's grunt as assent because she strode back to where Landon stood inside the door. "I'll keep track of your hours, and I'll provide your lunches while you're here."

As they stepped out onto the gravel path, a quiet "Score!" sounded behind them.

Landon nudged Anna. "Your cooking still rules."

"I'd better get at it, then. It's almost eleven."

A police cruiser purred into the lot and stopped where Meaghan had been parked.

Dylan climbed out, smiling at them over the car roof. "Landon, I heard you were back. I hope this time you can enjoy the best of Lunenburg with the petty nuisance activity behind us."

When they first met, the officer's lean, serious face had intimidated her until he flashed those poster-white teeth. She'd been concerned about his youth, too, but he'd been a major support for Anna.

He walked toward them and stopped, feet wide, a cop at ease but at the ready. "Anna, I wanted to thank you in person for bringing Corey in."

"You finally had a day off yesterday? I assumed you were out on patrol."

"I keep telling you, I do get them." His dark eyes sought Landon's face. "How was summer school?"

She couldn't stop a grimace. "Not good. But I get time with Anna now."

"All's well that ends well?"

"Something like that." She nibbled the inside of her lower lip.

Gaze intent, Dylan waited. Like what she had to say mattered and he wanted to hear it. He'd drawn out Anna this way whenever they'd called about the prowler, but he didn't need to listen to Landon's personal problems.

Another thought surfaced. "This isn't your area, I'm sure, but someone's been leaving fake reviews about the inn, and they're making people cancel. Is there anyone we can talk to? Some sort of internet department?"

"You're sure it's not actual guests?"

"Anna would know if she had that many dissatisfied customers. One mentions bedbugs, and she'd definitely have heard about that."

"You'd think." Thick black brows crowded down toward his eyes. "It sounds like cyberbullying, just not as extreme as what the schoolkids face."

Landon's memory burned with some of Ciara's choicest barbs. Bullying hurt. Anna didn't deserve it any more than Landon had. Less, in fact, with her kindness to all the misfits God sent her way.

The difference was that Anna, as an emotionally mature adult and a woman of faith, had resources most kids didn't. Except she was still off-balance from the harassment she'd experienced in June.

"So what can we do? Law enforcement's for the level of cyberbullying that triggers suicides. And exploitation." Landon rubbed the back of her neck. "I'm glad this isn't as dangerous, but it's still hurting Anna's business."

The sun-crinkles around Dylan's eyes softened. Did he recognize her unstated pain? Or maybe he heard her futile desire to protect Anna. "You can report it, and we can start the process."

Anna hugged her arms across her stomach. "I won't divert resources from more urgent cases. We're on our own this time."

The husky discouragement in her voice made the truth harder to hear.

On their own. With no way to track this reviewer and not even the chance to catch him or her in action.

Landon scuffed a sandal across the pavement, wishing for a stone to kick. Anything to release a bit of the energy building inside. "Unless it's a random crank, it's someone with a purpose. Hart or Quinn wouldn't dare with their court dates coming up. Would they?"

Dylan took a slow breath. "I hope not. I'll make a note, just in case. For now, keep track of what happens. I'll check in with you in a few days."

~~~

Landon and Anna sipped tall glasses of ice water on the deck, padded wicker chairs drawn into the table umbrella's shade. The air, still heavy with heat, vibrated with a cicada's high-pitched buzz.

As well as preparing a teenager-satisfying lunch, Anna had checked the review sites at least three times. Not only were there no new accusations, but a previous guest left a glowing new review on the inn's social media page and one travel site.

Anna trailed a finger through the condensation on her glass. "The boys soon need to wrap it up for the day. It's too hot."

The way her shirt clung to her back sitting in the shade, Landon agreed.
~~~

A mid-sized grey sedan drove into the lot. Anna rose, straightening the hem of her poppy-strewn white blouse. "That'll be our guests. I'll get their key."

Landon wasn't a host. She didn't need to greet them, and she didn't want to butt in on Anna's role. She wasn't a regular guest, either. Maybe being a personal guest tipped her nebulous status toward a support role. She'd go with that.

She scooted through the inn and caught up with Anna at the front door just as it opened inward.

A middle-aged couple entered, each pulling a wheeled suitcase.

Anna stepped forward. "Welcome! You must be the McNutts. I'm Anna, and this is Landon."

The plump woman's smile showed her teeth and reflected in her eyes. She practically bounced into the entryway. "Glenna and Ivan. We're booked for three nights."

Anna dangled a set of keys on a pewter schooner fob. "Let me show you your room."

Ivan McNutt hung back, glancing around as if something might jump out at him. Blunt fingers twisted one end of his short moustache. "We should see the room before we commit."

"Of course." Anna led them upstairs, chattering more than usual. When she came back, her expression mirrored Ivan's. "They won't stay. They must have seen the reviews too."

"Maybe he's just a nervous guy."

Footsteps sounded on the stairs. Landon squeezed Anna's arm.

Glenna led the way, her all-encompassing smile still in place, but Ivan hadn't lost his worried frown. She stopped in the entranceway and gazed around. "I'm sure we'll enjoy our stay."

She reached for her husband's hand. "We'll take our bags upstairs, and then could we have a tour?"

"With pleasure." Anna ducked out of the way of their cases.

When the McNutts returned, Anna led them into the breakfast room to the rustic white sideboard. "The coffee maker and kettle for tea are available all the time, and this little fridge has milk and cream. Just leave your mugs here when you're done."

She indicated the basket of assorted teas and hot chocolate pouches and the glass-domed plate of cinnamon loaf. "Help yourselves to a snack too."

Ivan examined a watercolour trio of local blooms—lupines, asters, and lilacs. His shoulders loosened as though the pastel shades reassured him somehow. "We stopped at the tourist bureau, and they were out of your brochures."

Anna opened a drawer in the sideboard and handed him a glossy pamphlet. "I'm surprised to hear that. I'll take in more."

He turned it over with blunt-tipped fingers, opened it, and skimmed through. "You don't mention the building's history or its builder. Here or on your website."

Landon hadn't thought to ask more about Captain Hiltz. Hiram a.k.a. Jack.

Anna leaned an elbow against the sideboard. "Captain Hiltz is best known as a rumrunner. When my husband and I started the Green Dory Inn, we wanted a sea-and-forest theme, but we didn't want to trade on the captain's notoriety. There are enough places in town focused on rumrunners and privateers."

Ivan fiddled with the corner of his moustache. "Not trading on his legacy is a plus, in my book." He dropped his hand in a hurry. Perhaps the moustache was a habit he was trying to break. "Still, one reason we're here is to do some research on Captain Hiltz."

Watching him, Glenna grew serious. Her arm moved as though to reach for him, but she held back.

Anna walked toward the entryway. "You'll find plenty of material in town, and we have a few books in the common room."

"I wondered about diaries." Ivan's jaw firmed. "Or personal accounts." His voice held a vague hurt-and-bewildered-by-it air.

Now Glenna did take his hand.

"His log books are on loan to the Fisheries Museum." Anna turned back in the doorway. "I haven't seen anything more personal, but we're going through what his daughter-in-law left in storage in the barn. I can ask the boys to lay aside any books they find."

"I should perhaps see the barn too. If that would be all right."

"Of course. But I'll warn you it's a mess. We had vandals last month. They didn't bother the inn or our guests, but they left a shambles out there."

Anna brushed her palms together as if to leave that in the past. Or to wipe it from the guests' memories, in case they worried about a repeat attack. "The police have made arrests. Nothing to worry about now."

Standing there, eyes on her husband, Glenna seemed like the only thing concerning her was Ivan. For all his earlier unease, he didn't show a reaction to the news. Instead, he asked, "Does he have family in the area?"

"Only Maria, his daughter-in-law. She's quite elderly now. There was a grandson who went missing a long time ago. He's presumed dead. It broke the old man's heart."

"What about locals who might remember Jack? Captain Hiltz?"

Landon wanted to roll her eyes. Did everyone know Hiram Hiltz as Jack, except her?

Anna tucked her hair behind one ear. "If you know his nickname, you've likely already heard about the pub, Captain Jack's, in town. They have a big portrait of him hanging there, on loan from the family." She caught

Landon's eye. "That's Jaclyn's place. She likes the play on words with their names."

Ivan made a sound like he'd swallowed something sideways. "There's a pub in his honour?"

"I wouldn't put it quite that way." Anna laced her fingers across her middle and spread her elbows, the same stance she took when she had to play peacemaker between Corey and Quinn. "You asked about people who remember Captain Hiltz. He's been gone for about forty years, I think. My neighbour Roy might have known him, but Nigel's probably your best source. Nigel Foley. He hears a lot and remembers it all. Next time he comes by, I'll introduce you."

She led them past the staircase into the common room. "You're welcome to enjoy this area as well, and you might find some useful books. I'll check the other rooms, too. Books do migrate."

Her finger traced the coloured spines on the bookshelf. "One that talks about Captain Hiltz is *Rumrunner Heroes*, if you'll forgive the title, but I don't see it."

Then she faced Ivan. "It sounds like you've already done some research. You understand the situation. Illegal, yes, but it let men support their families in the 1920s when the fishing dried up. Some of the men—and boys—who survived went on to build legitimate businesses or go back to fishing. One even became chief of police for a time."

A stubborn glint shone deep in his brown eyes, but he didn't argue the point.

Anna pointed to the painting of a schooner in full sail. "That's his ship. It's the only memento I've kept to display, although, of course, it's the property of the family."

Ivan approached the painting as if the vessel might open fire. He squinted at the details, then sucked in his breath. His whole body started to vibrate.

He spun and glared at Anna. At Landon, then back at Anna. The wrinkles outside his eyes pinched into dark lines.

"His ship is the *Pretty Young Thing.*" He spat the words. "What does that tell you about the kind of man he was?"

He practically ran from the room. The front door banged. Seconds later, he stormed down the driveway.

~~~

Turning from the window in the frozen silence, Landon struggled for something to say. Even Anna didn't have a response, although somehow calm still ruled her features.

Glenna's sigh broke the spell. Her normally jolly face red-stained, she spread her hands, palms up. "I'm sorry. Ivan can take things... personally. He'll walk it off and be back."

"I'm sorry the painting upset him." Anna crossed the room. "I'll take it down for your stay."

"No, don't do that. He just needs time." Glenna slipped a slim blue volume from the bookcase. "If it's okay, I'll take this upstairs to your cozy reading nook. I can watch for Ivan and learn a little local history."

"Make yourself at home. Take a drink up with you if you like."

When they were alone, Anna wandered to the jigsaw puzzle on the polished oak table. Within the frame, a lighthouse matched the picture on the box, leaving only a small flotilla of sailboats, the water, and the sky to complete.

She stirred the pieces with one finger and added a few to the sky-coloured pile. "I get these started, and if the guests aren't interested, I end up finishing them too."

It had been a schooner last month.

Anna frowned, obviously concentrating on more than the puzzle. "I wonder if I should warn Jaclyn she might have some trouble."

The back door banged, and a voice called, "Anna?"

"Be right there."

Corey stood in the kitchen. He drew a dark, wooden box the size of a brick from under his dust-streaked shirt and passed it to Anna. "Found this in the barn. It looks valuable,
~~~

and Quinn—" His eyes flicked toward the door. "I just thought it'd be safer in here."

"Thank you, Corey." Anna rotated the box in her hands. "The carving is beautiful. I don't remember packing this. Where did you find it?"

"In a shoebox, under some comic books. The balance felt off, so I checked inside. This was tucked at one end with a bunch of crumpled paper at the other like someone wanted to hide it."

Shoulders caved forward, he stared at the floor as if expecting to be accused of snooping.

If he'd spent enough time with Nigel to learn about the bunker, he'd probably absorbed more than that. "Thinking about Captain Hiltz's secrets?"

He nodded.

Anna groaned. "Does everybody think there's something hidden in my barn?"

"Maybe just Nigel." Corey spoke to the floor in a low mumble. "But he knows things."

In Nigel's case, the line between knowing and imagining could be a little blurry. Still... "You could have packed other hidden things, or there could have been something already out there. What if that's why Hart and Quinn broke in?"

Exasperation flashed in Anna's eyes. "They dumped everything to make a mess. They wouldn't have caused all the other trouble if all they wanted was to search the barn."

She held the box at eye level. "There's no obvious way to open this—not that it's our business. It's small enough Maria might want it in her room. I've been meaning to visit anyway. She should know about the vandalism."

Corey yawned. "Okay if we stop for today? I didn't sleep much last night. Quieter in the bunker."

Lunenburg wasn't exactly a nightlife hot spot, and it didn't have the perpetual sirens of a big city. Maybe his dad snored.

Anna made a shooing gesture with her free hand. “I was about to send you home when our guests arrived. Tell Quinn to go too. And since it’s not urgent, I’d like to keep Sunday not a workday. You two agree on a time, and I’ll see you Monday.”

She gestured Landon toward the exit. “I’d like to be out of Ivan’s way when he comes back. He might be embarrassed.”

Their half-finished drinks stood in condensation puddles on the smoked-glass tabletop. A rusty pine needle floated in Anna’s, and she fished it out with her index finger.

The umbrella’s shade had moved with the sun. They repositioned their chairs as the boys left, Corey on his bike and Quinn through the woods. The orange stray strolled a weaving path from the trees and circled to the front of the barn, almost as if he’d been waiting for the coast to be clear. He sat and stared at the doors Corey had just padlocked.

Landon’s spine prickled between her shoulder blades. “Nigel thinks the cat is Captain Hiltz. Because I didn’t know about the nickname and called him Captain Jack.”

When Anna didn’t respond, Landon sat straighter. “You don’t believe him?”

“Of course not. Although I don’t think Timkin will appreciate your captain invading his turf.”

“Could we feed him?”

Anna released a heavy breath. “I don’t want cats fighting outside at night. The last thing we need is more bad reviews.”

“He’s been around awhile. Has Timkin been fighting?”

“No, but why take the chance?”

Even at this distance, the stray’s ribs showed through his matted coat. “Because he’s hungry. And nobody wants him. Quinn seems sympathetic, but his grandparents don’t want a stray hanging around.”

Resting her water glass against the wicker arm of her chair, Anna sniffed. “So I should feed him to earn points with Quinn.”

Ordinarily, Anna would be inventing opportunities for a positive connection with the boy. She shouldn't need Landon to point one out. Landon gentled her tone. "Have you seen anything else to encourage in him?"

"Cats can fend for themselves. There are mice and voles and all kinds of little creatures. Timkin treats the forest as his personal buffet."

The cat was gone. "Will you at least think about it?"

Ivan stalked past the end of the house, hands jammed into his front pockets like rocks. Instead of veering off toward his car in the parking lot, he headed into the forest.

"So much for cooling down." Anna pulled out her phone. "I'd better text Jaclyn, just in case."

Chapter 7

Sunday

Landon smoothed her favourite skirt before fastening her seatbelt. The exuberant streaks of colour reinforced her confidence. She could do this. Not hide at the inn this summer, but find a temporary place in Anna's community. In her church.

"We'll just stop to pick up Roy." Anna signalled right from the inn driveway instead of left toward town.

"Bobby doesn't drive him?"

"My car's easier for Roy's leg. He can ride in the truck, but it's too high. And Bobby's Corvette is way too low."

"So they're both coming with us?" She'd have to sit with Mr. Disapproval in the rear so Roy could have the front.

Her conscience panged. Now who was having attitude trouble?

"When I take Roy, Bobby meets us there. I think he misses driving his car."

The white sports car was already gone when they reached the grey-green ranch-style bungalow. Roy waved from where he sat on his walker at the base of the back stairs.

Landon tossed her purse into the rear seat and climbed out of the car. "I'll load your walker into the trunk."

"Thanks. I'm glad you decided to join us."

The week she'd been here in June, she'd stayed at the inn Sunday morning while Anna went to church. Today, Meaghan had come in to cover any last-minute needs as the guests finished breakfast.

Each room's key ring included a key to the front door, and Anna had warned the McNutts they might need to let themselves in or lock up after themselves if her car wasn't there. Ivan had seemed calmer this morning, although a vague, emotionally bruised aura clung to him. Glenna's exuberance about another sunny day and getting out exploring had been enough for them both.

Anna put the car in gear and reversed to face the road. Passing the inn, she warned Roy, "You may have visitors later. Our guests were asking if anyone would remember Captain Hiltz. Did you live here then?"

"He was an old man when I met him." Roy chuckled. "Or so I thought, being that much younger. It was him, the son and daughter-in-law, and their son. At the end, it was just the captain and Maria. No love lost between those two, but she stayed to look after him until he died."

"Elva's family is the only other one that's been here long enough. Do you think she might remember any stories?"

He shook his head, his short hair rasping against the headrest. "Don't send them to Elva. She'd have been too young to have met him, and she doesn't talk about the past."

From their one encounter, Landon thought anything Elva did say would do Ivan more harm than good. That was hardly fair. Misery like that didn't spring from a vacuum.

Arriving in the church parking lot revived Landon's anxiety. A few people here would remember her as a child. Most her age and older would recall the missing person alert. Those didn't happen often in a small town.

At the time, whether they thought her a runaway or heard rumours of worse, they would have prayed. She owed them her thanks. But that first encounter was always awkward.

Sympathy and concern saw her as the victim she'd been, not the survivor she'd become.

Focused on a bright turquoise streak on her skirt, she drew in a long, slow breath and loosened her grip on her purse before her fingernails left permanent grooves. Shame didn't hold her anymore. Social awkwardness wouldn't, either.

Anna popped the trunk, and Landon sprang from the car before her nerves could root her in place. Together they unfolded the walker and brought it to Roy's door.

Landon swallowed hard. "Could we keep things low-key today? Let me be incognito?"

"Guess I should leave my welcome speech in the car, then." Roy winked.

She shot him a mock frown. "You're incorrigible."

"Heard that before. It's why I'm still alive."

She and Anna matched Roy's steps toward the plain white clapboard building. There were other churches nearby, magnificent stone structures, but Anna had been part of this congregation as long as Landon had known her.

A tall girl in shorts and flip-flops stood at the entrance with a plump, grey-haired woman wearing a blouse and skirt—with pantyhose in July. Their twin smiles told Landon she'd be welcome here, no matter what her style, outward or inward.

She responded when greeted but left the conversation to Anna and Roy, who seemed to know everyone. There'd be time to connect later.

In the sanctuary, long blue pads covered the hard wooden pews she remembered from childhood. Not that the kids had sat long with the lively action songs they'd sung before scattering into their activity groups.

Like a ghost from her memories, a child darted around her and zipped out into the foyer. A smaller girl followed, stubby blond braids bobbing. "Wait up!"

Pressure built in her chest. She hadn't paid much attention to the deeper side of summer Bible school, and when real school became too frustrating, she'd quit coming here. Told her mom she was too old. Still, without the love and whatever teaching she'd absorbed in those innocent summers, would she have been open to hearing the message from the people who later reached out to her in her brokenness?

She slipped an arm around Anna's waist and squeezed, leaning sideways until their heads touched. "Thanks for convincing Mom to bring me here." If only her sisters had received something God could use in their lives too.

Someday, she prayed, she'd have her family back.

For now, she leaned into Anna's return embrace and absorbed all the love she could.

"Is it really?"

At the feminine shriek, Landon cringed. Anna's arm tightened around her as a short, bulky woman in a pink flowered top surged up the aisle from the front of the church.

"Landon Smith, it is you, isn't it?" Her outstretched arms wrapped both Landon and Anna.

The scent of lilac teased Landon's memory, linked with a singsong voice for story time. And apple juice. The woman's name wouldn't come.

Heart racing, she freed herself from the embrace. The few people who'd noticed seemed unconcerned. Except Roy, who winked again.

The woman's eyes brimmed, and she clutched Landon's hands. "I'm sorry to make a scene, honey, but it's so good to see you. We prayed so hard—"

Her tears overflowed. Keeping a grip on Landon with one hand, she fished in her pocket and found a tissue to blot her cheeks. "You probably don't remember me. Ginette Shaw, from children's ministry when you were little. And I'm part of the midweek prayer group with Anna."

Ginette sniffed, then blew her nose and blinked at Landon through glistening lashes. "God did the impossible and brought you home, dear. He's so good."

"Yes, He is." Warmth filled Landon's spirit and left no room for stiffness or self-consciousness. God was loving her through this little woman's transparent joy.

She smiled from the inside out. "Thank you more than I can say, Ginette. For praying and for investing in all of us as kids."

"Moments like this are precious." Happiness glowed in Ginette's round face. "And there'll be so many more when we get to Heaven."

The loose sleeves of her top fluttered like little wings as she hurried to the front and through a side door near the platform.

One or two people still looked Landon's way, smiling. Roy poked her with a gnarled index finger. "Move along, miss. You're blocking the aisle."

Anna motioned her into one of the pews and slid in next to her. "It's easier for Roy to be on the end."

Landon sat and closed her eyes, taking in the sounds and atmosphere, thanking God again for putting compassionate souls like Anna and Ginette in her childhood in advance of what was to come. Some people would blame Him for what happened, forgetting the truth about free will. To her, the amazing thing was how many ways God inserted Himself into her story to bring her this far. And He did it for everyone if they'd only notice.

The seat pad shifted. Bobby had joined them from the row's far end. Clean-shaven today, he'd opted for a plain lime-green tee shirt. And running shoes instead of flip-flops. With a whispered greeting, he faced forward as the worship team began to play.

His judging words rose in her mind. *Girls like you.* She squeezed her eyes shut. Instead of singing, she let the song wash over her until it drew her back into awareness of God's presence.

The service was more traditional than the on-campus one she attended, but the songs, prayer, and teaching wove an encouraging theme to strengthen her heart.

After his closing prayer, the pastor invited everyone to stay for ice water and lemonade. "Or coffee or tea if you're not already hot enough."

She turned to Bobby. "Thank you again for helping Anna yesterday."

His shoulders jerked in a mini shrug. "It wasn't much."

"The moral support gave her something tangible she could do. She was so much better after that. And someone made a positive reply to her post."

"Great. Not that it'll stop this guy from doing more with his poison keyboard." His gaze flickered toward her. "Sorry. I'm not trying to be a downer."

Not about Anna, anyway. Or had he not noticed how his words had hurt yesterday?

When they'd been trying to stop the prowler, the lack of possible suspects felt like they were standing alone in thick fog with no landmarks, no path, no signs of any kind. The same blind helplessness enveloped her now.

They'd considered all Anna's friends and contacts for the previous incidents, and nothing had changed in the past month. Finding this faceless reviewer would be impossible. Especially if it wasn't anyone local. Maybe one of her guests did have a bad time and decided to take online revenge. But wouldn't Anna have noticed someone being dissatisfied?

As Anna and Roy filed into the aisle, Landon kept pace, aware of Bobby behind her.

A woman in a flowing tangerine blouse caught Anna's arm. "I'm sorry about your inn, dear. Will you stay in the area, or are you going to live near your children?"

Landon stopped short.

Bobby bumped her. "Sorry."

Catching his gaze, she nodded toward Anna's conversation.

The woman chattered on, hands waving and blond curls bouncing. "They said you were giving up the inn, that it's too much without your dear husband. Especially with your health the way it is."

Anna's elbows clamped into her sides. "Don't worry, Lylia. Everything's fine. That's an old rumour."

"No, no—this was yesterday, at the farmers' market."

"Well, if you hear it again, please tell people that I'm not going anywhere and the inn is still open for business." She excused herself and kept moving.

The fluttery woman studied Landon as if trying to place her. Then something else caught her attention, and she darted away through one of the pews toward a knot of people.

Landon and Bobby caught up to Anna as she reached the door where Roy stood talking with the pastor. The younger man held eye contact, bending forward to focus on Roy instead of hurrying him out to let the next people pass.

When Anna introduced her, his friendly handshake and warm smile offered genuine welcome without prying.

Outside, Bobby said goodbye and told Roy he'd see him at home. His Corvette glided out of the lot while Roy settled in Anna's car.

Anna had just shut the walker in the trunk when a white-haired man in a grey suit approached. "Anna, I'm glad I caught you. Have you already signed with another real estate agent, or could I come by and talk?"

One hand braced on her open door, Landon stood still.

Anna's head jerked from side to side. "Don't tell me—you were at the farmers' market too. I'm not selling."

He dipped his sunglasses. "Farmers' market? I had two calls yesterday asking when the property would be available for showing."

Anna stiffened. "Who's asking?"

"I didn't know either name, but I said I'd get back to them."

"You'll have to tell them no sale."

Thick white eyebrows drifted up above his glasses. "Sure thing. Sorry to bother you."

"I'm sorry someone's wasting your time with rumours."

As he walked away, Anna climbed into the car and slammed the door. "Bad reviews, vanishing brochures, fresh rumours..." She rested her forehead on the steering wheel. "I thought this was all behind me. I don't know what to do."

~~~

The rambling, honey-hued seniors' residence would have at one time been a private country home for a large family. Landon counted six pairs of narrow, white-framed windows on the upper floor, window boxes trailing bright red blooms. Six rooms in the front, and presumably another six in the rear.

A grey-roofed veranda stretched the length of the front, its squared white pillars hung with more flowers.

Landon hadn't been able to convince Anna to stay home and rest, so she'd invited herself along for moral support. After restocking the tourist bureau with Green Dory Inn brochures, they'd come to return the carved box to the inn's former owner.

Ignoring the accessibility ramp on the side, they climbed the broad, wooden steps to the veranda. A row of rocking chairs lined the open space. Two held elderly women with sharp stares.

"Good afternoon, ladies."

Anna's friendly tone didn't disarm them, but the one on the left dipped her head in a guarded nod.

Inside, Anna asked at the reception desk for Maria. A scrubs-clad man crossing the open space behind the desk veered toward them. "Maria is not very energetic today, but
~~~

some company will cheer her up. She's most likely in her room."

His warm bass voice flowed with a rich, African cadence. Landon wanted to close her eyes and ask him to read something. Anything.

The receptionist checked her screen. "She's in Room 6. All the residents' rooms are upstairs."

Maria Hiltz's tiny corner room contained enough space for a single bed and a few other pieces of furniture. A huge cultivated fern thrived in the natural light, spilling lacy shadows across the floor in front of her grey tweed swivel rocker. She laid her knitting in her lap and clicked off the television. "Anna! It's good to see you."

Her short, white hair kinked in wiry curls. Lines cut deep into her face, especially the vertical ones from the corners of her mouth down to her chin.

Anna clasped her hand, then stepped back. "I want you to meet my friend Landon. She's staying with me for the summer."

Behind Maria's blue plastic glasses, her gaze sharpened. "It's nice of you to come." She waved gnarled fingers toward the bed. "You'll need to sit there."

When they'd seated themselves on the bold geometric quilt, feet dangling, Maria leaned her head back on the rocker's thick upholstery. "How's the old house?"

So much for a light conversational opener.

Anna described a few changes to the decor and shared some things guests said they'd loved about the inn. "We did have some trouble a while ago."

Maria's fingers picked at the edge of her knitting. "What happened?"

"The house is fine, but someone broke into the barn and dumped all your storage boxes."

The old lady's face blanched. One hand flew to her chest. The other clenched her knitting, tangling apple-green yarn.

"I told you to keep everything safe. If they've taken anything—"

She glared at Anna. "I trusted you."

Anna spread her fingers on her knees. "We had a heavy-duty lock, but they cut it. I don't think anything's missing, just some damage. Bowls, pictures, things like that."

Blue eyes huge behind her glasses, Maria trembled visibly. "I'd packed things in smaller boxes. Nothing valuable, mind, but mementos. Things that would matter to David."

Longing throbbed in her voice as she spoke the name. David must be her son. The one everyone else thought was dead.

"Most of those went into the bigger boxes or into drawers in the furniture." The bed frame squeaked as Anna sat forward. "Please don't worry, Maria. The police said it was mischief, not theft."

She drew the carved box from her bag. "We found this in the cleanup. It's small enough I thought you might like to keep it with you."

Maria sat forward so quickly Landon almost reached out, afraid she'd fall out of the chair. "Give me that." She brought the box up to her face and slowly rotated it as if checking every inch for damage. When she placed it in her lap, one protective hand rested on top. "This belonged to Jack. It's to go to David."

Silence filled the space, a poignant waiting for a young man who would never come home.

Someone knocked. Maria flung the green square of her knitting over the box. "Come in."

The attendant they'd met downstairs entered with a tray. "We missed you at snack time, Maria. I've brought you some coffee and fruit. Would you like more to share with your visitors?"

"No thank you. I need to be alone." Her fingers curled over the hidden box. Once he left, she held it out to Anna. "Take this with you and keep it safe. In the house. Things can go missing here."

The weight of Maria's grief haunted Landon all the way to the inn. It took a strong will to cling to hope for so many years, but denial trapped the woman in her loss. "How old was David when he died?"

"In his teens. He died before Captain Hiltz, and that was at least forty years ago."

As they entered the inn, the phone was ringing. A low growl vibrated in Anna's throat. "I forgot to forward it to my cell again." She darted into the kitchen. "Hello, Green Dory Inn."

She strode into the hallway, handset pressed to her ear, and crossed to her sitting room. "What did he do?" She dropped her bag beside one of the recliners and flopped into the seat.

Landon kicked off her sandals and curled up on the couch, tuning into Anna's tense tone. "He" could be anyone. The reviewer?

Anna's forehead puckered. "I don't know any more than I told you, but I'll keep my ears open."

When she ended the call, she let out an explosive breath. "Good thing I warned Jaclyn about our guests. They showed up at the pub, and he went ballistic over the portrait of Captain Hiltz." She spread her hands to measure about twice her shoulder width. "It's a big painting in a heavy, gilt-edged frame, and he's staring out at you like he owns the world."

Ivan had been angry enough to see the ship. "That must have been quite a scene."

"Between the pub staff and Glenna, they got him off the property without needing the police. Hopefully, he'll calm down before we see him."

Landon grinned. "From your description, I take it you don't miss having the painting here to watch over the inn."

Anna cocked an eyebrow. "Maria didn't want to see him, either. Murdoch found it stuck in a closet, face to the wall."

"You could put Ivan in there if he keeps causing trouble." At least his negative review would be real.

"Or move him out to the barn." Anna lolled her head back in the teal upholstery and raised the recliner's footrest. "I've never had a guest like this. Picky, demanding, or rude, yes, but not actively hostile." She released a slow breath. "Two more nights and they're gone."

Whatever Ivan knew—or thought he knew—about the long-dead Captain Hiltz, his anger was personal. Maria hid the man's portrait, and Roy said she'd taken care of her father-in-law but hadn't liked him.

Landon shuffled around to stretch her bare feet in front of her on the couch, the floral upholstery tickling her heels. "We've assumed the fake reviewer is targeting you, but what if it's the inn? Something buried in the past?"

Anna massaged her forehead. "But why now? It doesn't make sense."

It didn't make sense that someone would be attacking Anna, either. "We should ask Maria about the family history."

As long as any trouble wasn't connected with her son.

Chapter 8

Monday

WHEN MEAGHAN BURST through the back door on Monday morning calling for Anna, Landon spun from the sink, splashing herself as she jerked the kettle out of the faucet's stream. "She'll be right back. What's wrong?"

Wide-eyed and pink-faced, Meaghan pushed straggling curls from her forehead and held her chunky braid away from the back of her neck. "Sorry I'm puffing. Hart dropped me off on the road, and it's already a scorcher. Anna's going to be so—"

Anna entered the room and laid a hand on her shoulder. "Slow down and catch your breath. Why do I think it's not good news?"

"I had this feeling I should check the website." Meaghan gulped air. "Someone's hacked it—it loads this filthy video. Complete with soundtrack."

Anna paled, and her jaw dropped, releasing a strangled whimper. "You're sure it's our site? You didn't mistype?"

"I'm sure."

Landon slid out a chair, and Meaghan guided Anna to sit.

Hunched forward, gripping her knees, she kept shaking her head. "I should have checked. With everything else, I should have checked."

Landon pressed a hand between Anna's shoulder blades, fingers spread for maximum contact. "It was fine Saturday. You showed me the room photos."

"Anyone who's seen it since this happened—"

Meaghan passed her a glass of water. "I hate bringing bad news."

Anna's fingers closed around the glass, her tremors clinking the ice cubes. "I'm glad God nudged you to check the website. It could have been weeks before we found out."

Meaghan's gaze fell.

Keeping her hand on Anna's back, Landon hooked a chair leg with her foot and drew it close enough to sit. "Bobby helped you with your site. We'll ask him to help now."

Anna's head came up, and she smiled like Landon had snatched rescue from thin air. "Of course. I'll text him right away." Her face clouded again. "I should have thought of that myself."

"You were still processing the shock. You hadn't started thinking about a solution yet."

Meaghan twisted the end of her braid. "If you're okay, I'd better get to work in case the guests come back early."

Ivan had seemed calmer this morning, grudge firmly in place but under control, planning more research. If he kept being tossed out of the local establishments, it could be a short day.

For now, his absence made it easier to deal with this crisis.

Bobby arrived a few minutes later, sandy hair thatched like he'd just crawled out of bed. He'd probably been writing for hours. With the barest smile for Landon, he leaned his elbows on the table across from Anna, who was picking a carrot muffin to pieces.

She slid the rest of the golden muffins toward him. "Thanks for coming."

He plucked one from the plate. "I have the login from when we were updating your site, but I'll likely have to talk to your web host. You'll need to call them and authorize me."

Anna brushed crumbs from her fingers. "I'll look up my contract number."

He reached out as if to warn her. "Just go to their site, okay? Trust me, you don't want to see your own right now."

"I'm not that delicate, you know."

"Neither am I, but I didn't need to see that this morning. Do what you want."

When Anna's desk chair squeaked in the sitting room, Landon leaned nearer so she could speak softly. "Sorry. She gets stubborn sometimes."

"This stress doesn't help."

"No, and she hasn't bounced back from last month. She has a doctor's appointment today, and I want to go along." She pressed her lips together and shook her head. "I don't know what to think."

"She could be depressed. Losing her husband, then these attacks..." He tugged a fistful of hair. "We'll never find a guest who's gone home, but it could be like we thought last time, someone local who wants to drive Anna out of business—for personal reasons or because they want to close the inn."

Landon jabbed at the glossy pine tabletop with her index finger. "Gord wanted to buy the property, but he has another place now. Jaclyn heard the sale rumour and phoned Anna about it last night. She'd take the inn as a tie-in to the pub. We should be able to rule out Hart and Quinn. The only other person I can think of is Elva because she doesn't like having an inn here."

Anna came back with a notebook and a pen. "Elva doesn't like a lot of things, but she wouldn't sabotage my livelihood. Besides, faceless reviews and rumours are one thing. Could she hack a website?"

Bobby's hand rasped against sandpapery jaw stubble. "Probably not, unless she's a computer geek. But anyone can hire a hacker."

Of course. His words rocked Landon's hope. They'd never figure out who this was.

But they had to try.

Once Anna authorized Bobby as her representative and he'd asked a few tech-heavy questions and scribbled some notes, he ended the call. "I'll work at home. That way you won't have to listen to me grumble when I hit a snag."

Anna plunked a zip-top plastic bag of plump muffins on the table in front of him. "Take these with you."

"Thanks. Maybe we should put Gramp on the suspect list. His motive would be your cooking."

"You're no slouch in the kitchen." A faint smile curved Anna's lips, then faded. "Bobby, I need to pay you for this. Your time is valuable, and this could take a bunch of it."

"We talked about this before, and my answer hasn't changed. You mean a lot to Gramp, and I want to do this for you." He ducked his head. "Travers could take this guy down. But at least I can fix this one mess."

His tone deflated as if he felt like a poor second.

Landon brushed a crumb from the front of her shirt. "We're just ordinary people, but we have God. That gives us the edge over a fictional hero—and over whoever's behind all this. It has to be the same person."

His focus didn't leave the floor.

Landon gave herself a mental shake. She shouldn't have minimized this Travers character, no matter what she thought. So much for the brief sense of being on the same side. "Cleaning up Anna's site isn't dramatic, but it's hero-worthy to us. Thank you for taking care of her."

The back of his neck reddened. "I'm glad I can help." Muffins in hand, he headed for the door. "I'll be in touch when I have a better idea of what I'm into."

Meaghan came back into the kitchen after he left and stowed her cleaning supplies. "If there's nothing else, I'll text Hart to pick me up. Are the boys coming to work on the barn?"

Anna slapped a palm to her forehead. "I forgot I have an appointment. I'll ask them to come later."

"And can Bobby help with your website?"

"He thinks so. It depends on what the hacker did. He said something about putting it in maintenance mode so visitors will see a blank screen with a message to come back later."

"Better than what was there." Meaghan tapped at her phone, then poured herself a glass of water. "As much as I'd like more hours, I'm glad to be done working in this heat."

Anna nodded. "I keep wondering about window air conditioners for the guest rooms. I'd hoped the ceiling fans would be enough."

With today's smothering humidity, rain would be a relief. Instead, unbroken sunlight poured in the windows.

Landon waited until Meaghan left before bringing up Anna's appointment. "I'd like to come with you. If the doctor has something complicated to say, a second pair of ears helps."

Anna's lips pinched, but then she nodded. "Murdoch would tell me not to be so independent. I'd appreciate your company. The only thing is... Elva is Dr. Nevitt's receptionist. But she's professional at work, and I can't see her being rude in front of patients."

Although Anna kept reaching out to the woman, Landon had been secretly glad Elva refused the potluck invitation. The idea of seeing her again, even in a supposedly safe place like the doctor's clinic, slid a shiver along the back of her neck.

She set her shoulders. "Ordinary women. Plus God. More than a match for Elva. Let's do this."

~~~

At the waiting room entrance, Landon did a quick headcount. Only seven people for the three doctors sharing the clinic. Enough to be a buffer with Elva, but not to suggest a long wait. A bushy-bearded man glanced up from his tablet, but
~~~

no one else made eye contact. In one corner, a tired-looking woman read a picture book to a toddler, her soft singsong punctuated by the child's listless whines.

Landon took a seat next to a shoulder-height, broad-leafed potted plant while Anna checked in. When Anna eased into the moulded plastic chair beside her, Landon ignored Elva's hard stare.

Anna leaned nearer. "She's good at her job. Dr. Nevitt loves her because she knows everything, and everyone's secrets, but keeps it to herself like a vault."

"She doesn't seem to miss much."

When Elva called Anna's name, Landon rose too. Elva's lips flattened to a brick-red line as they passed her desk, but she gave Landon a sharp nod.

Landon let out a breath she hadn't known she was holding. The doctor might also love Elva because she was a formidable gatekeeper.

They sat in thinly-padded chairs in a consulting room, surrounded by framed certificates and a beautiful dry-mounted poster of the iconic schooner *Bluenose II* in full sail.

The picture stirred a memory of sun-heated docks and salty air. Landon's parents had taken her and her sisters to visit the ship when it was in port. She'd held the smooth grips of the ship's wheel, spinning it and pretending she was a sailor at sea. Feeling the deck rock gently under her feet with the little waves hitting the pier.

The door clicked open, and Dr. Nevitt whisked into the room, his polished black shoes rapping a quick march. "Hello, Anna, what brings you in to see me?"

Tall, thin, and old-school enough to wear a white lab coat with a stethoscope poking out of one pocket, he projected brisk efficiency. His beaky nose and the way his posture curved forward reminded Landon of a flamingo.

Anna clasped her hands on top of her purse. "Doctor, this is my friend, Landon. She's here as my backup brain."

He dipped his head at Landon, then refocused on Anna as he lowered himself into his desk chair. "How can I help?"

"I just—something's wrong. I'm tired, I forget things, I hurt." Anna glanced sideways at Landon. "And my friends will tell you I'm moody."

He angled his head to the side, dark eyes intent. "Has anything changed recently? Something in your diet? Your activities?"

"No. But you might have heard about the trouble we had last month at the inn. Vandalism?"

One grey eyebrow arched. "I'm sorry about that. The stress could impact your health, but it should be short-term."

Purse clutched on her lap, Anna scooted her chair closer to the desk. "I thought the sleep deprivation and anxiety were behind my symptoms, but I'm not getting better. I might be getting worse."

The doctor fitted his stethoscope around his neck. "Well, let's check you out."

At the end of his assessment, he spun his chair to the desk and hunched over the computer keyboard, tapping keys rapid-fire. Chin lowered, he studied Anna. "You've had no sign of a rash or bug bite?"

"Not counting mosquitoes and black flies, no. If you're thinking about Lyme Disease, I'm careful after I've been in tall grass or the woods. The one time I found a tick, it hadn't attached."

"They show up in the strangest places. Pets can bring them into the house, or they can come in on your laundry."

Something tickled Landon's ankle. It wasn't a tick. For one thing, you didn't feel them. The power of suggestion, that was all.

The sensation persisted. She brushed at the spot with the toe of her other sandal and concentrated on the conversation. Lyme could be serious.

"I've seen three patients with Lyme in the past few weeks, and your symptoms are much the same."

"Minus the bull's-eye rash." Anna sat taller, arms crossed tight against her chest as if she could resist his words by force of will.

Anna lived alone. She wouldn't see the rash if the tick bit her on the back. Landon scuffed her sandal against her ankle again, but the irritation persisted.

"Minus the rash." The doctor nodded. "Which does not always appear. However, you're experiencing fatigue, muscle and joint aches, irritability, and perhaps cognitive issues." He ticked each one off on long fingers as he spoke. "Any headaches? Chills? Fever or swelling?"

With each symptom he listed, Anna's posture wilted. Her fingers slid from her purse. "Headaches. But I thought it was the stress."

"Stress would add to it." He scrawled on his prescription pad and tore off two sheets. "I want to see some blood work to rule out other possibilities, but I'm fairly confident this is Lyme—and not early stage, either."

He handed Anna the papers. "Have the blood test as soon as you can. And fill this prescription today and start it immediately. We'll reassess in two weeks. For now, I'm reluctant to waste resources on an antibody test for Lyme. So many come back with either a false positive or false negative, and if it's Lyme, we need you on antibiotics now."

The tickle at Landon's ankle made it hard to concentrate. It took too much mental energy to fight the image of a disease-infected tick biting her leg. She peeked down. Nothing. As she'd expected. She reached and gave the spot a good scratch.

Now the other thought itching her had space. "But, Doctor, if it isn't Lyme, won't antibiotics cause her harm?"

"Short-term, no." His Adam's apple twitched. "Anna can vouch I'm not a pill-pusher. I'm concerned about how long this disease may have been in her system. If she was bitten early in the season, it's been far too long without treatment. We need to be aggressive in fighting for her health."

Paler than when they'd arrived, Anna drooped in her seat. A sheen of sweat covered her forehead. The power of suggestion again? Or dashed hopes?

The doctor's papers fluttered in her white-knuckle grip. Determination—and faith—had powered her through losing her husband and then through last month's stress at the inn. But everyone had a breaking point.

Swallowing the emotion clogging her throat, Landon adopted a confident tone for Anna's benefit. "Is there anything else we need to know? Anything to speed up her recovery?"

So many Lyme horror stories... But the disease was recognized now. Anna didn't have to fight for a diagnosis. And her doctor knew the protocols.

Still, he could be wrong. With other Lyme patients fresh in his memory, he might be seeing a false match. Or maybe this was his obsession, and he saw it in everyone.

She pulled her thoughts back in line. If Anna trusted him, she should too. After all, the most straightforward answer was usually the best. Practically the whole province was high-risk for ticks now.

Dr. Nevitt rolled his chair nearer to Anna and clasped her hand between his larger ones. "Don't you give up on me. Lyme can be nasty, but it's not a death sentence. We'll have you back to yourself in good time. You're a praying woman, so do that too."

His birdlike eyes fixed on Landon. "See she fills that prescription and gets the blood work done. If anything in the report raises flags, I'll call right away, and if not, I want to see her in two weeks."

Anna faltered as she stood. Landon reached out, maintaining a light touch once the moment passed.

At least she'd be here long enough to help. Failing the course had an upside after all.

Dr. Nevitt unfolded from his chair and strode to the door. He opened it for them and whispered to Anna.

As the door clicked shut behind them, Anna straightened and put off Landon's supporting hold. At the end of the short hallway, she said a polite goodbye to Elva and walked steadily across the waiting room to the exit.

Landon added a friendly smile. Whatever the woman's problem was, they'd be living as near neighbours for the rest of the summer, and they needed to get along. Plus, Elva might know something about the inn's history to help their investigation.

Anna's health came first, but part of that health had to be finding—and stopping—whoever was trying so hard to ruin her business.

Chapter 9

Outside the clinic, a warm breeze curled around them, wafting the tips of their hair into their faces. Landon closed the door. "What was that about? The sudden bounce-back?"

Anna marched toward the neighbouring pharmacy. "Dr. Nevitt suggested the best way to fight the rumours of poor health and failing business was to appear healthy. Especially in front of known gossips."

"But you said Elva kept confidentiality like it was a national secret."

"Work-wise, she does. But outside the office, if someone said I wasn't well, she'd be happy to say she was worried about the way I looked without mentioning where she'd seen me. Other people were in the waiting room too."

In the privacy of the car, with the white-bagged prescription tucked into her purse on the back seat, she closed her eyes and breathed deeply through her nose. "I can do this. I have to."

Anna's words dropped like stones. No hope, just a rote mantra that couldn't carry her much farther.

The medication had better work fast.

When they arrived at the inn, the lot was empty. Anna sat for a minute before rolling up her window. "Thank God for small mercies. I don't feel up to playing host right now."

"I can cover for you if they need anything."

"This was supposed to be a break for you, not a working holiday. But today I won't say no."

The heat radiating from the pavement, and the high-pitched drone of a cicada in the trees, slowed Landon's steps. An ideal summer day, the air tasting of sun, salt, and pine trees. If any spot on earth could help Anna heal, it was here at the inn she loved.

If they could stop whoever was out to ruin it.

The thought came like a shove between the shoulders. With the doctor's diagnosis, she'd forgotten. They had not one problem, but two. Three, if she counted Ivan.

In the kitchen, Anna squinted at the label on the brown pill bottle. "This is a lot to process. I can't believe it's Lyme, but it would beat some of the alternatives."

After a brief internet search, Anna admitted the doctor could be right. From the way she focused on medical support sites and avoided anything more sensational, this wasn't her first time investigating symptoms online. Her health must have concerned her more than she'd let on.

Sympathy weighted Landon's chest, raw and scratchy like a sodden wool blanket balled up and pressing on her heart. Yes, Anna's faith was strong enough to carry her through whatever life brought, but they hadn't even reached the first anniversary of Murdoch's death. She'd endured an awful lot in a short time.

Before shutting down the desktop, Anna clicked over to the inn's website. An orange traffic cone sat in the middle of the screen. Below it, crisp black text declared *The Green Dory Inn is open for business, but our site's down for maintenance. Please check back soon or phone for immediate assistance.* Bobby had included the inn's toll-free number.

A cold shadow touched Landon's thoughts. He already had a login for Anna's site. What if he'd done this himself?

The helpfulness, and his easy manner with Anna, could be a cover for a deeper plot to ruin Anna's business. His attitude toward Landon could be frustration that Anna had moral support.

She focused on the bright orange image, sharp and clean. Okay, Bobby could have done it. But why? He had no reason for a vendetta against Anna, and his grandfather was her friend. Plus, if Bobby was the hacker, he'd have hardly come to the rescue so quickly. And why take down the video? He could have pretended to need more time.

The stress was making her paranoid.

Anna shut off the screen and rolled her chair back from the desk. "Too much to hope it was a simple enough fix to be done already, but clever of him to include a note to visitors."

The little frown lines between her eyebrows were less noticeable now, but her voice still dragged. "I don't have what it takes to manage Corey and Quinn today, no matter how good they were on Saturday. I'll text them to come tomorrow, and we can rest on the deck. I need some fresh air. If the McNutts come back, I can duck inside."

Landon poured two tall glasses of Anna's latest batch of iced herbal tea, pale gold and mint-scented, and followed Anna outside. Watching the tops of the high pines sway in a random dance with the breeze, hearing the hushed whisper of the air currents through their needles, brought a sense of peace.

A hummingbird darted for a sip from the garden feeder, sun catching its emerald back and the magenta glint at its throat. It zipped away. Nothing else moved.

"You're going to phone your kids, right? They need to know."

Face tipped to the sun, wisps of brown hair feathering her face, Anna didn't open her eyes. "I don't want to worry them, but at least I have a diagnosis and a treatment plan. Before, everything was so undefined."

Her daughter's family lived in Alberta, her son in Vancouver. Too far for frequent visits. They'd both been home to support her after Murdoch's accident, but with jobs, busy lives, and Anna's daughter wrangling young kids, there couldn't be a lot of time or money to be here for their mother if it wasn't an emergency.

That's why Landon had agreed to come in June when Roy called. Even though till then she'd vowed not to return. Anna had become a truer mother to her than her biological mom, who'd never gotten over Landon's abduction and the death of Landon's dad.

Not that Landon was over losing him, either. He'd died trying to find and rescue her. Nobody knew how he'd tracked the guy who'd taken her, but he did. And instead of calling the police, he tried to beat her whereabouts out of him. Except the guy had a knife.

Her dad died, the guy pleaded self-defence, and Landon's family shattered.

She learned it all later, after she'd been rescued and her mother refused anything beyond the most basic contact. Then Anna stepped in as her surrogate parent and mentor for her newborn faith.

Landon tried her drink. Cool mint with a background flavour she couldn't identify. Refreshing on a hot day.

Anna had helped so many people. Everybody loved her, except this person waging war on her through the internet. Well, Hart and Quinn had caused her trouble too, but because of their own issues, not for anything she'd done.

Maybe that was the secret, not to concentrate on Anna but on the people around her. Like Elva, who complained about tourists coming and going and wouldn't set foot on the property. And Gord and Jaclyn, each wanting to own the inn.

Of the three, Elva seemed most likely to use behind-the-scenes sabotage.

A seagull flew overhead, then wheeled back toward the ocean, its haunting cry piercing the air.

Landon thumbed condensation from her glass. Anna was too worn down to try to solve this problem, and she never wanted to consider friends and neighbours as potential suspects. Bobby was working on the website. Nasty or not, Elva was hers to tackle.

Light flashed on metal as a car purred into the lot. Landon tensed, but the McNutts' sedan was smaller. And grey, not silver.

Beside her, Anna's breath hissed. "I could have done without seeing Gord today too."

Gord waved from the slate path to the deck. "Ladies. Beautiful afternoon."

He dropped into the chair beside Anna. "How was your appointment?"

"He's given me medication to try, and I go back in a couple of weeks."

That was it. No mention of Lyme, blood tests, or any of the private fears Dr. Nevitt may or may not have put to rest.

Brow furrowed, Gord opened his mouth like he wanted to ask more. Instead, he reached for her hand. "Anna, you have good friends to support you. And faith. Give the medicine a chance and try not to worry."

A wan smile touched the corners of her lips. "I'm not worrying. I'm riding it out. But I'm tired. And on top of this, someone's been leaving fake reviews about the inn and hacked the website."

"Who? And why?"

Anna slid her hand from his. "If we knew, we could do something about it." Frowning, she pressed fingertips to her temples. "I'm sorry, Gord. I'm not myself today."

"No wonder." He sat back in his chair, seeming to think. Then he steepled his fingers over his stomach. "I can't help you heal, and I don't have the tech skills to do anything about your online woes. But let me help with the inn."

Before Anna could speak, he leaned in. "When you're better, you'll be able to fly solo again. But what about a temporary business partnership? Forward calls to me, and I could handle the paperwork and hire someone to fix your site. We'd increase Meaghan's hours to handle guests here."

He gestured toward Landon. "I'm sure Landon would help out with guests after Meaghan went home."

"Already on it. Anna's going to duck for cover when today's people come back."

A faint, ruddy hue spread across Anna's pale face. "Gord, I appreciate your care more than you know. But Bobby's already working on the website, and between Meaghan and Landon, we'll be fine."

Her jawline softened. "If things get worse, I may need to take you up on your offer. For now, I can keep up with the administrative work, and I need to feel useful."

Gord looked down, fiddling with the gold links of his watch strap. "You don't trust me."

Anna sputtered. "It's not about trust."

She clamped her lips together, drawing an audible breath through her nose. "I admit I can have trouble accepting help. But at present, I have enough helpers already on board."

His smile didn't return. "I'm worried about you, Anna. I wish I could do something."

Skipping the emotional blackmail would be a good starting point. Landon kept that to herself. Anna would remind her his heart was in the right place and say in business he'd been used to pushing for what he thought best. The line between manipulation and motivation stretched thin sometimes.

Anna slouched in the wicker deck chair as if to hint that one thing he could do was let her rest. Landon resisted the urge to grin.

Gord stood. Either he caught the implication, or his business sense dictated a strategic retreat. He nodded to them both. "I'll be thinking of you, and I'll check in later."

Before his car left the lot, Anna's eyes had closed again. "I'm not sleeping. Just recovering. Gord can be tiring, sometimes."

"He's young for retirement. If work was his driving purpose, he's probably lost."

Anna opened an eye and reached for her untouched glass of tea. It wouldn't be iced anymore. She took a drink. "Helping me would give him something to do, but he needs to find a different purpose."

Landon stared at a pine cone dangling at the tip of a high branch. The doctor had said two weeks. In that time, if Anna felt worse instead of better, she and Meaghan would be making breakfasts, even learning the bookkeeping side of things.

No matter what Anna had told Gord, she wouldn't be opening that up to volunteers when she had an employee and a trusted—if reading-challenged—houseguest. Even if he was more qualified for the task.

But the medication would help. The doctor had to know what he was doing. Anna had to get better.

Landon's part would be minimizing her stress by monitoring the review sites for new trouble and discovering who had motive and means to sabotage Anna's business. Starting with a visit to Elva this evening.

~~~

Ivan and Glenna hadn't returned when Landon finished cleaning up after supper. This time of year, it stayed light so late, they could be out for a few hours yet. If they'd spent the day on research, this was their time to enjoy some touristy activities. As pleasant as the Green Dory Inn was, they'd have no reason to hurry back.

Anna seemed to be adjusting to her diagnosis. Over supper, she'd mentioned how antibiotics usually started working within a few days, acknowledging they might make her feel worse before she felt better.
~~~

Despite the possible backward step, Landon took it as a positive. With all the unknowns crowding in on Anna, a clear plan of action must be a relief.

She topped up Anna's tea. "When's the best time to phone your kids?"

"Tomorrow." Anna drew the tall ivory mug nearer. "Daytime's better, and I wasn't ready earlier. Chase works late in the restaurant, so I have to catch him before he goes. I could phone Piper tonight. But then she won't sleep, and it's not right to tell one and not the other."

"You will tell them, right? Because otherwise, I'll pull a Roy and call them myself."

Anna's shoulders caved forward, and she leaned her elbows on the kitchen table. "I will. They need to know."

"Good." Landon dropped the mock-stern tone. "I think I'll take a little walk if that's okay. The McNutts could be out for hours yet, and they'll probably go straight to their room. I need some exercise."

All true. Her plan to visit Elva would only add to Anna's stress.

A brisk pace cleared the fuzziness from her thoughts and slicked her back with perspiration. She strode along the gravel shoulder of the two-lane road, tasting the sharp sea air. Out in the bay, a speedboat roared, its bow smacking each new wave it sliced. Laughter and yells drifted to shore.

When she reached the bottom of the hill, she turned and trudged back up the slope toward Elva's place.

Approaching the driveway, her feet dragged. She could do this. For Anna and for her own self-respect. But the vitriol Elva hurled held more power now than it had that night in June. At the time, the unexpected, attacking tone flash-froze her so the words couldn't stick.

Look at yourself—ruined for life. She filled her lungs with salt air and pushed it out, rejecting the memory. Refusing to allow Elva's judgment to stick.

The paved drive arrowed through short green grass with not a weed in sight. Landon sniffed. They probably didn't dare take root.

Elva's house was set back like the others along this stretch of road. With the summer tourist traffic, the distance was a good thing. A plain, white-sided colonial, it jutted abruptly from the lawn with no plants or shrubs to soften its stark effect.

Past Elva's compact Kia, a patch of vibrant colour peeked from behind the house. At this distance, Landon couldn't name the ground-level flowers, pinks and blues and purples and whites. They caught the early-evening sunlight, inviting her to see more, but Elva wouldn't appreciate her trespassing.

Her knock on the wooden screen door went unanswered. She knocked again. Elva might have seen her coming and be ignoring her out of spite, but the woman seemed too interested in other people's business to do that. She might miss something.

After another minute with no sign of movement through the door—presumably locked, but she wouldn't dare try it—Landon walked down the steps. It wouldn't hurt to try the back.

A drab-clad figure knelt at the far end of a flower bed brimming with petunias and begonias. Maybe this would be easier with Elva among the life she nurtured.

Grass whispering against her sneakers, Landon walked closer. "Elva?"

The woman's head jerked up, and her face hardened under the tight helmet of chestnut hair. She stood, pushing gold-framed glasses up the bridge of her nose.

Gardening tool in her other hand, she braced her feet wide as if poised to attack.

So much for finding a gentler side.

Landon's feet kept moving, but her lips froze shut. What could she say?

She couldn't come out and ask if Elva hired someone to attack Anna's website and leave bad reviews.

Anna was the key. Neighbourly relations should count for something.

Working some moisture into her mouth, she tried for a friendly smile. "Your flowers are gorgeous. I love bright colours." She hooked a thumb in the front pocket of her cherry-coloured shorts.

"Huh."

Not much of a start, but it beat being told to get lost. She stepped nearer. Slowly, like she'd approach the stray cat.

"You know Anna's not well."

A curt nod.

"Have you heard the rumours about her health and about her selling the inn?"

Another nod. The gloved hand holding the gardening claw fell to her side.

"This is new, not connected with what Hart and Quinn were doing in June. Whoever it is has also been posting negative reviews about the inn online, and they've hacked her website."

Elva bounced the garden tool against earth-stained khaki shorts. "What concern is that of mine?"

"Anna's a kind person. A good neighbour. You're alert to what's going on. Do you have any idea who could be trying to drive her out of business?"

Elva peered over the rim of her glasses. "Why should I talk to you?"

Landon held the eye contact. "I'm sorry you don't like me. But please don't let that be a barrier to helping Anna. She's not well enough to be asking these questions herself. I'm just trying to help."

"You should have known better. Kept yourself safe."

Why be surprised a woman with a gossip streak would know more than the news coverage? Or that someone bent toward nastiness would blame the victim? Landon inhaled, letting the woodsy scent from the back of the property infuse peace into her anger. Retaliating wouldn't help Anna.

She caught her ponytail and trickled the smooth blond hair through her fingers to rest on her shoulder. "Elva, I was a child. Fifteen. All angst and no sense. I was struggling in school, being bullied, and sure, I didn't handle it well. And I should never have trusted a stranger. But I had no idea what he really was."

Tears stung her eyes, and she blinked them away. "Please don't judge my today by my past—the poor choices or the trauma."

"Trauma." Elva spat the word. Her dark eyes glittered. "I was fifteen too." Her final words were barely a whisper.

Before Landon could process or respond, Elva tucked her chin and clamped her arms tight across her body. "Anna. I've heard nothing. Seen no one prowling the woods except Nigel. He thinks I don't know he's watching out for me."

Everything in Landon's heart wanted to stop this train of words, go back to that brief chink in Elva's wall, and offer care. From the woman's face and body language, that was not happening.

She let it go. There'd be another time. She'd pray for one. For now, she'd follow the other woman's lead. "Nigel keeps an eye out for Anna too. It's good to have people who care."

"If I hear anything, I'll call Anna."

"Thank you. It doesn't have to be someone with computer skills. They could have hired someone to hack the site."

Elva passed the garden claw from hand to hand. "How do you expect to find them? It's not like those two hooligans slinking through the woods."

"We need to find someone who's angry or upset with Anna. Someone who wants to ruin her business." Landon softened her voice. "Anna loves her inn. It gives her purpose. You may not like having an inn so near, but I can't see you doing anything to hurt her like that."

Surprisingly, it was true. Saying something nasty to Anna's face, perhaps. Spreading rumours behind her back. But not ruining Anna's livelihood.

Elva's thin lips twisted. "Thank you. I know what people say about me. But I haven't heard an unkind word against Anna."

Landon sighed. "That's the problem."

"If she does close the inn, would she have to sell?"

"I don't know." Landon waved a hand toward the inn and Jaclyn's home beyond. "Roy's neighbour, Jaclyn, offered to buy it. So did Gord Lohnes. I assume either one would keep it as an inn. You probably know Jaclyn, and Gord said he knew you in school."

The colour fled Elva's face. She opened her mouth, then closed it and shook her head. Her throat worked.

Had she thought of something? About Jaclyn or Gord?

She jabbed the garden claw toward Landon like a weapon. The tool wavered in her grip, but her face was granite. "Go away. I've said all I can."

"But—"

"Go. Now." Elva whirled and stormed into the house. The door slammed behind her.

Landon walked down the driveway, hands bunched in the front pockets of her shorts. She'd mentioned the possibility of a new owner reopening the inn just in case her instincts about Elva were wrong.

If Elva were behind this, wanting to close the inn, she might have shown disappointment or frustration. Instead, fear darkened her eyes and trembled on her lips before the angry wall slammed back up.

Businesses didn't frighten people. Other people did.

Back on the road, Landon kept to the shoulder, grinding pebbles beneath the heels of her canvas sneakers as she ground questions in her mind. Had Elva remembered something about Jaclyn or Gord, or about someone else wanting the inn? Something she didn't dare share?

No. Her reaction was too deep. It went beyond a crime directed at her neighbour.

It was personal. Primal.

A car whizzed past, flipping the tip of her ponytail to sting her cheek. She brushed it away.

Gord, Anna, Elva, and Nigel had all grown up in Lunenburg. They were close enough in age that they'd have known one another at school, even if at a distance.

At the potluck, Gord warned them not to believe everything Elva said. He'd known young Elva. Fifteen-year-old Elva? A traumatized girl who, years later, might react to the suggestion of her abuser moving in practically next door?

The back of Landon's neck prickled. Anna had told her Gord was a changed man, that he'd been a problem as a teen.

If this wild idea was true, his dismissal of Elva's value at the potluck said he wasn't as changed as Anna thought.

And Anna trusted him.

Chapter 10

The McNutts' grey sedan was in the lot when Landon reached the inn, and Ivan's emphatic tones carried through the open window in the common room. Great. Just what Anna didn't need.

She jogged up the shallow concrete steps to the front door, its cheery yellow a shot of courage. Inside, Anna and Glenna sat at opposite sides of the puzzle table. Anna had her professional hostess smile in place, patient and welcoming, but it pinched tight at the edges, more than a little frayed. At the sight of Landon, her brown eyes lost the hunted expression, and her fingers loosened their grip on the curved oak armrests.

Ivan paced between the dark-toned bookcase and the window like a caged tiger. He broke off his sentence for a quick nod at Landon, then carried on. "—tavern owner told me not to spread rumours. And today, at the museum and the library, they painted him as a pillar of the community."

Landon dropped into the brown leather club chair by the bookcase. "I hope you had a chance to enjoy a few of the tourist spots in town."

Glenna tipped an eyebrow. "Not as many as I'd hoped. Maybe tomorrow."

They'd be checking out in the morning, but they could explore before heading home.

As if she'd read Landon's mind, Anna gave her head the tiniest shake. "Glenna and Ivan are going to stay a few more days."

Landon nibbled the inside corner of her mouth. This could offset one or two cancellations, but at what cost to Anna's peace?

She put on a cheery tone. "That'll give you plenty of time to see the sights and take a few day trips."

Glenna directed a warm glance at her husband. "It's such a pretty town. It'd be a shame not to take advantage of being here."

Ivan spun from the window and widened his stance, hands clasped behind him. He rocked back and forth on his heels. "I would like to leave with a more positive feeling for the area. But everywhere I see the taint of Hiram Hiltz. Captain Jack, the hometown hero."

His perpetual motion was contagious. Landon nested her hands together to keep from tapping her fingers. "It sounds like you know more about Captain Hiltz than the locals."

He let out a low growl. "They knew. They did nothing about it. Except warn the girls to keep their distance." His motion stilled. "For some, that wasn't enough."

The bitterness in his words poisoned the room. Glenna rose and grasped his hand.

Anna sat forward, fingers pressing the hem of her lilac-patterned sundress against her knees. "Your mother was a local girl?" Gentle care laced her words.

Ivan's head snapped up. He jerked forward, then stopped, anchored by his wife's grip. His grey loafers shuffled on the hardwood floor. "Her family rejected her. Even though it was his fault. I was born in New Brunswick, and she never spoke of them. Her lawyer gave me a letter after she died. It was a horrible shock."

His free hand opened and clenched again. "He had a reputation. People knew. How could they not do anything?"

Sorrow shadowed Anna's eyes. "It was a different time. Families hushed things up and watched out for their own. They did what they could by spreading the word. Captain Hiltz was a prominent, popular member of the community. Maybe they thought the authorities wouldn't believe them. And people around here are proud and strong. Shame can be a powerful silencer. But it wouldn't happen that way today."

Glenna slipped an arm around her husband and leaned her head into his. "We hoped visiting the area would bring some closure, but it needs more time."

He blew out a ragged sigh that stirred the edges of his moustache. "That letter rocked my whole foundation. I need to find some good in her past because right now all I see is pain. She would have been sixteen, and from the dates on his fancy tombstone, he'd have been seventy-three. Old enough to be her grandfather."

That explained the vague sense of hurt and bewilderment radiating from Ivan—and the intensity of his outbursts. Chill feathered the back of Landon's neck. "And this happened here? In this house?"

Anna rapped her knuckles on the edge of the puzzle table. "Whatever was done here is gone. Murdoch and I went through, room by room, with our pastor. We prayed cleansing over everything. We had no idea what we were dealing with, but something didn't feel right. It's finished. Evil has no foothold here now."

Ivan twitched like he wasn't sure what to make of this spiritual talk. "My mom—Jenny Martin—said he'd meet her in the woods. It went on for years. She was just a child. He gave her gifts, told her she was special. Sometimes he wanted to do things she didn't like, but her childhood innocence thought it was just a strange, grown-up way of showing affection."

His hand was back to clenching and opening. "They ignored her at home. Until she got pregnant and they kicked her out. Didn't even ask who the father was. He gave her bus fare to Saint John and enough to set up in a rooming house. Hiding the evidence, but she thought he cared."

Landon's heart hurt for this young woman, frightened and alone. "When did she die?"

"This March." Ivan pinched the corner of his moustache. "She made a good life for us. Married an older man—not nearly as old—who was good to us both."

Glenna's chest rose and fell in a slow breath that rippled the thin gold chain at her throat. "She would never tell her age—I think so we wouldn't know how young she'd given birth. She never said anything about Ivan's father, but she didn't seem bitter or hurt. Somehow, she dealt with it and moved on." She tipped her face toward her husband. "And while it should never have happened, it gave us Ivan."

He stared at the floor, blond-brown brows hiding his eyes. Did he feel guilty that his life came from a wicked old man's abuse?

"I'm sorry for your loss, Ivan, and for the shock of your mother's secret." Anna's chin-length hair fell forward, covering her cheeks. "Does she have any family left in the area?"

His lips tightened at her words, but then he released a breath and looked up. "That's one reason we're staying on. When we talked to Roy, he didn't remember Mom, but he knew her family. I have an uncle living in town, Sandy Martin. I phoned him this evening, and he wants to meet for coffee."

Landon traced a seam at the edge of her armrest, her fingertip gliding up and down the bumps in the slick leather. "He should be able to tell you some good things to balance the bad."

"I hope so." Ivan reached for his moustache, then jammed his hand into the pocket of his navy pants. "And I hope he'll help me. My mother may have been the last victim, but some of the others could still be living. And other children."

His frown trenched into a scowl. "The old man's been gone for forty years, but the truth will discredit him. It's all the vindication we can hope for."

Vindication... for abused girls who lived in a time when being an unwed mother brought so much shame... for fatherless children growing up with that shame. Throwing the shame back onto Captain Hiram Jack Hiltz might be the closest thing to justice they'd find.

Yet—Landon prayed for the right words. His pain was still new. Raw and angry. "What if they don't want to reopen old wounds? They've built lives since then. Exposing the past could feel like a threat."

"You people are Christians. Don't you preach that the truth will set you free?" He glared through slitted eyes, leaning forward on the balls of his feet. "It's time to drag the truth out into the light. Whether they like it or not."

"If they've found a measure of healing, is it right for you to shatter it?" Landon hated the pain in her voice, but maybe he needed to hear it. She wrapped her arms around her ribs and pressed her spine against the chair back.

"He doesn't deserve to be shielded."

"And they don't deserve to be hurt again. I hope you find some who are ready to speak out, but the ones who aren't? Please respect them."

Red-faced, Ivan stalked from the room. Glenna flashed an apologetic smile before following.

Landon planted her elbows on the armrests and cradled her forehead between her palms. She'd offended Anna's only paying guest.

"At least we understand his turmoil now." Anna's hand settled on her shoulder. "Between troubled guests and this internet enemy, I don't know how much more I can take."

Chapter 11

Tuesday

"Anna?" Ivan's voice came from the front entrance. He sounded more curious than hostile this morning, but Anna didn't need to face him alone. Landon dropped the dishcloth into the sink and dried her hands.

She stepped into the hallway as Anna emerged from her sitting room, mild curiosity on her face. No anxiety furrows, so she couldn't have found any new bogus reviews. Although Landon had asked her not to check the sites, she'd insisted she could handle it.

"This must be for you." Ivan strode toward them, fingers looped through the handles of a mid-sized yellow gift bag. A splotch of green marred the front. "I found it on the front step. There's no tag. But that green thing could be your dory."

Anna accepted the bag and held it up to eye level. "Looks like someone drew it with a marker."

"Glenna's waiting in the car. Before we meet my uncle, we're going to tackle the local newspaper archives and see what births we can find."

When the door closed behind him, Anna gave a long, low whistle. "I understand his motives, but I'm afraid he's going to kick a hornet's nest."

"Me too. Their stories aren't his to share."

Anna swung the gift, about the size of a lunch bag, from her fingertips, the motion ruffling the white tissue paper tufted up between the handles. "Let's go see what my secret admirer left on the doorstep."

She had such good friends. Which one had brought this thoughtful pick-me-up?

In the sitting room, Anna placed the bag on the glass-topped coffee table and sank onto the couch, while Landon perched on the padded arm of the nearer recliner where she'd have a good view.

Humming softly, Anna pulled out the tissue. She tipped the bag and reached inside.

Her scream shot Landon to her feet.

Anna flung herself against the back of the couch. The bag shot across the tabletop and hit the floor in front of Landon.

"Don't touch it!" Panting, Anna pressed a palm to her chest. The hand she'd dipped into the bag scrubbed frantically against the pastel floral upholstery.

She swallowed hard. "It's—something dead. I think it's a bird."

"Dead?" Landon's initial jolt morphed into a heavy, clammy sense of unease. Sweat prickled her hairline.

A dark, shapeless shadow lay at the mouth of the bag. She dropped into the recliner seat hard enough to bounce, feet tucking up onto the chair as fast as her teacher's had done in grade three when a boy released a snake in the classroom.

The yellow bag lay where it had landed. They should pick it up. No, they should leave it for the police, in case there were fingerprints.

Whatever it held was dead. She squinted at the opening. The object didn't move.

Feet on the floor. Be brave. But it wasn't happening.

Anna stood, fingers spread away from her body. "I'll wash my hands. Then I'll phone the police."

Landon stared at the fallen gift bag while Anna splashed in the bathroom. It had to be connected to the person behind the rumours, the reviews, and the website.

This proved it was someone local, but she'd been pretty sure, anyway. That's why she'd visited Elva, why she wanted to follow up with Nigel to see if he had any ideas. He might deal in theories about aliens and conspiracies, but his sharp and suspicious mind could be their best hope of spotting someone with a motive to drive Anna out of business.

Anna came back and picked up the land-line handset. She shot Landon a wry grin. "Not many people have the nonemergency police contact number plugged into their phones. Hart and Quinn did that much for me."

When she finished the call, she said, "It'll be a while. Looking at websites on a phone screen is a pain. Can we use your laptop to check the rest of the review sites? In the kitchen?" She flapped a hand toward the bag. "I don't want to sit in here with that."

Landon coaxed one foot, then the other, to the floor and scooted into the hallway.

Anna laughed. "I'll take that as a yes. And I'll shut this door in case Timkin wants in. We can't have him eating the evidence."

Landon hadn't thought of the cat. Good thing he was already outside.

When she fetched her laptop from her room, Anna was tapping at her smartphone screen.

"Curiosity get the best of you?"

Anna's brow furrowed. "Mmm? Oh—I'm not online. I texted Corey and Quinn to postpone the cleanup again. There's no rush with it, and I'd rather not let this story spread."

The final site they checked held two new reviews, one positive and with a name Anna recognized as a legitimate guest, and one negative about a foul smell in the water.

Anna closed the laptop. "Perspective is everything. After that 'gift' up close and personal, a malicious review is a mere annoyance."

Maybe, but the reviews were still costing reservations. Beyond the cancellations, how many people had they scared off from booking in the first place? Landon kicked her heels against the chair legs, itching to reach into the computer, through the internet, and out the perpetrator's screen to grab him. Or her.

She tried to loosen the tension in her shoulders. "This is the first tangible evidence we've had. But it's not much of a clue."

Neither of them mentioned it could also be a threat.

Anna drifted to the kitchen window. "When Meaghan gets here, we won't tell her unless an officer shows up. She doesn't say much, but she has to be concerned about all this drama. Her job depends on the inn having customers."

Anna's livelihood depended on that same thing, and she was sick. But here she was, more concerned about another's need. It was who she was, why so many people loved her.

Still... Elbows on the pine tabletop, Landon studied her friend's stiff posture. "If I weren't here, would you have told anyone other than the police?"

Anna turned from the window, weariness etching her features. She clasped her hands in front of her forest-green tee shirt. "I told people last time, even when they didn't believe me."

Had Anna initiated those conversations, or had Roy and Nigel noticed her distress and asked? It seemed the more stress she felt, and maybe the stronger the Lyme Disease grew in her system, the more reluctant she was to accept help. After the barn break-in, she'd wanted to keep everyone out of the cleanup until Landon insisted she let them in.

Landon crossed the kitchen and wrapped her in a hug, breathing in the spiced-citrus scent of her shampoo. "We love you, and we want to help. Just like you'd help any of us in a heartbeat."

"I know. But Meaghan has enough problems already. I'd like to spare her this if we can."

Meaghan had come and gone before a police car arrived. Landon and Anna were sitting on the back deck in the shade watching Timkin stalk something in the grass. Landon had hoped to see the orange stray, but with the black and white cat on the prowl, the interloper might be wary of crossing his turf.

As the cruiser door thudded shut, Timkin pounced on his invisible prey. Anna winced. "I hope it's not a late june bug. They make him sick."

The crawly feeling touched Landon's ankles again. All it would take was one infected tick to hitch a ride into the house on the cat. They'd been at risk all along.

At least Dylan was the responding officer today. He couldn't do anything about ticks, but he'd been the main police presence with Anna's previous trouble. Despite being not much older than Landon, he had impressed them both with his diligence and compassion.

Now he climbed the steps with an easy grace, flashing a wry grin. "I thought I'd be here hours ago. What a day."

He took the seat opposite Anna and slid his notepad and pen from his uniform shirt pocket. "Walk me through what happened, and then we'll take a look at the bag."

His gaze stayed on her as she spoke. When she finished, he scribbled details and then rested his pen tip against the page. "And there was no note?"

"No. Landon checked around the doorstep in case it had blown loose, but there was nothing."

Dylan put his hands on his knees and then pushed to his feet. "Okay, let's see Exhibit A."

Anna led him into the house. Landon followed, closing the door just as Timkin trotted up the steps. The cat approached the door and sat, then mewed when Landon didn't let him in. "You'd better wait."

A slight narrowing of green eyes and the twitch of an ear communicated the equivalent of a hands-on-hips, full-out glare.

Chuckling, Landon walked into the sitting room where Dylan stood over the fallen yellow bag.

Hands sheathed in a pair of thin rubber gloves, he picked up the bag by one of the rope handles. "It's a bird, all right. One of those brown ones that hang out in flocks, about the size of a robin."

He retrieved the fallen tissue paper and tucked it into the opening. "I can't tell if it was killed for this purpose or found dead, and we're not laying it out on your coffee table to check for signs of trauma."

Anna summoned a feeble grin. "Thank you."

"When I have the lab report, I'll be in touch. We'll do a fingerprint check, too, but I'm betting the only ones we find are yours and your guest's." He sealed the gift bag into a clear plastic evidence bag, then peeled off the gloves and stuck them in his pocket.

He left the bag on the table. "I'd like to poke around out front."

They waited on the front steps while he explored the area, although with grass and a concrete walkway there wasn't much chance of footprints. Dylan returned empty-handed. "It was earlier when you came out. If the grass was still wet, did you see any kind of trail where our perp might have walked?"

"No, but why not stay on the driveway?"

"Maybe he did. What's the coverage area for the security cameras?"

Anna headed back down the hall, her loose tee shirt billowing behind her. "Let me get my phone."

She came back, frowning at the screen. "This app isn't as user-friendly as I'd like. Here we are. Okay, Dylan, I'm watching the camera covering the parking lot. If you want to walk up the driveway, I'll tell you when it picks you up."

He made it almost to the rear of the house before Anna called out, then came striding back, Timkin on his heels. "Well, that explains why the bag was left on the front step."

Landon crossed her arms over her ribs. "And it proves it's someone who's been here enough to know where the cameras are."

Anna scowled downward like a child who didn't want to hear what she was told. "Or it's someone who doesn't know I use the back door."

Expression neutral, Dylan caught Landon's eye. "Maybe, but then it's almost random. Random doesn't decorate the bag to match the recipient."

"Let's go back inside." Anna scooped the cat into her arms. "One of you put that bird up where Timkin can't reach it?"

Dylan placed the evidence bag in the kitchen sink. Anna poured three tall glasses of water, and they gathered around the pine table.

Notepad spread before him, he added a few words and peered at the page. Then he looked up, brown eyes serious. "The front door doesn't tell us if he knows about the cameras or not. Or if he wants to involve your guests. I think it's safe to assume the packaging means it's not for a guest, but for the inn's owner."

Anna nodded, grim-faced. The dark green of her shirt emphasized her pallor. "I'm glad I didn't open it when Ivan handed it to me."

"And you have no reason to suspect Ivan staged this himself?"

Her forehead puckered. "I don't know why he would."

"But he could have?"

"I suppose. He and Glenna had just gone out. For that matter, he could have been in and out a few times. I don't track my guests."

He flashed a quick grin. "It wouldn't be very hospitable of you."

"But he has no reason. If it were a practical joke, wouldn't he want to stick around and see my reaction? Besides, he's not the type. He's too bound up in his own issues."

His gaze sharpened. "Tell me more."

She pressed her lips closed.

Landon couldn't be as secretive. Not with a dead bird showing up at the door. "Ivan has a grievance against Captain Hiltz, the man who built the inn. He wants to discredit his reputation."

"What's his concern with a dead man? Never mind. I should hear it from him." His pen scratched Ivan's name darker on the page.

Palms to her temples, Anna pushed back her hair. "Ivan is confrontational, not subtle. And after our talk last night, he must know we're on his side."

True enough. Landon traced a finger around the rim of her glass, drawing comfort from the smooth, endless circle and the simple motion. "Even if he'd done, or hired out, the fake reviews and the website hack, I think he'd be targeting Captain Jack's more than the inn."

Dylan's hand rose in a classic stop gesture. "Website hack?"

Anna's eyes widened. "I forgot to report it." Her lips pinched at the edges.

"It was upsetting, and you had your appointment." Landon squeezed Anna's hand. "And—well, the day kind of fell apart."

Anna let out a slow breath. "It was one thing after another."

As she filled him in on the website and Bobby's promise to fix it, Dylan's brows came together. "Again, it's technically outside my scope, but it all seems part of one picture."

Landon ticked the pieces off on her fingertips. "Rumours. Reviews. Website. Bird. It's someone local."

"I agree." He pressed his fingertips together, palms apart. "Anna, you said something about Captain Jack's pub as another target?"

Landon quirked a rueful grin. "Apparently, everyone but you and I knew that Hiram Hiltz, builder of the inn and rumrunner extraordinaire, went by the name Captain Jack."

"I'll drop in at the pub." He made another note. "And I've checked with Hart and Quinn. They both deny being involved with the online trouble. They could be lying, but I don't see them as capable of a sophisticated website hack or affording to hire a hacker. Quinn, especially, is eager to appear clean."

He laid his pen diagonally on the paper, shifting his gaze between Landon and Anna. "We had a hard time finding suspects for the incidents in June before the tip that led to the arrests. I assume you don't have any names for me now?"

Landon nibbled the inside of her lip. "There are fresh rumours about the inn closing or being for sale. And about Anna's health."

She wanted to tell him the truth about Anna's health, but that was Anna's prerogative. "The only two people I know of who've expressed a desire to own the inn are Gord Lohnes and Jaclyn, who already owns the pub. But they're both her friends."

The lines around Anna's mouth communicated her displeasure, but how could Dylan help if they didn't give him every scrap of clue they had?

Landon went on. "Elva doesn't want an inn here. And Nigel has some sort of fixation about Captain Hiltz's secrets."

"Nigel would never harm a wild creature." Anna huffed. "If he found a dead bird, he'd bury it, not stuff it in a bag to terrorize me."

Dylan rested a hand on her forearm. "Anna, we've danced around this issue, but I'm going to lay it on the table. In the absence of a note explaining the intent, we have to consider this a threat."

He waited until she gave a guarded nod. "I need you to be cautious. This person has the power to reach you, but you don't know who they are. Keep a phone on you at all times and don't hesitate to call 9-1-1 if you think you're in danger."

His gaze shifted to Landon. "Don't try to solve this on your own. Any ideas, any clues, phone the station. Please."

She heard what he didn't say, that he'd rather investigate a threat than a murder. That two ordinary women wouldn't be a match for a person with intent to harm.

Heat crept up her neck. He didn't know she'd questioned Elva yesterday.

The problem was, they could be interacting with this person—likely were—without realizing it. Any complaint or innocent question could be perceived as a challenge. And if it was Ivan after all, he had free access to the inn.

Landon sat straighter, tiny hairs lifting at the base of her scalp. "Ivan and Glenna. Should we ask them to leave?"

"I won't do that." Anna's retort cut across whatever Dylan had started to say. "They're paying guests and decent people. Plus, Ivan has enough baggage right now without being kicked out of what was once Captain Hiltz's home."

Dylan grimaced. "There could be legal ramifications if he's contentious enough. He'd have to have a powerful motivation anyway to be our perp. It'd mean starting the online campaign before he even arrived on the scene."

He closed the notepad, fingers tapping briefly on the glossy blue cover. "Give us a call when he comes in? Routine questions about finding the bag should lead us into whatever his grievance is with the past. Then we'll have a better sense of how things lie."

As he retrieved the evidence bag from the sink, the faint crinkle of plastic lured Timkin from wherever he'd been hiding. Eyes alert, tail high, the cat fixated on the packaged bird.

"I'll drop this at the station. Then I need to get back on patrol, part of which will be a visit to Jaclyn to see if she's had any threats or trouble at the pub."

Chapter 12

Landon and Anna walked out with Dylan to the deck. Timkin paced behind him all the way to his car, keeping vigil until he drove away.

Lingering in the sun's heat, Landon tipped her face skyward, eyes closed. Slow breaths of pine-sharp air helped her exhale a bit of her tension, but she couldn't stop the questions from circling. Who would do something like this to Anna? And why?

A high-pitched whirring intruded, and it took her a minute to track the source. A drone flitted above them.

"Look at that." As she pointed, the little machine hummed over the roof toward the water.

"Someone has a new toy. I've seen it around a few times lately."

Anna's phone pinged, and she shaded the screen with one hand to read and respond. "Bobby's on his way over."

She plunked into the nearest chair and skidded it sideways into the umbrella's shadow.

Landon sat beside her, leaning into the thick chair pad. "I'm sorry for dumping my list of possible suspects on Dylan, but he needs everything we have. Even if we don't see how any of those people could be involved."

Anna gazed out toward the trees, twisting her wedding band. "You were right. I just can't believe this. Thank you for not telling him about my health problems."

"Your health isn't related to the inn trouble, but Lyme is nothing to be ashamed of."

"It's not contagious. People don't need to know."

Lips pressed tight, Landon released a slow breath through her nose. "Everyone can see you're not yourself. If they knew why, they wouldn't be concerned about something worse."

"They'll see me get better once the antibiotics kick in." Anna angled her chair so she faced Landon. "I had enough lecturing from Piper and Chase today. Let's talk about something else."

Good to know she'd spoken to her children.

The drone buzzed back across the roof, angling toward the homes nearer to town. She soon lost it in the sky.

Bobby's greeting from behind her made her whirl toward him. He climbed the stairs. "Your site's back up. The hack was messy but not as bad as I thought."

"Thank you more than I can say." Anna beamed at him. "You're a knight in shining armour."

Eyes downcast, he twitched his fingers, deflecting her praise. "It was good practice in case I have to go back to my day job. While I was in there, I tightened your security. Our friend's not playing in the big leagues, so I don't think they'll get back in."

Timkin strolled onto the deck and leaped into Anna's lap. She pushed back from the smoked-glass table to give him room and gestured to Bobby. "Grab a chair."

He sat, pale legs extended before him with ankles crossed. "The hacker was sophisticated enough that I couldn't trace him. Or her, as the case may be. And if we're dealing with a freelancer, they could be anywhere in the world. With no idea who hired them."

Stroking Timkin's glossy black fur, Anna gave a little shrug. "The police won't assign a cybercrime unit anyway, even if there was a way to identify whoever's behind this. It's not like those attacks that shut down hospitals and government agencies."

The McNutts' grey sedan eased around the side of the house, and Anna stood, transferring Timkin to the seat cushion. "They're back earlier than I thought."

Landon braced her hands on the rough-woven wicker arms of her chair. "Do you want me to come too?"

"I'm only going to say Dylan needs to ask about the bag. It shouldn't be a problem."

When the door closed behind Anna, Bobby straightened, tucking his feet beneath his chair. "What's up?"

Telling him about the dead bird brought back her anger. "She didn't look, just put her hand in the bag and touched it." Landon shuddered. "She's already upset about everything else. That could have sent her over the edge."

"She called the police?"

"They want to see if Ivan might have noticed anything before he picked up the bag. He's kind of volatile, but not toward Anna. I don't think he did this."

A corner of Bobby's mouth pulled down. "He's the same guy who came around yesterday asking Gramp about Captain Jack? I was tucked away working on Anna's site, but I heard. Nasty business."

He hunched forward, hands clasped between his knees. Did the captain's crimes remind him of whatever he'd gleaned about Landon's traumatic background?

She wanted to tell him to get over it. To see her as she was today, without sympathy, without judgment.

Instead, she relaxed her body into the chair pad, trying not to absorb his discomfort. "Ivan wants some kind of justice, but I'm afraid dredging up people's buried hurts is going to blow up in his face."

"Yeah." Bobby nodded, sandy wisps of hair screening the edges of his downturned face. "But he wouldn't blame Anna.

Even if he felt he had to burn the inn to the ground, he'd be sure you both were out first."

Heat prickled the back of Landon's neck. "He wouldn't." The denial came out in a choked whisper.

"Arson can make good vengeance. If he was conceived in the house..."

"He said it was always in the woods. The old man's son and daughter-in-law and their son lived with him, so I guess the house was too risky."

He straightened slowly and rotated his body toward the tree line. Searching for signs of taint? "Ivan's focused on Jack. Whoever's targeting Anna has something against her personally." He bounced a fist on the arm of his chair. "It's so frustrating having no idea who it could be. It's like we're just waiting for them to put her out of business or make her quit."

The same straining helplessness throbbed in Landon's heart.

Leaning forward again, elbows on knees, Bobby propped his jaw in his palms. One foot tapped in its flip-flop. "I wish I knew what Travers would do. He'd have a way to flush out the villain."

His hollow tone made it sound like he didn't think he was enough on his own. Like his fictional, larger-than-life hero who could do anything made Bobby into nothing in comparison.

Comparisons killed. She knew that, and he needed to know it too.

She filled her lungs with courage. "No matter how fantastic your imaginary friend is, you have a lot more going for you."

He went completely still like he was bracing for some kind of shot.

"You're real, for starters, and you seem like a genuinely caring guy." Except where she was concerned, but she didn't matter here. "You help Roy and Anna every chance you get.

Plus, everything Travers does must come from your imagination. Stop selling yourself short."

His hands twitched, but he said nothing.

He already didn't like her, so she had nothing to lose. "Restoring Anna's site was the most practical help anyone has been able to give her, and you brushed it off like it didn't matter. It's not my business, but maybe you should notice the good God does through you."

She recalled a conversation they'd had in June. "Anna doesn't need a high-tech tiger pit. Or a hero. She needs friends who do what they can."

His head shot up, and she could almost see the thoughts tumbling inside trying to place her words.

When his expression cramped into a frown, she spread empty hands. "Laser-something? When we were trying to catch Anna's prowler, you suggested a tiger pit." It was one of the few times he'd dropped his guard around her.

A smile smoothed the furrows from his face. "Laser lattice. I had a crazy time figuring out how Travers got out of that one."

"See? It's your brain behind his. Credit where credit is due. Give yourself a chance."

He was looking at her now, a full-on stare. Like he was trying to peer into her brain and decipher some kind of hidden meaning in her words.

She focused on Timkin curled in the chair beside her. "But if I thought a tiger pit would catch this guy, I'd help you dig."

His snort of laughter jolted the cat awake. Timkin's head shot up, ears alert. He sat up in the chair, yawned a silent tiger roar, and leaped to the deck. Tail high, he stalked down the steps.

Bobby stood. "I'd better get back to Travers. I'm behind on my word count. But don't tell Anna. She'd blame it on her site."

Once he left, Landon went inside. Anna and the McNutts weren't standing at the far end of the hall. Perhaps they'd gone into the common room.

Softly running water stopped her as she passed the kitchen. Anna stood refilling the filter jug. "They're going out later to meet Ivan's uncle, and they'll stop at the station before it closes. I'll follow up in the morning to be sure they did."

"And everything's okay?"

She replaced the pitcher on the counter. "Nobody wants to tell them anything, and they didn't get much from the newspaper archives. I think hearing about my day made theirs seem less of a problem. Bobby's gone?"

"Said he had to get to work. I guess writers aren't limited to business hours."

"Neither are innkeepers." She swept stray hair off her forehead. "I need a nap before supper."

"Go for it. Antibiotics always knock me out, even without the early starts we have here." Landon opened the closet and chose a pair of cotton gardening gloves, their fingers curled from use. "I noticed some weeds with the flowers. I think it's cooled off enough to tackle them."

Behind the inn on her knees, with the sun on her back and enough breeze to keep the flies away, she let her hands fall into a gentle rhythm of plucking and tossing. The mindless work left her thoughts free to pray for Anna's health and protection. They may not know how to find and stop whoever was harassing her, but God knew.

Motion to the side caught her eye. The stray cat stopped a few feet away and stood watching her, the crooked tip of his tail a pennant on a pirate's mast. His bent ear had been torn and healed with a notch in the side.

Slowly, she sat back on her heels. "Hey. Have you had any of the food I've put out?"

If he got used to a gentle voice, maybe he'd feel safer to come around. She had no way of knowing if he was the one cleaning out the food dish she left behind the barn. Anna had asked her to place it out of the guests' sight, but that meant out of camera range too.

The cat took one step nearer.

The breeze trailed a few strands of her hair across her cheek. It tickled, but she didn't dare move.

She stared back at the cat. "You look too much like a Captain Jack for me to think of you any other way, but I'd better not use that name around Ivan."

At the thought of Ivan's story, she couldn't stop a shudder. The cat twitched but didn't flee.

"Sorry. You'd think I'd seen enough evil this wouldn't shock me."

She prayed Ivan's vendetta wouldn't dig up more harm than good. Was he unstable enough to want to destroy the inn in some twisted revenge on the dead?

This malice felt deliberate. Directed. Not like an emotional backlash.

Pressure welled in her chest. The dead bird escalated the conflict, but who were they fighting? And why? All they could do was wait for Anna's enemy to make the next move.

~~~

Ivan wasn't a danger.

Landon was almost certain. But when he and Glenna drove away again late that afternoon, her entire nervous system seemed to pause and draw a deep breath like an army standing down from high alert.

Their departure may have refreshed Anna as much as her nap. She still allowed Landon to make supper, but she sat at the square pine table leafing through recipe books and making a grocery list. "I want to have Roy and Bobby in for a meal tomorrow to say thank you for all the website help. I wish he'd let me pay him."

"He'll be uncomfortable if you make too big a deal about it."
~~~

"Mmm. So, no cake decorated like a hero's medal with his name on it?"

Landon matched her grin. "That might be over the top."

Would he think about what she'd said? The world didn't need more arrogant people, but denying his value wasn't right, either.

After they'd cleaned up and carried cups of herbal tea out onto the deck, Landon stretched her arms wide and inhaled evergreen-spiced summer air. "I sure don't miss Toronto in the heat."

"You could transfer your degree to Halifax and ride-share from here. Plenty of locals commute to the city."

"Professor Iron-heart would think she won."

The sense of freedom vanished, smothered by concrete reality. To pass Tallin's classes, she'd have to pretend to adopt the woman's philosophy. Be determined and unyielding. And pray not to damage herself in the process.

Anna gazed at her over the gilt-edged rim of her china mug. "Professors must see a surprising number of student absences." One eyebrow angled upward. "I remember a classmate whose grandmother 'died' three times one semester."

Landon bristled, but Anna's musing tone and the warmth in her brown eyes convinced her to hear the end of the thought.

"All she had were your messages. It's hard to judge truth long-distance. Maybe it's not as personal as it feels. Maybe she's just strict."

"Then why delay processing my marks until my other course options were full?" Bitterness leaked out with the question, and she dragged a fingertip through the pollen dusting the smoked-glass tabletop. Anna wasn't the enemy. "Sorry."

Anna jumped up. "I'll be right back."

A minute later, she returned, rummaging elbow-deep through her striped canvas tote bag. "I know it's in here somewhere."

She sat, plopped the bag into her lap, and started clattering the contents onto the table. Hairbrush. Notepad. Screwdriver. The pile grew.

A lipstick rolled toward the tabletop's wicker rim. Landon herded it back toward Anna's belongings. "No wonder you're tired, carrying all that around."

"Never know what you might need." Anna frowned at a folded church bulletin and laid it aside. "Don't need that."

"You're a mini version of Nigel and his bunker."

Pens. A pocket-sized Bible. Tiny flashlight. The wooden box they'd taken to show Maria. Finally, Anna waved a brochure. "This is what I wanted. While you're here, we need to have some fun. I picked this up at the tourist bureau when we were in."

She passed the glossy page to Landon. Under a photo of a two-masted sailing vessel, it listed different tour options.

Landon's childhood wonder stirred. "A harbour tour?"

"What about the sunset one?"

"That would be amazing."

"What would amaze you?" Nigel climbed the stairs from the grass.

Landon flinched, and Anna gasped. "You're going to give someone a heart attack someday."

He raised his eyebrows, then blinked. "I thought you saw me."

Anna started refilling her bag. "Come and sit, Nigel. How are you?"

"Well, thank you." He crossed to the table. One hand shot out and grasped the wooden box.

He sat, rotating the box in his hands, studying it like an archaeologist with a rare artifact. "A puzzle box. Fine one too." His lips pushed out, then in. "Turkish, perhaps."

Anna plunked her bag on the empty chair. "We were talking about a sunset harbour tour."

"Ah." His gaze didn't leave the box. "You know how to open this, of course."

"No, actually." Anna leaned forward, fingers fluttering as if she wanted to snatch the box from him. "It belongs to Maria. Please be careful, Nigel. It could be valuable."

Sharp grey eyes glanced at her and focused again on the carved box. "Maria?"

"Corey found it in the barn. Maria asked me to keep it for David."

Nigel exhaled heavily. "He won't claim it."

"I still need to keep it for her. She may decide she wants it back."

The evening sun threw long pine and birch shadows over the barn holding Maria's legacy to her son. "What if he isn't dead like everyone thinks? Maybe she's not in denial—maybe she knows something no one else does."

Maybe he was back. And trying to scare Anna away from the family property.

Nigel's face darkened. "He's dead."

The bitter certainty in his tone chilled her. "How can you be so sure?"

"One who knows told me." His eyes narrowed to glittering slits. "One who was there."

"Have you told the police? Maria could have closure. David could have justice."

His glare pinned her, burning like one of Bobby's lasers. "I have no details. And I protect my source."

"But—"

"A vow of secrecy is sacred." One hand left the box to press his camouflage hat tighter on his head. "Please say nothing. Without a body, his mother won't believe. Everyone else already accepts the truth."

Hugging her elbows to her sides, Anna shifted in her chair. The wicker frame creaked. “This isn’t right, Nigel. Your source needs to come forward.”

He bent his head over the puzzle box, fingers working deftly. A section of wood slid out, then another. He plucked a brass key from its hiding place, then rotated the box and moved another bit of the wood.

Over Anna’s cry to stop, he inserted the key and twisted.

The lock clicked. Nigel raised the lid and removed a folded sheet of paper.

Anna sprang to her feet, hand outstretched.

Dodging her grasp, he read aloud. “ ‘Dear David, look in the tunnel. Love, Mother.’ ”

With a terse nod, he offered the note to Anna.

She took it, sputtering. “The contents of that box are none of our business.”

Nigel blinked rapidly, a pensive smile on his face. “The secret of Captain Hiltz. A tunnel. Of course. The perfect hiding place.”

“What’s this about a tunnel?” Ivan’s voice startled them all.

He bounded up the stairs toward them, Glenna on his heels.

Intent on the conversation, Landon hadn’t heard their car arrive.

Nigel and Ivan nodded as previous—if stiff—acquaintances. It made sense. Anna had suggested Nigel as a research source.

Anna refolded the note and clutched it close, but Nigel jabbed a bony finger at the open box on the table. “A hidden message for the captain’s grandson, telling him to look in the tunnel.”

Ivan’s eyebrows crept up. He focused on Anna. “A rumrunner might well have dabbled in other illegal things. Anything could be hidden in there. Even if it’s just ‘liquid assets’ they could be valuable. *Rum* was a catchall word for whatever alcohol they shipped. Some of it ages very well, indeed."

Anna's mouth tightened, and she sat straighter in her chair. "I've never seen a tunnel on the property."

"The captain's hiding place would be well concealed." Blinking rapidly, Nigel mashed his hat lower on his head. "He could have passed that knowledge on to his family."

Ivan poised on the balls of his feet, hands opening and closing at the sides of his walking shorts. "With your permission, Anna, I'll make a full search of the building and grounds."

"No." Anna's face bore a hard cast Landon hadn't often seen. She gripped the broad wicker rim of the table and pushed to her feet. "Everything that man touched, he ruined. I want nothing to do with him."

"But if he left hidden wealth, this is our chance to take it from him."

"He's already lost it. He's dead." Landon blushed. She hadn't planned to say it out loud.

Ignoring her, Ivan focused on Anna. "If you don't want his treasure, it could go to his victims. As compensation."

"Including you." Landon flattened her palms against the nubby weave of her shorts. This time she'd meant to speak. Anna needed support.

He shifted from foot to foot, the bewildered-little-boy expression back on his face. "I hadn't–" He reached for Glenna's hand and stuck out his chin. "Why not? It would be my mother's by right."

His free hand pinched the corner of his moustache. "He gave me nothing."

"He gave you life." A lilt of love warmed Glenna's soft words.

Red-faced, he seemed ready to spit. "At a criminal cost."

Glenna tugged her husband's hand toward the steps. "We should head up to our room. We didn't mean to intrude, but we heard raised voices and were concerned."

"This door leads through to the front. You can go in that way." Anna's innkeeper smile was back in place.

When the door closed behind them, Nigel coughed. "I've stayed too long." He extended a hand. "Shall I return the note to the box?"

Once Anna passed it over, he reversed the steps to seal the box and placed it reverently on the table. "Fine workmanship. Anna, if you decide to allow a search for the tunnel, please permit me to participate. Good night, ladies."

He walked down the steps and across the back lawn and disappeared into the trees.

Brushing at flyaway strands of hair, Anna wilted in her seat. "This place will be the death of me."

"Maybe we should ask the McNutts to move on. Staying isn't doing them any good."

"No, but I need the income." Anna slid her mug nearer, slopping amber-green tea over the lip. "How much worse can it get?"

Ivan could find the tunnel and unearth who knew what kind of skeletons from Captain Hiltz's past? "You're right not to hunt for the old man's hidey-hole. Better make sure the boys and Meaghan know Ivan's not to prowl around."

"Beyond the laundry area, the basement's mostly storage. I'd guess the entrance is hidden down there, but we should keep him out of the barn just in case."

The basement door didn't lock, and it was too late this evening to do anything about it. With any luck, if Ivan decided to search against Anna's will, he'd wait until he and Glenna were alone in the inn. Which meant buying a lock while Meaghan was here to keep an eye on him.

Landon drained the last of her now-cold herbal tea. "If word gets out about a tunnel, we could be fending off other searchers too." And word would get out. Ivan would see to that.

Whether Nigel was alone believing in Captain Hiltz's hidden secret or it was a local legend, with a rumrunner's mysterious tunnel, rumours would fly.

Her shoulder muscles pulled tight and hunched her forward, bracing against half-formed fears. She sucked a deep breath and forced her thoughts to follow the fear to its roots.

Real or imagined, treasure or tragedy, Captain Hiltz's secret could be a powerful lure. What kind of secret might he have had, and who could be after it now? Would they want it badly enough to drive Anna out of business and away from the inn?

Chapter 13

Wednesday

The next morning, Landon waited until they buckled into the car after Anna's blood test before raising the questions that had threaded her dreams. "We should ask Maria about the tunnel."

"I don't want her to know we opened the box."

She clutched Anna's arm to stop her from shifting into gear. "This trouble with the inn could be about Jack, something a person wants badly enough to ruin your business and drive you away. Maria might give us some leads."

Anna's wry smile came with a slow, sideways stare. "Leads to suggest to the police."

"I didn't mean we'd pursue them ourselves." Someone who'd send a dead bird as a threat... who knew what they'd do if confronted?

"I suppose we'd better ask."

Despite a light drizzle, when they arrived, the same two women rocked sentry-like on the sheltered veranda. Neither responded to Anna's friendly greeting.

Inside, the middle-aged receptionist tapped her chin with a plum-coloured fingernail. "Maria doesn't want to see any strangers, but I remember you. She's keeping close to her room these days. Go on up."

Through Maria's half-open door, faint music reached the hallway. Her grey-fabric rocker faced out the window. At their knock, she swivelled the chair. "Oh. Anna, come in." She gestured them toward the bed again.

A silver-framed photo of a gangly teen lay in her lap, and she cradled her hands above it like they hurt.

Anna clucked sympathetically as she perched on the edge of the bed. "These grey days are hard on a lot of people. Is your arthritis bothering you?"

"It's not good today. I'm glad to see you, though. I wanted to warn you."

"About what?"

They'd mentioned the inn trouble last time. Had the elderly woman thought of a suspect?

One gnarled hand rubbed the other. "A man visited me Sunday afternoon after you were here. Said he's staying at the inn." The lines in her face snaked deeper. "Don't trust him."

If Ivan confronted her about Jack's behaviour or told her he was Jack's son—

Anna's flinch rocked the mattress. She must have had the same idea. She pressed her palms into the lap of her denim capris. "He told us he was researching Captain Hiltz. I'm sorry he found you."

Maria's lips trembled, then firmed again. "I had the light dim, to see the television. When he came in, I thought for a second it was David."

Landon's chest ached at the longing in her voice. Nigel should tell this grieving mother what he knew and let her face the truth.

Maria cleared her throat. "A passing resemblance, but I've been low in spirit ever since. That man is nosing around for trouble. I kicked him out. Be careful."

No wonder Maria was upset. On top of disappointment, if she'd seen a family likeness, it could have recalled what she must have known about her father-in-law. She might even think Ivan came to steal her son's inheritance, if she had one to give him.

Rain trickled down the windowpane.

The mattress dipped as Anna shifted forward. Her breath came out heavy. "You remember Nigel Foley. He saw the box you asked me to keep, and he opened it."

Maria sat straight up. Her palms clapped her cheeks, her mouth an open circle between them.

Anna's fingers twisted together in her lap. "He read your note, over my protest. But it's back in the box now, and that's tucked safely out of sight in my room."

"You should never have let him see it." Sudden energy cracked in Maria's voice.

"I know. It wasn't planned, but... it happened."

The defeat in Anna's tone, like a scolded child, hurt. Landon jumped in. "We're concerned someone might try to find this tunnel. Where's the opening, so we can keep people away?"

The old woman gazed at the photo in her lap for an extended moment. "There is no tunnel. It's a code. David will know what it means."

A code, in a locked puzzle box hidden in another box. Right. "Please, Mrs. Hiltz. If someone wants whatever the captain hid... we're in the way."

They'd been picturing a dead-end storage tunnel cut to hide the captain's smuggled goods. But tunnels could also be passages. Cold shrouded her, and she rubbed her bare upper arms, staring into Maria's hard blue eyes. "If there's a tunnel and it has a second entrance, someone could get into the inn. Whoever's harassing Anna left a dead bird on the doorstep yesterday. A threat."

She watched Maria for any hint of a reaction. "We can't let that person find a way inside."

Maria's face could have been stone. Pale, cruelly sculpted stone. "There is no tunnel. You need to go."

On the way downstairs, they met the attendant who'd helped them the other day. He flashed a wide smile. "Ladies. So many people take the elevator, but it is so slow. Climbing stairs is good for us."

The rich cadence of his accent soothed the burn of Maria's curt dismissal. Landon smiled back. "Maria's pretty down today. I hope you can cheer her up."

"Oh, I have a trick or two that may help." He indicated the tray in his hands. "Starting with this."

He continued up the stairs.

"Poor thing," Anna whispered. "She's been waiting so long for David. I don't know what resemblance she saw in Ivan, but no wonder she's taking it so hard. He'd better not come back."

"She might put us on the blacklist, the way she denied there's a tunnel."

A tunnel that haunted Landon now more than ever. If it was a storage space, the contents must be scandalous, or Maria wouldn't try so hard to hide its existence. If it was a passage and their enemy found the other entrance, they were in danger.

~~~

Landon had the new deadbolt mechanism in place on the basement door, screwdriver in hand, when the back door swung open. A breeze ruffled the sheet of instructions on the hardwood floor at her feet.

Gord stopped in the doorway. "Smells good in here."

Anna called to him from the kitchen, but he walked toward Landon. "Need some help?"

"I've got it, thanks."

Anna had cut the hole for the lock before mixing up the fragrant spice cake now in the oven. Landon didn't have that kind of skill with tools, but she could decipher the illustrations to finish the installation.
~~~

She tightened the final two screws, then tried the key. The bolt shot out, then back in. The key worked as smoothly on the basement side of the lock. She shut the door, locked it, and tucked the keys into her pocket.

Gord followed her into the kitchen and crossed to where Anna stood chopping vegetables. He pecked her cheek. "Why put a deadbolt on the basement door?"

She flashed him a look. Either she thought the answer was obvious, or the kiss had startled her. "So I can lock it."

"I understand locking your living quarters, but the basement?"

Anna brushed hair out of her eyes with the back of her hand and resumed chopping. "Captain Hiltz may have had a tunnel, for storage or for coming and going. Logically, it'd be in the basement. Our guest is a bit too interested in the history of this place and wants to find it. I don't want him snooping."

Gord sniffed. "Let him snoop. The most he'll find are spiderwebs in the corners."

Anna grabbed another carrot. "If the tunnel's full of old booze, I don't care. But what if it opens to the outside? Whoever's been spreading rumours and hacking my website, I don't want them finding a way in here to do worse."

"Which is why you bought a deadbolt that's keyed on both sides."

He tipped his chin toward his yellow golf shirt, pale lips curving into a wry smile. "Let me set your mind at rest. When I was a teen, I had more courage than sense, so I took a boat and tried to find the fabled sea entrance to the captain's hoard."

So he'd heard the rumours too. They weren't confined to Nigel's head.

"I nearly drowned. Then I faced my father's wrath when I got home." Something hard flashed across his face and was gone. "I had a good, close look at that cliff. Cracks and fissures, to be sure. But no tunnel entrance."

Care lines deepened around his mouth. "Anna, you're a strong woman, but this is more than you should be carrying on your own. Murdoch wouldn't want you tied to this place, especially if someone's working against you."

"If?" Anna swung around, still gripping the knife.

Gord retreated, hands up like an actor in a robbery scene.

Blushing, she dropped the knife on the cutting board. "Sorry." Her chin kept its defiant jut, and her eyes flashed. "I wasn't imagining things last time, and I'm not now."

He had lowered his hands, but now he extended one toward her. "Websites get hacked. People leave negative reviews."

She planted her fists on denim-clad hips. "People leave dead birds in gift bags as threats too. This is not a persecution complex. It's real."

A bland expression smoothed his face. At his questioning glance, Landon nodded. His outstretched hand dropped to his side. "That's sick."

"That's why I'm not taking any chances on someone finding a way to sneak in."

Gord planted a hip against the counter. "Believe me, I hung around enough as a kid to know. There's nothing down there."

He sounded so certain Landon almost believed him. Maria's note could have referred to a tunnel somewhere else. There were sea caves a few kilometres away at The Ovens Park, so why couldn't there be other caves or tunnels? Secret ones?

But she'd lied about it. If the note referred to a hiding place away from the inn, she could have said so. They'd never find it. Her denial confirmed the message pointed to something on-site. Something she didn't want them to find.

Landon left Anna and Gord to chat.

The morning's rain had given way to a sunny afternoon, the air clean and fresh. A rake handle propped open one of the barn doors. Skirting Anna's flower garden, she wandered across the grass to check on the boys' progress.

Scuffing sounds met her ears as she poked her head inside. Corey was hauling a box to join the cluster against one wall. Dust motes danced in the air and tickled her nose with the musty-sweet smell of old hay.

The boys only worked a few hours at a time, but another few days should finish the cleanup. She stepped inside, sandals quiet on the stained wooden floorboards. "Great job, guys. Do you need something to drink?"

Quinn stopped sweeping and leaned on his push broom. "We're good. Thanks." He added the last word as an afterthought.

She stepped out into the sunlight, breathing deeply to clear the dust from her nostrils. Clover soft underfoot, she walked behind the grey building to check the cat food. Gone, but for whose stomach?

On her way back to the inn, she spotted the four-legged Captain Jack strolling toward her.

She eased to her knees in the grass. "Hey, Jack. I won't hurt you. Come say hello."

The cat's swaying walk brought him nearer, but he stopped well out of reach.

She kept talking in a low tone. When he didn't move, she brushed her fingertips across the grass tips and tried a shhh sound.

He flicked his bent ear and stalked away.

Behind her, Quinn barked a laugh. "You try too hard. He won't come when you do that."

His anyone-should-know-better tone cut. Landon pushed up from the ground and brushed grass from her bare knees. She levelled him a stare. "Thanks for the tip. Does he come to you?"

"Naw. Haven't really tried."

Gord trotted down the back steps. "Keep up the good work in there, boys."

He crossed the grass to Landon. "I appreciate all the support you're giving Anna. She won't admit she shouldn't be alone, but I'm concerned about how she'll cope when you go back to Ontario."

"I hope she'll feel more like herself in another week or so." If the antibiotics did their job, she would.

But her friends would worry less if they knew what was going on. Landon grinned at Gord. "For a gentle woman, she sure is stubborn."

"I'll say." He fished his keys from his pocket and headed for his car.

She stared after him. He genuinely seemed to care about Anna, and his wild, teenage years were long past. Still, she wanted to ask Nigel about him. Finding the tunnel note last time Nigel had come made her forget.

It wasn't like she suspected Gord of causing their trouble. But with what she knew about his past and Elva's reaction to his name, she needed to reassure herself he'd truly changed. Otherwise, she'd have to find a way to warn Anna.

As if Anna would listen to anything negative about a friend.

Chapter 14

ON SUCH A pleasant evening, Landon suggested they carry dessert outside to the deck. The spice cake that had smelled so good while it baked looked even better swirled with creamy white icing and a dusting of coconut flakes.

Anna had made coffee for Bobby and tea for everyone else. He waved his mug under his nose. "Ahh. This'll keep me going after that amazing meal."

She smiled. "Thank you again for salvaging my website."

Roy saluted with his fork. "Thank you for feeding us."

Slouched in her chair, Anna closed her eyes briefly, her pink blouse rising and falling in a deep breath. Naturally, she'd chosen a labour-intensive meal to show her appreciation. Her expression was content, though. No tension bracketing her generous mouth, no perpetual pinch to the corners of her eyes.

Landon broke off a piece of cake with her fork. Soft and dense, not too sweet, it invited another taste. "I'll need to buy new clothes if I keep eating like this."

Roy hiked an eyebrow. "You probably have one of those metabolisms that burn it all off." He patted his belly. "I used to be like that. The food caught up with me when I hit forty."

Landon grinned. "How fast were you running?"

"Huh?"

"When the food caught up."

Bobby snickered. In one of the chairs facing the trees, he craned his neck, peering over the deck rail. "There's that stray again."

The cat sauntered across the grass and disappeared behind the barn. Good thing she'd refilled the food before supper.

"I'm trying to make friends with him, but he won't come near me."

"Are you feeding him?"

"Trying to—I'm never sure what eats the food. Could even be one of Roy's squirrels."

Roy shot her a mock glare.

Bobby speared the last chunk of his cake. "What about putting a shirt or something under the dish? So he'll associate your scent with his food."

Roy patted his belly again. "The way to a man's heart... could work for felines too."

Timkin strolled around the side of the house. His ears came up, and he trotted for the barn.

She tensed. They hadn't heard any fighting, but the black and white cat couldn't be happy about a stranger on his turf.

As the minutes passed with no snarls or growls, her muscles relaxed. Captain Jack must have moved on. She leaned back in her chair, elbows propped on the wicker armrests, and tuned into Roy's latest anecdote.

A buzzing noise cut him off, and he stared skyward. The drone was back.

Instead of flying past, it descended to hover a stone's throw overhead.

A harsh, mechanical voice shattered the peace. "Leave now. While you still can. Go."

The machine shot straight upward and zipped off toward the water.

Landon hunched forward, eyes screwed shut.

Cold. She was so cold, locked in remembered terror. She couldn't move. Didn't dare. Her abductor had conditioned her. Like training a dog—or a slave.

A loud, dominant voice meant "freeze." And "obey." "Submit."

She fought for breath. Trembling took her, and she fought that too. Waited for a curse, a blow, whatever abuse was coming.

A hand gripped her upper arm, and she bit her lips to stop a moan.

"Hey, what's wrong?"

Her eyelids snapped open. A face—Bobby's—close to hers. Blue-grey eyes wide with questions.

She screamed and jerked away.

He jumped back.

Part of her mind registered the people staring at her. Bobby. Roy. Anna across the table, mouth open, hand to her heart.

Safe people. Safe place.

Shuddering sobs broke the paralysis, and she bolted from her chair. She caught her toe on something but kept her feet. The door banged behind her as she fled along the hall and upstairs to her room.

~~~

Hushed voices and the shuffle of movement on the deck carried through Landon's bedroom window. She wanted to shut it. Couldn't let them see her do it.

She lay on her bed, curled in a fetal position with the butterfly throw pillow pressed into her stomach. So much therapy, counselling, prayer, and still the right trigger could make her lose it.

Anna. Someone had just threatened Anna.

And instead of supporting her, Landon had fallen apart. Again.
~~~

An engine started in the parking lot. Roy and Bobby leaving. Landon hugged the pillow harder. She'd ruined the evening and driven them away.

Well, the drone had ruined the evening. But if she hadn't freaked out, the four of them would be sitting there now, strategizing while they waited for the police.

She dreaded facing them again. Roy seemed pretty unflappable, but Bobby—despite his opinion of her, he'd made casual eye contact a few times tonight. Finally starting to be comfortable around her. What would he think now?

He'd shown compassion in the moment. But then she'd screamed in his face.

She sniffled. As long as she was here, Anna's relations with her neighbours would be cramped.

A gentle knock tapped at her door.

No use pretending she was asleep. Landon drew a slow, shuddery breath. "Come in."

The door eased open, then shut again. "Hey."

Anna sat on the edge of the bed, dipping the mattress so Landon's curled-up body tilted toward her. She stroked Landon's hair. "Roy will explain to Bobby. And I'll phone the police as soon as I know you're okay."

"I'm sorry I ran out on you." More tears seeped through her closed eyelids.

Anna's touch paused briefly on her head like a blessing, then kept stroking. "A retreat to regroup is not abandonment. You couldn't help me until you helped yourself."

Landon dragged an arm across her eyes. She squinted up at Anna. "God's brought me so far, and then one moment undoes it. How can I show what He's done when I overreact to nothing?" She blew out a shaky breath that felt like her soul collapsing.

"That was hardly *nothing*. We were all frightened." Anna plunked a tissue box on the bed between them. "You were among friends. We see every day what God has done in you."

Landon yanked a handful of tissues and blew her nose. Her sinuses burned. "You see. Roy might. But Bobby's always holding back like he's waiting for me to crack and let the whole mess pour out." She sniffed and blotted her face. "I can't even help you. All I am is a liability."

"You don't need to do anything. And you're not a liability. That's the pain speaking, not the truth." Anna's hand stilled again on her head. "Our weaknesses can show God's strength. Let Him be strong in you."

Let Him be strong... He'd been strong, all along, every step of this road to healing.

Even during the worst of her trauma, when she didn't know He was there, He'd kept it from being worse. Kept her alive. And He'd brought the undercover cop who rescued her and given her the people and resources she needed to find life again—to find Him.

His presence still warmed her spirit. As she focused, the warmth grew. Her chest muscles loosened, and her breath came easier.

She prodded Anna with her knee. "Enough about me and God. Time to make your phone call."

"You okay now?"

"I will be. Thanks." Landon wadded up the tissues. "Let me wash my face, and I'll come downstairs."

Before leaving the room, she paused at the prints on her wall, the vibrant monarch and subtler tiger swallowtail. Her fingertip traced one of the swallowtail's yellow bands. Fragile limbs and paper-thin stained-glass wings that caught the light and reflected God's glory. To become all He planned, a butterfly had to survive a cage of darkness. No wonder she loved them. They gave her hope it was possible.

While Anna finished her phone call, Landon scrubbed the few pots that hadn't fit in the dishwasher. The warm water and repetitive motion soothed her still-jagged nerves. She kept glancing out the window for the feline Captain Jack, but nothing moved.

Something about this bedraggled, unwanted animal caught her heart. Despite whatever had happened to him, he walked proud with dignity and flair. Free, the way she wanted to walk.

The way she was learning to walk. His scars were external, hers internal, but maybe that was the connection.

As she was putting away the last pot, Anna returned. "You didn't need to clean up alone."

"There wasn't much to do." Landon hung the tea towel on the oven bar. "Are they sending someone?"

"Eventually. The dispatcher wasn't too happy about how long it took me to call, but the drone didn't stick around."

Landon peered out at the sky. Clear. "I need to go back outside. Before I'm afraid to go out at all."

Anna winced. "I hadn't thought of that. Smart girl. I'll come too."

"Thanks. It'll be easier together."

Stepping through the doorway caused a tingle of anxiety, but the tangy sea breeze cooling her cheeks gave her confidence. With another glance skyward, Landon crossed the deck and reclaimed the chair she'd fled.

Anna sat across from her, brown eyes warm with pride. "I don't think you recovered this fast the night of the barn break-in."

"It was night then." Dark and rainy, and she'd been determined to check for damage with Anna and Dylan. Until the wind blew the door shut on them and their flashlights weren't enough to stop a panic attack.

She'd shot out of the barn like her life depended on it.

If Dylan responded to tonight's call and heard why Anna didn't report the incident right away, he'd really think she was a weak link.

Her smile gentle, Anna tucked a lock of hair behind her ear. "All I'm saying is it's evidence God's working."

A police cruiser lumbered up the driveway and stopped beside Anna's sedan.

Other than Dylan, Landon had met two officers including the woman who'd reprimanded her and Anna for interfering in the previous investigation.

Before she could decide if she hoped for a stranger or a familiar face, the car door opened, and Dylan emerged.

Long strides carried him to the deck, and he joined them at the glass-topped table. He studied each in turn, his gaze lingering on Landon. "You're both okay?"

Heat rose in Landon's face. He knew. But his tone held no criticism, only acceptance. She forced a little smile. "We're good."

He nodded, but his eyes narrowed, the brown darkening. "I've read the basics of your story. You deserve to be protected, not terrorized by some faceless troublemaker with a fancy toy. All the more reason to stop him."

Gripping the wicker armrests of his chair, Dylan slid it closer. "When we were canvassing the area about Anna's prowler, one of the residents expressed suspicion of you."

"Elva."

His eyelid twitched. "I can't say. It was very vague, but I couldn't overlook anything that would help Anna. I did some digging." He held the eye contact, a smile creasing his lean cheeks. "We see so much darkness in our work. And we don't often see long-term, positive results. Success stories like yours keep us going."

Heat prickled the back of her neck. How could he call her a success story? He must know she'd just fallen apart again. But she owed her life to a man like him. A hero who fought the evil time and again—and this time, won. "Thank you for all you do."

"It's a privilege." Dylan laid his notebook on the table and angled toward Anna. "Walk me through what happened tonight, and then Landon can add her perspective."

Anna told the story. "I have plenty of witnesses this time. Roy and Bobby might be able to describe the drone better."

He underlined their names on his page. "I'll drop in on them next, in case they can add anything. Your cameras will give us visuals, though."

Anna blinked at him, and then her lips tightened. "They don't come on until ten. We're out here too often during the day. Sorry."

"Too bad. The image might have helped. Audio would have been even better."

"They're not that fancy."

Landon gripped the armrests of her chair until the woven edges bit her palms. "I won't forget those words. Anna had them right. The tone was... mechanical. Like it wasn't the person's real voice."

He scratched another note. "This incident confirms it's personal, Anna. It's not someone wanting the inn closed. It's someone who wants you gone."

"And I have no idea who." Anna pushed her bangs off her forehead, then let them fall back in place. "Or why."

"We're not going to let them win." Dylan clicked his pen closed. "I had a chat with your guest, Ivan. That's another nasty story. He has a serious hate on for Captain Hiltz."

"You could say that. But he knows we're on the same side."

Landon leaned forward, palms on her knees. "Unless he thinks you're not doing enough. He could want to buy this place and raze it to the ground."

"Motive is important, but we need to be careful not to speculate too much."

At Dylan's warning, her shoulders hunched. She studied the crisscross wrinkles in her shorts, stark proof she'd been curled into a hopeless ball upstairs on her bed. "You're right. And Ivan can't have a problem with the inn itself, or he wouldn't be able to stay here. Did Jaclyn say if there'd been any threats about the pub?"

She risked eye contact and found only acceptance, no rebuke for her wild words about Ivan.

Instead, a small smile tilted his lips. "Other than his outburst that day, she's had nothing. My gut tells me if he wanted revenge, he'd target the pub first." His jaw firmed. "She's traded on Captain Jack as some kind of local hero. That doesn't sit so well with me since I've heard Ivan's story."

A frown creased Anna's brow, and she rubbed her forehead. "She was shocked. Now, I think, she needs to know if it's true. All she has to go on is an upset patron who escalated until he was thrown out. Ivan is trying to find other victims or their children."

"I'm sure that's going over well." An eyeroll accented his dry tone.

"About what you'd expect." Landon drummed her fingertips against the glass tabletop, fingernails clicking gently. Something they'd said—she'd said—needed a second look. A vibration in her mind, like a seed about to burst and sprout into the light.

Focusing on the repetitive motion, she let her thoughts drift back over the conversation.

Suspects. Ivan. Motive.

Speculation. "Okay. Ivan forcing a sale for vengeance was a reach. But forcing a sale could be someone else's motive. Maybe it's not about Anna leaving. Maybe it's about the property."

Anna plunked her elbows onto the table edge and dropped her forehead in her palms. "We talked this to death last time, and it was just Hart and Quinn playing mind games."

"Unless—" Landon focused on Dylan. "The man trying to recruit a troublemaker kid to help 'play a joke on a friend'—what if that wasn't Hart? What if it was someone else, who hired them both?"

"It's possible. With their existing hostility toward Anna, Hart and Quinn would be easy picks."

Gord had nothing good to say about Hart's intelligence. Maybe there was another leader, after all. "That rules out

Ivan because he wasn't here then. But it still doesn't help. Gord and Jaclyn are the only ones who've expressed interest in owning the inn, and I can't see either of them doing this."

The last time Gord offered, it seemed more from a desire to ease Anna's burden than a need to own his childhood friend's former home. And Jaclyn needed to process the revelation about Captain Hiltz's personal life. She'd hardly be trying to acquire another site linked to the man if she might decide to cut her connection with him.

Anna bounced her palm on the table rim. "If it's someone who wants the property and they succeed in making me sell, then we'll know the buyer's the guilty one."

"This person schemes too well to be caught like that." Dylan clicked open his pen and scribbled a few more words. "If he wants the inn, he could have a middleman make the purchase and then resell. How many links down that chain might he go? Even then, other than proof of purchase, we'd have no proof of guilt."

Plus, the scheme might not work. Gord or Jaclyn could step up to buy the place in a private sale to help Anna, even if the timing was bad for them. Gord might even hire Meaghan to run the inn.

Then the villain would have to start over.

Dylan slid his chair back and stood. "Knowing Anna, I have an easier time believing this is an attempt to gain the property rather than a personal grudge, but we need to investigate both options. And you're right—it could be unfinished business from last month."

He tucked his notebook in his pocket. "I should head over to Roy's place before it's too late to stop in."

After he drove away, Anna pressed her fingertips to her temples and groaned. "I don't know if it feels worse to think this is the same person from June, so the ordeal is still going on, or if it's better because it's not a second person out to get me."

Even one person with a grudge against Anna was hard to believe. They thought last time had been about Meaghan, not Anna, because of Hart's desire to control her. And Quinn, he was just Quinn, like Elva was Elva.

Landon shivered despite the lingering heat. Who else was out there behind the scenes?

"Anna, if this is more about the property than about you, we should find that tunnel. If this person is after something hidden, we can locate it first."

Anna's countenance darkened. "Captain Hiltz had nothing that I want."

"So we dispose of it. Publicly. And whoever's after it will know it's gone."

Ivan's car rounded the side of the building.

Anna tipped her head toward the parking lot. "We're not going to hunt for a tunnel. And please don't mention it in front of Ivan. I don't want his vendetta spilling into our personal lives."

Landon had no authority to argue. But her instinct said the tunnel was key.

Chapter 15

Thursday

ANNA'S BREAKFASTS WEREN'T exotic, but the guests loved them. Landon's theory was that people didn't stop to cook in the morning. She never did at home. There was only time to grab something quick on the way out the door.

Coffee pot in hand, she went to check on Glenna and Ivan. The couple was still eating but they'd crammed everything onto one side of the table to make room for the map spread over the rest and propped against the adjacent window.

Landon set the coffee on the rustic white sideboard. "Let me clear some of this out of the way."

She shuffled as much as she could to the next table and refilled their coffee cups. "Planning some sightseeing?"

Ivan poked a spot on the map. "My mother has another brother living in Digby. Uncle Sandy phoned him and arranged for us to meet."

Glenna's smile crinkled the corners of her eyes. "We're going to make a day of it. Maybe even stay overnight. We want to keep our room here, but don't be surprised if we're not back until tomorrow."

"We'll definitely be here tomorrow. Uncle Sandy's taking us out in his boat." Ivan cut his eyes toward the white pass-through doors to the kitchen and lowered his voice. "A rumrunner's tunnel would connect to the sea. I respect Anna's wishes concerning her property, but there's no law against exploring the cliff from the water."

Gord said there was nothing to find. Still, if Ivan and his uncle discovered a way in, it could help Anna. "Even if you don't find anything, it should be a fun day out. And I'm glad you've connected with your family."

He tipped his cup to drain the last of his coffee, then waved away Landon's offer of more. "Sandy's so welcoming. I wish I'd met him last time."

Landon froze in place. Carefully, she arched her brows and affected a bland tone. "Last time?"

Angling her cutlery on her empty plate, Glenna bobbed her head. "Ivan came for a week in June."

His cheeks flushed a dark red, and he twisted the corner of his moustache. "I camped nearby. I wasn't ready to talk to anyone, but I came into town long enough to find out where Jack had lived. When I drove past and saw it was an inn, I didn't know what to think."

Glenna took his hand, wrapping him in a loving smile. "Being able to stay here and make positive memories has been good for you."

Ivan's ruddy face swam in Landon's vision, unnaturally clear, a bull's-eye in a swirl of grey. He'd been here in June.

He could have instigated their prowler trouble after all.

Her lungs heaved for air, and the breath rasped inward, burning her throat. Blindly, she collected their plates, the stack rocking in her trembling hands. A half-eaten slice of tomato slid onto the floor.

"But why come alone?"

"I needed time. To think." He focused on the map in front of him.

Glenna still held his hand. "Ivan's been off work since he read his mother's letter. It's been a rough spring."

"I can imagine." He still seemed broken. Landon forced a smile. "Well, have a wonderful day. I hope you enjoy your visit."

She clattered their utensils on top of the plates, then scooped the tomato into a paper napkin and quick-marched into the kitchen.

Anna glanced up from her tea. "What's the matter?"

Landon let the swinging doors fall shut behind her. "Not now," she hissed.

She rinsed the plates and loaded everything into the dishwasher. The rest of the cleanup could wait until the McNutts left the room.

Taking the chair beside Anna's, she kept her voice low. "Ivan was here. In June. He could be behind everything, after all."

Anna's worry lines deepened, but then she shook her head. "We don't know it was the same time as the trouble here. Even if it was, it's a coincidence."

"He said he found out this was where Jack lived and drove by. Saw it was an inn and 'didn't know what to think.' Like it upset him."

"But he knows there's no connection with the Hiltz family anymore." Anna flattened her hands on the pine tabletop, fingers splayed. "He wasn't here last night when the drone came, but he'd have no reason to send it. And I agree with Dylan. He'd go after the pub first."

Reasoning did nothing to calm Landon's jitters. Even though she wanted to believe it. Not having a suspect under their roof was a good thing. And Ivan didn't seem the type to terrorize Anna.

The patience in Anna's brown eyes urged her to agree. But to someone, somewhere, Anna—or her inn—was a target.

They couldn't let that person win. Landon walked to the window. Instinctively, she checked the sky. Clear. "I don't know how the police are going to solve this, but they'd better do it soon."

"Amen, sister." Anna's sigh was a slow wheeze. "This has been the worst year of my life. And I still have to get through Murdoch's birthday and the anniversary of his accident."

After Landon's dad died, she'd been warned about all the firsts. Birthday, Fathers' Day, Christmas, date of death. Not that things became magically easier after that, but the firsts did feel like mental or emotional benchmarks she'd had to pass.

She went back to Anna and tried to rub the tension from her friend's shoulders. "You can do this. With God's help, you're going to make it."

Anna flinched.

"Sorry. You have knots on knots in there." Landon rested her hands lightly on Anna's shoulders for a moment, then stepped away. "You need a serious spa day. Or a massage therapist."

"Or this faceless person to stop tormenting me."

Landon dropped into her seat. "That'd help." She studied her friend's pale face, the way her body slumped in the straight-backed chair. "Beating the Lyme Disease will help too. It's only been a few days, but do you feel like the medicine's doing anything yet?"

Anna touched her stomach. "Nothing good."

"Spa day. It'll make a difference. Trust me." Landon hadn't been to a spa. She couldn't afford it, and okay, she still had issues with strangers touching her.

One of the therapists who'd worked with her and the other girls had coached them for months until they'd allowed another of the therapy team—also a woman—to begin gentle massages. That had been another type of benchmark, learning to open up to a positive touch. The physical benefit, as heavenly as it was, had been temporary. The step toward emotional wholeness had been huge.

Landon braced an elbow on the table. "Roy might know a good massage therapist."

A little spark of fight gleamed in Anna's eyes. "Don't you dare."

She grinned. "I'll give you a couple of days to think about it."

The front door alert chimed. Ivan and Glenna must be leaving. Landon stood. "When is Murdoch's birthday, anyway?"

"Saturday."

"*This* Saturday?" No wonder she'd mentioned it.

Stroking the wedding band on her finger, Anna nodded.

"I'm glad I'll be here with you." She'd have to think of something special to do that day. Not to expect Anna to forget, but to help her find a bit of comfort. Or at least cry with her for the loss of a good man.

When Landon came back into the kitchen, Meaghan had arrived and was assembling her cleaning supplies.

"Good morning." Landon put the McNutts' cups in the dishwasher and unloaded the rest of her tray.

"Hi." Tendrils of red hair frizzed around Meaghan's forehead in the humidity, and her cheeks glowed. "You're still going back to school in September?"

"Definitely." No way was she letting Professor Tallin win. Was Meaghan afraid she'd stay on here and take over the housekeeping?

"I want to take a class this fall." Meaghan glanced at Anna. "Just one. To see if I can still do it. It wouldn't mess up my work availability."

Vulnerability softened her features. "Before I go today, could you give me an idea of where to start? Something useful, but not crazy hard?"

"Sure. And don't worry, wherever you go will have lots of support for students who've been out of school for a while."

Picking up her basket, Meaghan flung her braid over her shoulder. "Hart doesn't get it. And I don't want my dad to know yet."

Anna hugged her. “We’ll be quiet. I’m sure your father will support you, but it’ll be a nice surprise when you tell him.”

“Thanks. I’d better get to work.” Meaghan left the room.

Landon shared a smile with Anna. “Good for her.” Meaghan deserved to do something for herself instead of catering to her selfish boyfriend all the time.

Ouch. Landon brought her thoughts up short. She had no business judging Hart. Or Meaghan’s choices. But the other girl did seem discontented with her current situation, and if she dreamed of more education and a better job, now was the time to go for it.

A white bottle of shampoo stood on the counter. “Where did this come from?”

“Meaghan brought it. It’s a line of natural products she sells. Gord gave me some for Christmas, and she’s kept me supplied ever since. Smell it. It’s lovely.”

Landon unscrewed the cap and waved the bottle under her nose. “Mmm.” Delicate citrus with a trace of spice, not overpowering like some products. She closed the bottle.

“I’m going out to see if our stray needs more food.” Why did she have to name him Captain Jack, and then find out Captain Hiltz was called Jack—and what he’d done?

She stepped onto the deck and scanned the sky. No drone. Then the grounds. No stray, either.

Timkin lay curled on one of the deck chairs. He eyed her lazily.

“You, I’d call Mr. Superior. Or maybe Butler.” But she detoured to stroke his back before heading for the dish behind the barn.

The stainless-steel bowl was empty. She picked it up from the food-specked sweatshirt she’d sacrificed to familiarize him with her scent and knocked it against the barn to dislodge any insects from the underside. The first time, she’d taken a big spider into the house. Good thing only Anna heard her shriek.

They'd had a good laugh. After Anna corralled the spider and put it back outside.

When she rounded the corner of the barn, Nigel Foley stood watching her from a few paces away, metal detector resting on his shoulder.

He tipped the brim of his camouflage cap without actually removing it. "I didn't want to frighten you by speaking behind your back."

She pressed a hand to her chest, heart thudding against her palm. "I'm still a little startled. But thank you. Anna's inside. Have you come for tea?" She'd first met Nigel when he dropped in for tea. It had been an odd conversation.

He blinked twice, then twice more, like a signal. "First, a word in private."

"Okay."

Intensity glittered in his eyes—more than his usual direct stare. Tiny shivers prickled between her shoulder blades as he approached. "Is it something about Anna?"

"In a manner of speaking. I often see a car here. Belonging to Gord Lohnes." Resentment—or something dark—brewed in his tone.

Here was her chance to ask him about Gord. "How well do you know him?"

"Don't trust that one. Watch him around Anna."

Landon couldn't stop a quick peek at the house. Great. If Anna saw, she'd know they were talking about her—and think they were conspiring. "She said he was trouble as a teen, but he seems respectable now. Lots of people change."

"Some don't."

The words chilled something inside her. "Are you saying Anna's in danger?"

"That, I don't know. But she needs to keep her distance."

Landon tapped the cat's bowl against her leg. "Have you tried giving her advice lately?"

"I understand. This is not the Anna we know and love. You see no signs that he's influencing her?"

"Gord? No." If Anna would only tell her friends about the Lyme diagnosis, they'd stop dreaming up other causes. "She's a little run down these days, but she'll be okay soon."

A single bristly eyebrow slid upward. He wasn't convinced.

Landon checked the sky. Still no drone. Nigel might have seen it, too, but Anna could be part of that conversation. First, Gord. "You keep watch around Elva's place too, right?"

A single nod. "Why?"

"I visited this week, to ask if she might have an idea who's bothering Anna."

"She doesn't like you."

"I know. More to the point, when I mentioned Gord's name, it completely wrecked her."

Nigel hissed.

"Look, I don't want to pry, but that's serious hurt. If Gord did something to her back then, might he repeat it with Anna now?"

Nigel's face had gone inscrutable. Except for his eyes. What burned there pushed her back a step.

He didn't seem to notice. "He went to her house last night. If he reopened the old wounds..." His whole body jerked. "I have to see her."

From what Landon had seen, those wounds weren't closed. They were raw and festering. "Nigel, wait. Will you tell her—" Her voice broke. "Tell her I care. She knows I've been hurt too. Maybe if we talked, it could help her."

Elva would need more than that, but it could be a start.

The heat left his eyes. "She won't talk. But thank you." Another series of rapid blinks. "You're one of the good ones, Landon Smith."

He spun away and strode into the forest toward Elva's.

He hadn't answered her question. Landon walked back to the inn, dangling the bowl at her side. Praying for Elva and for Nigel.

Gord seemed like an ordinary guy, but she'd seen what people could hide.

She dodged those memories and opened the back door. Whatever lay in the past, present-day Gord was weakened by a heart condition and more mature than he'd been as a teen.

Her imagination was too stirred up by the mystery to believe her logic.

Chapter 16

LANDON WOULD HAVE enjoyed chatting with Meaghan about first-time course options if thoughts of Gord weren't crowding her mind. She couldn't very well ask the other girl if her father was potentially violent.

Instead, side by side under the striped deck umbrella, they browsed websites for universities and community colleges in Halifax.

Finally, Meaghan dropped her phone in her lap and ground her palm into her forehead. "Information overload." Rolling her shoulders, she dipped her neck forward in a slow stretch. "I'd better text Hart to come get me. He has plans this afternoon."

Hart was another line of conversation they couldn't share. Including how Meaghan put up with a guy who'd lost her one job and almost cost this one too. Still, it was good spending time with someone near her own age. Meaghan was probably twenty-one or twenty-two, not much younger than Landon.

When a car horn from the road announced Hart's presence, she rose and pocketed her phone. "Thanks again. I appreciate it."

Following her down the steps, Landon headed for the barn where Corey and Quinn were working. Anna insisted they only work when she was home, but so far, there'd been few conflicts.

Without an opening at the back for a cross-breeze, the stifling heat prickled her hairline as soon as she stepped inside. The boys probably wouldn't stay much longer.

Quinn broke off what he was saying—something about sports, by the sound of it—and stared at her. "Yeah, we'd love some water. Thanks." He smirked.

The dust-thickened air filled her mouth with grit and made her want to sneeze. She held the eye contact. "Apples too? Or muffins?"

Corey huffed. "We're gonna wrap up soon. We don't need anything."

"Muffins sound good." Quinn shook out a blanket and bundled it into a box.

Anna had said not to be too particular about folding anything, and they were taking her at her word. She'd also told them to stay hydrated. "I'll be back in a minute."

Landon returned with a tray of ice water and muffins and balanced it on one of the closed boxes near the door. "These are all the keepers?"

Corey hefted a glass in what she chose to interpret as a thank-you gesture. "The damaged stuff is in the ones over there. A lot more things survived than we thought. At least so far."

"Find anything interesting?" He'd think she meant Captain Hiltz's secrets, and in a way, she did. Specifically, had they found any signs of a tunnel?

"Nah."

While the boys chowed down on muffins, she roamed the empty spaces, scuffing her toes against the floorboards. No sign of a latch or a trapdoor.

Her circuit brought her back to the entrance to face twin stares. Quinn sneered. "Good enough for you?"

"There may be a tunnel somewhere on the property."

At last, a spark of interest in both pairs of eyes.

"Anna doesn't want it found, but if there's something hidden there, it may be what's behind the harassment. If you see anything, would you let me know?"

Corey jerked his head, flopping heavy blond bangs away from his eyes. "She'll chew us out."

"I'll take the heat. Just don't tell Ivan."

Quinn peered at her through one narrowed eye, the other fully closed. "So we find what this dude wants before he gets it."

"Or we prove there's nothing to find. Either way, if that's his motive, we finish it. Anna won't like it, but if it stops this trouble, she can have her life back."

Corey plunked his empty glass on the tray. "We can check for a trapdoor in here, but the entrance is probably out in the woods. Nigel should have found it, though."

Quinn snickered.

Corey shot him a dirty look. "He's okay." He made eye contact with Landon. "I'll ask what he thinks."

"Please. And ask him if he knows anything about a white quad-copter drone flying around. One broadcast a threatening message at Anna last night."

Corey's jaw dropped. "No way."

Quinn adjusted his ball cap. "I've seen it. Didn't pay much attention beyond wanting one of my own." He grinned at Corey. "Could have a lot of fun with one of them."

Corey shrugged. "We'll let you know if we find anything."

"Thanks, guys." Landon grasped the tray's hooped metal handles. "See you later."

Halfway to the inn, she glimpsed orange movement among the trees. Slowly, quietly, she moved to the steps and slid the tray onto the edge of the deck. Then she crept midway to the barn, farther from the entrance so the boys wouldn't call out.

She knelt and waited.

The cat stopped at the tree line and stared at her.

"It's okay. I won't hurt you. I'm the one who feeds you."

He cocked his head, bent ear high, one eye half-closed by an ugly bump. He paced a few steps nearer, an elegant dancer in a ragged costume.

A dark line of what could be dried blood snaked through the swelling.

"Ooh, that looks sore."

Without breaking eye contact, she inched her hand to her back pocket. In one cautious, fluid motion, she raised the phone and opened the camera app. "I need to see that wound, mister. A new name for you'd help too."

She snapped a quick picture in case he ran, then spread her thumb and forefinger across the screen to zoom in.

He'd flinched at the shutter click but held his ground.

The cut made her breath hiss. Surely he'd heal on his own. He already bore plenty of scars. But that wasn't an ordinary scab. It was crusty, discoloured. Although maybe that was normal for a cat.

She framed a close-up shot. No way would this wounded warrior let her take him to the vet. Still, if that cut was infected and so near his eye, he'd need care.

By now, he should know her voice and associate her scent with the sweatshirt under his bowl. With a prayer for the impossible, she stretched out her hand. "Come on, let me help you."

He sneezed, and a small whimper escaped as if jerking his head hurt. Tail erect with its signal-flag tip, he waded through the grass and disappeared behind the barn.

Poor thing.

"Landon?" Bobby's quiet greeting came from behind her.

She started but tried to cover it in a half-turn toward him. "The stray cat's behind the barn. I'm still trying to make friends."

"Can we talk?" His stance near the open doors left her a huge safety zone.

"Have a seat." She waved the hand holding the phone.

"Making a crazy cat video to post online?"

"He's hurt. The camera let me see him closer."

Bobby crossed the grass and lowered himself beside her. "That cat's survived a wound or two."

"This one's fresh. And nasty."

"Let's see."

After selecting a picture, she passed him the phone. His brows lowered. "It's not good, but he won't let us near him."

"I know. I just—I thought if he'd come to me—"

"You could grab him?"

Heat flooded her face. "I know it's dumb."

"It's not dumb. Well, it's sort of... impractical, but you want to help because you care."

Great. Now he was patronizing her. Landon stared at the corner of the barn where the cat had disappeared.

"Want me to dig you a tiger pit?"

She whirled.

His wide eyes and goofy grin disarmed her. "No spikes. Just to catch him. Or a thick sleeping bag. Grab him in that, and he can't scratch or bite."

When he pinched his chin between thumb and curled forefinger, she leaned a palm into the grass and gave her head a rueful shake. "Next you'll suggest we drug his food."

He threw his hands up in mock horror. "Have you never heard the joke about how to give a cat a pill? You're on your own with that one."

"He's been through so much. I want to see him have a happy ending." She plucked a few blades of grass, rolling them between thumb and forefinger. So what if that sounded dumb too?

Stretching out his pale legs in the grass, ankles crossed, Bobby leaned back on his palms. "That sounds pretty understandable, with what Gramp told me last night."

He stared straight ahead into the forest, stiffness etching his profile. His jaw worked a few times as if the words were stuck. " 'I'm sorry' doesn't begin to cut it. Sorry you lived what I can't imagine and sorry I upset you last night."

With anyone else, she'd touch his hand. Offer connection, support. With Bobby, that'd push him deeper behind his wall. "Thank you. And last night wasn't your fault. You wanted to help, like me with Cap—well, whatever I end up calling him. He can't be Captain Jack now."

"I suppose." Bobby waggled his eyebrows. "Call him Travers. You can't get more heroic than that."

"You've seen that cat. Travers would come out of your book and slap you. Hard."

"Point taken. Although it'd be worth it if he'd bring down our drone jockey." Now he met her eyes. "Are you really okay after that scare?"

"Mostly." She swept a palm across the tips of the grass, letting the tickling sensation relax her. "Triggers happen. I'm learning to handle them. Usually better than I did last night."

She pushed up from the ground and brushed loose grass from her legs. "He's not coming back. Sorry to keep you out here. And I'm sorry I screamed at you."

"In hindsight, I don't think it was at me." He did his own brush-down. "How's Anna doing?"

"Stressed but okay. Come say hi. I just want to check the food dish first and see how much our visitor ate. This time I know it's him."

At the top of the steps, Landon stooped to collect the boys' snack tray.

Instead of following her into the kitchen, Bobby tapped on Anna's open door.

When Landon joined them in the sitting room, Anna lay in her recliner in front of an oscillating fan, declaring herself to be fine. "Except for the fake reviews. Another one popped up this morning."

He dropped onto the couch and flung an arm across the back. "It must be the guy with the drone. The police should be able to trace him online. It's hard with the pro criminals like the hacker, but he'll be doing the reviews himself. A pro wouldn't waste the time."

Landon skirted the oval coffee table to the recliner beside Anna's, tucking her feet beneath her as she sat. The fan's breeze caressed her arm. She hitched sideways to face her friend. "No more cancellations, though?"

"Not yet. The new guests are coming any time."

"If they get here early enough, I'd like to go to the vet."

Anna arched an eyebrow. "We do have people doctors, you know. Mine would see you."

Bobby snorted.

Anna's sense of humour had weakened with her health. Maybe this meant the medicine was working.

Leaning over the padded arm of her chair, Landon pretended to swat her. "The stray cat's hurt. I can't take him with me, but maybe the vet could give me some medicine for him. I have a photo."

"You'd better make an appointment. I tried a walk-in once with Timkin, and the wait's terrible."

"I can drive you." Bobby tugged a grey throw cushion from behind him and eased back against the floral upholstery. "If you phone them now, I'll come back when it's time to go."

Landon hugged her knees to her chest. After his judgmental words when he was helping Anna deal with the reviews, she'd promised herself not to impose on him again.

Today, though, he'd tried to make peace. And she did need a lift. This was one of the few aspects of rural living she didn't like. At home, public transit took her wherever she had to go.

"Won't I interfere with your writing?" His lunch break, or whatever, must be nearly over.

He crossed an ankle over his other leg, navy flip-flop dangling. "I finished a key scene this morning. This won't take all afternoon, and even if it does, I can work this evening. Gramp and I were here last night. That's our social life for the week."

He didn't sound like he minded the slow pace. And if the cut really was infected, the sooner it was treated, the better.

Assuming there *was* a way to treat a feral cat. If giving them pills was nearly impossible, she could only imagine trying to smear ointment on the wound. Could she mix liquid medicine into his food?

"If you're sure..." She unlocked her phone. "What's the clinic called, Anna?"

Once Bobby knew the appointment time, he said goodbye. "If I don't hear from you, I'll be here at two thirty."

Anna smiled after him. "I have good neighbours."

Unless one of them was trying to scare her into giving up her business—and her home.

Chapter 17

BOBBY'S WHITE CORVETTE glided up the driveway just before two thirty. Landon left Anna waiting on the deck for the new guests. The humidity had eased, and in the sun umbrella's shade, there was no nicer place to pass the time.

Landon sank into the soft leather seat. "If I'd been able to catch the cat, we'd be in Roy's truck, right?"

"You know it."

She buckled her seatbelt and leaned back against the headrest.

Everything else about Bobby was low key. Clothes that probably came from a big-box store, down-to-earth attitude, ordinary conversation—except for his jokes. He didn't fit any of the stereotypes for a flashy car.

The breeze from the open roof teased her hair. "So how did you choose such a sweet ride?"

"Girlfriend insisted." His laugh erupted short enough to be a cough. "I didn't mind. On the highway, I kind of feel like it's a scout ship."

"Your girlfriend insisted?"

"She said it'd make me more interesting."

Landon schooled her expression back to neutral. Good thing he was watching the road and hadn't seen her reaction.

He didn't sound resigned, hurt, or bitter. More matter-of-fact. It made her angry on his behalf. "And this is a step up from the one who looks like me?"

"No comparison." The words rumbled low in his throat, almost a growl. He took a breath. "Jessie's okay. I know where I stand with her. She doesn't treat me like a—" His throat clenched. "Anyway, I got tired of attending author events alone."

They came up behind a boxy, rust-spotted sedan, and he dropped back a little. By the set of his jaw, he was still thinking about the past. Why had she brought it up?

Maybe she could find his sense of humour. She tugged on the sleeve of his faded tee shirt. "Does Jessie know you drive in old clothes and flip-flops?"

A faint smile cracked his scowl. "I'm sure she tries not to think about it."

A few minutes later, he bounced a fist on his thigh. "I'm sorry. Girls like you wouldn't understand mundane, commonplace relationships."

Landon hissed in a breath. The nerve of this guy! And after his so-called attempts to be kind.

Trembling started in her chest. "Girls like me. Who've been human trafficked. You'd judge us for that?"

Tires squealing, the car jolted to a near stop. His head jerked up for a rear-view mirror check, and their speed gently increased to normal.

"What? No, never." His face a death-white mask, he stared straight ahead. A tendon pulsed in his throat. "There's no room to pull over and talk this through. Not on these curves. I am so sorry—that came out so wrong. No judgment. Not for what they did to you."

One hand left the wheel to scrape through his hair. "Oh, man."

"Then what was that supposed to mean? Who are girls like me, Bobby? Worthless? Disposable? Trash?"

He didn't answer right away. They'd reached the outskirts of town, and as soon as parking spaces appeared at the curb, he signalled and stopped.

This time he pushed both hands through his hair and blew out an explosive gust that slumped him back against his seat, caving his shoulders forward as if the exhalation drained everything inside. He twisted to face her, still pale. "When I write, I can go back and edit. Once words are said, there's no do-over."

His weak attempt at a smile crumpled. He took another breath. Eye contact seemed to be killing him, but he did it.

Landon tried to get her own mental space in order. Whatever he'd meant, it wasn't what she'd heard. For one thing, the first time he'd said it, he hadn't known her past. "I shouldn't have overreacted. Those words are another trigger."

He shook his head, fast and frenzied. "It's not your fault. I was trying to dig myself out of one awkward moment, and I fell into a bigger one." Suddenly still, he raised an eyebrow. "One might say a tiger pit."

Landon wouldn't laugh. He wasn't getting off that easily. She pressed her lips together, eyes narrowed, and watched him squirm.

A mental image of Professor Tallin with that same critical expression made her want to slide under the seat.

He checked the dashboard clock. "Ten minutes, and the clinic's not far. Okay. Girls like you. Pretty and perky, energetic and popular. Slim and graceful." His chin dipped to his chest. "You were probably on the student council. Or a cheerleader." Something like dread hardened the last word, and it dropped into the space between them like a bag of wet sand.

Landon gaped at him. Never in a million years would she have been on track for what he described. "I was a half-developed, plain, ninth-grade student who was only popular as a target for the mean girls. Traffickers don't target the in-crowd. They want the kids who are marginalized. Exploitable."

Muddy red blotched his cheeks. "I didn't know."

"Count yourself privileged." Although everyone had wounds of one sort or another. She thought about his description. "You were talking about *her*, weren't you?"

"The one I called your evil twin." One finger tugged at the neck of his tee shirt. "What she did eviscerated me. If she hadn't been going for valedictorian, she'd have let the whole school in on the laugh. I can't face cheerleaders to this day. Even though she was one of a kind."

"Triggers are triggers. There's no logic in it." Only association and reaction. No wonder Landon's resemblance upset him so badly.

His lip curled. "I can't believe I'm complaining about my petty grievance to a person who's been through so much worse."

"Never minimize your pain, and never compare it to someone else's." Whether this went back to high school or university, he didn't sound like he was healing. "You never talked about it, did you?"

"Even a scrawny geek has enough pride to cover up his shredded heart."

He'd filled out physically and found success as a writer, but that heart was still dripping. "Bobby, no matter how much it hurt, if you let it go, she loses her power. She won't define you anymore."

"Easier said than done." He dropped his hand to the stick shift. "We need to go."

End of discussion. Okay. It wasn't her place to push.

She waited until he steered back onto the road. "So... no cheerleader here. No Miss Perfect Nightmare. Um... friends?"

"Friends."

"Then I'll admit your tiger pit line was funny."

A few minutes later, they reached the vet clinic, a long, white-sided building sharing space with a scuba shop and a health-food store.

After checking in at the reception desk, she found Bobby talking to Ciara, who held a purse-sized Chihuahua in her lap. Bobby gestured to the empty seat between them.

Landon sat, doing her best at a friendly smile.

"I didn't know you two were a couple." An undercurrent pulsed in that tone, one Landon had no desire to decode.

Nor did she want Ciara spreading gossip. "We're not."

Bobby leaned forward. "I drive the getaway car."

Ciara's brown eyes sparkled. "I've seen it. Let me know if you're looking for a passenger."

Her face lost some of its animation as she focused on Landon. "Isn't it customary to bring a pet?" A lightning glance at Bobby said she wanted to add a flirty comment but didn't dare.

He shuffled his feet as if he'd caught the message.

He was so quick with words, he'd probably have a snappy answer about her lack of animal companion. Claim it was invisible or something. The best Landon could do was put her hand to her mouth. "I knew I forgot something."

His snicker gave her courage, but she couldn't spin this any farther. "I've been feeding a stray cat at the inn, and he has a head injury. He's too wild to touch, but I'm hoping the vet can give me some advice."

"Dr. Alders is really good." She cupped the amber-and-white dog's chin. "Moxie's here for his s-h-o-t-s."

The animal shook batwing ears at her singsong tone, wide eyes rolling.

Bobby stood, holding his phone. "Sorry, I need to take this." He answered and walked outside.

"So. Rivals again." Ciara's words came out brisk, but bitterness seeped through.

Landon faced her. "What are you talking about?"

Ciara stared back, her full pink lips tight. "He's not really my type, but a girl can overlook a lot for a car like that—and the money behind it."

"He has a girlfriend back in Ontario."

"Which means she's not here. Game on."

Ciara's earlier words taunted her. "We were never rivals."

"Have you forgotten Zach?" Crooking a finger under the tiny dog's rainbow collar, Ciara slid her knuckle back and forth across his short fur. "I didn't need to be so nasty. He wasn't even worth it."

The other chatter in the room faded. "*That's* what junior high was about? You bullied me over a boy? A boy I didn't even like?"

None of the other pet owners were paying attention to them, although the chocolate lab in the corner eyed Ciara's lap ornament like a snack.

Landon gathered her hair into a ponytail and let it fall free. "Now would be a good time to tell you I forgive you. We can't change the past."

It wasn't a decision she'd reached easily, but it had been another step on the healing journey.

Ciara cradled the Chihuahua to her chest and pressed her face into the back of his neck. "It was just—" She peeked up, wide brown eyes haunted. "That's not why you ran away, though. Right?"

Landon swallowed the words she couldn't say. About not running away. Being taken. She couldn't lay all that blame on a self-centred fifteen-year-old. Honesty meant not denying it, either. She held the eye contact. "It was a contributing factor."

"But everything turned out okay." Her voice trailed up in a question. "Right?"

All the king's horses and all the king's men couldn't put Landon together again. She shook it off. The King of kings was remaking her as His child. "Everything will turn out okay, in the end."

Teal-glitter-painted fingertips mashed Ciara's lips. "I didn't know. I mean, I did it on purpose, but what does a kid really know about pain?"

Some kids knew. Corey, Quinn. Landon had known enough—before she learned more. Now, she nodded. "We're not who we were. While I'm here, we can try to start over."

Not that she'd be in a hurry to let Ciara too far into her life. Trust had to be earned.

Ciara exhaled a soft puff of air and cradled Moxie back into her lap. He swiped her hand with a tiny pink tongue. "Most of my friends are too busy with relationships. They don't want a single girl hanging around."

Anna was Landon's only friend here. Maybe Roy. Now Bobby too. "I haven't met many people my age since I've been back. Just Bobby. And Meaghan, who works for Anna."

Ciara leaned in, her shoulder butting Landon's. "At the potluck, Meaghan said she lost her other job, but she quit."

With Hart causing trouble with her boss, Meaghan may have been asked to resign. It amounted to the same as being fired. "How do you know?"

"They hired me to replace her." Ciara slid Moxie's sparkly leash through her fingers. "It's hard living up to her reputation. I still can't remember all the product details, and the owner has to arrange the displays himself."

This was new, a less-perfect side of Ciara. Maybe they had more in common than Landon thought. "How long have you been there?"

"About three months. It's not a long-term thing, anyway, but I'm used to being good at what I do."

Ciara had always excelled. That's why her words at school hurt so much. She didn't need to put Landon down to elevate herself. Landon's adolescent understanding had grasped that much—and believed it meant the words were true. Especially when her test scores agreed.

One side benefit to the counselling and support she'd received after being rescued was the diagnosis of her learning disability. Coaching and techniques had let her finish school and opened university to her as well. Something she'd never dreamed possible.

Tempting as it was to vindicate her younger self in her former tormentor's eyes, that might be better left unsaid. Instead, she asked, "What's your long-term plan?"

"It's... complicated."

A young man in pet-themed scrubs opened a side door and called Ciara's name. Clutching her dog, she sprang to her feet like she couldn't get away from the conversation fast enough. "Gotta go. Let's do coffee."

Landon rested her head against the wall behind her chair. She was used to being in the minority, age-wise, older than most of her classmates and younger than most of her support workers. Ciara was right. There weren't many women their age with time to build a relationship from scratch. Meaghan and Ciara might be her best hope for at least a surface friendship this summer.

The gender dynamic would keep friendship with Bobby on the surface too. She wouldn't have let herself get even that close, except he was safely committed.

He came back into the clinic and sank into the seat beside her. "Sorry. That was my agent, and I've ducked his calls the last two times."

The way his sandy hair stuck out like straw, he'd been mashing it again. "Are you the boss, or is he?"

"The publisher's the boss, and they want to bump up my book in the production schedule to fill a hole."

"The one you're behind on?"

"That's the next one. There's one in edits now, and they'll push it through faster." He sat forward and braced his palms on his baggy shorts, fingertips raised. "By the time I do what I need to do there, I'll be farther behind on this one—and they'll move that deadline up too."

The vet's assistant called another name. Most of the people here had arrived after they did. "It shouldn't be much longer. If you need to go, I can stay in town until Anna can come for me." Or ask Ciara to wait and drive her home.

"It won't make a difference. The scene I had this morning's done, and I'm stuck."

"What would Travers do?"

Bobby hunched forward, elbows on knees, hands dangling. "That's the problem. I don't know."

Ciara came back into the waiting room, cradling her dog. Moxie's eyes bulged even larger in his tiny head, and he whimpered. She stopped to pay, then walked toward them. "I have to get this poor boy home, but let's not be strangers. I'm at the Treasure Stop gift shop, next time either of you are in town."

Her gaze lingered on Bobby, now sitting up. Then she fluttered her manicure in a little wave and carried her pet to the door.

The vet assistant called Landon's name. Standing, she peered after Ciara. "You may have to bring Jessie for a visit to prove you're taken."

Bobby rolled his eyes. "Not when my deadline just imploded. I'll only surface now to eat and to chauffeur Gramp." He tipped his index finger toward her. "Or if you and Anna need me. Travers would insist."

Dr. Alders introduced herself as her gaze bounced between them. "Where is your pet?"

A slow-talking, gentle woman who could have been anywhere from thirty to fifty, she listened with a slight frown as Landon explained. "You understand I still need to bill you, even without examining the animal?"

When Landon nodded, the vet agreed to study the photos. She held the phone close to her face, her frown deepening. Then she returned it. "That laceration looks nasty. I'd like to clean it and assess the need for stitches. I can let you have our live trap."

"No cage." Landon heard the metallic click of a lock. She fought the memories, fixating on the vet's desk lamp. Light, not darkness. See the light. Breathe.

Dr. Alders said something, sharper-toned, but the words couldn't reach her.

A deeper rumble from Bobby.

Words, more words. Her heartbeat muffled them. They didn't matter.

Light. Air.

The light resolved into sun glinting off Bobby's car. Outside, in the parking lot.

Landon gasped another lungful of air. Bobby's eyes steadied her, blue-grey magnets stabilizing her in the here and now. Heat swarmed in her chest. This was the second time she'd freaked out in front of him.

Her hand ached—from clenching his.

She dropped it and stepped back. "I... thank you... I'm sorry... I..." She spun to stare at the blurred shapes of buildings across the street.

"It's okay. Let's drive."

She let him shepherd her into the car.

He'd have to get back to work. Or trying to work. She'd taken too much of his time and now embarrassed him by totally spacing out.

And the cat. No way could she face the vet again to help him. She'd have to ask Anna, leave it to someone else to clean up her mess.

She should never have come back.

The car reached the inn, but instead of slowing, Bobby blew past the driveway. "Watch the water," he said. "Feel the wind until the freedom gets inside of you."

He threw her a crooked smile. "It works for me. I'll take you home safe, but for now, let's drive."

Driving? It felt like flying, although a peek at the speedometer showed he wasn't much above the posted limit.

The two-lane road hugged the coastal curves, and they passed from ocean to trees and back again.

Eventually, Bobby spoke. "The vet said we could give him a couple more days. He may heal on his own." He slowed for a sharp turn. "If we have to capture him, I'll do it. He needs to associate you and Anna with safety."

"I..." Landon scooped her windblown hair into a ponytail, then let it fly free again. "Thank you." For the offer—and all he left unsaid.

They drove in silence with only the wind and the engine and the thrum of tires on pavement. It must have been an hour later when they looped back to the inn.

Landon felt grounded and somehow refreshed, and Bobby held the wheel in a more relaxed grip. Maybe he'd found some inspiration in the wind.

A thought hit her as she closed the car door. "The vet bill!"

"Handled. Don't worry about it."

"I'll pay you back."

"It's one thing I could do to help." His fingertips touched his brow in a mock salute.

She'd told him to notice the ways God helped others through him. No way could she refuse this. "Thank you. I'll pray for your deadline."

Finger-combing the worst of the tangles from her hair, she watched him drive away. Who knew speed therapy was a thing?

There was no sign of the stray cat, but Timkin yawned at her from his perch on the deck rail, furry stomach drooping over the sides. His black tail hung down, and he curled it lazily.

She stopped to rub between his ears.

Trapping the stray might be for the best, for his cut and his overall health. He could have picked up parasites or who knew what from living wild.

If she could afford it. Her student loans didn't leave much to live on, and it wasn't fair to ask Anna to pay for a cat she didn't want hanging around.

Especially when the pressures on the inn took Anna's full attention.

Landon let herself into the inn, praying the cat would heal on his own. And that the police would trace the drone owner before he attacked again.

Chapter 18

A blaring car alarm jolted Landon awake. Her feet hit the floor before her mind caught up. Guests. They had guests. She couldn't run downstairs in sleep shorts and a tank top.

She peered out the window. Security beams illuminated the yard, and beside Anna's sedan, the hulking SUV's lights pulsed with the alarm sound. Nothing moved.

She threw on yesterday's clothes.

At the top of the stairs, she met one of the guests, wild-eyed and rumpled. He waved a set of keys. "Sorry it woke you." He charged downstairs and took off out the front door before Landon reached the bottom step.

Her first thought had been vandals. But car alarms went off, usually for no reason. Here, it could have been a raccoon. Or even the stray. This place was making her paranoid.

Anna hurried along the hall, a brown terry bathrobe flapping at her calves. "What's wrong?"

"I didn't see anything. He's gone to shut it off."

Tight lines bracketed Anna's eyes. "I thought it was our drone again."

The door opened, and the man stomped in, swearing. He held up his hand, fingertips glistening red. "There's paint all over the cars."

Anna frowned. "I'll phone the police. I'm sure they'll be okay to come in the morning instead of ruining any more of your sleep."

He cursed again. "I need a hose to wash that mess off before it dries."

Landon hurried to the kitchen for a wet paper towel for his hands. When she came back, Anna was assuring him of a full refund for their stay.

Scowling, he scrubbed his fingers. "I can't believe my wife slept through this."

Landon reached for the soggy mass. "I'll help with the cars once the police see them."

"They'd better not waste time."

Anna relocked the deadbolt. "I'll phone it in right away, Mr. Sayers. Would you like coffee while we wait?"

After switching on the lights in the guests' common room, Landon left him pacing there. In the kitchen, she started the coffeemaker while Anna was on the phone. She pulled out a tray and was arranging muffins on a plate when Anna jammed the phone back into its cradle.

"This is two nights in a row I've called. Something has to give, and I think it's going to be me." Anna tugged at her robe's belt. "I'd better check the camera feed. And get dressed."

When she came back, she'd thrown on capris and a navy blouse and combed her hair. The drooping lines of her face radiated sadness. Despair. "Nothing. Whoever this is, he's smart enough to work around the cameras."

She braced her hands on the counter and stood staring out the window.

Timkin strolled into the kitchen and stared up at Anna, blinking. Landon rattled some dry food into his dish, but he ignored it and sat by the back door. "I'm assuming he stays in until the paint's dealt with?"

Anna dipped her head. "Let's not make this any worse."

Red paw-prints everywhere would not help.

"At least we'll only have two cars to clean. Ivan and Glenna chose a good night to be away." Landon curved an arm around Anna's shoulders, and she melted into the embrace, her hair tickling Landon's ear.

When the coffeemaker finished dripping, Landon poured a cup for their angry guest. Anna shook her head no, so she added a couple of water glasses to the tray. "Should I have made tea too?"

"It doesn't matter." Anna flicked off the light. "We might as well go wait together."

Stiff-backed in a chair in the common room, Landon crumbled a muffin and tuned out the man's complaints about property damage and vandals. His wife had come downstairs, and she curled, yawning, in the comfy brown club chair.

At last, headlights crept up the driveway. Anna rose. "No need for us all to go out. I'll ask the officer to step inside."

She left before Sayers could argue, probably to intercept whoever was on patrol tonight and ask them not to mention the other trouble if they could avoid it. She returned with Dylan, whose notebook was already out and in use.

He smiled at Landon but didn't slip out of professional mode. Instead, he interviewed the guests and tried to reassure them. "We've had no similar calls about vehicle vandalism, but you can be sure we'll keep our eyes open."

"I'll be on the phone to my insurance company first thing in the morning." Sayers glared at Anna. "Not that I'll be paying."

Anna's hands fluttered. "Of course not. I'm responsible, and it'll go through my insurance."

He sniffed. "I still want to see what'll wash off tonight. We have too many plans to wait around for a rental."

Dylan drew a thin flashlight from his pocket. "Give me a few minutes to examine the scene, and I should be able to release it." With a crisp nod, he left.

Sayers banged his coffee mug back onto the tray. "Should be able to. He'd better."

Landon focused on curling and straightening her toes, praying for peace to rule. The man's anger was justified, but he was making her tense. If he started yelling, she'd lose it again. Be no help to Anna and make things worse.

Anna caught her eye. "Would you please check Meaghan's cupboard? We should have plenty of rags. The hose is already hooked up."

Landon could have hugged her. "Sure."

She fled, whispering the Scripture verses that sometimes grounded her.

Armed with what she could scavenge, she filled one bucket at the sink and dropped in the rags. A squirt of yellow detergent pooled in the other, ready for hot water when Dylan gave the okay.

She lingered in the kitchen until the front door opened and Dylan's voice drifted her way. As she walked back to the group, he gave the all-clear to start cleanup.

To the other man's grumbled response, he added, "The security lights and cameras kept the vandal from approaching the vehicles. Debris at the site suggests he used a paintball gun, with the far side of the barn for cover."

He focused on Anna. "May I take a copy of your footage? Then I'll leave you to the car wash."

Anna sent Landon to help him with the files. Dylan followed as if he didn't know the way.

When he settled in front of Anna's desktop, he scrolled through the footage. "Nope, he's out of range. I'd hoped this wouldn't escalate to affect any guests before we wrapped it up."

Standing beside the desk, Landon shifted her weight from foot to foot. "What are we going to do? Anna's at her limit, and I'm no help."

His fingers paused on the keyboard. "You're moral support. That's huge. You do that job, and we'll do ours." He swivelled the chair, tipping his head to make eye contact. "Don't let him get to you."

A few more keystrokes, and he closed the program. "I've uploaded a copy, but it's not likely we'll find anything Anna missed."

He stood. "We'll be in touch. I'll say goodbye to Anna." His dark brown eyes locked her gaze. "Your guest is understandably angry, but if he gets belligerent, call in a domestic disturbance. You two are under enough pressure already. I'll stick close for the next little while unless I get another call."

The kindness warmed her, even though shame whispered the concern was more about her emotional instability than Anna's situation.

No matter the reason, she appreciated the care. "Thank you."

Chapter 19

Friday

GRITTY-EYED, LANDON kept a careful grip on the serving tray—and on her words—as she served breakfast. The guests couldn't be any better rested than she was, but they'd rejected Anna's offer of a delayed breakfast time because of a prebooked whale-watching tour. "As if we'll be able to keep our eyes open and see anything," the man muttered.

A daylight inspection showed red paint caught in a few seams around the windows and lights. The vandal must have hit Anna's car first. He'd only scored a few hits on the SUV before the alarm blared.

Mr. Sayers had already informed Anna that his insurance company would be calling her and that he and his wife had no intention of taking a second free night, even at a later date.

A fresh, scathing review would likely appear before the end of the day. Legitimate, this time.

He peered at her through sleep-heavy lids. "I checked with the police this morning, and there were no related incidents overnight. This was targeted."

Landon concentrated on refilling their coffee cups. "Two cars were enough. I'm glad the neighbours escaped damage."

Anna's car was hit worse, but that didn't seem to matter. Nor did the fact that they'd helped clean his before doing hers alone.

"If you've got vandals, you shouldn't take guests." His wife might have been complaining about mice or bedbugs.

Landon escaped to the kitchen as quickly as possible.

Grey pouches pillowed Anna's eyes. Her fingertips screened a yawn. "I've texted Meaghan to let herself in. The minute our guests go, we can crash."

"What about Ivan and Glenna?"

Anna rubbed her forehead with the back of her hand. "I don't think we'll see them until later today, but they have a key."

Landon poured coffee for herself and sank into a chair.

Anna frowned. "Not going to nap?"

"This is to get me through the next half hour."

She stared into the dark liquid and let her eyes lose focus. After a few minutes, she gulped half her drink. Smile in place, she went back to the breakfast room.

The couple's plates were empty. He tapped his fork against his water glass. "Forget about us?"

Not a chance. "I'm sorry." She made eye contact with him, then with his wife, mentally speaking grace and patience. "Can I get you anything else?"

"Just tell Anna we're ready to check out."

She collected a few plates and utensils but didn't try to balance a fancy stack. "She'll be right with you."

While Anna handled the final insurance details, Landon loaded the dishwasher and then downed the last of her coffee. It'd get her through a few more minutes. Half an hour was pushing it.

As soon as she finished resetting the breakfast room, she retreated upstairs. Sleep came fast, and she woke rumpled and sweaty with a sense of coming doom. A dull ache behind her eyes didn't ease when she showered.

She met Meaghan on the landing, dragging a vacuum from the newly vacated room. Landon hadn't heard a thing.

Meaghan tucked her braid behind her back. "What happened? Anna's text didn't say much."

When Landon told her, she scowled. "They didn't have to be so rude about it."

"No, but no wonder they're angry. Whoever's doing this to Anna has to be stopped."

Puffing out her cheeks, Meaghan released a slow, whistling breath. "Maybe she should sell. Before it gets worse. She needs to think of her mental health."

Anna wasn't the type to run away. But she was near the breaking point. Landon clenched her nails into her palms. "It's not right."

"No, it isn't. I'm afraid for her."

The turmoil in Meaghan's blue eyes mirrored the storm in Landon's heart. And there was nothing either of them could do.

~~~

Anna didn't surface until lunchtime, and after one glimpse of her heavy-lidded eyes and drawn face, Landon tried to shoo her back to bed.

Anna's lips firmed. "I need groceries. For now, let me power through. I'll lie down again later."

"Then I'll come with you. Two tired brains are better than one."

Armed with the list Anna had made the night before, they were back at the inn in an hour.

The McNutts' grey sedan arrived as they hoisted the last bags from the car. Anna closed the trunk. "I'd rather they didn't know about last night."

"What if he comes back? Shouldn't we warn them?"

"When has he done the same thing twice?" Anna edged closer to Landon. "Ivan's a challenge, but it's income. I don't want to scare them away."
~~~

She waited for the McNutts to join them. "How was your trip?"

A smile filled Glenna's round face. "We had a lovely visit. Ivan's Uncle Ralph is a hoot. He invited us to stay the night, then kept us up late playing cards."

Ivan had an overnight bag in each hand, and he swung them in time with each step. "He asked us to stay longer, but we didn't want to tire him. He's not as young as he thinks he is. Plus, Uncle Sandy's taking us out in his boat this afternoon."

As Anna led the way to the front door, keys jingling, Landon matched Ivan's pace. "If you find the tunnel entrance, would you tell me before you say anything to Anna? You know how she feels about it."

"Has something else happened?"

"No more surprises on the doorstep, but whoever left the bag is still making his presence known." Grocery bags weighting her arms, Landon hitched her shoulder to keep her purse strap from sliding off. "She's pretty stressed about it."

If the paint-bomber gave a repeat tonight, she'd feel terrible about not warning them, but this was Anna's decision as the inn's owner.

Anna unlocked the front door and hustled through to the rear of the building.

Ivan held the door for Landon. "Do you want to come on the boat? Sandy says there's lots of room. Glenna's not sure what she'll do."

"Depends on the size of the waves." Glenna's eyes twinkled. "I'll at least go with you to the dock. If I'm not up for it, I'll come back and pick you up when you're done."

"You know who you should take? Nigel Foley. If there's anything to see, he'll spot it."

Ivan bit his thumbnail. "He doesn't like me asking about Jack. I don't think he'd help."

Odd, where Nigel was so curious about Jack and his potential secrets. "He might do it for Anna's sake."

"He's hard to track down, and there's no time." Ivan paused with one foot on the stairs. "We need to leave in an hour. If you want to come, Uncle Sandy said to wear nonslip shoes and bring a jacket."

He started upstairs, Glenna behind him. Landon carried the remaining groceries to the kitchen.

Anna's reusable bags were folded on the table, ready to go back in the car. She stood in front of the window, a letter in one hand, with her other arm clutched across her stomach like a shield. A small pile of envelopes and flyers lay beside her on the counter.

Landon dropped her load on the table. "What is it?"

Anna's fingers bunched the thin fabric of her blouse. "A warning. But it doesn't say much."

She faced the paper toward Landon.

Someone close to you is not what they seem.

Landon reached for it, then pulled back. "One set of extra fingerprints on it is enough." The way Anna's mouth tightened made her pause. "You are going to report this, right? It means someone knows something."

"What are they going to do? Fingerprint the whole county?"

Crossing her arms, Landon stuck out her hip. "What would Dylan say if he found out you didn't tell him? Or Constable Ingerson, for that matter?"

Anna's huff ruffled her bangs. "All right." She laid the letter facedown on the counter. "I'll phone in a minute."

Landon put away the rest of the groceries. *Someone close to you is not what they seem.* "There was no return address, I assume. What about the postmark?"

"Lunenburg."

No surprise. "And you don't recognize the handwriting?"

"No. I'd guess female. And old enough they still taught cursive writing when she was in school. It's odd she didn't type it."

"Do you know anyone who wouldn't use a printer? Maybe that's a clue."

"Even Nigel uses a printer. He won't use a phone, and I'm not sure what his stance is on the internet these days. But he'd use a printer. Probably wired to his computer so the aliens couldn't intercept it."

Anna's tone held only acceptance. Nigel was who Nigel was, like Landon was who Landon was. The world needed more Annas.

Nigel had suspected aliens were behind the last round of Anna's troubles, and he'd seemed serious in considering the stray cat could be a manifestation of Captain Hiltz. Still, he noticed things. He might be key to tracking that drone or finding the tunnel on land or sea.

He appeared at the strangest times. If he showed up in the next few minutes, she'd ask him to consider the boat trip.

If not, should she go herself? An afternoon with Ivan in hunting mode would be a challenge, but it'd be fun to get out on a boat. And to escape the inn stress for a while.

A chime rang from Anna's purse.

Landon grinned. "That's a reminder to phone the police."

Anna retrieved her cell and tapped at the screen, then squeezed her eyes shut as if reaching for deeper strength. "I forgot Gord invited me out to dinner tonight."

"Don't sound so excited."

Anna tipped her fingers toward her face. "Would you want to see this while you ate?"

"I had expected to. Not that I'm any better." Landon squashed her unease about Gord. Anna trusted the man, and that had to count for more than the vague suspicions raised by Elva's reaction. "A few hours' sleep, some extra makeup, and you'll be good to go. If you feel like it. Once he hears about last night, he'll understand if you need to cancel, but a change of pace might help."

"I should at least try." A yawn broke free. "A nap does sound good. I'll phone about the letter first, and by the time they send someone, maybe I'll have slept enough."

"I'll talk to them. It was in with the regular mail. What else do I need to know? Oh. When did you pick up mail last?"

Anna checked the wall calendar. "Wednesday."

"There. Handled."

After Anna left, Landon slid a fork from the drawer and flipped the paper face-up, then snapped a photo with her phone. She turned it over again and dropped the fork into the dishwasher.

If she showed the picture to Anna's friends, might one of them recognize the handwriting? Might the writer give herself away by her reaction?

Nobody local would have written anything Anna would have kept. Except—Landon gasped.

Sympathy cards. Nearly everyone would drop a sympathy card in the basket at a funeral, and it sounded like the church had been packed after Murdoch died.

Anna would have saved them.

Landon took a quick step toward Anna's rooms before remembering Anna was asleep. She wandered into the guests' common room and tried to fit a few more pieces into the lighthouse puzzle while she waited for the McNutts to come back downstairs.

When their footsteps thumped on the stairs, she went out to meet them.

Ivan indicated her light sandals. "Not coming?"

"Thanks, but I'd better not. Anna's lying down, and I should be here if she needs anything. Good luck, though. And enjoy."

His eyes glinted. "I'll let you know what we find."

Chapter 20

LANDON WAS STANDING on the deck folding her laundry from the clothesline when the back door opened. She tucked a pair of socks together and dropped them into the basket as she turned.

Anna's chin-length bob looked freshly washed and dried, and her eyes weren't quite as sunken as they'd been. She'd chosen a flowing peach top in some sort of crepe fabric and crisp capris. The usual Anna sparkle was still missing, but between the Lyme Disease, antibiotics, and stress, no wonder.

She eyed the white plastic basket of clothes. "You should be taking it easy after last night."

Landon had spent most of the time sprawled in a deck chair, feet up on another, listening to a lighthearted audiobook on her phone. "I hoped the stray might show up." Hoped he wasn't curled up somewhere, in pain and getting worse.

At least the drone hadn't come back. Her plan was to video it with her phone if it did. If the first whir of its propellers didn't send her diving for the door.

"Is Gord picking you up, or are you meeting there?"

"He'll be here in about fifteen minutes."

"Constable Ingerson came for the letter. She didn't have any updates for us. But I had an idea—before you go, could you find the sympathy cards from Murdoch's funeral?"

The pinching around Anna's eyes made her falter. "May I go through them, or is it too personal? We might find a match for our letter-writer."

Anna's lips trembled, then firmed. "I haven't been brave enough to read them again. I'll go get the box."

Landon reeled in the few last articles of clothing and folded them quickly before following Anna into the house. As she opened the door, Timkin brushed past her ankles from behind. Facing her, he planted himself at the kitchen entrance, head and tail high, and mewed.

Checking the time now made her notice her own hunger. The cat usually came begging earlier than this. "I'll feed you in a minute. You'd better not have been eating the other guy's food out there."

She walked into the sitting room. Away from the kitchen. Timkin followed, complaining.

Anna indicated a clear plastic tote filled with paper, resting on the coffee table. "Take time to read what people wrote." Her eyes welled. "There are some precious tributes."

"I wish I'd been there." She'd been afraid of what coming back might do to her hard-won healing, and Anna had been surrounded by family and friends.

"You're here now, and I'll enjoy it while it lasts." Anna gave her a quick hug and slid her purse strap onto her shoulder. "Gord will arrive any minute."

"What's the occasion?"

Sadness lingered in her smile. "My friends have been so good, especially while I was here by myself, making sure I get out regularly. Sometimes it's one-on-one, and sometimes it's a group like the potluck to welcome the new neighbours. Speaking of whom, I should drop off some muffins or something on the weekend and see how they're settling in."

The back door opened. "Anna?" Gord's low call sounded like he wondered which room she was in. Not like Meaghan's boyfriend, Hart, who would have hollered and expected her to appear.

After they left, Landon fed Timkin in the kitchen and retrieved the stray's dish from outside. That food hadn't been touched, except by the flies she shooed away. She replaced it with a fresh serving.

The shirt she'd put down to familiarize the cat with her scent was matted and smeared with food stains and looked too far gone for even the bravest laundry detergent commercial. No way it still carried her scent. She'd have to sacrifice another one.

She lingered by the barn, watching the forest. "Come on, mister, where are you?"

When she went inside, Timkin trotted out. "Don't mess with our guest." Oddly, he hadn't seemed to, despite his territorial attitude toward any spot Landon had seen him place a paw.

After a quick meal, she plunked down on Anna's couch and drew the plastic container nearer. Reading the first one made her cry. She allowed a few minutes of sadness out of respect for Murdoch, then wiped her eyes and found a bit of distance. No more reading the messages. Not tonight. Handwriting was harder for her than typed print, anyway, and as much as Murdoch deserved her to spend time honouring his memory, he'd understand she was on a mission.

She studied each card's writing, then laid it aside. A few were close to the image on her phone, so she placed them in a separate pile.

A knock at the back door made her jump. Nigel, too late to send on the boat?

When she entered the hallway, Bobby beckoned through the window in the door. Landon stepped outside, darting a quick check skyward and tree-ward.

He chuckled. "I did the same thing. How's the patient?"

"I haven't seen him." Admitting it brought back her anxiety.

"He's pretty random, though, isn't he, about when he comes? I haven't seen him at Gramp's today, but I often don't." He backtracked to the stairs. "Has he touched his food?"

"Not earlier."

"Let's see."

He'd sympathized about the cat's wound, but he hadn't seemed worried. Landon caught up with him. "What about your deadline? Is this some sort of avoidance behaviour?"

He gave her the eyes-narrowed, lips-flat, chin-stroking look that conjured images of a cartoon villain plotting victory. "Maybe." Then he sobered. "Actually, I wanted to talk to you. Away from Anna." His gaze flicked toward the house.

"Anna's out for supper." Landon peeked behind the barn at the cat's dish. Still full. Where was he? She headed for the deck. "What's up? Did you think of a way to stop all this?"

"I wish. But there may be more going on than we thought."

"Great." Not. Unless it gave them a clue to who was behind it all.

They sat at the outdoor table. Bobby leaned in, forearms on the tinted glass top. "So here's the thing. My deadline's messing with my head, so I started playing around with a few complications that might jump-start the plot."

He flattened his hands on the table, palms down, fingertips drumming. "What if Anna's being poisoned?"

Where had that come from? "Anna's on medication, and we think it's helping. Her doctor identified the problem—it's treatable—but she doesn't want to tell anyone. I really had to pressure her to tell her kids."

Bobby sat for a minute, fingertips still tapping. "That's a relief." His eyes narrowed again. "I still think we should check for poison. A friend of mine can run some tests. All he needs is a few strands of hair from her brush."

"But the doctor said—" Anna's secret wasn't hers to share.

"And you said you *thought* the medicine was working." Bobby leaned nearer, holding her gaze. "You'd do anything for Anna. Why not this one little thing? We know someone's acting against her and has been at least since June."

A chill swept Landon's arms. She rubbed her hands up and down them until the friction erased her goosebumps. "This is crazy."

"So's what's happening. It would have to be a slow-acting poison, and the person would need regular access. Perhaps one of Anna's friends isn't what she thinks."

The letter. Landon gasped and covered her mouth with both hands.

"What is it?"

She brought up the picture on her phone and handed the device across the table.

Eyebrows pinching, he read it aloud, each syllable heavy. "Where did this come from?"

"With the mail Anna picked up today. The police have the original. Local postmark, but she doesn't recognize the handwriting. I was going through the cards about Murdoch to see if I could find a match."

"Brilliant." He passed the phone back to her. "Any luck?"

"Not so far. But at least someone knows something."

"Or it's the person causing the trouble planting more."

"Thanks for that."

"Well, it could be. If she starts mistrusting her friends, it's harder for us to help her."

"Either way, if we find out who wrote the letter, it's someone to ask." Landon scuffed her feet under the table. "Come with me if I find a match?"

"If you find something, let the police handle it."

"Says the guy who wants to sneak a hair sample and test for poison."

"That's different. They'd think I'm nuts." He slapped his chest, rippling the sunburst on his tee shirt. "*I* think I'm nuts. But the idea's stuck in my head. If the letter's legit and someone close to Anna's up to no good, it could well be poison."

His hands roamed through his hair, leaving sandy tufts like a bad mowing job. "Please. It costs us nothing, and if my buddy finds something, then we have a clue the police can take seriously."

At least he hadn't suggested this to Anna. She didn't need paranoia on top of everything else. "Okay, but we'd better be quick. I don't know when she'll be back."

He drew a clear plastic bag from his pocket and offered it to her. "Let's go."

Nothing like being prepared. She kept a wry grin from her face. No point making him think she was mocking him.

Holding her breath, she crept into Anna's bedroom while Bobby hovered in the doorway. This felt wrong. Like a violation of Anna's personal space.

A green-handled hairbrush lay on the dark-stained bureau, near an eight-by-ten framed photo of Murdoch. Careful not to touch anything else, Landon picked up Anna's comb and drew it through the brush bristles. She dropped a few hairs into the plastic bag and repeated the motions.

She replaced the comb and shifted the brush a tiny bit. As she backed away, she studied the layout. Was it right? What if Anna noticed?

This was crazy. Anna wouldn't organize her bureau with pinpoint precision. And she was tidy enough there were no dust outlines to worry about.

From the doorway, Bobby hissed, "I hear a car."

She streaked across the room and thrust the bag at him, then closed the door as quietly as she could. As he sealed the bag and stuffed it into his pocket, Landon threw herself onto the couch. "We'll never make it out of the room. Sit and help me with the cards."

"She won't mind me reading them? They're personal."

"She'll mind it less than you having a sample of her hair in your pocket."

Landon showed him the reject pile and the separate group she wasn't sure of. She opened the photo on her phone and laid it on the seat cushion between them.

They each grabbed a card from the container. "It's easier not to read them. Just look at the shape of the letters."

"That's my story if she's mad. Not reading, just looking."

Three cards later, Landon's heart rate was almost back to normal. "You're sure you heard a car?"

"I thought I did. Fine burglar I'd make."

The front door opened. "It's Ivan and Glenna. I want to hear how it went. His uncle took them out in his boat to search for a sea entrance to the tunnel."

He gave a low whistle. "I'm sure Anna was thrilled."

"That's why I want the scoop before she's back. Come on."

The couple stopped at the bottom of the stairs as Landon and Bobby approached. Glenna spread her arms wide. "I decided to go on the boat after all. It was fantastic."

Landon introduced Bobby as a neighbour and ignored the speculative twinkle in Glenna's eye.

Ivan's face had seen too much sun today. He stuck out his hand. "You're Roy's grandson? Missed you when we visited."

Bobby shook his hand. "Good to meet you."

Inside, Landon felt like a child jumping up and down in anticipation. "Did you find it?"

"No." The corners of Ivan's mouth lapsed into that air of vague disappointment he often wore. "Uncle Sandy couldn't get as close as he wanted. We spotted a few cracks that might widen out inside, but you'd need a smaller boat and the tide just right. He said he'd take us back, but he's not hopeful."

Glenna swatted his arm with her sun hat. "Take *you* back. I'm not getting into a rowboat and smashing against those rocks."

He started up the stairs. "Truth told, I'm not crazy about squeezing into a crack and getting stuck. As amusing a photo as it'd make for the local papers."

Landon slid her fingers into the back pockets of her shorts, elbows wide. No secret access to the inn was a relief—nothing for Anna's enemy to find. But on the other hand, they still lacked a way into the tunnel to bring out whatever this enemy might be after.

They needed some type of progress. Tonight, she should have searched the basement while Anna was out. The cards could have waited. She'd poked around when she went down to do laundry, but with Anna napping, she hadn't risked knocking on walls or any of the things they did on-screen to hunt for secret passages.

"Well, I'm glad it was a fun afternoon, even though the search came up empty." She smiled at them both. "The fresh air will help you sleep well tonight." Assuming the mad paint-ball artist didn't return.

The McNutts headed upstairs, Glenna saying she might be back to make some herbal tea.

Landon hissed under her breath. So much for thinking Bobby could stand guard and she could hunt downstairs. She started back down the hall to the sitting room. "I can finish the cards on my own. You probably want to get back to your writing."

"Sometimes the best way to catch a good idea is to let it sneak up on you. I seeded a few things into my imagination today, and I need to see what sprouts. Tomorrow's time enough. After an early-morning run to courier a package to my friend."

Side by side on the couch, they tackled the rest of the cards in the box. A few more landed in the Maybe pile, but most were rejects.

Landon opened the next one and froze. "This is it."

She angled it for Bobby to see while focusing on the signature. "Elva Knapp. Anna's neighbour. It has to be. There can't be more than one Elva here."

"May I?" Bobby took the card and studied the writing. "Gramp could tell you for sure. She sent him a letter about my 'reckless driving.' "

"You're not serious." Elva had complained to Landon and Anna about it, with no basis in fact, but to send a letter?

"Yup. He wouldn't have kept it, though."

"What did he do?"

"I think he phoned her and promised he'd keep me in line." He chuckled. "Of course, this is a man who's been chased by dogs, bulls, and squirrels, so his idea of 'keeping in line' might not match hers."

Landon placed the cards back in the box with Elva's on top. "Elva doesn't want an inn here, but I really don't think she'd do this to Anna."

He shifted sideways, tucking one foot in the crook of his knee. "She seems more of a complainer than the sort to launch an attack. Even though it could be a woman behind the drone. All she'd need is a voice changer."

"So you agree it's a genuine warning?"

"I think so, but show the card to the police. They'll know how to talk to her."

"Dylan might be able to charm her, but Constable Ingerson's too direct." Landon pressed her palm into the couch's pastel floral upholstery and rubbed against the grain, the brushy fabric rough against her skin. "Elva reached out to Anna. I think Anna's the one she'll open up to."

"Ingerson's the one who told you off about the posters, isn't she?"

Technically, the issue had been Landon and Anna putting up posters asking for information without first asking for the investigators' approval. The posters generated a tip about a man trying to recruit troublemakers, which eventually led—they thought—to Hart and Quinn.

Ingerson didn't want civilians interfering with professionals. Landon respected that, but still... "Can you see Elva responding well to that kind of approach?"

"I can see Constable Ingerson giving you another earful. Let them handle it."

This time, Landon heard the car outside too. "Here's Anna, now."

Bobby rose to his feet. "I'd better head back. Let me know what you two decide to do."

She walked outside with him and scanned the tree line. No sign of the cat.

Bobby trotted down the stairs and stopped briefly to chat with Anna before heading toward the path to Roy's place. He waved to Gord as he passed the car.

Anna hurried up the stairs, her smile as tightly in place as if she'd glued it there. "I didn't expect to be so long. We took a drive, and Gord wanted to talk."

If he tried anything—

Panic flared in Landon's chest, but Anna looked stressed, not like she'd been in a fight.

"You're not upset about Bobby being here, are you? He was helping with the cards."

Anna flapped both hands in a shooing motion. "Certainly not. I felt bad thinking you were here alone and bored."

Landon stopped with her hand on the door latch. "Then what's wrong?"

"Let's go inside." Heels clacking, Anna strode into the kitchen. "Chamomile tea. Do you want some?"

"No thanks."

Foot hooked on the rung of her chair, Landon watched Anna's jerky motions as she filled the kettle and dug out a huge striped mug and a tea bag.

Finally, Anna carried her steaming drink and perched on the chair across from Landon. Elbows anchored on the tabletop, she released a body-shaking sigh. "Nothing's wrong, just—unexpected."

Her brown eyes wide and unfocused, she repositioned the mug, then slid it back to where it started. "Gord proposed."

Landon's mouth opened. She caught her jaw before it dropped.

Proposed. Marriage. "Wow."

Anna began nodding gently, more a rocking motion than anything else. With a little sigh, she raised her eyes. "He'd picked a nicer restaurant than my friends usually choose, but he can afford it. Over in Mahone Bay. I thought he'd found out tomorrow's Murdoch's birthday and wanted to distract me."

She lifted the striped mug and blew on the steaming surface of her tea, then put it down untasted. "He distracted me, all right."

Tears shone in her eyes, and she blinked hard. "I didn't know what to say. It came out of nowhere."

"Tell me." Landon reached across the glossy pine surface and squeezed her hand. "It'll help you process."

"We had this lovely meal, and over dessert, he said with his health improving, he's thinking about the future. Good, I thought. He's taking a new job. Retirement bores him."

She took a slow breath. "Then he asked me to marry him. Soon, because we're not getting any younger."

Landon bit her cheek to stop a smile. "Well, not everyone's a romantic. He's kind, though. We see how good he is to Meaghan."

"Oh, he is. He's a fine man. Just not for me."

Given the amount of time he spent here and his repeated offers to help, he obviously cared for Anna. "Anna... is he in love with you, or is this his way of looking after you?"

Anna rotated her mug by the handle until she'd made a full circle. "A little of both, I think. He said he knows it's too soon for me to have feelings for him, that I'm still grieving, but we're fond of each other and the fondness would deepen over time. Whether we lived here or at his place, I could keep the inn, and I wouldn't have to carry all this alone."

"The businessman in him presents a good case."

"Oh, he presented eloquently. And at length. Every time I said no." She tried a sip of tea. "He even said he'd go to church with me."

Anna and Murdoch had shared such a close spiritual bond. If she found another man, he might be completely different, but being a committed Christian would be nonnegotiable. Faith wasn't part of Gord's life. No way could he understand it went deeper than Sunday mornings.

And Anna wouldn't want to make him feel she was judging him, so she couldn't give him the one reason he couldn't argue around.

Her fingernails clicked against the sides of her mug. "Driving home, he kept floating ideas about how it could work. I got rattled, and I—" Her chest heaved, and she met Landon's eyes. "I told him, when the boys finish with the barn, I'm going to renovate it. Add more guest rooms. And a suite for you."

This time Landon couldn't keep the shock from her face. Anna knew she was flying home next month.

Pink tinged Anna's cheeks. "He kept going on about me being alone. I needed something to stop him before I lost it and hurt his feelings."

Only Anna would be concerned about his feelings by that point. This went way past any definition of polite boundaries. "So if he asks, you want me to pretend I'm staying?"

"I'm not asking you to lie. I just wanted you to hear it from me in case he brought it up."

Her brows lowered, and a mulish set stamped her lips. "I *will* do the renovations. And show whoever's tormenting me that he can't kill Murdoch's dream."

"Anna..." Landon prayed for the right words. "This is wearing you out. Murdoch wouldn't want you carrying all this opposition. It stinks to let this guy win, but maybe you should sell. Let someone else run the inn. Move out West and enjoy your grandchildren."

Anna's eyes brimmed, and tears slid down her cheeks. "Don't make it harder. Please."

"I'm sorry... I—"

Landon reached for her, but Anna fled the room.

With a groan torn from the depths of her soul, Landon pillowed her head on her forearms. "God, I know You've got this, but she can't take much more."

Chapter 21

Saturday

LANDON WOKE FROM a dream about a tunnel full of crates, with gold coins scattered on the floor like pirate treasure.

Daylight streamed around the edges of the window blind. She cancelled her alarm and sat up in bed, yawning.

Anna's enemy might be the only one who knew what Captain Hiltz's tunnel held, if even he knew. But if Anna wouldn't leave the inn, Landon had to stop him. Finding the tunnel—and exposing what he hoped to gain—was her best shot.

As soon as Ivan and Glenna left the inn today, she was taking Anna's big flashlight and searching every corner in the basement. With or without Anna's blessing.

The thought of upsetting Anna lodged a weight in her chest. Especially on Murdoch's birthday. But they couldn't sit helplessly and wonder what would happen next.

When she reached the kitchen, Anna flashed a strained smile. "I'm sorry I overreacted last night." She slid her hands into oven mitts and pulled a tray of muffins from the oven. "I do intend to stay, but I know you weren't trying to pressure me."

Landon waited until Anna set down the muffins, then hugged her.

Anna held the embrace an extra moment as if sealing any cracks in their friendship. "Your presence here in this mess means more than I can say."

"I haven't been able to do anything."

"Moral support means a lot. With this faceless enemy and difficult guests... and decompressing after out-of-the-blue proposals." She swept her bangs away from her forehead.

"Was Gord hurt?"

"A little. Mostly, I think he couldn't understand why I wouldn't agree. He kept trying to solve my objections."

"Proposing right before Murdoch's birthday wasn't smart."

"He couldn't have known, or he'd have chosen another time."

"Do you think we'll see less of him now?"

Transferring the muffins to a cooling rack, Anna shrugged. "I don't know. And I don't know what I'll do if he keeps trying to convince me."

The muffins' warm scent had Landon's mouth watering. "What kind did you bake?"

"Cranberry-orange. Murdoch's favourite." Her chin wobbled, then firmed. "Today, I want to honour his birthday with positive memories and be happy for what we had. Not sad for what I've lost."

"Good for you." And if a few tears sneaked in, too, that would be okay.

Landon was sampling a muffin when the guests' voices carried from the stairs. The sound moved into the breakfast room. A chair scraped the floor, and cutlery clinked. She lowered her voice. "Do you know how much longer they're staying?"

"No. Most people only stay one or two nights. They must be getting tired of my menu options by now."

Anna smoothed her sailboat-print apron and picked up the coffee pot. "I'll start them off."

When Landon served their breakfast, she noticed Ivan's sunburn extended to the patch of thinning hair on top of his head. Today's overcast sky could be a good thing.

Despite yesterday's failed search, he had the same uncomfortably-determined cast to his mouth and a hint of a frown around his eyes. "I didn't say anything to Anna about not finding the tunnel. It's disappointing, but maybe it's for the best."

"I'm glad you tried." She topped up their water from the pitcher on the sideboard. "What's on for today?"

Ivan flexed one hand into a fist, then spread his fingers wide. "I haven't found anyone to speak out against the captain. Small-town mentality—hide the shame instead of fight for justice."

It was too late for justice, with Captain Hiltz dead, but breaking the bondage of silence, finding vindication and support, did sound like a positive idea.

Ivan was still talking. "I've decided to show my mother's letter to the owner of that pub." He practically spat the final words. "It's the only evidence I have. If I'm not willing to bear exposing my own situation, I have no right to ask anyone else to do the same."

He sliced off a strip of fried egg and popped it in his mouth. After a quick chew and swallow, he sniffed. "I won't enter that establishment again under that name, but Ms. Carstens said she'd meet us here this morning."

So much for the hope they'd go out quickly so she could search the basement.

Back in the kitchen, she warned Anna Jaclyn would be coming. "It's a lot to ask, to change a business name, but I can see Ivan's point."

Anna finished drying the muffin tin she was holding. "People are probably so used to it, they don't even think—those who know that side of his character. Although now that I know, I'm not comfortable keeping the painting of his ship in the common room. Not with the name he gave it."

"Maybe the museum will want it." Sticking it in the uninsulated barn with Maria's other belongings would ruin it. The thought sparked another question. "If you convert the barn into more guest space, what happens to Maria's things?"

"We committed to keep them until she dies, so I'll have to put them in storage."

"For her son who's not coming back."

"Even if he's still alive and decides to come back, there's nothing of any great value."

"Except the note in the box." Landon took a quick breath. "If the tunnel is what your enemy is after, we have to find it first."

Anna frowned toward the white swinging doors to the breakfast room and put a finger to her lips. In the brief silence, the tones of the McNutts' conversation continued unchanged.

Landon stepped nearer to Anna and spoke just above a whisper. "When they leave, I want to search downstairs."

She held up her hands against the argument she read in Anna's face. "Maria left something valuable for David. If that's what this guy is after, the only way to protect it for her is to find it before he does. It may be the only way to protect you too."

~~~

When Jaclyn arrived midmorning, Landon jogged upstairs to knock on the guests' door.

The vivacious pub owner had never been high on her suspect list, but that could be a mistake. Unless they closed the common room door, some of the conversation might carry. Jaclyn's response should give insight into her character, at least. How determined was she to have her way?

Ivan lingered in the doorway and beckoned to Landon. "Come and join us."
~~~

She slipped into the room and took one of the straight-backed wooden chairs by the puzzle table.

Anna sat beside Jaclyn, presumably as a stabilizing neutral party. Glenna had left a seat between herself and the pub owner, but instead of taking it, Ivan chose the leather club chair beside the bookcase. Highlighting the conflict between them, or wanting a clear view of her reaction?

He clutched the folded letter in his lap. "Ms. Carstens, I do appreciate you agreeing to talk to me again." Colour seeped into his cheeks, and he hooked a finger into his collar. "I embarrassed us both last time."

Jaclyn's pale-gold eyebrows tipped upward, and her lips twitched.

He jerked to his feet and crossed the few paces between them, the letter extended like a knife. Jaclyn pinched it between her fingers. Once he sat back down, she brushed the folded pages against the fingers of her other hand. "What you've said puts me in an awkward place. I can't ignore it, but I can't believe everything I hear, either. Thank you for trusting me with your mother's private story."

Ivan gave a stiff nod. His toes tapped, one foot at a time, bobbing his knees in a rapid bounce as she unfolded the paper.

As she read, Jaclyn's expression hardened. The intensity in her blue eyes, the grim set to her mouth, and the straight line of her blond brows projected a Viking warrior, fierce and strong.

The back of Landon's neck prickled. Before today, she'd only seen Jaclyn's clear-eyed openness and full-lipped smile. But this side of her... this side would have no trouble taking the inn.

Landon gave her head a mental shake. Assessing for motive was one thing. Letting her imagination create shadows was no help at all.

"I need to think about this." Jaclyn folded the letter carefully. "I'm disgusted by what the man did, and if he crossed my threshold, I'd throw him out personally. With a few well-placed kicks. But I don't know if that needs to affect the rum-running theme at Captain Jack's. I play on the name, but the regulars call me Captain Jack too."

A dull reddish hue stained Ivan's face. His fingers worried the edge of his moustache. "He doesn't deserve anyone making him into a folk hero. Or a role model."

"Not for that aspect of his life, no." Jaclyn passed him back the letter, her silky claret blouse billowing. "All I'm saying is that it's complicated. I have no desire to endorse a child molester, but that's not what the pub is about."

Landon hadn't been inside, but from what Ivan said about the big portrait and the nautical decor, even someone who knew the worst of Jack's life should sense the seafaring theme.

The portrait... Jaclyn's Viking warrior expression had softened, but traces remained in her ice-blue eyes.

Landon sat forward. "The painting of Captain Hiltz—"

"Exactly." Ivan's fist pounded his knee.

"That's not what I meant." Landon focused on Jaclyn. "What about a replica, but with you? A new Captain Jack? Some period clothes, a photographer... it could work."

Jaclyn stared long enough for heat to crawl up Landon's neck. Then the woman laughed. "I like it."

One glossy fingernail tapped her chin. "Maria would never allow me to use the original frame, but the antique shops are loaded with things like that—so are some of the locals' attics. That's how I decorated the pub."

She stood, smoothing narrow black dress pants. "Speaking of which, I'd better get to work before the lunchtime rush starts. I'll ask some of my regular patrons what they've heard. Maybe they all know but were afraid to bring it up. I'm an outsider, after all."

Ivan's muttered goodbye was less than gracious, but Jaclyn didn't acknowledge his sulk. Fishing keys from her purse, she grinned at Landon. "Thanks for the idea."

The group stepped into the hallway as Meaghan came downstairs with a basket of laundry. She glanced from Glenna to Ivan. "I'm nearly done in your room, just need to empty the garbage and do the floor. Should I wait for later?"

"Give us fifteen minutes. We're on our way out." Ivan started upstairs, the letter still in his hand. Glenna followed.

As relieved as Landon was to hear the coast would soon be clear, she hoped they had pleasant plans for the day. Not more trying to resuscitate the pain Jack's victims had hoped to leave behind.

When the front door closed behind Jaclyn, Landon drew Anna aside. "I didn't tell you last night. Bobby and I found a match for that warning note."

"Who is it?" The catch in her voice could be relief or fear.

"I'll show you." She led Anna to the sitting room and opened the storage container of cards on the coffee table.

Elva's card bore a single white lily. Landon flipped it open and handed it to Anna before finding the photo on her phone to compare.

Anna's gaze darted between the two, slower and slower, as if she was hunting for a discrepancy. Finally, she sighed. "Elva. But why?"

" 'Someone close to you…' She could just be sniping at me like she did before, but the timing's too coincidental." Landon counted back in her head. "I talked to her on Monday, and it upset her, so it could be me. But what upset her was mentioning Gord, so she could mean him."

She flopped onto the couch and stared up at the ceiling. "Or Meaghan or Roy or the new neighbours… I don't think she'll talk to the police, but she might open up to you."

Anna laid the card back in the box and replaced the lid. "If she'd wanted the authorities to know, she could have written them directly. I've worked too hard to build a bridge with Elva to destroy it over this. But you're right, a visit might help."

"It might even be another piece of your bridge. The thing is, you shouldn't go alone and she won't want to see me again." Not after Landon had invaded her garden, clearly a place of solace, and triggered such deep fear.

"What about Tricia?" Tricia and Blaine—Quinn's grandparents—were Elva's neighbours on the other side. An impish expression crossed Anna's face. "Or would you feel left out of the investigation?"

"Hey, I have a basement to explore. Do what you need to do."

Anna nestled the box on the floor between the desk and the wall. "This goes downstairs, but I think I'll keep it here for now. People wrote such kind things about Murdoch, reading the cards might be a good way to celebrate him today."

Landon had thought to suggest they visit some of his favourite spots, maybe prepare a special meal. Reading the tributes would be bittersweet, but Anna's idea showed she was healing emotionally. Now if the medication cured her Lyme and they could identify her enemy, Landon could go home with only school to worry about.

Repeating the course with Professor Tallin made that enough.

While Anna was on the phone with Tricia, the front door chime sounded. The McNutts must have left. Landon strolled into the breakfast room to watch them go, then found the heavy-duty flashlight Anna kept in the kitchen.

When she went back to the hall toward the basement door, Anna was coming out of the sitting room. "Tricia can't go until after supper. Quinn's playing baseball this summer, and he has a game this afternoon."

Good for him. Maybe he'd make some better friends than the ones he hung around with now, the ones he blamed Corey for leaving behind.

"Did you tell her why?"

Anna shook her head, then gestured at the flashlight in Landon's hand. "I'll help, but don't get your hopes up. It was pretty empty down there when we moved in, and we didn't see anything."

"You wouldn't have been looking for a hidden door then."

As Anna had instructed, Meaghan had locked the deadbolt when she came back from starting the laundry. Landon unlocked it and stuck the key in her pocket. "The last thing we want is for her to think she forgot and lock us in."

"Agreed." Anna flicked the light switch and started down the stairs.

In the basement, Landon spun a slow circle. "It looks like someone started to finish this and gave up."

Dark wood panelling screamed early sixties. Thick orange curtains bracketed the small windows, letting in daylight. Instead of a sub-floor and carpet, the concrete floor, painted long ago, was now a mottled brown and grey. With what Landon had seen of retro styles, the lack of carpet might be a very good thing. Plus, this way a trapdoor would have a visible outline.

Overhead, age-darkened floorboards and joists lent a rough, cavernous feel, swallowing some of the light from the bare, dangling bulbs.

The washing machine vibrated in a corner. It was as good a place to start as any. Landon played her light along the panelling, where extra lines could indicate a hidden entrance. She leaned on top of the appliances and aimed the light behind them, even though the plumbing and wiring should rule out an opening.

Next came a length of floor-to-ceiling shelving. Filled, naturally. Landon tugged at the end. "This is attached to the wall, isn't it? Was it here when you came?"

"No, Murdoch built the shelves. But he'd have noticed if a patch of wall was hollow."

"I hope so." Landon swiped the back of her hand across her forehead. "Grab me a hammer or something from the workbench? I'll tap a few spots, just in case."

"Would you know the difference in sound?"

"Maybe? If we're doing this, we need to do our best."

Anna handed her a rubber mallet. "Try this."

Landon reached between the boxes and tapped the wall, which sounded the same every time. Together they shifted some boxes to shine the light on the panelling.

Reaching the end with no sign of a door was a relief. They worked their way around the open space, tapping and peering at cracks with no results. Against the far wall, near the furnace and boiler, was a rectangle of unpainted floor. "I wonder what was here."

"I think the oil tank used to be." Anna pointed diagonally up and out. "It's an exterior tank now. Maria had to replace it a few years before we bought the house."

A door opening into an oil tank or against the side of the furnace wouldn't be much good. Landon played the light across the wall anyway but didn't see any suspicious cracks. Beyond the furnace lay Murdoch's workbench and an impressive collection of tools and equipment. She crawled under the bench and peered at the panelling.

Above her, Anna said, "There was a smaller workspace here when we came."

Unless it had been built to swing out with the door, that meant this section of wall was solid. Landon checked anyway, then backed out carefully.

"What are you doing?" Meaghan's voice came from the top of the stairs.

Landon jumped. Good thing she'd been clear of the workbench.

Anna sniffed. "Chasing rumours."

Landon brushed cobwebs from her knees. "There's a tunnel somewhere on the property, and if I were a rumrunner with something to hide, I'd put the entrance in my house where it would be secure."

Meaghan clumped down to their level. "Is this connected to the trouble about the inn?"

"If he wants what he thinks is in there, it could all be about scaring Anna away from the inn so he can get it."

"Any luck?"

"Not so far, and we're nearly done."

The boys hadn't seen a trapdoor in the barn, either, and if it was outside, and well-enough hidden that Nigel hadn't spotted it, they'd never find it. Neither would Anna's enemy.

There'd be a satisfying irony to him driving Anna away from the inn and then being unable to locate the tunnel. If the tunnel idea meant anything at all. Landon examined the next section of wall.

Wet laundry thudded into the dryer, and the door banged shut. After the machine started humming, Meaghan said, "I'm going back upstairs. You have the key, right?"

Landon patted her pocket. "We'll lock up."

Trudging up the stairs a few minutes later, Landon told herself at least the wasted time ruled out a possibility. But did it, or did she simply not know what to look for?

If Maria's tunnel note wasn't a clue, they had nothing. "I almost wish the drone would come back. Maybe we could chase it."

"Only if it followed the road." Anna took the flashlight while Landon locked the door. "I'll put this away."

Landon followed her into the kitchen for a drink of water. "I hate waiting for him to attack."

As she put her glass in the dishwasher, she faced the window. Nigel strode along the tree line. "Be right back."

She hurried outside. "Nigel!"

He stopped, and she jogged to meet him. He touched the brim of his hat. "I saw your cat from a distance."

"Today?"

His answering nod eased that concern. The stray was still alive and on the move.

"Did the boys ask you about the tunnel?"

Eyebrows climbing, he tugged his hat more firmly onto his head. "I haven't spoken with them."

When she suggested an outside entrance, he squinted at her, followed by a series of rapid blinks. "Impossible. I would have found it."

Landon's sigh came from the very depths of her lungs. "That's what I thought. We can't find it inside, either. But you saw the note. It has to exist."

Nigel tipped his head to one side like a robin hunting a worm. "The note didn't stipulate the tunnel was on this property."

"Ivan's been researching Captain Hiltz. I could ask if he found a reference to another location." Other than the ship's wharf, which wouldn't offer much hope for a tunnel.

His lips pinched, his eyes flashing black fire. "That one should mind his own business and not rake up other people's pain. The captain was a complicated man who did the unforgivable. Yet he used his gains for good."

The passion in his voice sent her back a step. For Nigel, this was a long speech. She risked another question. "What kind of good?"

"Envelope of cash in the mailbox. Box of groceries at the door. Not often, but he seemed to know when the need was dire."

Nigel still lived with his mother. Landon had assumed his father had either died or left them. She tried to keep her expression from changing as she thought it through. Gord's snide remarks suggested they'd been in school together. That put Nigel maybe ten years older than Ivan.

It could be.

If Jack was Nigel's father, Nigel knew it. That explained the intensity of his objection to Ivan's questions.

Asking would hurt him. Even if she was wrong. Landon used her gentlest voice. "He must have been a wealthy man. That's why I want to find his tunnel. I think Anna's enemy is after what's inside."

His dark eyes glittered. "If I could help Anna, I would."

"I know, Nigel. Friends like you keep her going."

His gaze shifted past her shoulder. "Your cat is back."

Holding her breath, she turned slowly. The stray crouched at the food dish behind the barn. "I need to get closer."

Nigel didn't answer. She glanced back, and he was gone.

Sliding her phone from her pocket, she eased toward the barn. She pitched her voice soft and friendly. "Hey, mister, I've been worried about you. Where've you been?"

One ear twitched in her direction. She crept nearer, still talking. When she got as close as she dared, she knelt, opening the camera app and zooming in.

Eventually, he looked up at her, tongue catching the last bit of food around his mouth. She snapped a couple of quick shots.

His good ear stiffened at the shutter sound.

The cut was swollen and nasty, the orange fur matted around it, but it didn't seem any worse. "What are we going to do with you?"

He held the pose another moment, then stalked away like an offended dignitary.

She pushed up from the grass and headed back to the inn. Relief that he was still alive couldn't stop her wondering about Nigel.

The odd man must have been an odd boy, ripe for torment from peers like Gord. Rumours about his parentage would have made his childhood even more of a nightmare.

She was guessing, but the idea fit like a puzzle piece. If she was right, his fascination with Captain Hiltz could come from a father craving. Especially if the man had sometimes provided for him and his mother. A child might not have recognized the gifts as an attempt at a payoff or to salve an attack of conscience.

If he'd carried a subconscious dependence on the captain into adulthood, the man had nothing left to give him—except the family property and anything hidden on it.

A shiver chased along her spine. If Nigel were another of the unacknowledged children, he might very well resent Anna and Murdoch buying what he thought of as his father's house—a house he might have convinced himself was rightfully his inheritance.

Nigel, too, fit Elva's warning of someone close to Anna.

Chapter 22

LANDON COVERED THE leftover salad from lunch and slid it into the fridge, still thinking about Nigel. Mentioning her suspicions to Anna would only put her on the defensive, but Roy might know the answer. Best to ask him in person.

The phone rang before she could tell Anna she was going for a walk.

Behind her, Anna said, “That’s very sweet of you, Meaghan, but today’s not… Oh. Well, thank you, then. See you in a bit.”

She ended the call and blew out a deep breath. “Meaghan invited us for tea. She’s already baking brownies, and she sounded so disappointed when I tried to say no, I just couldn’t do it.”

Hands nested, she rubbed her wedding ring. “I wanted a low-key, stay-at-home day to remember Murdoch’s birthday and not have to put on a brave face.”

“Want me to call her back and explain? Let Hart eat the brownies. They might sweeten him up.”

“I don’t want to hurt her feelings. Besides, she said Hart won’t eat things with a lot of sugar. He’s into strength training and healthy eating.”

For a little guy, Hart was strong. He'd moved some heavy furniture in the barn during the break-in.

"Anna, you don't have to be everything to everyone. If you need today at home, Meaghan will respect that. The brownies will keep until tomorrow. It's not your problem."

The determined glint flared in Anna's eyes. Standing taller, she straightened her blouse. "It won't hurt me to go. Maybe God doesn't want me to stay home and mope. She asked us both, but I didn't commit you."

Landon pretended to study the calendar. "Saturday, hmm... relax, watch the trees grow, figure out who's harassing you... I think I can fit it in. If we're not gone too long."

Anna's lips twitched. "Well, as long as you're free."

The sun had come out since Landon talked with Nigel. Humid and hazy, the air hung thick, sticking her tee shirt to her spine on the short walk to the car. Sweat prickled her hairline, and she bunched her hair in one hand, holding it free of her neck.

An angry buzz overhead pulled her attention skyward.

Fighting the urge to duck, she whipped out her phone and opened the camera app. "The drone is back." Feet braced, she targeted the approaching white object and started recording.

It shot upward.

Maximum zoom couldn't capture a clear image. She lowered the phone but left the video running in case the drone swooped back. At least she'd get a recording if the voice came again.

"Did you get a picture?" Wide-eyed, Anna stood with a hand to her chest.

"I think so. Man, that thing moves fast." Landon opened her car door, and a wave of heat hit her in the face. "It's a sauna in here."

Driving along the road with the windows down generated enough breeze to cool them off. Landon replayed the drone video, slowing the speed. "The first second or two are pretty clear. I'll email it to Dylan when we get back."

"Meaghan probably has Wi-Fi."

"Let's have a nice time without—"

Anna yelled. The car shot to the right.

They were tumbling, falling. Over the bank. Into the ocean.

"Seatbelts." Landon jabbed the button to release hers.

Anna's hands still clutched the wheel. Landon clicked the driver's seatbelt open too. "We have to get out—"

They hit water.

Landon's side of the car hit first. Water splashed her from the impact, but the angle had been shallow. The car flopped flat on the surface, upright but already beginning to sink.

"Anna, now—through the window."

Landon gripped the window frame, ready to launch herself out. She paused long enough to see Anna crawl into position, then kicked free.

The cold made her gasp, and then she was choking and sputtering. She dashed salt water from her eyes and peered across the roof of the sinking car. "Anna?"

Anna's head and shoulders were free, but she wasn't moving clear of the car. "I'm stuck."

Praying, crying, Landon swam around the front of the car to Anna's side. "Stuck how?"

"Leg. Seatbelt. I think." Anna's breath came in gasps.

Her motions must be tightening a loop in the belt. Landon grabbed the side mirror and pulled herself nearer.

Anna flailed at her. "There's no time—get clear."

Growling, Landon squeezed between Anna and the door. "Slide back inside. Just a bit."

Her questing hand found the strap around Anna's ankle. As the pressure eased, she tugged the loop wider. "Now."

Anna's foot shot free, the shoe left behind.

They swam as fast as they could, parallel to the rock wall that fell away from the road. When Landon glanced back, only the car's roof remained above water. Then it was gone.

Paddling in one place, she tried to catch her breath.

Anna's face was pale, her lips grey-rimmed. "We'll never make it to a safe landing." Her words burst out in a wheeze.

The rock wall was fissured and broken, too low here to be a cliff but too high to climb. Maybe they could find handholds. But how long could they cling there, waiting for someone to notice them?

"Hey!" A man's voice rang from above. "Hang on. 9-1-1's on the way."

Anna's gasp could have been a sob.

Landon waved her arm to show they'd heard and locked onto Anna's eyes, huge in her white face. "You heard him. Hang on. You want to swim to the rocks?"

"They might come by boat."

They stayed in place, treading water, hauling lung-knifing gulps of air. The waves weren't high or pounding, but the cold jabbed needles into Landon's feet and calves.

With the Atlantic currents, the beaches around here were cold even in high summer, and this water was much deeper. She hadn't minded it as a child skipping in the shallows, but Anna's teeth were chattering, and hers would be soon.

"Come on, people." She gritted out the words, jaw tight.

A wave slapped her in the side of the head.

Time blurred until at last the roar of an approaching powerboat gave fresh hope. The deafening rumble cut, and the boat eased into position. Strong hands hoisted them aboard, wrapped them in blankets.

Landon tried to answer questions from a kind-eyed man, but the warmth and the boat's vibration lulled her into a half sleep. She was hazily aware of being transferred from boat to ambulance to hospital. Of gloved hands poking and prodding. Muted voices, calm but serious.

Her body jerked, and her eyes snapped open.

A middle-aged woman in polka-dot scrubs bent toward her, her thin tan face softening in a smile. "Hi, there. Can you tell me your name?"

"Landon. Landon Smith. Where's Anna?"

The woman's dark eyes warmed as if getting her name right was worth a prize. Perhaps after being hauled out of the water and collapsing, coherent thought was a victory.

"Landon, I'm Dr. Sharma. Anna said she saw a flash of light that caused the accident, so we're running some tests on her vision. She's a little disoriented, but otherwise, she's fine."

"She has Lyme Disease, she's overstressed, and today's her dead husband's birthday. And we nearly drowned. No wonder she's disoriented." Landon sniffled. That came out way sharper than she'd meant. "I'm sorry, Doctor. I was pretty scared too."

The doctor's expression hadn't changed. "I understand. It was just the two of you in the car?"

"Yes, we—Meaghan. We were going to visit a friend. She'll be trying to reach us."

"One of the nurses can call and let her know you're okay."

"I don't know her number, and they probably don't have a land-line to look up. Our phones—" An image of the car roof slipping beneath the waves brought hot, rolling tears. "I'm sorry. I—"

A wad of tissues pressed into her hand. "It's okay. Let it out."

"I can't even give you my health card. Everything's at the bottom of the ocean."

"Don't worry. When they retrieve the car, you'll get your belongings back." Dr. Sharma patted her forearm. "Why don't you try to rest some more? We'll check on you later, and I'll ask Anna about a contact number for your friend."

Landon couldn't rest. Her muscles were heavy from the exertion, like waterlogged tree trunks, her throat seared from gasping for air and from the salt water she'd swallowed. Her brain kept flashing pictures of the sinking car and her lost phone—with the video of the drone.

She should be thanking God for saving them, instead of reliving this kaleidoscope of terror.

Gratitude was there. Definitely. But for now, everything else was louder.

Bouncing her head lightly against her pillow made a soothing rhythm that at last slowed her thoughts. She must have slept. Or zoned out. Next thing she knew, a familiar male voice spoke outside her curtained cubicle.

"I'll take them home. I'm glad they're all right."

Gord? Meaghan must have worried when she couldn't reach Anna by cell or at the inn. Of course she'd phone her father, especially if she didn't know Anna had turned down his proposal.

Odd that he'd have checked the hospital so quickly—and that they'd let him into the emergency ward. But with her and Anna disappearing in the short distance between the inn and Meaghan's apartment, maybe an accident was a logical guess.

Landon sat up carefully and swung her legs over the edge of the bed. The room didn't spin, but the top-heavy feeling in her head made her cautious.

Her clothes were gone, replaced with a thin, mint-green hospital gown. She eased her bare feet to the floor, flinching at the cool tiles. She found her sandals under the single chair, but they were squishy enough she'd go barefoot until it was time to go outside.

Holding the gown closed behind her, she poked her head through a gap in the curtain. A stick figure sign halfway along the corridor gave the needed direction.

As she washed her hands, she studied her reflection. Her hair hung as stringy and wrecked as she'd imagined, but the purple shadows under her eyes surprised her—those and the livid scratch down one side of her face. She should have felt that.

Still... she and Anna were alive.

She padded back to her bed, glad she'd left the curtain ajar so she didn't blunder in on a stranger.

A petite nurse hurried toward her, holding out her clothes. "We threw these in the dryer for you."

Landon hugged the neatly folded pile to her chest, inhaling the fresh, crisp scent. "Thank you so much. May I see my friend, Anna?"

"I'll check while you change."

The dryer's warmth had faded, but dry clothes beat damp and clammy.

"Knock, knock." The nurse was back.

"I'm ready." Landon hooked her fingers into her sandal straps. Even if Anna was still being tested, they'd want this bed for someone else.

The nurse led her along the corridor to an actual room with a door. "Did the doctor tell you she was a bit unsettled? We thought a quieter environment would help her stabilize. Go on in, and I'll bring another chair."

Landon slipped inside and stopped at the sight of Gord in the visitor's chair. Anna lay pale but awake, brown hair splayed on the pillows elevating her head. Landon rushed to hug her. "I'm so glad you're okay."

Shaky fingers cupped her cheek. "Thanks for getting me out."

"Thank God the windows were open. We wouldn't have had time."

Landon straightened and met Gord's eyes. "Meaghan must have called you. How did you know where to find us?"

"I had a bad feeling. If something had come up, Anna would have contacted Meaghan." His chin dipped. "I had to tell them I was Anna's fiancé for them to let me in. A lie, but for a good cause."

A hard lie to tell when Anna had only said no last night. For all Landon's concern about Gord, he'd impressed her today. Unless he was using this as an opportunity to press his case.

She banished that ungrateful thought as the nurse returned with another chair. "Thank you."

Seated, she searched Anna's eyes, still wide from the ordeal. "How do you feel?"

"I have a nasty headache, but I'm ready to go home. Since I don't have to drive."

Gord held up a key. "I fetched this from Meaghan, hoping I could take you home, but knowing otherwise you'd likely want something from the inn."

Anna's cheeks pinked. "I hadn't thought about how we'd get in."

Her lips veered down as if she were angry with herself, but Landon hadn't thought of it, either. That would have been something, them waiting on the doorstep for the McNutts to come back. "Do we have to stop and file an accident report?"

Trembling fingers plucked at the white sheet across Anna's chest, and her face crumpled as if she might cry.

"I'll take you home, and you can phone from there." Gord pointed to Anna's clothing, piled on the counter beside her bed. "I'll wait outside."

When the door shut behind him, Landon said, "Let's see how steady you are on your feet. If you don't need help, I'll go out too."

Anna took a slow approach to standing and pronounced herself fine. Landon hugged her again and stepped into the hallway.

"I'll go get the car." Instead of moving, Gord held her gaze, eyes intense. "What caused the accident?"

"I don't know. One minute we were driving, the next we're going over the bank."

He gave his head a slow shake. "With Anna's health, I've been worried about her driving, but I never expected this.

There should be a guardrail all along that road. Not just on the heights."

Shoulders sagging, he walked toward the exit. Landon leaned against the wall, frowning after him. Anna's driving had been fine—until today.

Chapter 23

THE INN'S PARKING lot was empty when they arrived, and Landon released a breath she hadn't known she was holding. Ivan and Glenna had become much easier to deal with, but right now, she and Anna needed the comfort of coming home. Not reporting back to work.

A soft sniffle came from the front passenger seat. Gord reached sideways to Anna. "We'll have you settled in no time."

When she refused to go to bed, he found a light blanket and tucked her into her recliner.

Landon kicked off her wet sandals and padded barefoot into the kitchen. Waiting for the kettle to boil for tea, she rooted in the freezer and found a slab of homemade lasagna.

When she carried the tea and a plate of muffins into the sitting room, Anna and Gord were talking quietly. Leaving the tray on the side table between their chairs, Landon snagged a muffin for herself and curled up in a corner of the couch. "We missed supper, but this can be a start. I'm thawing lasagna."

Anna clutched a wadded tissue. She pressed it to her eyes. "Comfort food."

Gord checked his watch. "A meal might encourage the police not to linger."

Suddenly famished, Landon devoured her muffin before responding. She made one last swallow. "You called them?"

Anna nodded slowly. "I want to get it over with. I phoned Tricia too. We'll get together another time."

The meeting with Elva. Anna's choice of words meant she didn't want Gord to know Elva wrote the letter. Good. If he involved himself and upset Elva, she'd never tell Anna what she knew.

Halfway through their meal, the doorbell rang. Gord waved his hands at them like he was shooing pigeons. "Stay put. I'll get it."

He led an unfamiliar officer into the kitchen. "Constable Zerkowsky, this is Anna Young and Landon...?"

"Smith." Even Constable Ingerson would have been easier than a stranger, although she'd hoped for Dylan.

Constable Zerkowsky looked like he'd barely met the height requirement to join the force, but his broad physique seemed all muscle. He surveyed the half-eaten meals, then pulled out the fourth chair and perched on the edge as if he was afraid to break it.

Like Dylan, he positioned a notepad and pen on the edge of the table. "I apologize for my timing. Perhaps you could tell me what happened between bites, and I'll save my questions until you're finished."

Gord arched an eyebrow. "Isn't it just a matter of Anna writing a report to file? She hasn't had time yet."

"Ordinarily, that would be true, but her statement to the doctor raised a flag." Zerkowsky faced Anna with an unhurried air, forearms resting on the tabletop's rounded edge. "I'd rather not say more until I hear your story."

Anna took another bite of lasagna and laid down her fork. "First, can I offer you a cup of tea or coffee?"

"No thank you." He gave an exaggerated sniff. "But I'm glad I've eaten. Your lasagna smells as good as my wife's."

A smile flickered and died. Hands wrapping her water glass, Anna cleared her throat. "We'd reached the base of the hill where the guardrail ends, and there was a bright flash—I don't know what it was—I jerked the wheel." A shudder rocked her. "Then we fell."

Landon skidded her chair closer and put her arm around Anna, squeezing her shoulder through the thin blouse.

Bright light? She met Gord's troubled gaze.

As Anna took a trembling sip of water, Zerkowsky angled his pen toward Landon like a microphone. "Anything to add?"

"I was looking at my phone. I didn't see anything until we went off the road." She told about her experience exiting the sinking vehicle and untangling Anna's leg. "I'm so thankful that motorist saw us and called for help."

Memory of the icy water brought back a shiver.

Across from her, Gord reached for Anna's hand. "I would have driven you to Meaghan's today. I wish you'd called me."

Anna sat a little straighter. "I'm fine to drive. Landon, have I ever worried you?"

"No." Not until now.

Gord patted Anna's hand and withdrew from her space. "You're a trooper. But you do have some health concerns, and you're not getting proper rest. Those things affect us."

Anna faced the officer, dabbing her eyes. "I'm not crying. My eyes have been watering since the accident—it must be the salt water. My doctor is aware of my health concerns and has said nothing about not driving. I did not fall asleep or lose focus. I saw a flash of light, which caused the crash."

She flattened her hands on the pine tabletop, fingers spread, the tissue sticking out beneath one palm. "It makes no sense, but that's what happened."

Zerkowsky's expression gave nothing away. Dylan hadn't believed Anna's initial experiences, either, before the events leading up to the barn break-in. Tonight, Gord's concern for Anna made her sound less than credible. And in her still-frazzled state, she wasn't at her best to offset that impression.

A faint line appeared between Zerkowsky's heavy brows. "Tell me again about the light, and anything else you noticed at the time."

"It all happened so fast. I saw the flash and jerked the wheel to the right. Which sent us over the side."

"Why to the right?"

"Away from the flash? I think—" Anna closed her eyes, forehead furrowed. "It was a reaction. Bright light—it felt like an impact. I knew the water was there, but I flinched away from the light."

She opened her eyes and stared at the officer, hands clenched as if she expected him to reject what she said.

The line between his brows deepened. "So the light came from the left. What did you see to the right?"

"Nothing. It blinded me."

"Landon, you saw nothing, even peripherally?"

"I was looking down at my phone." She'd told him that. What was he fishing for?

Zerkowsky steepled his fingers, resting the edges of his palms on the table. "Had there been a bright flash—like a strobe light or a flare, for sake of argument—would you have caught it at the edge of your vision?"

"Maybe? I looked up when Anna yelled, but she'd twisted the wheel. All I saw was the water, and everything tipping— " She stared at the lasagna sauce smeared on her plate, trying to anchor in the present.

Gord cleared his throat. "I don't see where this is going, Officer. These women have had a difficult experience, and they need rest. Not questions."

Zerkowsky's nod showed no impatience. "I respect that, sir. However, the test results revealed no issues with Anna's eyes." He smiled at Anna. "You still need to see your family doctor as soon as possible for the official verdict, but the hospital gave us an unofficial report earlier today."

"You believe me." Anna blotted her eyes again.

He finally cracked a smile. Briefly. Then he stared around the group one by one. "Because of the harassment and threats Anna has already received, this incident merits extra scrutiny."

The air around Landon seemed to chill. He thought it was intentional. "But how? At night, someone could use a spotlight, but it was a bright, sunny day."

Gord hitched his chair nearer. "Sunlight could have reflected off a piece of glass or even metal. There's always some fool throwing litter out the window."

"That's one possibility." Zerkowsky's brows bunched like crags over his dark eyes. "Another is this—while I can't speak to this incident, there have been cases where a driver has been intentionally blinded by a focused laser beam—like a laser pointer. What Anna describes are typical details, and watering eyes are often one result."

His broad fingers folded together. "It's reasonable to suspect this was a deliberate attempt on her life."

Anna gasped, sharp and harsh. The colour drained from her face as tears brimmed. She blinked rapidly, her whole face trembling as she fought for control.

Holding her closer, Landon drew Anna's head against her own.

Anna leaned into her for a moment, then straightened, drying her eyes with the crumpled tissue. "Constable Zerkowsky. My husband died in a car crash last November. The cause of death was listed as unknown, presumably driver error."

A ragged breath shook her frame. "Please. Review his file. Murdoch Young. This could have happened to him too."

Anna collapsed onto the table, sobbing.

Landon sprang to her feet and bent over Anna, pressing her arms and torso around her like a shield. Holding, absorbing the shuddering grief.

Murdoch had died before any of this started. It couldn't be connected, but the mere thought of his death being deliberate would tear Anna's heart to pieces.

Gord's chair scraped. "Anna, you're overwrought. You need rest. Constable, she can't take any more. You'll have to leave."

Landon straightened, sliding her hands along Anna's shaking shoulders. She faced Gord, then Zerkowsky. "You should both go now. Constable, we can finish this tomorrow."

Zerkowsky's steady gaze measured her. "Of course. We'll need to follow up once we have the report on the car. The best thing for you both now will be a good night's sleep."

"The car—when they pull it out, we need our purses back. Our ID, our health cards—"

"The car's been retrieved, and your belongings are secure. I haven't been to the site yet, but we'll get your things back to you. Before that, I'll start the process for the other accident. We have no way of knowing what Mr. Young experienced at the time, but there may be other indicators."

He extended his hand in an after-you gesture to Gord. "We'll show ourselves out. It would be wise to lock up behind us."

From Gord's scowl, he wanted to stay. "Call me if you need anything. Any time."

Once the front door clicked shut, Landon squeezed Anna's shoulders and let go. "I'll be right back."

She locked the front, then opened the back door. Timkin slept on one of the chairs, and she coaxed him inside. "You're needed."

In the kitchen, Anna's head lay pillowed on her arms. Her shoulders still quaked, but the storm seemed to be easing.

Landon stroked her hair, sticky from the salt water. "Let's go into the sitting room before the McNutts come back."

Anna shuffled beside her, and Landon guided her to the couch. Timkin leaped onto Anna's lap, and Landon fetched a box of tissues and then sat beside her, arm around her waist.

"We don't know about Murdoch, Anna. You were right to bring it up, but let's not go there until we know."

Anna dried her face, but fresh tears spilled. "I feel it. In my spirit. Who could hate us this much?" A shudder rocked her.

Now was no time to argue. "Let's pray for the truth to come out, for Murdoch and for today." And for the peace they needed to sleep.

Landon prayed quietly. Anna didn't add much, at least aloud, but slowly she calmed. Her tears stopped, but her face remained a puffy, pasty grey.

The front door opened, and the welcome chime sounded. Landon stood. "I'd better let them know we're here since the lot was empty."

She closed the sitting room door behind her and hurried through the inn.

Glenna gasped. "What happened to you?"

Landon's grimace shot a twinge through her scratched cheek. "We had an accident today. We're okay, but Anna needs to rest. And without her car parked outside to show there's someone here, we locked up."

"Poor Anna, she's had such a rough time lately." Sympathy clouded Glenna's usually sunny face.

Ivan clicked the deadbolt. "No other guests tonight? This way you won't have to remember later."

Landon waited until they'd gone upstairs before double-checking the lock. She found Anna where she left her, one hand resting on the cat's furry back, the other still clutching a tissue. A small pile of wadded-up ones lay beside her on the couch.

"The guests okay?"

"They're fine. I told them we'd had an accident to explain the car being gone, but I didn't say anything more."

"Good. They don't need to worry." Anna's face puckered into a frown. "How could he have known where to find us? Or was it random, and I'm paranoid?"

"I don't know—I just assumed it was connected to everything else." A memory clicked. "The drone. He could have had it circling up high for hours waiting for us to go out. And town's the logical direction to set up an ambush."

"That must be it." Anna slid the dozing cat onto the seat cushion beside her and crossed to take Landon's hand. "I'm sorry I dragged you into my trouble. We could have both died today."

Landon clasped her other hand over the back of Anna's and gave their combined grip a little shake. "But we didn't. God protected us."

"He did." Anna's hold tightened. "This is the first time my enemy tried to hurt us. I hope the lights and cameras will keep him away from the inn."

"I'm camping on your couch again tonight. And we should each take one of your land-line handsets since our cells are gone. Just in case."

Chapter 24

Sunday

Landon stepped out onto the deck, shaded from the morning sun, filling her lungs with pine-and-ocean-flavoured air. In the forest, a squirrel scolded. A blue jay flitted to a leafy branch, what looked like a peanut held in its beak.

She could use about three days of sleep to make up for yesterday. One night, splintered by jumping up to check every time a nocturnal creature triggered the motion-sensor lights, did not cut it.

Somehow, she and Anna had produced a respectable breakfast for the McNutts before the couple left for an extended family picnic Ivan's uncle had arranged. Glenna had insisted it be a no-axe-grinding day so Ivan's family could know more about him than his drive for justice.

Anna had phoned Roy to tell him they couldn't drive him to church today, giving the bare minimum about the accident. She seemed… brittle, somehow. And distracted. The sooner the police ruled out a laser attack on Murdoch's car, the better. She had enough to deal with already.

Landon still struggled to believe it was a serious consideration for their own accident. Anna wouldn't have imagined the light blinding her, and it must have been intense for her to react so strongly. But it felt like something out of one of Bobby's books. Not real life.

Still, the drone operator had spotted their departure, and he'd seen Landon taking pictures. Maybe she'd made him angrier by fighting back.

Her sandals rapped the wide stair planks. Too bad if he didn't like it. They'd fight back. They had to.

Once she'd refilled the stray's dish, she flopped into a deck chair. The occasional call of a bird or chatter of a squirrel made a gentle backdrop, and she closed her eyes.

A bump against her ankle sent her halfway out of the chair.

Timkin blinked up at her.

"Yeah, like you never sleep during the day." She kneaded a kink from her neck. At least he hadn't jumped into her lap. If she'd screamed, Anna would've thought it was another attack.

She reached down and scratched behind his ears. "Seen your buddy today?"

Right on cue, the orange cat strolled from the forest and disappeared behind the barn. Timkin backed out from under her hand and leaped onto the deck rail as if taking a sentry post. Strange, how he tolerated the interloper.

Landon crept down the steps toward the barn. She stopped in sight of the stray and knelt in the grass, speaking softly. In the shadow from the building, she couldn't get a good view of his wound.

Other than a twitch of his good ear, he ignored her. Eventually, he raised his head and stared at her, licking the food from around his mouth. He took a few slow steps nearer, walking like a tightrope artist, then sat just out of reach. Raising a paw, he started cleaning his face.

The wound did seem better, and the swelling had decreased a bit. "I guess you're going to make it on your own. Anna says we'll have to let the feral cat people trap you anyway."

Trap, neuter, and release—in an ongoing battle to control the feral cat population.

The cat paused in his bath, paw curled over his nose, and shot her a one-eyed glare.

"You did not hear what I just thought, and it'll be for your own good. If you're less aggressive, you'll fight less." Unless he'd been someone's pet and already had the procedure done. That might explain why he and Timkin, who'd been neutered as a kitten, coexisted.

If he'd been a pet, he'd lived on his own long enough to let his earlier battle scars heal. He was evasive, watchful, but more wary than frightened of her. Did he remember human kindness?

Landon dropped her hands into the grass in front of her. Slowly, she shifted forward, still talking. She stretched out a hand. If Bobby's theory worked, the cat would associate her scent with food and decide she was safe.

He declined to sniff her reaching fingers, so she kept moving. She'd barely touched the fur on his back when he bolted for the trees. Sitting back on her heels, she stared after him.

"I'm sorry." The whisper brought a lump to her throat and the burn of tears behind her eyes.

One simple goal. Gain the animal's trust. And she'd ruined it.

She trudged back to the inn and found Anna watching from the chair she'd vacated. As if to underscore her failure, Timkin sat tall in Anna's lap, as smug as only a cat could be.

Anna's plum top reflected a hint of colour into her cheeks, and her hair shone soft and clean. But puffy eyes and strain lines around her mouth revealed the truth. She managed a wan smile. "You're making progress."

Landon dragged out another chair. "I blew it."

"Hardly. He ran, but he didn't attack you."

Landon clasped her hands together. She knew better than to touch a wild animal. "What was I thinking?"

She could have been begging Bobby for a ride back to the hospital—in Roy's truck, so she didn't bleed on the Corvette's interior—for a tetanus shot. Still without her health card.

Timkin eyed her, then stood and trod in a dainty circle before folding onto Anna's lap. She rested a hand on his glossy black fur. "He's jealous of your attention."

"Not jealous enough to fight the competition."

"We can be glad of small mercies." Anna combed her fingers through her hair. "Speaking of which, the insurance company approved a rental. I wasn't sure if they'd have to wait for the police report."

From the hollow expression in her eyes, Anna was thinking about Murdoch's accident more than her own.

An approaching engine and the glint off a police cruiser nosing around the side of the house saved Landon from a fruitless attempt to distract her.

Moments later, Constable Ingerson sat across from them at the patio table. She'd brought a bag with their waterlogged belongings from the car, but she didn't have much to add to what Constable Zerkowsky said last night.

When she spoke of the possibility of a laser strike, her tone suggested she didn't share Zerkowsky's opinion. "In light of the hospital tests, the idea is being given careful consideration."

She gave Anna a tight smile. "And the file on your husband's accident has been pulled as well. One of the things I need to follow up on today is whether there were any other incidents, however small, from before his death up to when you first reported trouble this June. In hindsight, something may stand out."

Elbows on the smoked-glass tabletop, Anna cradled her chin in her hands. Finally, she sighed. "I've been thinking about this since last night, but I don't know. They were such little things when I did start noticing."

She tapped her pinky fingers against her cheeks. "The sounds and letting me catch sight of him before he disappeared... those didn't start until June. There may have been some pranks, to make me doubt myself, but I'd have just chalked them up to grief and not thinking straight."

Anna's tiredness had started before June, and who knew when grief gave way to a different cause for her moodiness? If the doctor was right about Lyme, that meant nothing. But if Bobby's friend found poison in her hair sample, that could point to a longer-term attack.

Bobby's idea, Bobby's follow-up. Landon would not be the one sharing that tidbit with Constable Ingerson.

Another car arrived, stopping beside Ingerson's. Gord.

Anna's lips compressed and her eyelids flared. Her neutral expression was back in place before he joined them.

After a quick introduction, he took the empty seat. "All right if I stay? I brought them home yesterday, so I'm already in the loop."

Ingerson cut him a narrow-eyed glance that suggested she wasn't thrilled, but she could have merely been assessing him. Or perhaps she'd seen Anna's reaction. "We're nearly finished. Anna, until we get to the bottom of this, it's important to treat it as a deliberate attempt to cause harm. Be extra vigilant, both when you're out and when you're at home."

Gord leaned back in his chair. "I'm glad you have the security lights and cameras."

So was Landon. Yes, they'd woken her regularly last night, but without knowing they were there, she might not have slept at all.

After the officer left, Gord asked if she'd shared anything new.

Anna smothered a yawn. "Not really. She did confirm they'll review Murdoch's crash too."

He stared down at his hands, then seemed to brace himself and met her eyes. "I wonder if that's wise. Without a witness, they could never prove it was intentional. All it does is plant doubt and make your loss even more painful."

"Gord, I have to know. Especially if the same person is after me."

A faint smile touched his lips, somehow sad. "I sincerely hope this was an accident. The other incidents have been bad enough. Still, it's good to have investigators who'll explore every option. We need to keep you safe."

He rested a hand on her shoulder. "You also need wheels. Can I drive you in to pick up a rental?"

"I would love to take root right here on the deck, but yes, please. And now that we have our ID back, I'm sure the hospital records people would like to see us."

Gord drove them to the hospital first, then to the car rental agency. One more round of paperwork, and the clerk handed Anna the keys to a compact red sedan.

After adjusting the seat and mirrors, she scowled. "Gord's still here. I told him I need to rest. If he comes back to the inn and keeps fussing over me, I'll—"

Landon chuckled. "Take a nap. That'll make him leave, and you probably need one."

"Amen to that."

He followed them to the inn but kept going once they turned into the driveway.

Anna sputtered. "Don't know what he's worried about my driving for."

"I don't know either, but today maybe it's about being a bodyguard. That might not be a bad idea."

A note wedged in the back door invited them to Roy's for a home-cooked supper.

Landon stood back for Anna to let them in. "You do have good friends."

They locked the inn and slept all afternoon. The shady forest walk to Roy's cleared their heads, and casual chatter over comfort food left Landon feeling calmer than she'd been since the accident.

By the time they returned to the inn, Anna was yawning again. It was only seven thirty, but Landon encouraged her to go to bed. "Worst case, the McNutts wake you when they come in, but they're pretty quiet."

"I feel like I'm abandoning you."

"I want to sit outside and see if our stray comes back, but I won't be up late, either."

Ivan and Glenna arrived soon after Anna went to bed. Now that Anna wouldn't be alone, Landon locked up and walked down the driveway. Yesterday's accident kept Anna and Tricia from confronting Elva about the anonymous note. Going by herself might be crazy, but Landon's gut said Elva meant the message as a warning, not some kind of threat.

Still, her heartbeat picked up as she passed Elva's parked Kia and climbed the shallow, grey-painted front steps. This place was the size of Anna's inn. A family home, with Elva the end of the line.

The inside door stood open. Landon knocked on the wood-framed screen. After a minute, she knocked again.

Brisk footsteps rapped the floor, and a shadowed figure approached. Elva glared at her through the screen, arms crossed. "What do you want?"

Landon kept her distance from the door, arms loose at her sides, as nonthreatening as she could be. Her words would be threat enough. "Who isn't what they seem?"

Elva's eyes narrowed even more. She sniffed. "I don't know what you're talking about. Get out of here, or I'll call the police about a trespasser."

Landon anchored her weight in her heels. "All right, I'll wait and talk to them instead."

"You have nothing to say."

Drawing a deep breath, Landon focused on how it filled her lungs and buoyed her frame. "We know you sent Anna that note. Now someone's trying to kill her."

A ragged gasp escaped Elva's thin lips. "What happened?"

"He caused an accident that nearly drowned us." In her bones, she felt Anna's and Zerkowsky's suspicions were true.

"She should leave while she can."

"She won't leave. You must know that."

Doubt flickered in Elva's dark eyes. She pushed her glasses closer to her face. "I don't want her to be hurt."

"She's already been hurt—by the attacks on the inn and now an attempt on her life. You know who he is, Elva. Please."

The woman's head shook so rapidly, she could have been trembling. "I can't say."

"You cared enough to warn Anna. If you want to help her, help her. We can call the police right now. They'll take the information and arrest whoever it is before he can hurt you or Anna."

Elva opened her mouth, then snapped it shut. She shook her head again. "I can't say. But... it's good you came back to help Anna. I was wrong to be so hostile."

She slammed the inside door.

Landon whirled. Whatever hold this guy had on Elva didn't matter. In the morning, she'd phone the police and identify the letter-writer. Stalking back down the driveway, she took small comfort in Elva's apology.

Back at the inn, she burned off her frustration by weeding around the pansies and marigolds in the green dory on the front lawn. Then she parked on the deck, watching for the stray until mosquitoes gathered with the dusk and drove her inside. Bedding down on Anna's couch again, she hoped she was overreacting. Whoever was behind this hadn't attacked the building yet. Although he hadn't attacked Anna until yesterday.

She was nearly asleep when the land-line phone rang. She fumbled for it and jabbed the On button before it could wake Anna.

"Hello?"

"Anna?" A woman's voice, low, intense.

"No, it's Landon. Anna's sleeping. Can I help you?"

Silence. Then the caller said, “It’s Elva. Come tomorrow. Alone. I’ll tell you.”

The connection clicked off.

Chapter 25

Monday

LANDON WRESTLED THE breakfast grill into the cupboard. There. Cleanup done, time to get some answers from Elva. This could be over today.

A rap at the back door brought an annoyed huff. If it was more police follow-up, she'd have to stay. Without mentioning Elva. For once, she hoped it was Gord. Then she could slip away.

Nigel followed Anna into the kitchen. The man's black hair stuck out at all angles beneath his camouflage hat, which clung to his head like he'd mashed it there in some kind of frenzy. His face had a sallow cast beneath day-old salt-and-pepper whiskers. Had he been roaming the woods all night?

Anna herded him to the nearest chair. "Sit, and I'll make some of your tea." She brought the glass jar for his approval, but he barely sniffed at it.

The first time Landon had met Nigel, she'd learned how particular he was about his specially-prepared blend of tea. To break his quality-control ritual, he must be seriously upset. She slid into the chair beside him. She didn't dare say anything trite about it being okay. Not to this level of distress, not without knowing what lay behind it.

Nigel folded bandaged hands on the pine tabletop, blinking rapidly at nothing. When Anna placed an oversized red mug in front of him, he flinched. Then he seemed to collect himself.

"Thank you." He nodded crisply to Anna, then to Landon. He grasped the mug awkwardly with the bandages wrapped around his palms and most fingers, closed his eyes, and inhaled the steam.

With another round of blinks, he sat taller, spine erect. "Elva is in hospital."

His dark eyes, always bright, held a sheen of tears. From the set of his mouth and the ice in his tone, he was angry.

Landon held back her questions. Anna and he had more history.

Anna had muffled a gasp. She dropped her hand from her mouth, leaning forward. "We heard sirens overnight. What happened?"

"Attempted murder." He sat so straight, shoulders rigid—he could have been in a witness stand. Or at a prosecutor's bench.

Glittering eyes flickered from one to the other. "I was patrolling around eleven thirty. Saw an unnatural glow from her kitchen. The door was locked, so I had to break a window." His breath rasped. "She was lying on the floor. Four pans of flame on the stove."

He closed his eyes as if to block the sight that was only in his mind. Then he found his control. "I dragged her away, extinguished the fire, but I couldn't wake her."

Anna whispered, "What did you do?"

"Called 9-1-1."

Landon didn't want him to think she was mocking him, but... "You don't use the phone."

"I did what had to be done. Aliens may have captured my voice, but I have no regrets." In his eyes shone the avenging warrior who'd rescued a woman from death.

"And the bandages on your hands are from the fire." From Anna's matter-of-fact tone, she knew sympathy for his own hurt would not be welcome.

"Another small price." He gulped a mouthful of tea.

He'd said eleven thirty. Not long after Elva had phoned to say she'd expose Anna's enemy. The hairs on Landon's forearms rose, each one prickling her skin. If she hadn't pushed, Elva might still be safe at home.

Blindly, Nigel rattled his cup onto the table. "They took her to the hospital. She's still unconscious."

Anna's lips thinned. "We should pray for Elva. Now."

Either Nigel was a believer, or he was willing to go along with anything that might help. Anna's brief but fervent prayer echoed Landon's cry for Elva's recovery. In the silence of her spirit, Landon added a request for the full healing Elva needed for whatever hurt lay in her past and for protection for Anna and herself.

Someone else knocked on the back door.

Anna's breath hissed. "Amen."

She returned with Dylan, and his confident, familiar presence brought a measure of calm. Landon's lungs expanded.

Never mind he was the youngest member of the force. He'd listened patiently to Anna even when he'd thought it was all in her head. Then he seized the first evidence of an actual prowler and never stopped digging.

A brief smile split the all-business expression on his face. "Guess I'm late for the meeting."

Anna gestured toward the fourth chair. "We were just praying for Elva."

His lips slid back to neutral. "That's a little outside my expertise. But I'm glad you know about Elva."

Sitting, he angled his body toward Nigel. "If you hadn't found her, she'd have burned to death. Well done, putting out the fire."

Pink tinged Nigel's ears. He cupped his bandaged hands around his mug.

"And I'm glad you two are okay after Saturday." Dylan focused on Anna. "Naturally, the attack on Elva is going to pull resources from our investigation here, but we'll continue to work on both cases."

"Umm." Landon's voice came out in a squeak. Faced with three pairs of eyes, she anchored on Dylan's as the safest. Anna would be upset she'd done this alone, and Nigel could be furious.

"The warning letter." Hands clenched in her lap, she tried to keep her words from piling up on one another. "Elva wrote it. I confronted her last night, and she sent me away. Then she called and said to come back today and she'd tell me."

She fought the need to see Anna's and Nigel's reactions. *Focus on Dylan. Just get it out.* "That was maybe ten, ten fifteen. If he was monitoring our phone—or hers—"

Her control broke. She looked at Nigel. "It's my fault—"

Smudges of brick red stained his cheeks. "The fault is his. His alone. And he will pay."

The certainty in his tone chilled the air.

Dylan tapped his fingertips on the wooden tabletop, firm and measured. "Nigel, you need to leave this matter with the police. Please. For your own safety and because I don't want to be arresting you for vigilante actions, no matter how justified. We will find this person, and we will stop him. Or her. Are you with me?"

The silence stretched. Finally, Nigel pushed back his chair. "Find him before I do."

He stalked from the room. The back door shut firmly, but not with the slam anyone else would have given it.

Dylan studied Landon and Anna. "Did he say anything to suggest he knows—or suspects—who this person is?"

"I think if he knew, we wouldn't be having this conversation." Landon's scalp prickled. This gentle man she'd sworn wouldn't hurt even a bird... she didn't know him at all.

And Elva. If the woman died because of Landon's questions... She curled her fingers around her hair, tugging gently. "Elva called from a cell. She wouldn't let this person have access to install some kind of spy app."

That left the inn land-line. It'd be risky to interfere with the outside wires in the brief times nobody was home. Other than Anna, Landon, and Meaghan, the only ones alone inside recently were the McNutts.

Realization slapped Landon like a wave of cold seawater. "Ivan! Best chance at tapping Anna's phone. And if he silenced the entrance chime, he could have sneaked out last night. Anna and I were sleeping in the back."

She stared at Dylan, heart thudding in her ears. "They checked out this morning—all of a sudden. Maybe this is why."

"What was his behaviour at breakfast?"

"Well... normal. They enjoyed yesterday with his family, and he said he felt bad taking all of Glenna's vacation for his search so they were off to Halifax for a few days."

She was being crazy, overreacting. Imagining things. Unless she wasn't. If something with Elva made Ivan snap, who knew what he'd do next?

"What if they didn't really leave? If they hide somewhere nearby? Until Ivan—" *Finishes the job.* She swallowed the words in a lump of fear.

Holding her gaze, Dylan nodded slowly, deliberately. Landon forced her breaths to match the repetitive motion.

As she calmed, he stilled, brown eyes glowing with approval. "It's most likely a coincidence, but we'll talk to him. We have his contact information on file. In the meantime, we'll put a guard on Elva, and I need you two to keep your doors locked and watch one another's backs. Is there a deadbolt on the front that's separate from the guests' keys?"

In case Ivan made a copy?

Anna had been uncharacteristically quiet. Now, she cleared her throat. "There is. But you didn't come to tell us about Elva."

"No." He leaned forward, giving her his full attention. "I'm afraid there's no easy way to say this. After Murdoch's accident, the investigation ruled out mechanical malfunction and weather. And heart attack or anything similar." His palms bounced gently on the table. "Driver error is the catchall in those situations, and we'll never know. But it could have been a similar laser attack."

Tears tracked Anna's cheeks.

"So, what now?" Landon took her hand.

"Now, we pursue this individual who has attacked you both and presumably Elva as well. With an awareness that he may also have attacked Murdoch." His lips flattened in a grim line. "When we find him, we will ask him."

He drew his notebook from his pocket. "For the record, how do you know Elva wrote the note?"

"It matches the handwriting on the sympathy card she sent after Murdoch's death."

A slow smile creased his lean cheeks. "Well played. May I see?"

Landon squeezed Anna's hand and released it. When she brought the card to Dylan, she placed a tissue box next to Anna. "We know you'll need to take the card as evidence. Please bring it back?"

"Of course." He rose. "Once we can talk to Elva, we may have all we need. I'm hopeful she saw—and recognized—her attacker. If it's the same person she wanted to warn you about, we'll have our connection."

"Nigel said something was burning on the stove. There's no way Elva was just cooking late at night and fell?"

"Four saucepans of cooking oil with the burners on high?" Dylan pressed a finger to his lips. "Pretend Nigel told you that. He found it. It points to an argument that got out of hand and impromptu arson to cover the crime. Although I can't understand why he thought she was dead."

Unless he didn't care she was still alive and wanted the fire to fix it. Landon shivered.

Chapter 26

Landon waited for Meaghan in one of the padded patio chairs, hoping for a sight of the elusive stray. After Dylan left, Anna had shuffled to the sitting room and shut herself in.

She could imagine a lingering hint of smoke from the fire at Elva's, but the breeze teasing her cheeks was soft and light, free from the earlier humidity. All that heaviness had seeped into Anna's heart—hers too.

When Meaghan arrived, Landon followed her into the kitchen. "Anna's not feeling well, so it's just you and me."

"Is it from the accident?"

"It's everything, piling up. But the McNutts have checked out, and nobody's coming for tonight. I hope she can rest." Now she and Anna would be alone, and for who knew how long? There'd been a flaming review from the guests with the paint-balled car, on top of the ongoing fake ones, and at least one more reservation had cancelled. Others weren't booking in the first place.

"What happened? Dad said you went off the road."

As Landon described the crash, Meaghan's face blanched. Fear lurked in her wide blue eyes. "And they think it was deliberate?"

"Likely."

Lips trembling, Meaghan hugged herself so hard her thin white tee shirt billowed over her forearms. "She needs to get away from here. At least until this stops."

Hands jammed in the pockets of her shorts, Landon jerked her head toward the sitting room. "Tell that to Anna. You know how she gets."

"I do, and I'm afraid for her." Shoulders bowed, Meaghan collected the basket of cleaning supplies from the cupboard. "I'd better get to work."

After making Anna a cup of mint tea, Landon carried it into the sitting room. She found her huddled in her recliner with her Bible open in her lap. Despite the room's warmth, she clutched a light shawl around her, its bright yellow tulips out of place with her gloom.

When Landon deposited the steaming mug on the side table, Anna lifted her face, brown eyes dim like she wasn't focusing. Or like the sadness in her spirit was too deep to see through.

Landon sank into the chair beside her, angled sideways so her cheek rested against the soft fabric. A silent presence could do more than empty words.

They sat for a long time. Finally, Anna scuffed her heels against the footrest. "I've failed him. Murdoch."

"How so?"

Staring straight ahead, Anna slouched lower in her seat. "I should have pushed for an investigation. Should have been able to stop what's been going on since then." She drew a long, shuddering breath. "It's time to admit defeat. Close the inn and accept the death of his dream."

Landon nibbled the insides of her lips to keep them closed, praying for the right words. Yes, she and Meaghan had just spoken about this. It wasn't right to let the enemy win, but neither was the inn worth dying for.

Except losing the inn would be severing a tangible tie to her husband. More grief.

"Would you go to your daughter's?"

"Not broken like this. She has enough on her plate. I don't know where to go. Somewhere."

"Anna, if the inn closes, it's not because of you. It's because of a faceless bully who wants something that's not his."

Head lolled head back against the teal upholstery, Anna closed her eyes. "I can't fight this anymore."

Landon ached to comfort her, but this wasn't a skinned knee or a splinter. This was one of those dark nights of the soul a person had to work through on their own. Nobody could make the dawn come faster, and right now, Anna likely didn't believe it even existed.

That didn't mean her friends were powerless. Landon pulled her knees to her chest and rested her forehead against them, praying for Anna until her own tears came and passed. When she reached a place of assurance that God did have this—did have Anna—and would work His own good purposes in the mess of it all, she uncurled and gently stretched her complaining back muscles. She stood and padded around the room until her circulation returned.

"Let's get through today before making any big decisions. If Elva regains consciousness soon, the inn's troubles should be over."

Grief for Murdoch wouldn't end, but on its own, it would be manageable. If whoever was behind this could prove he had nothing to do with Murdoch's death, the weight would be that much less.

Anna's fingertips fluttered the gilt edges of her Bible as if she couldn't read it but couldn't put it aside, either. "I'm done. That's not going to change."

"No. But acting on your decision takes energy too, and I don't think you want to go there right now."

A quiet huff broke from Anna's lips. "Not likely."

"So we rest today. Is it okay if I put on some soft music?"

"Suit yourself."

Landon chose a CD of instrumental worship music. If Anna's memory supplied some of the words, it might help. She picked up the now-cold tea. "I'll get rid of this."

In the kitchen, she stared out the window. Perched on the barn roof, a crow rocked back and forth as it cawed. Nothing else moved.

It felt like the inn was holding its breath, waiting for Elva to wake and tell what she knew.

No one else had anything to say that hadn't already been said. Except Maria. Possibly.

Landon snatched the land-line handset.

She heard Meaghan come upstairs from the basement and waited until the sounds of movement continued toward the upper floor. Then she found Bobby's number in the phone memory and hit the call button.

His voice mail activated, and she almost disconnected. How could she put this into a coherent message?

She gulped a quick breath and plunged in. "Hi, it's Landon. If you get this and you both have time... Anna needs a visitor, and I need to beg a ride. Again." She clicked off before she started apologizing for being needy.

Knowing how much Anna hurt and not hovering over her felt callous, but sometimes people needed space. She puttered in the kitchen, making muffins that came out of the oven lopsided, childish caricatures of Anna's perfect offerings, and assembling a salad for lunch.

Meaghan stopped to say goodbye. "Tell Anna to let me know when she needs me again. Without reservations, the schedule drops way back."

"Will you be okay with less hours?"

"For a while." Meaghan flipped her thick red braid behind her back. "I can pick up something part-time if I need to." She headed for the door. "Give Anna my best. I hope she feels better soon." Worry darkened her tone.

Anna refused lunch, so Landon made her a smoothie with fresh strawberries and yogourt. "Your body's still trying to recover from the accident stress. Don't make me stage an intervention."

She used a playful tone for Anna's benefit, but meant the warning too. Respecting Anna's need to work through the pain didn't mean allowing her to self-sabotage.

The phone rang, and Landon snatched it, hoping it was Bobby. Instead, it was Tricia. She covered the mouthpiece. "Anna, can you talk to Tricia?"

When Anna shook her head and mumbled no, Landon carried the phone outside onto the deck. "She's pretty down today, Tricia, and doesn't feel like talking. Can it wait?"

"Dear, I wanted to tell her Elva's in the hospital. The sirens last night? We went over, but there was nothing we could do."

She scanned the tree line for the stray. "Nigel told us this morning. I hope she'll be okay."

They chatted a bit, and Tricia ended the call with a promise to pray for Anna.

Landon was finishing her lunch when an engine purred outside. Too smooth to be Roy's truck. Dylan or another officer with news? She checked the window. Gord's silver Lexus.

For all his good intentions, Gord's pushy streak was not what Anna needed right now. She met him on the deck. "Anna's not up to company today."

He carried a bouquet of mixed flowers. "Meaghan said she's struggling. I won't stay long." He stopped in front of Landon as if waiting for her to move aside. "Sometimes if we put on our cheerful face for a visitor, we feel better when they leave."

"The accident shook her, Gord. And now the police say Murdoch's could have been deliberate too. She's grieving."

His brows drew together. "I wish I could spare her this pain. I promise, if she asks me to leave, I'll go."

Today might be the day Anna would do just that.

Instead, she mustered a faint smile and invited him to sit. With a mental shrug, Landon offered to put the flowers in a vase. When she carried it back into the sitting room, there wasn't much conversation happening, but they both seemed content. She positioned the flowers on the coffee table in front of Anna and watched a small smile curve her friend's lips.

The phone saved her from deciding whether to stay or leave. One handset rang from Anna's bedroom, but she jogged to the one she'd left in the kitchen.

"Hello?"

"Hey, it's Bobby. Gramp's at a friend's, but I can provide one genuine getaway driver, at your service."

She'd trust Roy to sit with Anna while they talked to Maria, but Gord? Still, Anna hadn't sent him away, and if Landon didn't do something to find their answers, she'd explode.

"What about your deadline?"

"I can have writer's block anywhere. It's pretty flexible that way." His laugh rang hollow. "Your message sounded urgent. Let me help. Or do you also need someone to stay with Anna?"

"As it happens, Gord came by a few minutes ago." She walked into the breakfast room, pitching her voice lower so it wouldn't carry back to Anna. "Maria—Captain Hiltz's daughter-in-law—knows something about the tunnel. Anna's falling apart, and it's the only thing I can think to pursue."

"If Gord can stay, I'll be there in five."

"I'll ask." She backtracked through the kitchen and left the phone on the table.

Gord broke off what he'd been saying and looked a question at her. Anna barely glanced in her direction.

Landon clasped her hands, then unclasped them because it felt like a child's posture asking a favour. "Anna, are you up for visiting longer, or do you need a rest?"

Gord sat taller, hands braced on his crisp khaki pants. "Anna needs only say the word, and I'll be on my way." She'd offended him, but his tone stayed mild.

"Actually, I hoped you could stay. I need to go out for an hour, and Anna shouldn't be alone."

He eased back in his seat. "I have the time, and if she needs to lie down, I can watch television or something."

"Thanks. I'll be as quick as I can." She hurried back to the phone in the kitchen.

Bobby arrived within minutes. "Where to?"

Landon gave Maria's address. As he headed for town, she told him about the attack on Elva and the possibility that Murdoch had been murdered. "Anna's given up. She's handled so much, but that tipped it. I hope she just needs to process, but I don't know."

"An accidental death would be hard enough. The thought of it being deliberate must add a whole new level of pain."

"It's got to be the same guy. We can't let him win." She twisted her purse strap. "Anna can't fight, so her friends have to fight for her. And we can't even see the enemy."

"Here's hoping you can convince Maria to tell what she knows. And that finding whatever's in the tunnel will give a clue to who this is."

When they reached Maria's residence, Bobby slowed at the parking lot entrance and gave a low whistle. "Nice place."

The honey-hued siding glowed in the sunlight, warm and inviting. A hummingbird zipped to drink from one of the hanging baskets of bright red geraniums, then darted away.

Landon scanned the shaded rocking chairs. "Those two old ladies on the veranda must be there all the time."

"Guards. The one on the left has a shotgun in her bag to chase off undesirables."

His matter-of-fact delivery made her snort. "Do you have to be nuts to be a writer?"

"It helps." He shut off the engine. "Want an escort, or would you rather go in alone?"

"Company'd be good." She shot him a grin. "Unless you're afraid to face the guards."

"That's right, question my courage. I'm in."

Inside, Landon checked in with the receptionist, who sent them up to Maria's room.

The door stood ajar, the sounds of a talk show filtering out. When Landon knocked, the volume decreased. Maria called, "Come in."

They stepped into the cramped room, leaving the door as they'd found it.

Maria squinted at them from her chair by the window. "Do I know you?"

Landon took another step nearer, into better light, keeping her body language open and nonthreatening. "I'm Anna's friend Landon—"

"I meant your companion."

"Bobby Hawke, ma'am. I'm Roy's grandson."

She pushed her blue plastic glasses closer to her face. "I thought you reminded me of someone. Roy used to visit me. Haven't seen him in a while."

"He broke his leg a few months ago, and he's navigating in a cast. I'll tell him you were asking about him."

"What happened?"

"He had a run-in with a squirrel. The squirrel won."

Maria snorted. "That's Roy." A square of knitting lay in her lap, pink today, and she picked up the needles like she was bracing for battle. "Now, what do you want?"

Direct and to the point. Okay, if the elderly woman wanted it that way. Landon stood tall, shoulders braced. "Anna's on the verge of emotional collapse. Whoever's after the inn tried to kill us on Saturday."

She let the words hang there. Maria's knitting didn't falter, but her breath hitched. "Was she hurt?"

"Not badly. A touch of whiplash and some muscle pain. We think the same person was responsible for Murdoch's accident."

Bobby moved closer to her side, the warmth of his presence reassuring.

Landon held out her hands to Maria, palms up. "Anna's enemy will win if you don't help us. The tunnel is a key. Either he wants what's hidden there, or he could find another entrance and attack us. Please, Maria."

Maria hauled more yarn from the pink skein at her side and knit ferociously, lips pressed in a grim line. Finally, she threw down her needles. "You're worrying for nothing. Jack barred the sea entrance years ago. The opening doesn't look like more than a crack, anyway."

So Ivan had been right. There was a secret way into the inn.

"We should seal the inn end, just in case, and we need to see if Captain Hiltz left anything there this person could be after."

Maria tipped her head to the side, eyes narrowed upward as if she was reviewing memories. "I don't know if even my husband knew about the tunnel. Before Jack died, he said he'd shown it to David."

Her lips pinched. "I saw Jack come out of it once. Startled me badly. The door is well hidden. I'd never have found it if I hadn't seen it open." The lines in her face etched deeper. "It will remain a secret until David comes back. Don't worry about your enemy finding it."

Landon clenched her teeth and fought for calm. "That's small comfort if he drives Anna away from the inn—or if he kills her. He nearly killed Elva last night."

"Elva Knapp?"

"She sent a warning note about someone close to Anna. Last night she said she'd tell me who it was. Less than an hour later, she was attacked and left in a burning house."

"How terrible." Maria's hands picked at the pink square of knitting as if she wanted to hold it but couldn't connect. "How would Elva know who this is?"

Bobby said, "We don't know, but we have to stop him before he hurts anyone else."

The blue-veined hands stilled. "There's nothing in the tunnel to help identify this person. I'm sorry."

"But—" Arguments and pleas boiled in Landon's mouth.

The steel in Maria's eyes cut them off.

Defeat closed in like a thick fog. Chilling. Impenetrable. Smothering Landon's last hope to find a clue.

Elva could still end it, but only if she regained consciousness before Anna gave up. And before the unknown enemy struck again.

Chapter 27

The child in Landon wanted to stomp down the stairs from Maria's room. Instead, she opted for a brisk pace. Brisk and silent.

In the car, she blew out a huge lungful of tension. "That went well."

Bobby swiped the screen on his phone. "Makes me wonder just what's in that tunnel she doesn't want anyone else to find."

"Could we convince the police—"

His exclamation cut her off. "Sorry. Text from my researcher buddy. It's poison. Lead. Hair sample suggests this has been going on for months."

He stared at the phone, eyes wide as if he hadn't truly expected a positive result. "He says it's sometimes found in traditional remedies or cosmetics, like kohl—did I say that right? K-o-h-l. Maybe even hair dyes. Or of course, old, lead-based paint, but Anna's not the type to be chewing on window ledges."

Landon ignored the joke and sifted through the rest of what he'd said. Picturing a bottle of shampoo on the kitchen counter. Shampoo Meaghan supplied.

Despite the open top on the car, sweat popped out over her whole body. Yet her mouth went paper-dry. She worked up enough moisture to swallow.

"How likely is this to be accidental?"

Slowly, he shifted focus from his phone to her face, his forehead creasing. "You have an idea."

It couldn't be Meaghan. She was an ordinary girl. She'd been good to Anna.

She kept Anna stocked with special shampoo. She'd invited them for brownies—insisted they come—the day of the laser attack.

Landon forced a swallow that hurt like a huge wad of gum. "Meaghan. But I want to be wrong."

"Tell me."

He listened, bouncing the edge of his phone against the leg of his shorts. Gaze never leaving hers.

When she finished, she waited, desperate for him to argue.

Instead, he slid the phone back into his pocket. "Could she do it alone? Or maybe Hart's not as out of the picture as he'd like us to think."

"She might not know. He could be using her."

Creases pinched the outer corners of his eyes. "I get that you don't want it to be her, but we have to tell the police. They'll do their own tests, but maybe they'll question her in the meantime."

"She wants to go back to school, to make her life better. Why would she do this?"

"Landon, Anna has to come first."

"Of course she does!"

Ouch. She squeezed her eyes shut. "Sorry. I'm just—I can't believe it. Couldn't we ask Meaghan ourselves? We don't know it's the shampoo, but we could ask where she gets it. If she's selling it to other people too and they're having the same symptoms, then it's the source that's tainted."

"You know what the police would say about that. And not just Constable Ingerson."

True. Still, she took a deep breath. "Yes, but if Meaghan's a pawn in this, she'll talk to me faster than she would to a uniform."

Bobby started the car. "Where to?"

Saturday had been their first invitation to Meaghan's apartment, but Landon remembered the address. The GPS on Bobby's phone led them across town to a three-storey wooden building with faded brown paint.

He drove into the parking lot, but only used the visitor spots to turn around. He parked on the street, facing back the way they came.

Landon's nerves tingled, prickling every hair on high alert. "You're taking your getaway role way too seriously."

"Did you see how narrow those spaces were? No door dings for this baby."

They climbed the concrete steps to the building. Landon found the apartment number and buzzed in.

"Hello?" Meaghan answered.

"Hi, it's Landon. I'm in the lobby. Can we talk?"

"Sure." Surprise carried through the speaker. "Come on up."

The security lock buzzed, and Bobby cracked the door before it locked again. "We're in."

The building had no elevator, and their footsteps echoed in the cinder block stairwell. Nostrils pinching at the dank, sour air, Landon wished she'd checked the lot for Hart's car. From what Meaghan said, though, he didn't spend much time at home.

Meaghan stood at the open door to her apartment, hip propped against the doorjamb. "I thought you were alone."

"I don't have my licence, and Anna's not in any shape to be driving today."

A slight frown clouded her face as she let them into a small but neat room with a tattered brown couch facing a big-screen television. She swept a hand toward the couch and flopped into a matching chair, elbows resting on her knees. "You're worried about Anna."

Now that they were here, Landon didn't know what to say. Her stomach in knots, she sat so close to Bobby they were practically touching.

He leaned back, not saying a word. At least he hadn't sent her up here alone.

She scrubbed her palms against her shorts. "We know what's making Anna sick. It's lead poisoning."

The colour left Meaghan's face like a white curtain falling. Against the sudden pallor, her red hair seemed to glow. "No."

"That's what the test showed." No point revealing it was an unofficial test, not admissible as evidence. Landon gulped air. "The shampoo she gets from you—do any of your other customers have the same sort of symptoms? Tired, moody, a bit forgetful... although maybe it's different for different people."

How could they differentiate between the results of grief and stress and the results of poison?

Meaghan bunched her hands in her lap. "Of course not. My other clients are fine."

Bobby shifted forward and the couch creaked. "Then someone has deliberately tampered with the bottles that go to Anna."

His backup firmed Landon's confidence. She sat tall. Unbending.

She'd seen a movie once where the detective's success came from out-waiting the people he questioned. It was fiction, but nervous people did tend to let their words run away with them.

Meaghan's blue eyes filled. Rapid blinks kept tears from her cheeks. Her chest heaved as if she couldn't get enough breath.

Lips clamped, she glared at them.

Nobody spoke.

Choking on a cry, she dashed to the window and stood facing away from them, rocking on her feet, hands clenched at her sides.

Finally, she whirled, her face tear-streaked. "I'm not going to jail for him."

Hart. He'd fooled them all.

She dashed her forearm across her eyes. "Anna's a good person. He made me leave the gift shop to spy on her. The shampoo—he said it wouldn't kill her, only make her sick. And Saturday, inviting you here, I thought he just wanted to make trouble at the inn."

Red hair haloed against the sunlight, she stood like a trapped animal, but there was nowhere to run. "He caused the accident. Then he said I was in too deep because I'd lured her into his ambush. I didn't dare go to the police."

One of the inner doors burst open. Hart charged across the living room toward Meaghan. "Enough."

Landon was on her feet, Bobby at her side. Hart was strong for his size, but they couldn't let him hurt Meaghan.

Meaghan flung her arms around her boyfriend, fingers twisting into the dark-blue fabric of his muscle shirt.

Her action froze Landon in place. Bobby stopped a pace ahead of her.

Hart pulled free of Meaghan's grasp and stepped back, hands fisted. "No more doing what your father says and ruining our lives. I'm already risking jail time."

Landon stared at them, mouth open, trying to fit the pieces together.

If Gord was behind this—and Gord was with Anna now—

Hart grabbed Meaghan's hand and steered her toward the open door. "You have five minutes to pack." He whirled on Landon and Bobby, legs bowed in a half-crouch. "We're leaving. And don't worry about us warning Gord." He spat a curse. "He's on his own."

"But..." Landon found her voice. "Without your testimony—"

Hart's lip curled. "We'll contact the police once we're out of his reach. And we'll testify. It's our only chance to reduce our own charges."

The pieces still didn't fit. Or maybe her mind was too overloaded to cope. Landon stood shaking her head.

Bobby started for the door. "We have to get back to the inn."

The urgency in his voice unlocked Landon's feet and planted a single, burning mission in her brain.

Protect Anna.

Chapter 28

Landon had barely fastened her seatbelt when Bobby cranked the engine and rocketed away from the curb.

"Gord's been alone with Anna before." He sounded like he was trying to convince himself not to panic. "But if he's behind the accident, something's changed. Maybe he's out of time for what he wants, or maybe he's out of options."

She clung to the car door as they whipped around a corner. "He proposed on Friday, and she said no."

"This isn't a rejected lover. It's been going on too long."

They rounded another corner into the flashing overhead lights of a crosswalk. Brakes squealing, the Corvette jolted to a stop that threw them forward against their shoulder belts.

The two little girls crossing the street spun toward the sound. One giggled and waved, but the other scowled and took off for the sidewalk.

"That was too close." Bobby's voice shook. Still, once the street was clear, he launched forward. "Now would be a good time to pray."

"I have been. Bobby, we have to get back there."

"I'm working on it." He spoke through clenched teeth.

She held her breath, straining at the tightness in her chest.

A stop sign, another crosswalk, a wait to turn left across traffic—they were through town in less than five minutes, but it felt like trying to run through chest-deep water.

They hit the coastal road, and the engine roared. Bobby shifted gears. "Phone Anna. Make sure she's okay."

Landon's phone was at the inn, sitting in a bag of rice in hopes it might dry out. "I need yours."

The car swerved as Bobby wrestled his from his pocket. He wrenched one-handed back into their lane, narrowly missing an oncoming SUV. The other driver's horn blared.

She snatched the phone, but it slipped from her fingers and bounced off her thigh. Her frantic grab missed, and it slid between the gearshift and her seat. "No!"

Wedging her hand into the gap, she caught the case's edge with her fingertips just as the car accelerated. The motion shot the phone out of reach.

"I'm sorry. I—" How could she be so useless? She shrank against the door, anticipating Bobby's fury.

He leaned forward, knuckles white on the wheel. "I can't stop to find it. We need to get there."

Landon held onto the armrest and rode out the swerves, praying they'd make it in one piece—and find Anna safe.

Finally, they reached the hill before the inn. Bobby slowed to a normal speed. "We can't act like we suspect anything. You're back, and Gord is free to get on with his day. Can you do that?"

She brushed a rogue tear from one eye. "I'll have to."

The driveway was long enough for three deep breaths. She needed more.

As soon as Bobby parked beside Gord's Lexus, Landon fell to her knees on the hot asphalt and rummaged under the seat for the phone.

Bobby helped her up. "Remember, we're not in a hurry."

"I'm not stupid." She thrust the phone at him, and his face sagged.

"I'm sorry. I didn't mean it that way." He tucked the phone in his back pocket and shoved his hands through his hair. "I'm trying to coach myself. I've never faced down a potential murderer."

He squared his shoulders. "Let's do this."

Walking slowly toward the inn when she wanted to run strained Landon's willpower to the breaking point. She tried to control her breathing, but a thousand butterflies flapped in her lungs.

Inside, everything was quiet. In the sitting room, Gord looked up from his phone. He put a finger to his lips. "Anna's sleeping."

He grasped the light jacket beside him, then stood and stretched. "She's taking this so hard. Sleep will let her escape it for a while."

The sympathy in his voice made Landon want to scream at him. He'd been trying to poison, terrorize, and now kill Anna—yet he dared pretend to be a caring friend.

Hope whispered this was a good thing. He was still pretending. Not ready to reveal his hand.

And he was walking to the door. All they had to do was let him leave.

Then lock the doors and report him.

Landon stepped into the room to give him a clear exit. Her racing heart drummed a panic beat.

Bobby followed and flopped onto the couch like he belonged there. Tension lines around his mouth revealed his stress, but Gord wouldn't know him well enough to read him.

A whisper of air was Landon's only warning before Gord seized her upper arm in a death grip. She screamed and tried to twist free, but his fingers dug into her biceps.

Bobby had catapulted from his seat. He froze in mid-lunge.

Landon backtracked his gaze to the weapon in Gord's hand. A deadly-looking gun. In a very steady hand.

Gord jerked her arm. "Party's over. Sadly, Anna has taken too many sleeping pills, trying to forget her troubles. You—" His fingers gouged deeper. "You were an inconvenience from the start."

"How did Elva know it was you?" *Keep him talking.* So many people had dropped in since Anna's accident, maybe someone would come. But if he'd drugged Anna, there was no time.

His laugh sent cold pebbles down her back. "That nutcase Foley has to sleep sooner or later. Elva may not wake. And if she does, she'll think twice about crossing me again."

"What does Nigel have to do with it?"

"Nigel." He spat the name. "Lines his hat with foil, you know. So the aliens can't read his brain. He's set up camp outside Elva's door as a self-appointed guard."

The fire in Nigel's eyes when he'd left this morning... Landon's sight misted. "Good for him."

Gord jabbed the gun in Bobby's direction. "You try anything, she gets the bullet. Let's go."

Teeth clenched, Landon stomped on Gord's instep. In light sandals, it hurt her foot, but he didn't flinch.

He shook her hard enough to jolt her neck. "Do. Not. Mess. With me."

The commanding tone was the same as from the drone. Landon's mind was screaming, but she couldn't move. Feet planted on the floor, she stood quivering.

"To the door." He gestured with the gun, and Bobby backed toward the door.

He shot a wild look at Landon.

Gord tugged her forward. Shivering started under her skin, vibrating her bones.

Her body followed Gord's orders. Out of the inn. Down the steps. Toward the barn. She tried to speak, but her brain blanked. Terror left only a whimper.

Bobby glanced at her again, slack-jawed, helplessness plain on his face. He was still walking backward, casting quick looks behind him. He caught himself before he backed into the building.

Gord stopped a pace away. "Open the door."

"It's locked."

"I removed the lock already. Open the door and get inside."

The weathered door creaked on its hinges.

Landon's knees fused. Gord snarled and yanked her forward into the barn.

Her breath came in rapid bursts. Almost whistles.

The lights clicked on. Then he closed the door. Anna's big orange flashlight sat on top of one of the boxes, and he used it as a pointer.

"Now. Sports-car boy." He played the beam across a tall chest of drawers near the back of the barn. "See that? You're going to push it sideways."

Bobby didn't bother arguing. With a last hollow glance at the gun, he shuffled past the boxes. Gord led Landon close behind.

Hands spread at its edges, Bobby leaned into the hulking piece of furniture.

Nothing happened.

"Try harder. Or do I have to persuade you?" Gord twisted Landon's arm, and she yelped.

Muttering, Bobby repositioned his hands and set his feet. Tendons stood out on his neck. The bureau squeaked sideways. Not much, but enough to stir a cloud of dust.

Bobby doubled over, coughing.

Landon blinked grit from her eyes. Her nose tickled. Her desperate prayers for help seemed to ricochet around inside her skull.

Something deep in her spirit held fast, whispering they'd be okay. In Heaven, sure. But her trembling, rebellious body was not ready to die. Not when she'd just started to live again.

The bulky piece of furniture lurched in bits and stops. This was the one Hart had moved during the barn break-in. At the time, they'd thought he was trying to tip it over as part of the vandalism.

There must be another reason.

Her brain found it just as Gord barked, "Stop."

The tunnel. It wasn't in the house after all.

Gord shoved her closer to the cleared space.

Bobby stood panting, shoulders hunched, hair matted with sweat. Something grim darkened his eyes. He'd reached the same conclusion. And expected to die in that tunnel.

He straightened and took a shaky step toward them.

Gord ground the gun into Landon's shoulder just above his hand. "Try it. The first shot won't kill her."

For a second Landon saw Nigel's avenging fury in Bobby's face. Teeth bared, chest heaving, he trembled visibly. Not afraid. Trying desperately to master himself.

He planted his feet hip-width, shoulders back. Standing down from attack. His smouldering gaze lanced into Gord.

Gord jammed the gun harder against Landon's shoulder. "There's a pry bar in the top drawer. Open that hatch."

The wide floorboards' edges hid two sides of the opening, but seams marked the other two sides. With the end of the pry bar wedged into one of the cuts, Bobby levered the edge high enough to get his fingers under it. He shifted the wooden square sideways.

Darkness yawned in the gap.

"All the way open." Satisfaction rang in Gord's voice.

The loose section grated onto the solid floor.

Landon's lips were stone. Her whole body shuddered with the effort to break them open. "How did you know where to find the tunnel?"

"Old Man Hiltz showed David. Who showed me."

David. Maria's missing son.

Bobby eased a half-step nearer. "If it was a family secret, why show you?"

"We were friends. I had a plan."

Gord's fingertips pulsed tighter into Landon's flesh, lancing pain the length of her arm. "First, you spooked Hart into thinking for himself. Breaking into the barn made Elva suspicious. I handled that, but you couldn't stop interfering. You'd have had Anna renovating out here, and she'd have found the tunnel."

His laugh was a cold, satisfied rasp. "Instead, her grieving offspring will need to sell this heap, and what more trusted buyer than her selfless, supportive friend, Gord?"

He shook Landon's arm. "Certainly not her troubled young protege, who stole from her and then ran off with the neighbour's grandson. Especially since the young lovers will never be found."

Bobby flinched. "My car's in the parking lot."

"Too recognizable. Clearly, you had alternate transportation. Perhaps you stole Anna's rental, if I can arrange it quickly enough."

Bobby had moved nearer, knees bent to tackle Gord.

Landon tensed for the pain of a bullet.

Gord snarled at him. "Into the tunnel. Now."

The gun shifted against her shoulder. "She'll follow, bleeding or not."

The look Bobby sent her brimmed with sorrow, and his hands fluttered upward in helpless surrender. He sank to his knees and leaned toward the opening. "There's a ladder."

Slowly, as if each motion cost him, he extended a leg into the darkness. Then the other leg. He climbed down a few rungs and stopped with his shoulders still above the floor.

His gaze burned at Gord. "Watch your back. But you still won't see it coming."

"You're in no position to threaten me."

A half-smile shaped Bobby's mouth. "It doesn't have to be me."

His eyes met Landon's. He didn't speak, but his fractional nod told her she could do this.

Then his head disappeared below floor level.

Landon shivered.

Gord pushed her toward the opening, her feet compliant even though her mind was slushy cold.

The ladder top was almost as black as the tunnel. Below, Bobby's face was a pale blur.

She was numb. Her feet barely felt the rungs. The thought of being caged underground froze to her core.

Gord stepped nearer. "Move. Or I'll help."

Her heart seized.

Gripping the rungs so hard her hands ached, she stared at him through tears. "Why are you doing this?"

"It's business. There's good money in smuggling."

His face twisted. "The syndicate used my heart attack to push me out. Once I open a pipeline to bring in drugs and guns, they'll have to reinstate me." He kept the gun aimed at her. "Before the first run, we'll give you a burial at sea."

He took another step, and she retreated another rung.

Below, Bobby said, "You have room, but I'll stay close."

She wouldn't die in here alone. But that meant Bobby would hear when she lost it.

Gord's silhouette loomed over the opening. "The ladder leads to a passage to the sea. That end is blocked. I expect you'll go down anyway. Don't step on David's bones."

The floorboards were above Landon's eye level now. Her vision faded in and out—or maybe that was the dim light.

"David?" The single word vibrated with all her questions.

With a scrape, the door slid over a corner of the opening. A cry filled Landon's mouth, trapped behind her teeth.

"His job was to get the tunnel secret from his grandfather. I didn't know Elva was the price." Gord swore. "His teenage girlfriend—the old man was eighty."

A tiny piece of Landon's soul shuddered for Elva. It was all she could spare.

"Old Hiltz used her and left her there, crumpled in the corner, while he showed David the entrance. When he went back into the house, I sneaked into the barn. David took exception to something I said. We fought. He fell."

The door covered half the opening now, sealing them in. Cutting off hope.

"If Elva told my part, she'd have to tell her own. Instead, she ran away."

Only a small triangle of dim light remained above.

Gord coughed. "We were fine until you started playing on her sympathy. If she dies, it's on your head."

The door slammed into place.

Darkness swallowed them whole.

Chapter 29

BLACK. COMPLETE. THICK enough that it cocooned her skin.

Her eyes went dry from flaring wide for a glimpse of light.

Scrapes and thuds echoed overhead. Gord, piling things on the entrance.

She lunged upward, pushing the trapdoor with everything she had. The rough wood bit into her palms, but it didn't move.

A faint whistling drifted through the floorboards. Then footsteps, walking away.

Another sound filled her ears, and it took time to realize it was her own keening wail.

Her hands ached from their grip on the rough metal ladder. She squeezed tighter, afraid to fall. Afraid she'd knock Bobby to the bottom of this hole.

Forearms shaking with the strain, she pressed her forehead into one of the rungs.

She couldn't breathe. Lights flashed in her vision. Here in the dark.

Not real light. She was passing out. *Can't fall on Bobby.*

She wrapped her arms around the ladder and twisted her hands back toward her chest. Leaned in with her last bit of strength.

Tried to stop whimpering. Tried to breathe.

Sound reached her. A voice.

Fervent. Urgent. Familiar.

Bobby.

Tuning into the words hurt her head. But she needed to hear.

The flow of words was a current, carrying her.

He was praying. Bobby was praying. For her.

"...You can see in the dark. Let Landon know You see her. You're holding her. Light of the World, speak Your peace to Your precious daughter—Your peace beyond understanding..."

The words went on. Washing her. Warming her.

Her breathing slowed. The spots faded from her eyes. She saw black instead of the grey edges of oblivion.

Tears welled from the depths of her soul. Huge tears, slow and warm. Salty, and somehow healing.

This wasn't the gulping, heaving, sobbing mess of fear and trauma.

It was a rhythm matching the determined voice echoing off the tunnel walls.

It was release.

Arms locked on the ladder, she drew a deep breath. The air tasted damp, metallic, and a little like dirt. But it filled her lungs, expanded her chest, and loosened her locked muscles and joints.

"Bobby?"

"Right here."

"Thank you."

A noisy breath floated upward. "I didn't dare touch you, but I had to let you know you weren't alone."

A final tear slid down her cheek. "That was the most beautiful thing anyone has ever done for me."

He cleared his throat. "Um… Did you try the door?"

"He put stuff on top."

"Yeah, I was afraid that's what I heard. Okay, downward it is."

"But that end's blocked too."

"If it's only barred, I might get cell reception." Scuffing sounds beneath her suggested Bobby was climbing down.

"I'm following you… warn me if you stop."

"Yup." It was more of a grunt than a word.

They moved steadily downward until Bobby called a halt. "Found the bottom. I'm going to use my flashlight app for a minute. You okay to stay there?"

Flashlight. And they'd made this descent in the dark. But phone flashlights ate batteries like crazy.

Her arms shook with fatigue. She wrapped them around the ice-cold ladder again. "I'm good."

A glow warmed the walls around her. Rough-hewn, like a natural fissure. Black and rust-coloured streaks ran in diagonals and zigzags. Here and there, pinpricks of rock shone greyish white.

Shuffling below. "Okay, come down. You have five more rungs."

When she'd counted down to one, Bobby said, "Now squeeze left and step down hugging the wall. Take a few steps sideways before you come to my light."

She followed the instructions, then bolted forward and clung to him.

Her breathing picked up again. Reaction. Face buried against his shoulder, she inhaled through her nose, consciously slowing her respiration. Focusing on the feel of her lungs expanding. On the earth-stained, damp sweat from his shirt.

Bobby squeezed her ribs, the cell in one hand a hard rectangle. "You good?"

"I think so." She stepped back. "What was with the fancy move at the bottom of the ladder?"

"I found David."

So it was true about David. And Elva. And Jack. Bile burned Landon's throat. She pushed it down.

No wonder Elva was so damaged. All these years keeping such horror inside. It must have been Elva who told Nigel David was dead. Protecting his source made sense now.

Bobby aimed the light into a relatively level tunnel. Away from the ladder's base. "We should leave this on from here, in case there's a sudden drop."

The passage was wide enough for two. They jogged along a slight downward incline, racing the light.

Ahead, vertical bars closed the passage—an iron gate, anchored to the tunnel walls and secured with a rusted padlock.

They shook the bars, but everything held firm.

The opening continued beyond the gate to an apparent dead end. Landon squinted at an extra line of shadow along the right-hand edge. "It must veer sideways."

So much for the gate being near enough the opening that they could wave a shirt or something through the bars as a signal.

Bobby clicked off the flashlight and tapped the glowing screen. "Nothing." He stuck his arm between the bars, waving the phone. Still nothing.

Landon pressed her face tight against the cold black metal and screamed for help. A hollow echo bounced back at her.

Her tremors started again, and she clenched the pitted bars with both hands. If she lost it now, there'd be no coming back. *Concentrate.* On the rough metal biting her palms. The damp of salt and rock. The slosh and smack of water.

Water.

She spun toward Bobby, who was doing something with his phone. "What if we only need the tide to go down? If it's covering the opening—"

His hands stilled. "Of course. One chance left."

The phone cast a creepy glow on his face until he dropped his arm to his side. "I disabled everything nonessential to slow the battery drain and set the screen to dim but not time out. Will this be okay? Think of it as a night light."

She wanted the flashlight. A floodlight. A way out. "Good idea."

He aimed the screen back the way they'd come. "I want to try the ladder again. Will you be okay... with David?"

Landon's skin pebbled. "He can't hurt us. But I gave the trapdoor everything I had, and it didn't budge."

"I thought we might get a signal at the top of the ladder with only the barn floor blocking us."

They could have tried that in the first place. If Landon hadn't been a hot mess of terror.

She stepped away from the gate. "Hurry. Anna might not have much time left."

The mental image of Anna breathing her last, alone at the inn, haunted her. Anna was so much more than a friend and a mentor. She filled all the places in Landon's life where a mother should be. Losing her to Gord's twisted plot—

They ran back, the dim light barely illuminating their steps.

The ladder appeared out of the gloom. Bobby started upward. "Sorry, the phone has to come with me."

"Right behind you."

At the base of the ladder lay what might have been a pile of rags and sticks. David's remains.

No need to look twice. She jumped toward the ladder and climbed at Bobby's heels.

"I'm at the top."

She stopped beneath him, waiting. Hoping.

"Nothing." Disgust rumbled in the word. "Take the phone a minute?"

He lowered it into her upraised hand, then ascended another rung. Grunts echoed downward, then a defeated sigh. "Don't bother with 'I told you so.' I had to try."

"I know." Defeat left her voice husky.

He stepped down to the rung above her. "Let's go back."

Their footsteps dragged on the way to the gate. Bobby tried the phone again—no luck. They sank to the floor with their backs against opposite walls, Bobby's cell on the ground between them.

The chill seeped through Landon's shirt. "We're okay for a while, but Anna needs help now. Even waiting for the tide to go down could be too long."

Bobby's face was shadowed. "Pray Meaghan and Hart report Gord fast."

"Even if they do, they didn't know he was with Anna. Or what he did." Her voice rose in a shriek.

"Landon." Urgency sharpened his voice. "We're scared. Anna's in danger, and so are we. But we can't afford to panic."

She drew a shuddering breath. He was right, but that didn't make it any easier.

He reached forward and picked up his phone. "Tides are twice a day. Worst case, if the opening's low and was just covered, we could be waiting six, eight hours or more for it to be clear. We don't dare leave this on that long."

The thought made her shiver with more than the cold. The short time they'd been in the dark on the ladder felt like an eternity. "I can't—"

"Yes, you can." Confidence firmed his tone. "And that's worst case. It might only be twenty minutes. When it starts to open, we'll see the change in light."

He held out his free hand. "Come sit beside me. We won't feel so alone."

Landon shuffled across the passage on her palms and heels and sat with her shoulder pressed against his. The shared body heat brought a sliver of comfort.

With one last peek at the glowing phone, she screwed her eyes shut. "Okay."

Even through her eyelids, the sudden black hit like a slap. Pitch darkness magnified the weight of the rocks and dirt above them. Pressing. Crushing.

She couldn't help a sniffle. "Can I hold your hand?"

"Okay." Clammy fingers threaded hers. He was trembling too.

Blindness made the other sensations more intense. The rough, unyielding rock at her back and beneath her. The smell and taste of the air, damp, earthy, a blend of minerals and decay. Overpowering it all, the rasp of their breathing and the ocean slapping stone.

"What if the tide comes in here?"

The pressure of Bobby's grip increased. "I didn't see a high-water mark on the walls, and there'd be shells or bits of seaweed."

David's remains wouldn't still be at the bottom of the ladder if the water reached that far. They could retreat if they had to.

David. Landon tried to work some moisture into her dry mouth. "If—*when*—we get out of here... can we not tell them about Gord and David? For Elva's sake?"

"But Gord killed him."

"It could have been an accident. There'll be other charges against him, with evidence, but it's our word against his for David. Elva's the only witness, and you know he'd drag her into it. They'd make her testify."

His shoulder shifted against hers. "Maria deserves closure."

"She'll at least know her son didn't abandon her."

"Would you be satisfied with that?"

"Can we wait to see if Elva wakes up? And warn her first?" Landon propped her head against the rough rock behind her. "Maybe it won't come to that. Maybe when Meaghan and Hart tell what they know, Gord will confess."

Bobby snorted. "Maybe he'll let us out too."

The swift comeback stung.

Silence grew between then like a chasm. When she could trust her voice not to hold hurt, Landon bounced their linked hands in a little pulse. "I'm sorry I dragged you into this."

"I'm sorry I didn't call 9-1-1 before we faced Gord."

Landon shivered. By the time the water went down far enough to let a cell signal out, Anna could be dead. If they were close enough to the tunnel mouth for a signal to reach.

If not, they'd die down here.

Slowly. Hungry and blind, dying while the sound of water amplified their thirst.

She couldn't let her mind go there. She grabbed the first safe thought that occurred. "What would Travers do?"

Bobby snorted a laugh. "No sweet clue. But he'd find a way out. Or he'd have seen through Gord's act in the first place. He definitely wouldn't die in a hole in the ground."

"When you prayed for me—was that a Travers thing?"

He didn't answer. Was he embarrassed to pray aloud? Or afraid if she remembered how she'd felt, it would trigger another panic attack?

Finally, he exhaled. His shoulder slouched forward away from hers. "No. That was 'what would Bobby do.' I didn't write Travers with faith."

"Why not?"

His arm moved up and down as if he'd shrugged. "People read my kind of books for fun. Adventure. They're not looking for God."

Landon blinked in the blacker-than-midnight dark. "I'm glad God looks for us. I wouldn't last five seconds in here without Him."

She imagined Jesus in the tunnel with them, perhaps sitting at her other side, holding her hand.

The thought didn't stop her being scared. Or slow her desperate mental countdown toward Anna's last breath.

It did warm her spirit. And stir a memory of other coping skills. She breathed deeply, tasting the damp, metallic air.

Not fighting it, desperate to escape. Noticing it. Accepting it as something she couldn't change.

What she could change were her thoughts. Fighting this fear should be the same as fighting memories of abuse.

Except her mind was as blank as her vision.

"Bobby? Give me a Bible verse?"

Heat rose in her cheeks. Bobby couldn't see that, but he'd have heard the higher pitch in her voice.

"Um. Coming up empty here."

She drew her knees up to her chest. A whimper broke through her lips.

" 'Behold, I stand at the door and knock... if you hear me and open the door, I'll come in.' " He shifted beside her. "That's the gist, anyway. The verse that inspired that painting." He grunted. "Sorry. Not much of a comfort verse. It rubs our faces in the whole not being able to open the door."

The gate. The trapdoor. More than just locked, they were impassable.

Trap. Door.

Landon stiffened. Her breath hissed.

"What is it?"

"I don't know. Let me... maybe..." The thought crystallized. "If you walked into the barn and saw someone open the tunnel, what would you call it?"

"A tunnel?" He sounded cautious, like he thought she was losing it again.

"No. Sorry. What would you call... what the person moved to open it?"

"A trapdoor. Maybe a hatch?"

Energy zipped in her veins. "But you wouldn't call it a door. Because it's in the floor."

"Okay..."

Landon half-turned and clapped her free hand over their joined ones. "Maria said she saw Jack open the door. Not the trapdoor. The door. What if there's another exit?"

He let out a soft whistle.

But instead of helping her to her feet, he slumped lower against the wall. "We've been from one end of this passage to the other. It doesn't branch."

"Sideways. It doesn't branch sideways. We didn't look up."

A different type of fear took her. If she was reading too much into Maria's choice of words, if the woman had meant the floor entrance in the barn, the dashed hope would break her.

Chapter 30

Memories of sun and fresh air filled Landon with a craving she couldn't contain.

If Bobby wouldn't try, wouldn't risk his phone battery—

He stirred. "It's possible. Weird, but possible."

Landon climbed to her feet, numb from sitting on the damp, hard rock. She was shaking her legs and trying to loosen up when the phone glowed again.

Dim light outlined Bobby's smirk. "Nice dance." He swept the phone toward the tunnel depths. "Shall we?"

The tunnel floor was fairly smooth, but between checking her footing and watching the rock above her, Landon felt like a bobble-head doll. They must be nearly to the ladder, and other than a few darker patches on the rock overhead, they'd found nothing. She fought to brace for another disappointment. Inside, hope trembled with such force it might shatter.

A new dark patch loomed above, wider than the others.

She held her breath as Bobby angled the light.

The black smear became a hole. Along one side, a different texture of night could be a ladder.

She gripped Bobby's hand. "You see it too."

"I do." The words came out in a whoosh of air.

Her breathing had sped up to match her heart. She stood on tiptoes and stretched up with her arm. "How do we reach the ladder?"

"I need the flashlight for a second. If you want to keep your night vision, cover your eyes."

And miss whatever he wanted to see?

The light hurt. Blinking like an owl, she stared upward along its beam.

To a shaft with a ladder.

Bobby closed the flashlight app.

Waiting for the purple splotches to fade, she rubbed the chill from her arms. "Did you see what you wanted?"

"I think the bottom part of that ladder's supposed to extend down. If I hoist you on my shoulders, can you grab it?"

"To get us out of here? You'd better believe I can."

"That's the spirit." He squatted in the middle of the passage and placed the phone glowing upward in front of him. Fingers braced against the tunnel floor, he said, "All aboard."

Landon slipped out of her sandals and climbed onto his shoulders. "Slowest elevator ever, okay?"

As he rose, she teetered and wobbled, feet flexing, fingers clutching his head for balance.

Finally, he stopped. In the dusky light, she couldn't see as clearly as she'd like, but the hole was obvious.

She forced one hand to release Bobby's hair. "Sorry, that must have hurt."

"Small price." Strain tightened his voice.

Careful to keep her balance, she extended an arm upward. "Can you shuffle forward? Very slowly?"

Seconds later, her fingertips brushed cold metal. "Stop."

Extending both arms to their limit, she seized the bottom rung. "Got it."

"Good. When you're ready, I'll duck out of the way. The sudden weight should jar the extension free."

She locked her hand muscles. "Now."

His shoulders fell from beneath her. An electric jolt ran the length of her arms as they stopped her fall.

The ladder gave a metallic screech. It jerked, then held.

"Bobby?"

"Okay. Plan B. I'm going to hold you and add my weight. Any inappropriate touch is accidental."

Her shoulders creaked. "Hurry."

"Let's go." His arms clasped her thighs in an iron band.

The strain to her joints brought tears to her eyes. She tried pulling up toward the bar like a crazy chin-up. Anything to relieve the agony in her shoulders. She would not be a weak link here.

Teeth gritted, panting, she was about to cry out to stop when the ladder jerked.

It only budged perhaps the length of her little finger. But it moved.

"Give me a minute... I need your shoulders again."

"Huh? Oh. How's this?"

The force around her legs didn't change, but now instead of bearing down, he supported her.

"Okay." As soon as the pain dulled, she braced herself. "Round two."

By the time they had the ladder extended halfway into the tunnel, Landon felt like she'd been on the losing end of a fight. The way Bobby stood hunched over, hands on knees, he wasn't in any better shape.

She didn't care. They had their way out.

Together. If the ladder hadn't dropped, one of them would have had to climb up with the cell to call for help. Leaving the other alone in the dark.

Bobby straightened and swiped his forehead with the back of his hand. "Funny it's not cold down here anymore."

He swept a palm toward the ladder. "Ladies first."

"If there's another hatch to push, you're stronger."

"Then let's go." He handed her the phone. "I need both hands to get started, and then if you pass it back, I can light our way."

He scuffed his palms against the sides of his shorts, then grabbed the ladder and hauled himself upward into the shaft. When his feet caught the bottom rung, he leaned sideways, extending one arm for the phone.

On tiptoes, Landon stretched up with the device in her fingertips.

Bobby caught it in a pincer grip and climbed far enough to give her room before pausing to shine the light downward. "Your turn."

She grasped the highest rung she could. Lunging upward, she caught the next one with one hand, then brought the second hand to join it. Her feet still couldn't catch the bottom rung.

One more time, gasping with effort, shoulders screaming. Crunching her stomach muscles tight to tuck her legs up.

The toe of one sandal scraped the bottom rung. It slipped, but she jammed her foot hard against the metal and used the leverage to position her other foot. Heart pounding, she scooted her hands up the ladder until she was standing.

"Wait a minute." She locked her arms around the ladder and rested her forehead against a rust-roughened rung, panting.

Anna needed them. She could do this. "I'm ready." Despite the urgency burning in her heart, she barely kept pace. Her arms and legs dragged, leaden and clumsy.

They climbed in silence, the only sounds the scuff of feet on metal, the strained gasps for breath, and the pounding of Landon's pulse in her ears. Finally, Bobby hissed, "I found another hatch."

He passed down the phone.

Landon held position and leaned into the ladder while he worked to open the trapdoor. His muffled grunts echoed in the hollow space.

If this way had been sealed too—but it couldn't be. Maria had hidden something behind the door for her son before selling her home.

But they were banking on Maria's door being a vertical opening in a wall. Captain Hiltz could have sealed this trapdoor years before he died.

Please, no…

"Ha." Wood scraped overhead. Bobby started coughing.

Grains of dust—or something—rained on her head, filling her mouth with grit. Choking, she gripped the ladder.

His breath still rasping, Bobby was moving again. As soon as he cleared the opening, Landon swarmed up the final rungs, slapped her hands against the ground around the shaft, and launched herself out.

In the phone's glow, shadowy shelves lined the walls. Not slowing to investigate, they ran along the passage until they came to a vertical barrier.

"Wood. Maria's door." Bobby's whisper barely met her ears. He traced the light around the edges of the door. A protrusion in the wood might be a handle.

Instead of touching it, he tapped the phone screen. Then he motioned Landon back down the tunnel. Bending his head close to hers, he whispered, "I had a cell signal at the door. We should phone 9-1-1 from here in case Gord's still in the inn."

Everything inside her screamed to shove him aside and burst out of here. Run to Anna. But he was right. "Okay."

He checked the phone again. "Only one bar. Here goes."

Landon winced at the shrill electronic tones. The door must lead into the inn's basement. Gord wouldn't hear. But what if he did?

"You've reached 9-1-1. What is the nature of your emergency?"

Bobby held the phone tight against his head, and the words filtered around his hand. "Hello—I'm—" He stumbled through a request for an ambulance and an explanation of what had happened.

The story sounded so crazy, Landon prayed the dispatcher would believe him.

"And what is the victim's current condition?"

Bobby smacked his forehead. "We're locked in a tunnel under the inn. I can't see her. All I have is what our attacker said."

"Gord Lohnes?"

"That's correct. Please, if you'll log this and send help, we'll try to get back into the inn and check on Anna. I'll update you then."

"I need you to stay on the line until help arrives."

"It's on the way?"

"Yes, please stay on the line."

"Sorry. We have to get out." Bobby cut the connection and pocketed the phone. "Let's hit that door."

He eased it inward with the care of a midnight burglar. Bright light streamed through the widening crack, bringing tears to Landon's eyes. She crowded against Bobby's shoulder, squinting past him for her first glimpse of freedom.

Blocking with his arm as if he knew how badly she longed to dart into the house, he put his ear to the gap. If his heart was storming half as loudly as hers, he wouldn't hear if Gord stood on the other side mocking them.

At last, he opened the door.

Clean household air flooded in, replacing the dank, musty scent of the storage tunnel as they crept into the basement. The furnace blocked most of their view. Light, not so blinding now, filtered between the open curtains.

Nothing moved.

They raced to the window facing the parking lot. Bracing his foot against the edge of one of the storage shelves and levering up from there, Bobby peeked outside. "His car's gone. Anna's and mine are still there, so he might be back."

Landon reached the stairs before her brain caught up. She let out a low growl. "The basement deadbolt needs a key on this side too. We didn't want someone coming in through the tunnel and surprising us."

"Okay." He scanned the room. "The window over the workbench. Easier than the shelves."

Murdoch's work corner had two small ground-level windows. Landon scrambled up and spread the curtains even wider on the one facing the road.

It opened toward her with a creak. Fresh air poured through. Sun-heated, ocean-salted air. A siren wailed in the distance. Hope.

The benchtop creaked as Bobby joined her. Within seconds, they hoisted the window free and propped it against the pegboard of tools.

Bobby grinned. "After you."

Landon's palms hit the grass. She lowered her face to the soft green carpet, filling her senses with the fresh, living scent and the moist topsoil at the roots. Then, with a grateful glance at the sun, she sprinted for the deck.

The sirens sounded close now.

Bobby's footsteps thudded behind her.

Together they raced up the back stairs. He flung open the screen door and tried the inner one. "Locked."

The kitchen window was open. Not wide, but they could crank it open enough to crawl through. "Do you have your car keys? If we cut the screen—"

Two police cars screamed into the lot. An ambulance stopped beside the path to the back deck.

Everything inside Landon wilted. She didn't have to be strong anymore. Help had come. She and Bobby ran to meet them.

Two police officers rounded the ambulance. Dylan and Zerkowsky. At the sight of Dylan, Landon's tears started.

He strode nearer. "Door's locked?"

Landon nodded. "The kitchen window—"

He took her hands and squeezed them, firm and comforting, before letting go. "We've got this."

Then he tipped his head toward Zerkowsky. "Take the front."

Scenes from cop shows flashed through Landon's mind. "It's not a raid—do you have to break down both doors?"

"We shouldn't need to force any doors. Those etched-glass panes framing the front entrance? Break one in the right place, and you can stick a hand in and unlock it. Messy, but quick. Easier than landing in the kitchen sink."

Moments later, Zerkowsky opened the back door from the inside.

Dylan threw Landon a look. "You two stay here." He ducked past Zerkowsky. "This way."

The male paramedic followed the officers, pulling a wheeled stretcher. Landon ducked inside before the door closed.

At the entrance to Anna's room, her feet froze. If she lost Anna—

Dylan's and Zerkowsky's backs screened the bed from view. She crept nearer.

"She's unresponsive, but I have a pulse. Breathing is faint."

"Thank You, Jesus." Landon's words pushed through trembling lips.

Zerkowsky whirled. "You shouldn't be in here. This is a crime scene."

"I had to know."

Phone raised as a camera, Dylan advanced around the side of the bed. Anna lay on top of a pale rose duvet, slack-jawed, her face a sickly white. Gord had folded her hands on her chest in a classic funeral pose.

Landon knuckled her lips to stop a whimper.

The paramedic made brief eye contact. "Besides the sleeping pills, do you know if she's taking any other medication?" One blue-gloved hand pointed to the tipped-over orange pill bottle beside a pastel green porcelain mug on the night table.

"She's on an antibiotic for Lyme. And—and she was being poisoned with lead in her shampoo."

Dylan lowered his phone. "Gord told you?"

The police would roast her alive for this. She gulped a deep breath. "Meaghan did. A sample from her hairbrush will prove it."

His gaze locked hers, his face impassive except for the telltale eyelid. "And you know this how?"

She moistened parched lips. "A friend of Bobby's tested some of Anna's hair for us—just in case. It seemed like a crazy idea, and we didn't want to upset Anna if it wasn't true. Today we found out. But Gord was here alone with Anna. And we had to get back here first, and... and then we'd have reported the poison and Gord and—"

Dylan extended his palm like a traffic cop. "We'll finish this conversation at the hospital once you've been checked out."

Zerkowsky emerged from the bathroom with three pill bottles and the shampoo in a clear plastic evidence bag. He showed it to the paramedic, who grunted, face tense.

Anna lay so limp, so... lifeless. The paramedic knew his job, and God had the ultimate authority. Still, it was hard to form the words. "Will she be okay?"

The paramedic glanced up with a calming smile. "She has a good chance. You can help by letting my colleague check you over. It'll speed up our turnaround to the hospital."

"I'm—" Her muscles and surface scratches wouldn't let her say it.

"Fine?" Dylan's dark eyes still smouldered, but a corner of his mouth quirked into the ghost of a smile.

Her cheeks heated. "Fine compared to being trapped in that tunnel. I'll be outside."

When she opened the back door, Bobby sprang from his seat, the question clear in his eyes.

"She's alive. Unconscious, but he said she has a good chance."

His shoulders lifted and fell with a huge breath. "We made it."

"Yeah." Landon's knees melted. She dropped into the closest chair with enough force to scrape it sideways on the deck.

Bobby took a half-step toward her and stopped. "You okay?"

She nodded, suddenly unable to meet his eyes. Their experience in the tunnel was too intense, too much shared. In that space, they'd poured everything into the common goal of survival.

Now, she needed distance. Room to process what had happened. He likely felt the same.

Time to reset the boundaries. Keep to the surface, avoid the depths. Anchored in her chair, Landon surveyed his dirt-streaked face and arms and rumpled hair. Somehow, he'd bent his glasses. "Do I look as bad as you?"

The second paramedic, a stocky woman with a round face, chuckled. "I'll save your hide, Bobby. You both look like you've spent the afternoon crawling around underground. Now, my dear, I need to know how you're feeling."

Bobby stepped off to the side, phone in hand. "I'd better tell Gramp what happened."

Once the paramedics wheeled Anna from the inn, Landon rode with her in the ambulance. Zerkowsky stayed behind to secure the crime scene, and Dylan and Bobby followed in their cars.

The debriefing was every bit as painful as Landon feared. Especially when she admitted they'd gone to confront Meaghan.

It didn't help that Dylan was right. Or that she suspected a large portion of his anger was at Gord. His previous words, almost tender, about wanting to protect her whispered in the back of her mind, but tenderness was completely absent now.

Eventually, he snapped his notebook shut. "I'm going to check for an update on Gord. You two stay put this time."

Landon grimaced at Bobby. "It's like being back in school and having detention."

Bobby removed his glasses and tried to bend them back into shape. "Kind of anticlimactic after thinking we were going to die underground."

He hadn't said anything about Gord and David. She wouldn't fool herself that the argument was over—wasn't even convinced she was right to protect Elva this way—but it could wait for another day.

When Dylan returned, his frown was still in place. "Gord was apprehended about twenty minutes ago. We still haven't heard from Meaghan and Hart."

Landon squirmed in the hard plastic chair. "They promised they'd call. It's for their benefit too."

"We'll see." He stood in the doorway, feet spread. "When Anna wakes, I need to get a statement from her before you can visit. Zerkowsky's at the inn. Now would be a good time to go collect a few things. You'll need to stay somewhere else tonight."

"I'll be okay to stay alone."

Dylan rasped a knuckle across his chin. "It's a crime scene. And you may feel different at two in the morning."

Other than answering direct questions, Bobby had been quiet. Now he rubbed at a dirt smear on his panda bear tee shirt. "Gramp has another bedroom. You can stay with us."

He'd gone back to avoiding eye contact. Definitely feeling the awkwardness too. But Roy would insist, and where else could she go on a moment's notice?

As well as packing a bag, Landon put out food for both cats. On the way back to the hospital, Bobby detoured through a fast-food drive-thru. They carried coffee and sandwiches past the nurses' longing glances and had almost finished eating when Dylan stuck his head in the room.

He inhaled theatrically. "Coffee, the universal cure."

His face was still tense, but frustration no longer tightened his voice. "Anna's ready to see you now. She knows you were trapped in the tunnel, but she's pretty drowsy. Best not to go into details yet."

Bobby stayed in his seat. "One person will be enough. Tell her Gramp and I send our best."

Anna lay propped up on pillows, an IV in one arm. Her face was still pale, the skin sunken around her eyes. Her smile was a shadow of the one Landon knew.

But she was alive. Landon bent for an awkward bed hug. "Thank God you're all right."

"And you and Bobby too." A tremor shook Anna's shoulders.

Landon slid the visitor's chair closer and cradled Anna's hand. "When you're better, we can talk about it. For now, let's be glad to be alive."

Anna's brown eyes filled. "Gord... and Meaghan... I don't know what to say. And Dylan said it was about using the tunnel for smuggling."

"For what it's worth, Meaghan genuinely seems to care about you. Gord was controlling her."

The first tears fell. "They both seemed so kind."

Landon massaged the back of Anna's hand with her thumb. "It's over now. You'll be home in no time. Let us pamper you for a few days, and you can boss me around instead of Meaghan for the rest of the summer."

"If we have any guests."

"The fake reviews will stop now. That'll help."

Anna raised her head from the pillow, then flopped back. "The damage is done."

Such finality in her listless tone. And no spark in her eyes. Landon's hope seeped back into the tunnel. The air changed to the dank, metallic salt she'd tasted underground.

If Anna gave up, then Gord won. Even from jail and without taking her life. He'd have crushed her spirit.

Pleading in silent prayer, Landon stroked Anna's cheek and willed confidence into her voice. "First, let's concentrate on recovering from today. We can deal with the future when we get there."

Chapter 31

Wednesday

THE TIMER BEEPED, and Landon slid a tray of misshapen muffins from the oven. She glared at them, but the fault was hers, somehow. The recipe worked fine for Anna.

Anna would be home soon. Landon had spent most of yesterday at the hospital, keeping her company between other visitors. Last night the doctor promised to sign the discharge papers this morning, so instead of going to the hospital, Landon moved back into the inn from Roy's place.

Today Anna's bed had fresh sheets, and her bathroom had been scrubbed hard enough to remove every last one of Gord's fingerprints.

Timkin had staked claim to Anna's recliner like a sentinel guarding his post. Two days and nights outside hadn't hurt him, but he seemed to distrust Landon being here on her own.

An engine hummed outside, and Landon hurried toward the door. As she opened it, Timkin brushed past her ankles and shot across the deck.

He stopped in Anna's path, head high, then twitched his tail and bounded into the forest.

Still pale, Anna managed a faint smile. "I'm not sure if that was 'Welcome home' or 'It took you long enough.' "

Landon swept her into a hug. "Welcome home."

She waved her thanks to Tricia in the driver's seat before reaching for Anna's overnight bag.

Anna relinquished it with a sigh. "I feel like a wrung-out dishcloth."

No surprise, after the sleeping pills they'd flushed from her system—and the build-up of lead poisoning.

"But you're alive, and we can put this behind us."

The doctor had begun treatment while waiting for the toxicology report to reveal the severity. In the meantime, Anna had been taken off Lyme antibiotics. Meaghan and Hart had finally contacted the police, accusing Gord of staging Anna's accident and Murdoch's as well. Anna would have a lot to deal with as she recovered.

Landon waited until Anna was ensconced in her recliner with tea and a muffin before fetching the land-line handset and plunking it down in her lap. "Time to call your kids."

Anna rested a hand on the phone. "Thank you for respecting my decision to wait until I was home."

She wouldn't have if the prognosis had been dire.

A hint of colour washed Anna's face and her chest rose in a deep breath. "I have to tell them their father was murdered." She blinked back tears, tapping her nails against the black plastic phone. "Gord pretended to be so kind, right to the end. I'd told him about the pills, that I hated to take them. He must have sneaked them when he went to the bathroom. Then he made me some tea, saying I looked so frail."

Her throat worked. "It was herbal and it tasted odd. But he said he'd found it on the shelf. I assumed it was Nigel's special blend. Nigel claims it has health benefits, so I didn't think twice. When I felt drowsy, he suggested I lie down, and… I woke in the hospital."

"Will you be okay to sleep in your bed tonight?"

"He is not scaring me out of my home. Not now."

"Good." Landon folded her arms across her chest. "And while your courage is up, call Piper and Chase."

Anna made an exaggerated scowl and picked up the phone.

Once Anna said hello, Landon left the room to give her privacy. She took Anna's gardening gloves and escaped into the fresh air. She'd been outside as often as possible since the tunnels, even when it rained. This afternoon was a perfect July day. High in the pines, cicadas buzzed. It would be too hot inland, but the coastal air kept the temperature bearable.

From the front of the inn, the ride-on mower droned its relaxing rhythm. Corey must have arrived while she and Anna were talking. She'd have to let him know Anna was home. He'd been so upset to hear what happened. The poor kid didn't have many positive role models, and Anna's near miss likely brought back his loss of Murdoch.

She walked across the grass and knelt at the edge of Anna's flower garden. Sunlight fell across her shoulders like a heating pad, softening muscles and drawing out her lingering tension.

Anna was alive and on the mend. The doctors said it would take time to clear the poison from her system, but she should have only minimal long-term effects.

If any. Landon was praying for a full healing.

The barn had been declared off-limits to Corey and Quinn until the tunnels could be sealed, although Nigel had begged to lead them on an "underground expedition" first.

Landon uprooted another weed and dropped it in her bucket. According to Dylan, Maria had tearfully identified the clothing at the base of the first ladder as David's. As soon as the crime-scene tape had been removed from the inn, Landon braved the house end of the tunnel with Anna's big flashlight. It was hard to resist cracking open the rough wooden crates on the shelves, but that was Anna's privilege, not hers. Instead, she retrieved the plastic-lined metal box Maria left for her son—filled with bank notes.

When Landon phoned to tell her about Anna and reassure her the money was safe, Maria asked her to keep it a little longer.

Also in the tunnel were racks of Captain Hiltz's prohibition-breaking alcohol. That could wait until Anna was ready to deal with it.

Elva had regained consciousness and was expected to be home by the weekend. Nigel still checked on her regularly, even though Gord was no longer a threat.

Now that Landon knew why Elva wouldn't set foot on the inn property, she'd asked Roy to host a welcome-home gathering for the two women. They chose a date for next week, and Elva had shocked Roy by saying she might come.

Of course, that had been before Landon and Bobby reported Gord as David's killer. If Gord dragged Elva's name into the investigation and the police required a statement, she might cut herself off from them again.

Landon had asked Nigel to warn her there could be questions. Nigel had been coldly furious, but Bobby was right. They couldn't withhold information about the death, whether it was accidental or deliberate.

All Landon could do now was pray Elva would open up to counselling—and healing.

Motion in her peripheral vision froze her hand on a stringy green shoot. The stray cat was back. She resumed weeding, keeping her motions slow and unconcerned. Pretending she hadn't seen him.

He advanced, tail high with its crooked tip like a sailboat pennant. A questioning sort of half-mew came from his mouth.

Carefully, she turned her head. "I'm sorry I scared you the other day."

At this range, his wound appeared to be healing well. The lump had mostly gone. Another few steps put him within reach, but she wouldn't make that mistake again.

Sitting back on her heels, she dropped her hands to her shorts, hardly daring to breathe.

He strolled forward and butted her forearm with the healthy side of his head.

Landon swallowed a squeal of surprise. "Hello to you too."

With glacier speed, she raised her hand. He retreated half a pace, then stretched his head nearer to sniff her gloved fingertips. Then his head whipped toward the driveway. He bounded away.

She twisted in place as Roy's truck rumbled to a stop. Rotten timing, but maybe she'd have gone too far and scared the cat again. This way they'd parted on a good note.

Roy waved from the passenger seat. "Did Anna get home?"

"About an hour and a half ago." She stood, knees protesting, and peeled off her gloves. "She was on the phone. I'll see if she's finished."

Bobby came around the truck's tailgate. "Gramp's been to visit Maria." When he was close enough to speak quietly, he said, "She asked us to bring her the box she hid for David. Is that okay?"

"I'll get it for you."

"She'd like us to deliver it this afternoon, but if Anna's up for company, we can stay a few minutes first. She probably doesn't want anyone sticking around too long."

"No, she's pretty tired."

As they passed the sitting room, Anna was still talking. Landon continued to the basement door, unlocked now. "It's down here."

"You put it back in the tunnel?"

"Not with the police coming and going. It doesn't need to be in the chain of evidence." She crossed to the shelving unit and pulled out a big plastic tote marked Christmas Lights.

Bobby narrowed his eyes and stroked his chin like a plotting villain. "Suitably sneaky. I like it."

She cracked open the lid and removed a layer of neatly coiled and tied strings of lights. "How's your writing going?"

Staying at Roy's, she'd barely seen Bobby. Last night at supper, he confessed he'd been holing up in his room to write. Something in their tunnel experience had sparked what he needed for his novel.

Not that he'd told them what it was. Apparently, talking about it before writing diluted the inspiration.

His eyes lit, and a broad grin stretched his stubbly cheeks. "It's been nonstop except for chauffeur duty, and I used the writing app on my phone while Gramp visited Maria. Unless I hit another snag, I'll finish in time. The other book's edits are coming next week."

Landon retrieved Maria's box and handed it to him. "I'm glad Roy went to see Maria. She sounded pretty broken up when I called her about the box."

"Are you going to the burial on Monday?"

She replaced the lights and slid the tote back onto the shelf. "If Anna's not up to driving, Tricia and Blaine will take us."

Bobby seesawed the grey metal box in his hands. "I barely know Maria, but it feels wrong to stay away."

"I'm sure she'll appreciate your support. There may not be many people there since David's been gone so long." Nigel had emphatically refused when Landon mentioned it. How much Elva had told him, and how much he intuited, they'd never know.

When they passed the sitting room, Anna had the phone to her ear. At the truck, Bobby handed the box through the window to Roy.

Roy tipped his chin toward the inn. "Anna still talking?"

Landon nodded. "She's finally telling her kids what happened. It could be a while."

"At least she's telling them."

"Gramp, please." Bobby slammed his door. "I called Mom and Dad. I'm not ready to talk to Jessie about it yet. Besides, I'm on a deadline, and she fusses."

Roy fixed Landon with a sea-blue gaze. "Since I'm playing the meddling old man, and you like me too much to hit me—what about letting your mother know?"

His tone was gentle, but the question nailed Landon in the heart.

He stuck a hand out the window and squeezed her shoulder. "Think about it."

She was still gaping when the truck reversed and headed down the driveway.

Chapter 32

Monday

THE FOLLOWING MONDAY dawned grey and drizzly. Fitting for a burial, but it wouldn't help Maria's arthritis to spend time outdoors in the damp. By ten, a watery sun appeared, and by the time Anna and Landon left the inn in Anna's rental car, the pavement was drying.

Maria had elected a simple graveside committal. The pastor from Anna and Roy's church greeted them and wrapped Anna in a hug. "I'm glad you're recovered enough to be out today." Releasing her, he smiled at them both. "It'll mean a lot to Maria to see you. Friends will make this bearable."

A burnished mahogany coffin hung poised above an open grave, a small cluster of people standing to one side. Someone had arranged a row of folding chairs, most of which were occupied by elderly people, likely Maria's friends and fellow residents. Including the rocking chair warriors. Roy sat on his walker at the end of the row, Bobby standing beside him.

Tricia and Blaine hadn't arrived yet. Would Elva come with them?

Landon had slipped away from the inn on the weekend to see Elva and encourage her to attend the burial, if only for the symbolic act of putting David completely out of her life.

Elva had been less angry than Landon feared about the police report. Maybe after the attack in her home, she wanted to dig Gord in as deeply as possible. Still, her words were stiff as if she resented Landon knowing her pain.

Landon didn't try to talk about it. All she did was offer to stand with Elva at the burial, in solidarity and defiance of the past.

Elva snorted and shook her head, but her face lost its hard edge.

Now Landon followed Anna to mix with the others. Voices were hushed yet cheerful in the absence of the grieving mother. People caught up on one another's news and speculated about the identity of David's killer.

Anna deflected questions about her own ordeal. "Today's for Maria's pain, not mine."

A rustle in the small group hushed the conversation and focused all eyes on the black sedan creeping as close as possible to the grave. When it stopped, a dark-suited man helped the stooped, black-clad woman exit and escorted her to a seat in the middle of the row.

Murmurs of sympathy rose around her.

As the others gathered in a horseshoe behind the chairs, Landon spotted Tricia and Blaine. They must have arrived while everyone was talking.

Her gaze swept the group. No sign of Elva.

Heaviness filled her chest. Maybe she'd been wrong, and this wouldn't be good for Elva. But healing couldn't come while Elva hid from the pain.

The pastor shared a few of Maria's memories of David. Landon tried to concentrate on the glimpses of who David had been, a boy who loved fishing, a teen who made his parents proud. Over it all, the thought of what he'd done to Elva spread like a poison stain.

Her gaze caught Bobby's. From the pinch around his eyes, he shared her thoughts.

As the pastor moved into what he promised would be a brief message, Landon scuffed the toe of one sandal in the still-damp grass. It must be difficult to offer hope when he knew nothing about the deceased and had met Maria only to plan for today.

A final Scripture verse and prayer, and then time to lower the coffin. The creaking winches added to the soundtrack of mourning.

The sound drilled cold through Landon's body. Had it been that way for her father's funeral too? Or had he been cremated? Her mother hadn't said in the brief communications they'd shared once Landon was rescued.

Landon rubbed the back of her neck. This was Maria's day to honour her son. Not a day to prod unhealed wounds.

Concentrating on her breathing, she studied the faces around her. Several graves away, a lone figure leaned on a cane. Something about the shape—

Elva. Landon eased away from the group. Approaching Elva was as risky as approaching the stray cat. But the woman had come, and Landon had promised to be her support.

Elva spared her one glittering glance, then set her face toward the still-lowering coffin as if pushing it into the ground by force of will.

Silently, Landon stood beside her, their shoulders almost touching.

When the lowering mechanism finally ceased its dirge, Elva sniffed. She nodded briskly at Landon and shuffled away.

"Wait a minute." Bobby jogged toward them.

Elva advanced toward the road.

Bobby stopped at Landon's side. "You couldn't make her wait?"

"It cost her to be here today, Bobby. What did you want me to do, tackle her?"

His eyes flashed. Then he shook his head. He extended a padded manila envelope. "Maria wants her to have this. See if she'll take it?"

Landon caught up with Elva before she reached Tricia and Blaine's car. Good thing, or the woman would probably have locked herself in and refused to talk.

"Elva... this is from Maria." The envelope was squishy in her grip, thick enough to hold a paperback novel. Or a stack of bank notes.

Elva's lips pinched like she wanted to spit. "I want nothing from that family."

Landon locked gazes with her, envelope outstretched. "Please."

"She knew. When I came back, she told me the old man died in pain. As if that could help."

"I'm sure it didn't hurt."

A curt laugh split Elva's brick-red lips. Her face hardened. "It did not."

"So maybe see what she has to say today? In your space, on your terms?"

Elva's fingers closed around the package. "If it's a memento of David, I'll burn it."

"Fair enough. But she doesn't know he shares the blame." Landon stepped back. "I'll see you around."

She walked back among the grass-covered graves to David's, open with a mound of dirt beside it. Anna stood chatting with the others, apparently in no hurry, so Landon waited for the chance to speak with Maria.

When the old woman finished her conversation, she excused herself and limped toward Landon.

Landon held out her arms. "May I hug you?"

Maria's chin quivered, then firmed. She nodded. Behind her glasses, her eyes glistened with unshed tears.

Landon embraced her gently, like she'd hold a bird, and whispered, "I'm so sorry for your loss."

The polyester blouse shifted under her palms at Maria's ragged breath. "At least I finally know why he didn't come home to me."

Before releasing her, Landon spoke in her ear. "Elva has your envelope."

"Good. I hope she'll read my note and not throw it all in the trash."

"Money from David's box?"

Maria nodded. "I have more for the others. Including your guest since his mother has passed."

Was there a packet for Nigel's mother? Landon couldn't ask. "You knew?"

"Never in time to prevent it. You'll say I should have told someone, but at the time, it wasn't done. We all lived in the same house and I did what I could... pressured him to pay support, tried to keep him away from possible victims. I hadn't known about your guest's mother. And Elva... I was horrified. How did he ever get near her? He was crippled with arthritis."

Mercy stopped Landon's words. The grieving mother didn't need to know David had supplied Elva to the old man to gain access to the tunnel. Another reason to hope it didn't come out at Gord's trial. Although if it did, Ivan would have his victory of publicly discrediting Captain Hiltz for his crimes.

A scowl twisted Maria's already contorted features. "I hope his victims saw the justice in his death agony. I knew there was more behind the pain than his joints. Was glad to see the cancer take him."

She straightened to her full height, chin lifting from the black ruffles at her chest. "His hands were so bad he couldn't open his pill bottles. I felt no guilt withholding his pain medication. Still don't. And he knew it. I saw it in his eyes. He hated me. Well, it went both ways."

Landon let her talk. Maria had probably kept this inside since the old man's death.

"Jack told me he showed David the tunnel entrance, so I hid the box inside. Maybe I was selfish to keep the money for David, but it should have been his. It wasn't his fault his grandfather was evil incarnate."

The irony was, she'd hidden the box at one entrance, but David knew the other one.

Maria released a sigh like death itself. "And now I'm alone."

Landon hugged her again. There were no words, not now in the depths of grief.

Maria stirred in her arms and pulled free. "I was angry with you for insisting about the tunnel, but you were right. You're good for Anna. Come with her to see me sometime."

"I will." As Maria limped back to the group, Landon spotted Bobby standing alone. He probably didn't know many more of these people than she did.

She crossed the grass toward him. He'd shaved for the funeral and traded his tee shirt for a button-down that had even been ironed. And gelled his haystack hair into submission. "I'm sorry I snapped at you about Elva."

"No worries. Although the image of you tackling her is worth a chuckle." The glint left his eyes. "She's carried that pain for so many years. No wonder she's bitter."

"I hope today brought some closure."

"She knows you know. Do you think she'll open up to you? Not keep the poison locked inside?"

"She needs professional help." A little breeze wafted strands of blond hair across Landon's face, and she slid them behind her ear. "If I can share the difference it's made for me—and the difference Jesus has made in me—maybe she'll reach out."

"Maybe." Bobby scowled. "Gord wasn't part of that if he's to be believed, but he knew and still terrorized her for his own gain. And tried to murder her. If Nigel hadn't pulled her out of the fire and then guarded her hospital room, we'd have two funerals. Nigel's a hero."

"Yes, he is." Lifting her chin, she fixed on his blue-grey eyes. "So are you."

His gaze dropped.

Landon braced her core. No way was he deflecting this. "You were a hero down there, Bobby. You kept me sane. It wasn't flashy or swashbuckling, and there weren't any lasers or tiger pits. But it was heroic. And it got us out of the tunnel. Thank you."

"It was your idea to look up. And it took two to budge that ladder."

She'd been so focused on making him see his strength that she'd missed her own. Cheek muscles straining with the width of her smile, she stood a little taller. She wasn't the helpless girl who needed rescue. Not anymore. This time she was one of the rescuers.

Ruddy-cheeked, Bobby sketched a rough salute. "Guess we make a good team."

"Two of us to equal one Travers?"

"Now don't get carried away." His eyebrows wrinkled, and his lower lip pushed out. "You know who you should really thank? That prof who failed you. If you weren't here, Gord would have won."

The truth of his words filtered into her soul.

Professor Tallin's vindictive streak had saved Anna's life.

The injustice still rankled, but how could she stay angry when she saw what was gained?

She filled her lungs with good, Nova Scotian sea air. "Failure's a small price to pay for a friend."

Author's Note

There are **sea caves** in the Lunenburg area, most notably at The Ovens Park, but none where I've placed the inn. The land and road where the inn would be is much closer to sea level, with no room for cliffs and caves. One of the perks of writing fiction is being able to adjust the facts as needed, for the purposes of the story. I hope you'll have the chance to visit Lunenburg someday, and that you'll forgive the liberties I've taken with the landscape around the inn.

Another deviation from the facts: passengers at Halifax's Stanfield Airport must now collect their checked baggage before leaving the secure area.

Lyme Disease is real but don't let fear of it keep you from visiting the beautiful province of Nova Scotia, billed as "Canada's Ocean Playground." Ticks are found in many parts of North America now and are one of many things to watch for while enjoying the great outdoors. The Canadian Lyme Disease Foundation (canlyme.com) offers information on prevention and symptoms.

Human trafficking is all too real a problem, both for sex and for labour. It's possible for survivors to heal as well as Landon is healing, but I didn't find very many positive reports. The truth is ugly and frightening, and sex trafficking victims can be girls and boys as young as 12. Or younger. One way to fight back is to support your local programs for at-risk youth.

A few sites for background information:

- Canadian Centre to End Human Trafficking canadiancentretoendhumantrafficking.ca
- Public Safety Canada canada.ca/en/public-safety-canada/campaigns/human-trafficking.html
- Canadian author K. L. Ditmars lists more resources on her website: klditmarswriter.com/resources

If you are or someone you know is a victim of human trafficking, please reach out for help!

- In Canada: Canadian Human Trafficking Hotline canadianhumantraffickinghotline.ca
- In the US: National Human Trafficking Hotline humantraffickinghotline.org/get-help
- In any country: in your internet browser, type "human trafficking help" and add your country.

To end on **a brighter note**: here's the quote Bobby paraphrases in the tunnel:

> Behold, I stand at the door and knock. If anyone hears My voice and opens the door, I will come in to him and dine with him, and he with Me. (Revelation 3:20, NKJV*)

Finally, a favour if you're so inclined: Could you drop a **brief review** on Goodreads or your favourite online bookstore? Nothing fancy, just mention what you liked or didn't like, and why. No spoilers, please!

Read on for **discussion questions** and a peek at the next Green Dory Inn mystery, ***Bitter Truth***. Thanks for reading!

Janet

ACKNOWLEDGEMENTS

I'm deeply grateful to the many people whose insights shaped my raw story into one I'm proud to share with readers. Obviously, thank you to Deirdre Lockhart at Brilliant Cut Editing and Emilie Haney at E.A.H. Creative for their work. Thank you to my husband and son, Russell and Matthew Sketchley, for early reading and significant brainstorming input, and to beta readers Ruth Ann Adams, Janice Dick, Ginny Jaques, Heidi Newell, and Beverlee Wamboldt for their eagle-eyed typo hunting. Any lingering errors are my own.

Multiple thanks to the members of my local writers' group for help distilling the back cover summary and for insights into the running of a B&B. Thank you for being a safe place to share early segments and plot struggles. The night you let me talk through my sudden need to keep Elva alive—when I realized who'd guard her and it choked me up—you understood.

Thank you to my newsletter readers and to my family for having some fun with me discovering how Roy broke his leg.

Russell, Adam, Amanda, Andrew, Adrianne, Matthew, Mom & Dad W, Mom & Dad S, you mean the world to me and your encouragement is priceless.

Jesus, my chain-breaking, life-giving Saviour, thank You for the gift and privilege of writing. I pray there's something in these pages You'll use to touch hearts.

Discussion Questions

1. Landon leaves the city and everything that reminds her of her toxic professor for the rest of the summer. How does a strategic retreat allow a person to rest, recover, and regroup? When is it wise to simply withdraw from a situation?

2. Landon and Bobby will remember the inn's tunnel with fear, but tunnels and secret passages can be places of wonder and adventure. What sorts of places do you like to explore?

3. How do you see the feral orange stray as a mirror for Landon?

4. Relationships and experiences in our youth can impact us for years to come. Landon can tell Bobby hasn't spoken of his past hurt. Hers was so severe that she's spent significant time in counselling, therapy, and prayer. Is she just projecting on Bobby, or do you think he'd benefit from telling a trusted confidant about what happened?

5. Because Landon has been working through her traumatic past, she can recognize the need to address and forgive Ciara's school-aged bullying. Do you find that clearing up the larger troubles in your heart helps you be more sensitive to correcting the smaller ones as well?

6. We may ask Jesus to heal us in one touch, yet often He accomplishes much of this work through trained professionals in the physical, mental, emotional, and spiritual fields. What are some of the benefits and impacts of these "ordinary miracles"?

7. Ivan claims the whole community knew about Captain Hiltz's crimes and did nothing except warn young girls to stay away. Today we'd report an abuser to the police and encourage his victims to testify. In the past, there was often a culture of "this is wrong but we have to live with it or deal with it in our own way." As unbelievable as that sounds in a case this extreme, can you recall a situation in your own life that you look back on now and ask why nobody (perhaps yourself included) spoke up?

8. What do you think about the effect of Ivan's desire to drag Captain Hiltz's past crimes into the public eye? And about Landon's concern for the victims who might not be ready to speak?

9. What do you think of Nigel's attitude toward Captain Hiltz as a complicated man who did the unforgivable but also did good?

10. Roy's concern for Anna in the previous story brought Landon back to Lunenburg. Now he asks Landon to tell her mother about nearly dying in the tunnel. When is it interfering to advise others on what to do? When might it be necessary? How might we offer insight or input in a supportive way?

11. Corey thinks nobody believes in him. He can't hear Nigel's praise. Landon challenges him to "show them." How is this good advice, and how could it be bad?

12. Bobby compares himself to the larger-than-life action-hero in his novels and he can't see his own value. How might a right perspective on Travers inspire rather than diminish him?

NEXT IN THE GREEN DORY INN MYSTERY SERIES:

BITTER TRUTH

Who would want Ciara dead? And why?

Against all odds, Landon Smith and her ordinary-hero neighbour Bobby Hawke survived a murderous plot six weeks ago. Now, she's determined to leave solving mysteries to the experts—like handsome local police officer Dylan Tremblay.

But when a friend is nearly killed in a daring daylight attack, Landon can't sit this out. Not when she knows the anger of being a victim.

Her faith tells her to leave room for God's vengeance. Her heart says to retaliate.

The fight to expose Ciara's enemy will uncover secrets and betrayal that could cost Landon her life.

~~~

Order your copy now in print or ebook from your favourite retailer, or request it from your local library.
~~~

YOU MIGHT ALSO LIKE JANET SKETCHLEY'S REDEMPTION'S EDGE SERIES:

Heaven's Prey (book 1)

A grieving woman is abducted by a serial killer—and it may be the answer to her prayers.

Despite her husband's objections, 40-something Ruth Warner finds healing through prayer for Harry Silver, the former race car driver who brutally raped and murdered her niece. When a kidnapping-gone-wrong pegs her as his next victim, Harry claims that by destroying the one person who'd pray for him, he proves God can't—or won't—look after His own. Can Ruth's faith sustain her to the end—whatever the cost?

Secrets and Lies (book 2)

A single mother with a teenage son becomes a pawn in a drug lord's vengeance against her convict brother.

Carol Daniels thinks she out-ran her enemies, until a detective arrives at her door with a warning. Minor incidents take on a sinister meaning. An anonymous phone call warns her not to hide again.

Now she must cooperate with a drug lord while the police work to trap him. Carol has always handled crisis alone, but this one might break her. Late-night deejay Joey Hill offers friendship and moral support. Can she trust him? One thing's certain. She can't risk prayer.

Without Proof (book 3)

"Asking questions could cost your life."

Two years after the plane crash that killed her fiancé, Amy Silver has fallen for his best friend, artist Michael Stratton. When a local reporter claims the small aircraft may have been sabotaged, it reopens Amy's grief.

Anonymous warnings and threats are Amy's only proof that the tragedy was deliberate, and she has nowhere to turn. The authorities don't believe her, God is not an option, and Michael's protection is starting to feel like a cage. How will Amy find the truth?

Janet Sketchley is an Atlantic Canadian writer who likes her fiction with a splash of mystery or adventure and a dash of Christianity. Why leave faith out of our stories if it's part of our lives?

Janet's other books include the Redemption's Edge Christian suspense series and the devotional books, *A Year of Tenacity* and *Tenacity at Christmas*. She has also produced a fill-in reader's journal, *Reads to Remember: A book lover's journal to track your next 100 reads* (available in print only, with two different cover design options). You can find her online at janetsketchley.ca.

Subscribe to Janet's newsletter at bit.ly/JanetSketchleyNews, or follow her on BookBub at bit.ly/JanetSketchleyBookBub.

Manufactured by Amazon.ca
Bolton, ON